The
Birthday
Party

First published in Great Britain in 2010 by Orion Books,
an imprint of The Orion Publishing Group Ltd
Orion House, 5 Upper Saint Martin's Lane
London WC2H 9EA

An Hachette UK Company

A CIP catalogue record for this book is
available from the British Library.

Typeset at The Spartan Press Ltd,
Lymington, Hants

Printed and bound in Great Britain by
Clays Ltd, St Ives plc

The Orion Publishing Group's policy is to use papers
that are natural, renewable and recyclable products and
made from wood grown in sustainable forests. The logging
and manufacturing processes are expected to conform to
the environmental regulations of the country of origin.

www.orionbooks.co.uk

The Birthday Party

Veronica Henry

One

There was a joke, a plagiarised version of the one about the Sixties, that went: 'If you can remember the Raffertys' wedding, then you weren't there.'

Delilah could remember, however. Every last magical moment of it. The sun had rained down liquid gold all day, before evaporating into a deep pink sunset that melted into velvet black. Then the stars had come out, more than anyone had ever seen, and there were some guests who swore they could see the bride and groom's names spelt out amongst the constellations.

Delilah and Raf.

They had only known each other two months before they were married. There had been no question about it. She wasn't even entirely sure he had officially asked for her hand. It had been a given. It was meant to be.

Raf Rafferty, the hell-raising heart-throb who could down seventeen pints of Guinness then deliver a Shakespeare soliloquy in a mellifluous, husky half-whisper that had his audience weeping. And Delilah MacBride, his co-star, the copper-haired ingénue, the only woman who had ever stopped him in his tracks.

It still made her shiver, the memory of standing next to him at the altar, her tiny hand in his, as he slid the band of gold onto her finger; melting into his hypnotic blue eyes as he drew her towards him for the sealing kiss. She'd tasted the whiskey on him already that day, the peaty kick of Paddy's. But that was part of the package. She'd known that all along.

They'd barely done any organising for the wedding. No official invitations, just word of mouth amongst their coterie of friends and a few phone calls to lure people across the Channel or Atlantic. No formal catering: the food was thrown together in a languidly haphazard fashion. No seating plan – not even any seats to speak of. Just a hot summer afternoon in the medieval monastery in Herefordshire they were renting while they finished the movie they were making. They'd had no idea who was going to turn up, nor did they much care. There were barrels of cider, a cellar full of wine, Delilah barefoot wrapped in twenty yards of diaphanous silk organza held together with giant safety pins aeons before Elizabeth Hurley was even a twinkle in Versace's eye . . .

It was a million miles from the party she was planning today: her fiftieth birthday, just over two months away. A lavish extravaganza to recognise her half century, a fact which, with her typical and refreshing honesty, she had emblazoned across the invitations. It was something to celebrate, not hide. Delilah had never had a problem with age. Why bother worrying about something you had no control over? Life threw enough at you without inventing problems.

Mind you, some people would say it was all right for her not to worry, when she barely looked forty. Her skin was wrinkle-free, still creamy, lightly dusted with freckles. Her eyes were unlined, her lips full, her cheeks still plump, her hair long and thick and lustrous – sure, she had it coloured, but not to hide grey, just to add streaks of amber and topaz to her natural chestnut. She knew she was lucky. By now she should be haggard and drawn, her complexion dull. She put it down to good genes and the generous application of Jo Wood organic products.

She was sitting at the kitchen table, her bare feet resting on Doug the Pug, surrounded by brochures and menus, price lists and guest lists and check lists. She had her MacBook in front of her, her iPhone at her side, the lid off her Shanghai Tang fountain pen as she scribbled furiously, writing out all the details that she needed to check – all the minutiae that were going to make this party perfect.

It had to be perfect. The party represented a turning-point in her life. Everything was . . . well, just as it should be. Her last cookery show was a ratings winner – again – and the accompanying glossy recipe book had shot to the top of the bestseller charts – again. The girls were all settled – each in jobs, flats of their own. And Raf.

Raf was about to make a comeback.

She looked at the Fornasetti clock on the wall. He should be meeting Dickie Rushe right about now. Raf would completely flip if he knew about all the clandestine conversations she had had with Dickie. The director had approached her first, because everyone thought that she wore the trousers in the Rafferty house, which actually wasn't true at all. They were a team, a proper partnership. It was just that she tended to be the mouthpiece, and she was far more in the public eye these days, so people often thought there was no point in running something past Raf if Delilah hadn't approved it first.

And she did approve. The time was right. Even a year ago, she would have thought it a potential disaster. But Raf was strong enough. He was ready. Of that she felt certain. They'd talked it over, long into the small hours, for over a week now. It was going to mean upheaval, added pressure, unwanted publicity, a gruelling schedule, days and nights apart, but on the plus side, it was a challenge, a project for Raf to get his teeth into, the glamour and excitement that a film shoot always brought, new friends . . .

Oh, and money.

Delilah would never have dreamed of voicing it, but for her this was the biggest plus. She was tired of being the breadwinner, which she had been for the past ten years. And she knew Raf didn't have any real idea of what it cost to keep the Rafferty machine afloat. The fuck-off mansion on Richmond Hill, the flats for the girls, the cars, the staff, the clothes . . . She spent five hundred pounds a month on fresh flowers alone

3

– probably the mortgage repayments for the average family in Britain.

She would never, ever have used this to push Raf into making a decision about his career. She hadn't complained once about the pressure she felt to fill their coffers. She was very cautious not to push him over the edge. For all his manliness, for all that testosterone that made women weak at the knees, Raf was fragile. He needed cocooning. And Delilah had built that cocoon, carefully spinning the silken threads around him to protect him from the real world.

Her iPhone burbled at her. She flicked her eyes at the screen: Coco. The first call of the day. There would be anywhere between fifteen and thirty between now and midnight. Coco might be the eldest of her three daughters, but she needed constant reassurance.

Violet, the middle one, never called. She didn't even have a mobile. Delilah kept buying them for her, but she left them in cafés, in bookshops, on the tube. And Tyger, her baby – Tyger called when she felt like it, usually at three in the morning when she was on her way home in a cab, bubbling with excitement and gossip and laughter.

They were so different, each of her daughters. She wouldn't have them any other way, but she worried about them non-stop. One was too dependent, another too independent. One was too focused, another too dreamy. One worked too hard, another not enough. There was always some issue to keep her lying awake. Like any other mother, she supposed.

She answered the call.

'Hey.'

'Hi, Mum. I'm on my way to the studio. What's new?'

'Party planning. Are you bringing anyone, by the way? I need to know.' Delilah's pen hovered over the guest list, which was at three hundred and rising. 'Plus ones have to be named. We can't have random people turning up. The security guys will go nuts.'

'No. In fact, I don't know if I'll even be able to come.'

4

Delilah rolled her eyes. This was typical Coco. Drama queen. Emotional blackmail all the way. Don't rise. Don't rise.

'Why not?'

'It's on a Thursday, isn't it? We film late on Thursdays. And start at six the next morning.'

'Surely you can talk to the producers? Book the time off?'

'I don't want to piss them off when I'm still new.'

Delilah didn't protest any further. It wasn't worth it.

'All right,' she replied, non-committal. 'Just let me know nearer the time.' You couldn't force Coco into anything. It had to come from her. 'Did you sleep OK?'

'Mmm . . .'

Coco had always had trouble sleeping. Right from birth. Even now she was up half the night, falling into a troubled slumber two hours before it was time to get up. Delilah didn't know how she was coping with her relentless shooting schedule. She worried about her driving home at night exhausted. She worried about her driving to work in the morning exhausted. She worried about her not eating . . .

Although Coco's constant calls drove her mad, at least when she phoned she knew she was all right.

'You're coming tomorrow, aren't you?' she asked.

Lunch at the Raffertys' on the first Saturday of every month was a ritual. All the family turned up, together with an assortment of current beaux or friends and whoever Delilah and Raf had invited to throw into the mix. It started at midday and finished – sometimes – at midnight, though it had been known to carry on until the early hours of the next day.

The girls turned up religiously. For which Delilah was grateful. It was the only way she could keep a proper eye on them these days. Only today Coco was prevaricating. She was in one of her uncooperative moods, which meant she was unsettled.

'Maybe,' she replied cautiously. 'Depends whether we get through the shooting schedule. It's pretty tight.'

Delilah frowned. Of course they would get through the shooting schedule. They had to. No studio could afford to run over these days. They couldn't cough up the money to bring in actors and crew on a Saturday, not to mention location caterers. Coco was bullshitting . . . But she was new to all this. For God's sake, her scenes hadn't even been aired on TV yet.

'Got to go, Mum. I'm nearly at the studio.'

'OK. Bye, sweetheart.' But Coco was gone. Delilah looked at the phone suspiciously. What was up? Was she entangled with some new bloke who wasn't yet ready for the Rafferty circus? Was she heading for one of her dark spells? Or did she just want to spend the day in bed?

The phone rang again.

'Is Tyger coming?'

Delilah was instantly wary. Coco and Tyger could be the best of friends or the worst of enemies. You could never tell. Was this the root of Coco's reticence – a feud with her little sister?

'I haven't heard from her,' she replied truthfully.

'OK.' Coco rang off.

Delilah rolled her eyes. It was such a typical Coco call – no greeting, no goodbye, just a curt question. Sometimes she found her eldest daughter irritatingly self-absorbed. Or maybe Coco felt so close to her that she didn't need to be polite?

She went back to her planning, and her heart quailed. This party was going to be a fracas, no matter how carefully she planned it. There would be squabbles and scenes and tantrums, about who was wearing what and who was bringing who and who was sitting where. The Rafferty sisters could be guaranteed to make a drama out of a crisis. She supposed it was her own fault. She'd brought them up to be feisty and independent, able to voice their own opinions, so she shouldn't complain when she was on the receiving end of it. And they would all be as good as gold on the night, she was sure of it. She knew perfectly well Coco would turn up in the end.

As she looked down the list for the hundredth time, racking her brain to see if she had left anyone off, a thought occurred to her. She *hadn't* heard from Tyger, for over a week. She usually phoned every couple of days, her breathless, rushed tones imparting the latest scandal, but there had been nada since . . . Delilah couldn't remember when she'd last spoken to her.

Delilah scrolled through the names on her phone and pressed dial. It went straight to voicemail: *Hi, it's Tyger. You know what to do.*

Delilah hung up. There was no point in leaving a message. It would be one of a thousand. She'd see her tomorrow. Of all the girls, Tyger was the most loyal, even though her life was lived at a hundred and ten miles an hour. She lived in a whirlwind of business meetings, press launches, PR stunts and parties. She never returned anyone's phone call, but she got away with it because of her impish charm. And because most people needed her more than she needed them.

But she never failed to turn up for the Saturday lunch. Never.

The Presidential Suite at the Bellagio looked as if it had been turned over by the Las Vegas Police Department. Open suitcases disgorged a trail of clothes that led to the bed, the bathroom, the wardrobe and back again. Plates of half-eaten food – sushi, Caesar salad, pizza, melted ice-cream – were strewn over every available surface. In the middle of the floor was a half-eaten three-tier wedding cake. Iced in red, white and black and studded with treble clefs and musical notes, it proclaimed around the bottom layer, 'I Love Rock 'n' Roll'. Two champagne glasses lay amongst the crumbs, accompanied by several empty bottles of Krug. A phone in the corner of the room rang insistently, then stopped, tired of being ignored.

Room service had tried to get in but the 'do not disturb' sign had been up for thirty-six hours, and the management had advised the cleaners to steer clear.

Honeymooners. They'd set off the smoke alarm six times with their cigarettes. And the noise of the music . . . Even now, at half past eight in the morning, Audioslave blared out from the sound system. On the bed, a young man lay strumming along on his guitar. He was skinny and sinewy; the physique of a man who burned his fuel before it even hit his stomach. He wore ripped jeans and a leather waistcoat, his torso bare, covered in a mass of tattoos. On his head was a battered top hat.

A girl came out of the bathroom. She had a spiky peroxide crop and a cute little face with a turned-up nose and freckles. She looked about twelve, dressed in a red polka-dot dress with sky-high scarlet stilettos. She bounded across the room, scrambled onto the bed and straddled him. She could feel the buckle of his belt digging into her and she rubbed against it, enjoying the sensation of cold metal against her hot clit. He ran his hands over her taut arse appreciatively, sliding his fingers under the skimpy lace of her knickers. He twisted the flimsy fabric in his hands and gave a sharp tug. The knickers came away in his hand.

'Cheap shit,' he commented with a grin.

'Cheap shit that retails at sixty-five quid.'

'You were robbed.' He held up the flimsy scrap disparagingly.

The girl lowered her face down to his and wrinkled her nose.

'Cheap shit that's paid for this room.'

They locked gazes for a moment.

'So, Mrs Dagger,' he said softly, 'what do we do now for kicks?'

Two

Coco chucked her phone on the passenger seat and put her foot down. Her white Scirocco responded eagerly. It wasn't her choice of car, but her mother had insisted on something safe and practical that didn't attract too much attention, and Coco had finally given in. And she had to admit the little car was nippy and comfortable, with its truffle leather seats and all the gadgets she needed. White was a questionable choice of colour, but she soon had a deal going with one of the guys who looked after the vehicles at the studios. He was quite happy to boast that he washed and valeted Coco Rafferty's car. She hated mess, but not enough to muck out the empty cans, gum wrappers and cigarette packets herself.

She pulled up at the security gates of the studio compound. A passer-by would never guess that behind the unassuming grey breeze-block wall was the lot where one of Britain's most popular dramas was shot. *Critical but Stable* was young in comparison to some of its long-running competitors, but its steamy storylines, featuring the staff and patients of a fictional London hospital, had made it must-see viewing for an incredible six million viewers per episode.

Coco had been drafted in to build on that success. The producers never let themselves get complacent. They knew they had to work to keep up their viewing figures, so they were always looking for ways to improve the show. Coco was under no illusion that she had been employed for her acting ability, but for her name and her body, which were equally hot. She was, after all, the daughter of living-legend Raf Rafferty. And her perfectly proportioned physique looked dynamite in that navy nurse's uniform, her waist cinched in with a webbed belt, a watch pinned to one of her 34C breasts.

She played Sister Emily Farraday, a virgin who was destined to break the heart of every surgeon, consultant, anaesthetist and registrar in the hospital, not to mention the lowlier porters and security guards. She was saving herself for her boyfriend Zak, currently on a life-support machine at the hospital following a tragic surfing accident.

Each episode began with Sister Farraday sitting at Zak's bedside, filling him in on her life, the hospital gossip, her thoughts, her dreams and her prayers for him to come back to her. And throughout each episode, Zak sent her messages from limbo – not only could he read minds where he was, but he could see into the future. So Emily found herself interfering with Fate on a daily basis – more often than not steering her colleagues away from the wrong decisions and saving patients' lives in the process.

It was a complicated and risky premise that sat nicely between traditional medical drama and the more experimental shows that dabbled in the dark side. A hybrid formula that the production company were hoping would prove a hit with all ages, harnessing both the populist and the cult. With Coco's episodes in the can but not yet transmitted, it was too soon to say whether the risk would pay off.

Needless to say the rest of the cast resented Coco somewhat, because her character was becoming the main focus of the show. The producers had done their market research. She would be a role model for the younger viewers, a bit of eye-candy for the older men, and the heartbreaking romance of her situation would be a sop for the middle-aged housewives. It was no wonder that the other actors were miffed. They'd been working hard to establish the show over the past two years, after all – they had to take some credit for the existing loyal fan-base. Coco sensed they felt it was a cheap stunt bringing in a celebrity, complete with column inches courtesy of her infamous parents. But it wasn't her fault. She couldn't turn the part down on the basis that the role of Emily Farraday was a cynical marketing ploy.

Now she was on board, she desperately wanted to break down the barrier she felt existed between her and her colleagues. As the new girl she felt isolated, but because of the status that had been thrust upon her, she found it well nigh impossible to break through and become accepted. For a start, everyone knew she was being paid a vast amount of money, and that she'd insisted on her own dressing room. None of this would endear her to them. Especially as she wasn't all that experienced as an actress – she'd only left drama school nine months before, having enrolled at the age of twenty-two. To be fair, it was her agent who had negotiated her immorally high fee, but the dressing room had been the deal breaker for Coco. Everyone else had to share, but she desperately needed her own space. Quite simply because she was crippled with nerves.

She was good, she knew she was good, and they wouldn't have taken her on if she couldn't act. But she was inexperienced and lacking in confidence. Every day she woke up feeling sick to her stomach at the thought of having to face the cameras. She would have loved to have gone to the catering bus at lunchtime and sat with the others eating free-range chicken and ratatouille, but she couldn't eat, not until the day's filming was over. Instead she went back to her tiny dressing room and sat in a beanbag going over and over her lines for the afternoon, doing her breathing exercises to relax her.

As a result, the others thought she was snotty. She knew she should try to break the ice, go out with them one night to the pizza place they frequented near the studios, have a few drinks and let her hair down, let them see the real her. They saw evidence of it often enough in the tabloids and gossip magazines. The problem was she couldn't wait to leave the studios every night. She escaped as soon as the floor manager told her it was a wrap, fled to her car and drove as fast as she could back to her flat, where she could finally face food. And although she knew she should stay in and get an early night, she so longed for non-judgemental company that she often ended up taking a cab into town, meeting friends in a club or a bar, then dancing till two in the morning. She'd been out last night, to her favourite private members' club in Dean Street, and glugged down one too many lychee martinis. Not enough to give her a hangover, but enough to make her feel groggy.

She found a space in the car park, switched off the engine and slid out of the car. She was wearing a grey tracksuit and an outsize satin parka, her honey-blonde hair tied back in a loose ponytail, her face make-up free. Despite her late night and overindulgence, she still looked a million dollars. Great bone structure, her mother's flawless skin and her father's swimming pool eyes. God bless good genes.

Inside, she felt a wreck. She felt light-headed and her stomach was churning, as it always did first thing in the morning. Her nerves were shredded. Would she be able to remember her cues? Would her performance be up to scratch? Would there be an unexpected cut that she wouldn't be able to take on board? It always threw her when the director changed things at the last minute, which he inevitably did. The script was constantly being altered because of continuity or because it was running too long or because the executive producer wanted to change the nuance of a story. So Coco could never be certain that the lines she had learned would be the ones she was expected to deliver.

She clutched today's scenes to her chest as she made her way down the long passage between the warehouses that held the scenery, then in through a non-descript door and along a corridor. Either side of her were doors leading to costume, make-up, the prosthetics department: inside she could see people already beavering away industriously. It never ceased to amaze her how many people were involved in getting *Critical but Stable* onto the screen. They all put in such long hours, and most of them weren't even getting a tenth of what she was getting.

She turned left down another long corridor that was lined with stills from the series. It unnerved her, seeing her co-stars peering out at her. Finally she reached the door to her dressing room. It was dark and poky. The window looked out onto a dingy courtyard filled with dumpsters. She'd done her best to make the space her own: a chenille rug to cover the threadbare beige carpet, some framed prints, a big silver beanbag, but it was still no better than a prison cell.

Anyone who thought acting was glamorous was seriously deluded.

She put the scenes she had to go through down on the dressing table, shrugged off her parka and sat down.

She stared at her Marc Jacobs tote.

She could almost sense the tiny little bag inside burning a hole in the soft leather.

Last night, after three martinis, she'd finally confided in a friend. She'd known Harley for years, so she trusted him enough to reveal her insecurities and anxieties. She explained about the torture she felt, day in, day out. How she desperately wanted to belong to the team, but how she felt so far from being a team player. He'd found it hard to believe. Coco Rafferty, so bright and sexy and confident when she was out with her mates, crippled with doubt?

But he'd come up with a solution – a very practical one. To go with it, he'd given her a list of strict instructions: she must ration her use, not become over dependent, and, above all, must make sure she wiped her nose clean every time she used it.

'You'd be amazed how many people come out of the toilet with white around their nostrils,' he'd said, slipping her a little package under the table.

Coco got it out now and stared at it. She'd never been a big drug user. She and her sisters had always been more than aware of the dangers of addiction, whatever the substance.

This was just going to be an ice-breaker, to get her over her self-consciousness and give her the confidence to make friends. And maybe forget her nerves. Harley hadn't given her enough to develop any sort of habit, anyway. She would be fine. Lots of people she knew were light users. You didn't become a complete coke-head with a rotting septum overnight.

Of course, she'd have to take care. There were people all around her just waiting for her to make a wrong move. At least she had her own space. She jumped up to make sure her door was locked, then chopped out a line with precision. Not too much. Then she brought out a pink straw she'd pinched from the cocktail bar the night before and carefully snipped it into quarters with her nail scissors.

For a moment she hesitated. She thought she could hear a tiny alarm bell in the back of her mind. Think of Dad, she told herself. Look how he destroyed himself. Images of that terrible time replayed themselves like a montage. Her mother's tears. Her father's protestations and empty promises. Rows. Pledges. Shattered hopes. Knowing looks from her classmates; sympathy from her teachers. Embarrassment. Lying under the covers praying he would stop . . . Which he eventually did, but not before he had done a lot of damage and ruined one of the most promising acting careers of the twentieth century. Presumably he had started just like this – one small drink, to give him confidence. She didn't know. She had never spoken to him about it. As far as the Rafferty family were concerned, those years were ancient history, not to be revisited. A decade and a half of wanton destructiveness had been swept under the carpet.

Raf hadn't wanted her to act, she knew that. Which was why she had tried several other things before finally going to drama school, but in the end she couldn't shake the desire. He hadn't stopped her, but he certainly hadn't encouraged her. Presumably he was afraid that she would take the same path as him, that she would inherit his weakness and his fear and his addiction.

But she was different. Her father hadn't been in control. He had let drink take over completely. That wouldn't happen to her. Coco knew exactly what she was doing. This was a calculated risk. Not even a risk, in fact. A tactical move to help her survive.

She bent her head and snorted up the line carefully.

Looked in the mirror and checked for evidence.

Breathed in again deeply and smiled, as the magic powder whooshed into her blood stream.

Would anyone be able to tell? Shit, would they all look at her and see straight away she was as high as a kite? She'd be sacked on the spot. There was zero tolerance on the set, though the producers didn't go as far as random testing, not least because the backlash of someone testing positive would be such an inconvenience. The perpetrator would have to be disciplined, given a warning, the press would find out – the press always found out, no matter how confidential these matters were kept.

For a moment, she panicked. Someone would sniff her out straight away. They were all out to get her, after all. Then she told herself to stop being paranoid. She'd had a little line, a tiny pick-me-up – barely enough to even count.

She took a deep breath and waited a little longer for the cocaine to take effect.

'Bring it on, baby,' she said to her reflection.

There was a knock at the door. She answered it with a radiant smile. The little girl who did her make-up looked at her in surprise.

'We're ready for you, Miss Rafferty.'

'Call me Coco, darling,' she said cheerfully. 'I'll just get my bag.' Moments later she glided down the corridor, ready to take on the world.

For once, Coco enjoyed having her make-up done. Usually she was quiet and withdrawn, as once you were in make-up it was only a matter of time before you went onto the set. She used the time to go over her lines yet again. She lived in terror of drying up in the middle of a scene and letting her fellow actors down. They were ruled by the clock in the studio, with a set number of scenes to get through each day, and woe betide anyone who held up the process.

Other people fluffed their lines. Of course they did. It happened all the time. But Coco was a perfectionist. She wouldn't allow herself to fail. She had to have an unblemished track record. After all, everyone was waiting for her to slip up.

Today, however, she let herself relax. Ruby, her make-up girl, had all the tools of her trade spread out around her – brushes, tweezers, sponges, eyelash curlers. The actual make-up was piled up in a huge muddle on a shelf, but Ruby's deft fingers knew exactly which tube she wanted, which mascara, which powder. As she played a nurse, Coco's make-up was fairly toned down and neutral, but it took time nevertheless.

As Ruby worked, George Michael's 'Faith' was blaring out.

Coco smiled and clicked her fingers in time to the music. 'God, I love this song.'

Ruby looked at her in surprise. Coco was usually mono-syllabic – she'd given up trying to chat with her – and she certainly never started a conversation.

Ruby flicked a glance at the other two other actresses having their make-up done in neighbouring chairs.

'George Michael. What a waste,' she sighed.

'My mum says he's lovely,' offered Coco. 'She did a photo shoot with him once.'

'Oh yeah – she used to be a model, right?'

Coco nodded. 'In the eighties. Before she met my dad.'

'Wow. I bet they've got some stories.'

Coco's lips curled into a little rueful grin. 'You could say that.'

She took a sip of her coffee, not wanting to say much more, because she never spoke about her family, but feeling pleased that she had made the first move for once. Deftly she switched the conversation.

'Where do you get these eyelash curlers? They're amazing – I can never get mine to work.'

'I'll get you some if you like,' offered Ruby. 'I've got to go to the warehouse to pick some stuff up.'

'That would be great,' answered Coco, feeling warm inside. She felt, almost, like one of the girls.

Ruby picked up a lipstick.

'How about we try this colour today? Just for a change.'

Coco nodded, just as Neal bounded in. He played Zak, the boyfriend in a coma, so he needed a suitably corpse-like complexion, which took hours to achieve.

'Hey, girls, you ready for me?'

'Hey, Neal.' Coco greeted him with a smile.

Neal took the cue and put both of his hands on Coco's shoulders, kneading them lightly. Whereas before she would have shot him an icy glance in the mirror, she gave herself up willingly to his fingers, tipping her head back.

'Mmmm. You're good at that.'

'I am.'

He looked straight at her in the mirror.

'You seen next week's scripts?'

'Not yet . . .'

Coco never looked ahead, in case she got confused. She got the week's filming out of the way, then read the following week's scripts as soon as she got home on Friday night, to embed them in her brain as quickly as possible.

Neal leaned forward and grinned.

'We have sex.'

'How? You're in a coma!' Coco feigned horror. 'Emily's not going to turn into some kind of . . . necrophiliac, is she?'

Everyone burst into laughter and again Coco felt gratified that she had made a joke. This was great.

'Relax.' Neal grinned. 'It's a dream sequence. It's Emily's

fantasy. And she turns out to be one hot little mama under that uniform.'

He winked at her reflection.

Coco couldn't be sure if Neal was winding her up. This was exactly his sense of humour. He liked to think he was a bit of a joker, but in fact he was a bit of a prat, as the rest of the cast and crew had already found out. Behind his drop-dead-gorgeous surfer looks, he was as insecure as the rest of them.

She wasn't going to let him think she was fazed, however. She responded gamely.

'Wow. That's going to be a ratings puller – Sister Emily finally gets her knickers off.'

Neal flopped down in a spare chair and pushed his shoulder-length blonde locks back from his face.

'It's going to make a change from me lying still on the bed trying not to laugh.'

Coco looked at him.

'It must get boring.'

'It's not what I went to drama school for.'

Ruby gave her face a final dusting with Cornsilk powder.

'You're done.'

Coco stood up.

'Cheers, Ruby. See you later.' She'd be back in after lunch for a touch-up. The make-up never lasted long under the bright lights. She wiggled her fingers at Neal. 'And if you think we need some rehearsal time for those steamy scenes . . .'

As she went, Neal looked round at the others with a raised eyebrow.

'Someone's been on the happy tablets . . .'

Coco bounced into the green room, her mood still buoyant. The cast were sitting around, some of them nibbling on the plate of Danish pastries and croissants, others on fruit. They were variously perusing the daily papers, texting, going through their lines. One was actually knitting, supporting the myth that this was the preferred activity of waiting actors.

'Hi!' she offered gaily, and her colleagues looked up in surprise. Coco rarely ventured into the green room.

'Is there an apricot Danish left?' She rushed over to the plate and picked one out, sat in a chair and began to munch. 'Are they nearly done?'

She indicated a screen in the corner showing a feed through to the studio, where the cast and crew were running through a scene about to be filmed in the operating theatre.

'They've rehearsed. It shouldn't be too long. It's only a two-hander.'

Coco walked over to the noticeboard, which displayed a variety of adverts for lodgings, invitations to parties, stuff for sale, yoga classes, and incriminating photos of cast members. There was a poster announcing a social night at a local bowling alley.

'Anyone got a pen?'

The knitter put down her knitting and burrowed in her bag, proffering a chewed Biro.

'Thanks.' Coco took it gratefully and added her name to the list of people attending. 'Should be fun.'

Mike, a twinkly eyed round fellow who played one of the hospital porters, nodded. 'Yeah, well, you know what they say. All work and no play.'

'I haven't had much chance to socialise since I've been here. I've been having some work done on my flat – I always need to get home and survey the damage, clear up the mess . . . To be honest, it's been stressing me out. But it's done now.'

The lie was effortless. Coco hoped it was convincing. Maybe they'd swallow this explanation for her standoffishness and word would get round.

'Well, you'd better get in training if you're coming out for the night with us lot. It can get pretty hairy,' Mike warned her.

'Don't worry. I'll stay the pace.'

She heard the floor manager call her for the next scene on the Tannoy, jumped up and raised a hand in farewell.

'See you all later.'

As the door shut behind her, everyone looked at each other.

'Has she had a personality transplant?' offered Mike.

Coco teased Neal all the way through the rehearsal, trying to make him laugh as he lay in his coma. She cooed over the floor manager's pregnant bump, gossiped with the medical adviser who sat through every scene to make sure it was totally authentic, chatted through a couple of changes with the director – normally she would have freaked out at any suggested alteration, but today she could handle it.

She could totally handle it. All of it. She felt as if she could take anything they threw at her. She went at the scene with a renewed energy. She always gave a good performance, but this time she lifted it just a little higher. Her mood seemed to be catching – everyone reacted off her and the scene they finally got in the can was a scorcher.

Coco left the studio feeling elated. She had just begun to get a headache, which wasn't unusual. The lights in the studio, the concentration, the stress – but it didn't matter. Today she had given the performance of a lifetime – and enjoyed it! And if she could do it once, she could do it again and again and again. Thank you, Harley, you bloody little genius, she thought, as she opened the door of her dressing room and slipped inside.

Three

The great thing about the Soho Hotel was, no matter how famous you were, there was always someone more famous than you in there. But no one ever batted an eyelid, because it was uncool to be starstruck, or stare. If you saw Daniel Craig waiting for the lift, you had to pretend not to notice.

So it was the perfect place for Raf Rafferty and Dickie Rushe to meet. They wouldn't be bothered for autographs, but it was a given that word would be out before they had even finished their meeting – a discreet whisper would insinuate its way through the streets of Soho and reach the ears of every other producer and director who had their offices in the hallowed streets of London's media-land.

Raf stretched out on the apple-green sofa in the drawing room and nursed a tall glass of soda with freshly squeezed lime juice and crushed ice. One of the problems with giving up the booze had been the question of what to drink, and this was the concoction he had finally settled upon. It looked as if it could conceivably contain alcohol and it tasted pleasant enough, and he enjoyed giving instructions to the bartender – a whole lime, plus two wedges from another and a grating of zest. Ritual was everything when you were on the wagon. It helped take your mind off the longing. The longing that never left you.

He looked over at Dickie, who was perched on the edge of a squashy pink armchair. Dickie was tall and gangly with horn-rimmed glasses: a bundle of gentle enthusiasm and nervous energy, all knees and elbows. His first two movies, *Bed Head* and *Bad Hair Day*, had been cult hits on both side of the Atlantic, with their kooky charm and naive wit, but despite his success, he still dressed like a penniless student. Today he was in jeans, a V-necked jumper that was four sizes too small and battered desert boots. Raf was in essentially the same outfit – a fine gauge sweater in pale pistachio, jeans and Paul Smith brogues – but he felt positively overdressed in comparison.

Dickie was so immersed in his work, so passionate, that he didn't bother with small talk, for which Raf was grateful. He spent enough time talking nonsense with all the hangers-on that were in their lives. Raf was good at chit-chat, but it was a relief not to have to bother. Dickie cut straight to the chase.

'OK, so here's the pitch. It's called *Something for the Weekend*. An ironic title, because it all predicates around Hugo – that would be your character – forgetting to use a condom when he sleeps with his mistress. Because he's not from the condom generation – he hasn't slept with someone else since he got married to his wife in nineteen seventy-nine. So what happens then is his mistress gets pregnant. Oops. And that wasn't the plan. She was just supposed to be a mild diversion for his mid-life crisis – he's been faithful until now, but he can't cope with his once-glamorous wife hurtling into jam-making and comfy shoes. Thirty-something Saskia seemed the perfect answer, happy to have no-strings sex. But now things are complicated – and made even more so by the fact that Hugo's oldest daughter has announced she is pregnant, too: he's about to become a grandfather . . .'

Dickie sat back with a smile and looked to Raf for his reaction.

He gave an amused grimace. 'There but for the grace of God . . .'

'Exactly!' Dickie leaned forward again, clasping his hands and resting his elbows on his knees. 'This could conceivably be you.'

'Except I'm not being unfaithful to Delilah.' Raf fixed him

22

with a stare. He wasn't going to be a walkover. He would make Dickie sing for his supper.

'No. But you have been in the past.' Dickie knew he had to stand up to Raf. If he didn't he would have no hope of getting the actor on board. And it wasn't as if Raf's former infidelities weren't common knowledge. They had kept the nation enthralled for years. 'So you understand the temptation. And the ramifications. Just imagine you took up with that waitress over there . . .'

Dickie gesticulated towards the very attractive blonde who was taking an order from a sofa full of businessmen.

'And then Coco or Violet or Tyger announced she was pregnant at the same time as she did . . .'

Raf sighed and stretched out his legs. 'That's pure fantasy. It's no better than saying imagine if I'd discovered the cure for cancer.'

'It's not that impossible! Come on, play the game.' Dickie's desperation was making him irritable. 'It's perfectly feasible. You've still got lead in your pencil. And your girls are getting to that age—'

Raf unleashed his famous blue gaze – the one that bored right through you, so you couldn't be sure what he was thinking.

Dickie squirmed. 'Come on, Raf, give me a break. I'm talking to you first because I think you'd be perfect. You'd walk it. And it's a winner. There's something for everyone: you for our generation, Pandora Hammond for the next generation, cutting-edge sound track, great locations – three months' filming in Bath. What's not to like?'

Raf swirled the drink in his glass. Dickie didn't realise it, but he was acting a part now. Playing the reluctant star. He wanted this part, desperately. Acting was in his blood. He longed to pick up the script, absorb every word of dialogue, immerse himself in the character, find all the little nuances that would make the role his.

There was just one huge and insurmountable problem. He had never acted sober in his life.

For all he knew, without the crutch of drink he was as wooden as the bloody table the script was sitting on. He didn't know if he could do it. And he was reluctant to take a risk with a director he genuinely admired.

Frankly, it was astonishing that Dickie wanted him to so much as carry a spear. But Raf wasn't a fool. Dickie wasn't doing this out of the kindness of his heart. This was a gamble, and if it paid off, Dickie would be credited with resurrecting the career of one of the best-loved actors of the twentieth century. Like Tarantino had with John Travolta in *Pulp Fiction*. Except John Travolta hadn't been a pisshead . . .

It was ten years since Raf had trashed the epic, multi-gazillion-dollar production of Homer's *Iliad* with his legendary binge. He had been carted off the location and slung into rehab, and he hadn't set foot on a film set since that day. No one would touch him. He was a liability.

Raf picked up the script. His heart was pounding. It felt so good – that weighty sheaf of A4 paper, each page unfolding another step of the story. He scanned the first page. You could always tell straight away if a script was going to be a turkey or a diamond. At least he could. Which was why he had chosen hit after hit. Until the bloody booze got the better of him.

He scanned the stage directions and the dialogue. By the fifth speech he was already smiling, and could feel the fizz in the bottom of his stomach – the fizz that made him want to carry on reading. He put the script down hastily. He didn't want to look too eager. Any glimmer of enthusiasm and Dickie would start working on him. It had been a long time since he had been courted. It was only too easy to be flattered and cajoled. He wanted to make this decision with a clear head.

It was strange, being a household name yet not carrying on the work for which you were famous. It was like being in suspended animation. He felt as if he was half living. And he knew one thing – he didn't want to carry on as he was, playing second fiddle to Delilah. Immersing himself in tennis and rowing, writing film reviews for that poncy arts magazine, sorting stuff out for the girls and their various ventures, teaching himself guitar – he kept himself busy on the surface but nothing had ever filled the vacuum.

This was the opportunity he had been waiting for. He knew without reading it that the script was a winner, because he trusted Dickie's judgement. He completely understood what he was trying to do with this film. It would be romantic, heart-warming, sexy, thought-provoking. It would make you laugh and it would make you cry. And he knew he was perfect for the role of Hugo. He knew he could portray Hugo's agony, the dilemmas of an attractive man of a certain age. He knew he could make Hugo sympathetic even though he was being unfaithful to his wife.

By taking the role he would be taking a huge risk. Not because he thought he couldn't do it, but because the very thought of doing it made him want a hefty slug of vodka in his soda and lime, and it was all he could do not to beckon the waitress over. And he hadn't even started acting yet.

He put his glass down carefully.

'Who's going to play my wife?'

This was an important question. If the actress was a contemporary, there was every chance that Raf would have had an affair with her. He didn't particularly want to open any of those cans of worms.

'Genevieve Duke.'

Dickie couldn't help shooting Raf a triumphant look. Genevieve Duke was his ace. She was better known for theatre than for film, notoriously picky about what she chose. She was the thinking man's crumpet, incredibly sexy in a way that couldn't be pinpointed. Icy reserve, fabulous tits and a voice like dark treacle, all combined with a scathing wit. Sexually voracious, too, if the legends were to be believed. One famous actor had a particularly filthy anecdote involving a very short ride in a lift.

25

More than anything, though, Genevieve Duke was a wonderful actress.

Raf could almost feel himself salivating. The chance to work with Genevieve was tempting. Their paths had never crossed in his acting days. She had spent most of her time treading the boards at the RSC in Stratford or the National. If he was going to make a comeback, she was the actress to do it with. And Dickie obviously knew that only too well. They would be dynamite.

He wasn't going to let Dickie see his excitement. Instead, he frowned.

'I can't see Genevieve Duke playing a fifty-something woman who's gone to seed.'

'Ah, but here's the twist: when she hears about Hugo's affair, his wife re-invents herself and runs off with a man ten years younger. And at the same time Saskia – the mistress – realises that Hugo has feet of clay and dumps him. So by the end of the movie, he's lost both his wife and his mistress. The final scene is him alone in the park with a double buggy containing his daughter and his granddaughter. And there's no one to share the experience with him.'

'The moral of the story being . . . ?'

Dickie grinned wryly. 'Always wear a condom.'

Raf laughed appreciatively as Dickie leaned forward again.

'No – seriously. It's a tale of our times – about how we give in to our mid-life crises all too easily. And it's about life being a cliché – how we all fall into those traps, even though we swear we never will.'

Raf leaned back in the depths of the sofa and shut his eyes. His mind was racing. He loved the pitch. He could see the film already. It probably wouldn't be Oscar material – it was a little too lightweight and fluffy – but it would definitely be a hit. And he would be re-launched. He would get his pick of roles. He could be a star again – someone to be revered instead of a has-been trailing in the wake of his glamorous wife.

He picked up the script. Dickie looked at him expectantly.

'Who will you get to play Hugo if you don't get me?'

Dickie looked him in the eye. Actors, they were all the same. Insecure. Egotistical. He'd already checked out Bill Nighy's availability, but he wasn't going to tell Raf that.

'I haven't even thought about it. To my mind, there is only one Hugo and that's you.'

Raf looked at him through slightly narrowed eyes. The guy did a great job.

'I'll read the script and I'll get back to you.'

Dickie smiled. 'It's a done deal, then. The script's fantastic.' He handed Raf his own spiral-bound copy in a heavy-duty envelope. 'Call me when you're done.'

The two men shook hands. Each had a feeling in their guts that this meeting was going to change the course of their lives, but neither of them voiced it just yet. There was still a long way to go.

Raf walked out into the streets of Soho. The air smelled of last night's sesame oil and cigarette smoke. People were jostling each other: workers on their way to lunch, media types and strippers, waitresses and voyeurs. Triple-X movie theatres sat next to edgy boutiques and fashionable bars. There was an energy mixed with the scent of decadence. Raf loved Soho. It made him feel alive. You could be anyone here. Or no one, if that's what you preferred. Mad, bad Soho, where anything goes. You could have a Michelin-starred meal or buy a pair of size-twelve skyscraper stilettos. Or both, if you had the budget and the predilection. Nobody judged you here.

Raf grabbed a table outside his favourite café. It was still a little chilly, the April sunshine was lacking in confidence, but he wanted to enjoy the few rays it was throwing out. He ordered a coffee and a smoked-salmon bagel from the waitress, pulled the script out of its envelope and began to read.

No one took a blind bit of notice of him. There was a time when he couldn't have gone anywhere without being mobbed, or at least hassled for his autograph. Now he had a more low-key status as an underground icon. If anyone looked at him now, it probably wasn't because they recognised him but because he was still startlingly good-looking.

In his heyday, he'd had a wild mop of curls which he kept long. At the first hint of grey three years ago he had gone straight to the hairdresser's and had every lock shorn off. He was surprised to find that it suited him better. The curls had been so much part of him and his raffish gypsy bad-boy image, but the close crop set off his angular features – the sharp cheek-bones and the hypnotic eyes – and made him look, if anything, more beautiful. Those looks, together with his immaculate dress-sense – he'd been voted Best Dressed Man of the Year twice – meant he often received admiring glances.

It wasn't enough, to be a bit of iconic eye-candy. He was no longer known for what he did best. He was in the shadow of his dazzling wife. Nobody knew what a struggle it really was. He was the envy of everyone he knew – not having to do anything but swan about and look the part – but the truth was he was in a gilded cage.

His life was entirely at the mercy of Delilah's schedule. His house was over-run by a film crew six months of the year. He couldn't sit and read the paper in his own kitchen half the time. He was wheeled out to any number of award ceremonies, premieres and after-parties – and all he really had to think about was what to wear. It was hardly stretching.

So *Something for the Weekend* was a proposition he had to take very seriously. He didn't want to melt into middle-age a nonentity. He wanted something for himself, something he could be proud of and that stretched him. His renaissance was long overdue.

The part had to be right, of course. In his time, he had played bad boys, scoundrels, lovable rogues, smooth-talkers. There had even been talk of him becoming the next James Bond. He'd had the looks. He'd perfected the art of the ruthless stare. He'd had the animal magnetism. The killer body – fit, lean, not too obviously worked out but panther-like. There was no doubt it would have taken him onto a whole new level, but he'd blown it.

Did he regret the error of his ways? Would he have swapped those wild years of excess for the chance to be 007? He didn't think so. Raf didn't believe in regret. The party years had made him what he was today, and even if he wasn't totally enamoured of who that was, here in front of him was a chance to change, to be who he wanted to be once again.

Half an hour later, his coffee untouched, he picked up his mobile, scrolling through till he found the right number.

'Dickie? It's Raf. You're totally wrong about this script. It's not fantastic.'

There was a disappointed silence at the end of the phone. Raf grinned.

'It's totally fucking out of this world.'

Four

Polly Fry's legs were pumping furiously. Her heart felt as if it was going to burst out of her not insubstantial chest, but she had to keep going. This was going to be the regime that worked, she knew it. She'd snipped up her bus pass so she wouldn't be tempted to hop on. She'd bought a huge cagoule so the weather could never provide an excuse.

Surely cycling three miles to work and back every day would have an effect? It was bloody torture, so there ought to be some payback. She was halfway across Richmond Bridge now – nearly there, though she still had that ghastly hill to navigate. She knew she would probably have to get off and walk, but that was still exercise, wasn't it? And she would arrive at work red-faced and panting, but no one would mind. It had been Delilah's idea, after all. It was Delilah who'd ordered the bike for her birthday, after she'd found Polly sobbing in the cloakroom two weeks ago.

She'd polished off the rest of the cranberry and coconut cookies after the afternoon's shoot – even though they had been under the bright lights all day. She hadn't been able to resist. She'd been good all day – porridge for breakfast and a salad pitta bread for lunch. But the cookies had smelled so delicious. And once she'd had a bite of one – sugary, buttery, slightly salty, soft but crumbly – that was it. The whole lot had to go.

Why hadn't she been able to stop at one? Or even two? Like a normal person? She had to trough the whole lot, until she felt sick. And she couldn't even be sick. She didn't have the nerve to stick her fingers down her throat and chuck it all up. She wasn't bulimic; she was just a pig. She ate like a pig and looked like a pig.

Working with beautiful people didn't help. Delilah wasn't thin, she was curvaceous, but it was all in proportion, the classic hourglass figure. And the girls were all perfect – not an ounce of fat on one of them. If Polly wanted a reminder of her gluttony, she only had to compare herself to one of the Raffertys.

She'd worked for them for nearly ten years. She'd been taken on when Delilah was writing her first book. The publishing company had sent her along to collate the recipes, check them and make sure the measurements were correct. It had been hard work, deciphering Delilah's elaborate scrawls with the asterisks and squiggles and scratchings-out. Most of her recipes were from her head. But Polly was a plodder, meticulous and organised, and had done the most brilliant job.

She had been shocked at the chaos of the Rafferty household. Gradually, over the three months she had been employed, she had sorted out their lives. The girls had all lived at home then, which only added to the confusion. Polly had established some sort of order, starting with a huge calendar wall-chart she put up in the kitchen with a sticker system – a different colour for each of them. They had all been astonished at the difference it had made, and clearly thought Polly was a genius.

When her contract came to an end, Delilah had begged her to come and work for them full time and Polly had agreed. She didn't have a title. She wasn't a PA, because she could turn her hand to anything. Cook, chauffeur, hairdresser, sticker-on-of-false-eyelashes: her job description covered every eventuality. She never knew what she might be asked to do when she turned up in the morning. And she never knew quite what time she might go home at night. And she loved it. She loved being at the heart of this mad, noisy family

She had a stock answer when people asked her what the

Raffertys were like. 'They're lovely, absolutely lovely.' And that's all she would ever say.

She could never leave. Polly Wolly Doodle Dolly, they used to call her. They were her family, her social life, her entertainment, her sounding-boards. Her parents and her children in one. And in return they couldn't live without her. Her calm, her common sense and her meticulous organisation had kept the Rafferty family afloat for a decade. She was the voice of reason in a house full of neurotic mayhem.

Her parents and some of her friends had often expressed concern. They felt she was living in the Raffertys' pockets, that she had no identity of her own, and that they exploited her good nature. Her father thought it was incestuous and her mother felt the family were too dependent on her, given that she wasn't paid a huge salary, though the perks were spectacular. If the truth was known, Polly would have worked for them for nothing. She adored the girls – they were like sisters to her. Naughty little sisters who came to her for advice. She worshipped Delilah. And as for Raf . . .

She would walk over burning coals for Raf. Stick pins in her eyes. She adored him, unreservedly. Of course she knew he was out of her reach. He and Delilah belonged together. But as long as she could be near him, feast on him with her eyes every day, breathe in the same air that he breathed, then she was happy. Besides, he would never look at a pudding like her.

All in all, Polly was perfectly content with her lot, except for her wretched weight. It was getting out of hand. She was no fashion plate, but even she knew that size-sixteen stretch jeans with elasticated waist bands were hideous. She wore them with a rotation of baggy sweatshirts, topped with a padded waistcoat when it was cold. And loafers. She knew she dressed like a frumpy English cliché, but girls like her didn't have much choice when it came to fashion. The baggy layers were an institution to hide behind. There were carbon copies of Polly all over the Home Counties – women to whom skinny jeans were as inaccessible as the moon. Her face was pretty – round, with twinkly eyes and a mass of unruly curls that she tied back in a scrunchy – but she felt sure no one saw beyond the massive arse and wobbly stomach. Not to mention the thunder thighs.

She reached the bottom of Richmond Hill. There was no way she would be able to cycle to the top. Her legs were already trembling, so she climbed off and began the ascent.

'*I will not ask a lovelier dream, A sweeter scene, fair Thames, than thine . . .*' she murmured as she looked down at the famous view – the only view in England to be protected by an act of Parliament. And rightly so – the sight made her heart soar every time. The lush green meadows, the mighty trees, the silver thread of the river pushing its way determinedly through the verdant landscape, and in the far distance, on a clear day, the outline of Hampton Court. It was a slice of English countryside in the middle of town, and the reason why so many celebrities had made Richmond their home. With the centre of London only twenty minutes by train, yet the splendours of the Thames and Richmond Park on your doorstep, it was the perfect compromise. And the spattering of high-end boutiques, delis, restaurants, the theatre, and the Green – what more could a wealthy, aspirational family ask for?

Eventually, panting and perspiring, she reached the crest of the hill and came to a halt outside the electronic gates of The Bower. Delilah and Raf had resisted this type of security for years, but had eventually capitulated, after several attempted break-ins, prowlers and press intrusion.

The house was an estate agent's dream. Queen Anne listed, it was perfectly proportioned, a large family home that was neither ostentatious nor unmanageable, with every twenty-first-century luxury sympathetically integrated into its gracious walls. Polly pressed the code that allowed her access through the tradesman's gate, pushed her bike through and left it propped against the garage wall before slipping through another gate into the garden and down the path that led to her office, housed in a little lodge that also contained a gym and the massive laundry room.

It was Friday, which meant she had to order up food for tomorrow's lunch, as well as flowers. She needed to check with the housekeeper that scented candles and soaps were all in stock. She needed to organise deliveries from the butcher, greengrocer, cheesemonger, wine merchant and bakery, depending on what Delilah had decided to cook. Extricating this information from her was the most difficult task: Delilah hated to be pinned down, but unless Polly got the menu from her by midday, she wouldn't get the ingredients. The days of Delilah having either the time or the inclination to wander into Richmond and do the shopping herself were long gone. And Polly knew her likes and dislikes only too well by now, her preferred brands and varieties.

She flicked on the lights, booted up the computer and pottered across the garden, into the main house by the back door then through into the kitchen.

This room was familiar to nearly everyone in the land, as it was where Delilah's cookery show was shot. Nearly thirty foot by twenty, it was fitted with hand-built cupboards painted in rich cream, limestone flooring and a semi-circular island topped with white marble, behind which Delilah cooked the mouth-watering food that was emulated in virtually every kitchen nationwide. The canary-yellow Lacanche cooker into which she slid her concoctions was almost as famous as she was.

Adjoining the kitchen was the orangery where Delilah's guests were filmed devouring the food she made in each episode. This in turn overlooked the walled garden, where a stone terrace looked down on a series of three tiered ink-black pools. Here and there were dotted pieces of antique statuary mixed with more modern pieces of garden sculpture – Raf's passion – the pride of which was an entwined couple made of wire. This had been Delilah's twenty-fifth wedding anniversary present to him.

Delilah was sitting on a high stool at the island, her para-phernalia around her. She was just hanging up her phone. She looked pale, slightly shocked.

'Delilah?' Polly rushed forward, anxious.

'It's Raf . . .'

Polly's heart gave a lurch. What had happened to him? Had there been some sort of accident? An image flashed into her mind, of Raf's beautiful body crushed under a lorry. She couldn't bear it. Her mouth was dry with panic. She could barely speak.

'What's happened?' she croaked.

To her relief, Delilah smiled. 'He's doing the movie. He's taken the part.'

Sweet relief flooded through Polly. 'That's . . . fantastic,' she breathed, still feeling a bit shaky.

'I know. I think . . .' Delilah replied. 'It's going to be . . . weird.'

For a moment she looked totally at a loss. Then she slapped her hands decisively on the worktop. Delilah was never thrown by anything for long.

'Right,' she said, 'action stations. We need to get Tony over here for a meeting as soon as. And Miriam. Work out when we're going to announce this. And who to. Get on to the film company – tell them part of the deal is we control the publicity. Ask Dickie Rushe for lunch tomorrow. And Genevieve Duke – she's going to play Raf's wife . . .'

Polly had already grabbed a notebook out of her bag and started writing notes. She'd been expecting a quiet day, and now it was going to be anything but. The Rafferty machine was whirring into action.

Tony was the Rafferty publicist, responsible for keeping bad things out and getting good things in to the press. Miriam was the Rafferty family's agent – although Raf hadn't acted for years, she still dealt with various things he was asked to do, occasional public appearances and voice-overs. She would be negotiating his contract, just as she had recently negotiated Coco's.

Delilah was running her hands through her mane of hair, looking slightly overwhelmed. Polly knew her mind would be working overtime, working out all the ramifications of this new departure. There was no doubt it was going to have a huge impact on all of their lives.

'The girls . . .' she was saying. 'We need to tell the girls.'

'They're coming tomorrow, aren't they?'

'I think so. Coco's being tricky. I don't know what's up with her. I'm sure Violet will come. And I haven't heard from Tyger all week.' Delilah looked at Polly. 'Track her down for me, will you?'

Polly nodded, scribbling furiously. Any thoughts she'd had of a restorative cup of tea were out the window. Any thoughts she'd had of escaping early tonight to attend Weight Watchers at the local primary school were out the window. Life was going to be full-on for the duration. Still, when it was hectic there was less opportunity to eat.

Welcome to the Rafferty diet . . .

Having given Polly her orders, Delilah ran up the sweeping staircase and along the upstairs corridor to the master bedroom. She threw herself onto the bed, shutting her eyes and breathing in deeply to try and calm herself.

Why did she feel so horribly unsettled?

Ever since Raf had phoned to tell her he was doing the movie, she'd had a tight knot in her stomach. She should be ecstatic, jumping up and down for joy. She was the one who had encouraged him, after all. Instead, she felt nothing but dread. Now it was a reality, she suddenly wished she'd told Dickie it was out of the question when he had first mooted the idea.

Had she secretly hoped that Raf wouldn't take the bait? That he wouldn't have the courage? What kind of a bitch was she, that she couldn't be happy for her husband? Was she . . .

jealous? She knew he was going to be in the limelight. Was there some kind of green-eyed monster lurking in her that was resentful of his incipient success?

He would be successful. Of that she had no doubt. The formula was practically tried and tested. With all those talented people on board, the film was hardly going to bomb at the box-office. And that would lead to other things. More roles. A higher profile.

Wasn't this exactly what she wanted? To be relieved of the responsibility of being the breadwinner and to take a back seat? She'd felt so tired of late. Not physically, necessarily, though it did take a little more effort to bounce out of bed in the morning than it had in her youth. But mentally. She was tired of juggling everything in her head. Trying to assess what mental state each of the girls was in. Trying to assess what mental state Raf was in. Finding ways to keep her show fresh and exciting and inspiring, as well as her books, in a market that was fiercely competitive. Keeping herself looking good, without resorting to anything extreme. Did anyone have any idea how much work it took to look youthful, to keep her figure just the right side of fulsome without running to fat? It was easier to be thin than aesthetically curvaceous. If she dieted too much it instantly went off her breasts, yet if she ate too much her stomach ballooned. Being the woman every woman wanted to be and the woman every man wanted to shag was exhausting. You didn't get a day off, you couldn't go out looking anything other than fabulous, even if it was an artless fabulous that suggested she had just thrown on the first thing that came to hand. Those sneaky photos that made you look bloated and unkempt could do untold damage, and the papers and magazines seemed particularly enamoured of them these days, as if they were trying to reassure their readers that glamour and beauty were just smoke and mirrors.

Which, of course, to a large extent they were. You had to tick a few boxes to begin with, but walking out of the house looking a million dollars took time, effort and money, even if you went for the casual, natural look. *Especially* if you went for the casual, natural look and you were breathing down the neck of fifty.

Fifty. Where had all those years gone? Somehow it was only when something momentous happened that you took the time to look back and wonder how you had got here.

Delilah was originally Deborah, an ordinary girl from Bradford on Avon with extraordinary looks who worked in a travel agent. She and her friends had gone on a day trip to London, where she had been spotted by a talent scout at the Hard Rock Café. On her agent's advice, she'd changed her name from Deborah to Delilah (her mother was a Tom Jones fan), and it had taken her more than six months to remember to respond to the name when someone called her. She had taken to modelling like a duck to water, being unselfconscious and imaginative, but most important of all hardworking.

She'd come to the public's attention when she'd starred in a series of television adverts for a popular chocolate bar. She'd been filmed devouring it with sensual pleasure along with uninhibited moans in a variety of inappropriate places – in a box at the opera, at a board meeting, in the middle of a wedding – and the ads had developed a cult status, sending sales of the chocolate bar soaring. Delilah had found herself a public figure overnight, unable to walk down the street without people humming 'Mmmm . . .' as she passed. A whole new world had opened up to her. She'd worked hard and played hard, jetting all over the world, never out of work because of her versatility, her professional attitude and her constant smile.

Then one day she was offered a part in a film. She had shied away at first, until she learned that she didn't actually have to act. She was to play the object of the leading man's obsession – a fantasy figure he lusted over from afar, in a bucolic coming-of-age love story that ended in tragedy. It was being heralded as the next *Tess*, a sensual, passionate tale with 'tasteful' nudity. Delilah had agonised over whether she should agree to being filmed without her clothes on, but the director's credibility was so high that in the end she gave in. Polanski hadn't done Nastassja Kinski any harm.

Everyone had warned her about Raf: her agent, the director, her mother, the milkman. Good for nothing, ne'er-do-well womanising drunk was the general consensus. She'd been quite certain that she would be immune to his looks and his charm. She'd fought off enough come-ons from men who thought they were God's gift. Raf Rafferty wasn't going to cause her any problems.

He took her breath away on sight. Nothing could have prepared her for the depth of his blue eyes, the clarity of his skin, the perfection of his bone-structure. She had never seen anything so close to a deity, and this was a woman who mixed with perfection in her job every day. And she hadn't been prepared for his sincerity, though a little voice inside her told her he was an actor, that it was an act, that this was what he did day in, day out for a living, and she shouldn't be fooled. When he looked at her, she felt her soul trying to fight its way out of her body and into his. When he told her – *told* her, not asked her – he was going to kiss her three days into the shoot, she was lost.

Everyone working on the film saw it. It was as if they were the only two people who existed, with an invisible force field around them. The crew rolled their collective eyes at the predictability of it – there hadn't been a leading lady yet who Raf hadn't worked his magic on. But this time it was different. This time he wasn't playing a role. This time he truly was in love, and it shone out in his performance, as his character burned with an unrequited passion. There were even hushed rumours of an Oscar. And by the end of the film, they were Mr and Mrs Rafferty. The cast and crew attended the wedding; the photos were on the front page of every newspaper in the world.

The first six months of married life were bliss, as both Raf and Delilah decided to take some time off. They bought a huge garden flat in Kensington, furnished it from antique stalls, went out for dinner, caught up with their respective old friends and made new ones, took little trips to places they'd never been – Florence, Marrakesh, Portmeirion. And then Delilah had discovered to her delight that she was pregnant. She couldn't wait to become a full-time mum. The film had bought and paid for the flat between them; she had plenty of savings. And Raf was thrilled to be becoming a father. They did a sumptuous shoot for Nigel Dempster, Delilah in a floaty chiffon dress leaning back on Raf, who had a proud hand on her stomach. They were the golden couple, fêted by everyone, a fairy tale.

And the drinking wasn't a problem. Yet. Of course she knew Raf drank. It was like breathing to him. But he seemed to have it under control, because he was content. On the set, he hadn't raised hell, because he had been absorbed in the pursuit and capture of Delilah, much to the relief of the director and producer. It had been the easiest Raf Rafferty movie to shoot, and the industry kept its fingers crossed that Delilah had tamed him, and that from now on casting him would not be so fraught with fights, hangovers and broken-hearted actresses who had fallen for his charms and then been dropped like a hot potato. For the time being, his drinking was something he did a lot of, but in a sociable, acceptable way. Sure, there were always empty wine bottles piled up, but they were a newly married couple having fun.

It was a marriage made in heaven . . .

Delilah felt tears well up as she remembered the simplicity of those days, pottering about with her burgeoning bump, a paintbrush in one hand. It had always seemed to be sunny, though of course it wasn't. The biggest decision she ever had to make then was what to cook for Raf's supper—

'Are you OK?'

She jumped. Polly was standing in the doorway.

'I've brought you up a cup of tea – and some things to sign.'

Delilah sat up wearily. Couldn't she even have a lie-down without someone interrupting her? But it was her own fault. She had got into the habit of Polly coming up to her room to go through paperwork while she got ready in the morning. Delilah was a firm believer in multi-tasking – if she could get through her mail while she did her make-up, then she was ahead of the game. Her bedroom had become like a second office.

'I'm fine, Poll. I've just got a bit of a headache.'

Polly looked concerned. It wasn't like Delilah to feel unwell.

'Why don't you have a sleep? I'll leave this stuff with you to look through. We can go through it later.'

She put the papers down on Delilah's bedside table, pinning it down with an Emma Bridgwater mug full of peppermint tea.

'Thank you.' Delilah shut her eyes, willing Polly to go. She wasn't in the mood for explanation.

As Polly left the room, she turned over and buried her face in the pillow.

The marriage made in heaven soon became hell.

The honeymoon was over. Raf went back to work: a three-month shoot in New York. Being pregnant, Delilah decided she would stay in England, preparing the flat for the baby's arrival, and without Delilah at his side Raf slid back into his old ways: carousing in the local bars every night, drinking till dawn. Photographs of him with various women hit the press. Rumours of on-set affairs emerged via dubious sources: make-up girls, the leading lady's body double. If you were to believe what you read, he was insatiable and indefatigable. On his return he protested his innocence. Yes, he'd been socialising, but only because he was away from home and lonely and that was how he coped. And as for the girls – yes, there'd been girls when he went out, but he hadn't done anything with them. It was just the press stirring it all up, looking for a story where there wasn't one.

Delilah wanted to be reassured. It was impossible not to

believe him, with his beseeching blue eyes and his contrition. And when he was by her side, he was beyond reproach. Attentive, dutiful, loving, funny, generous. He came shopping for baby things: they bought a beautiful antique cot, and he restored it and put it up in the nursery and she filled it with beautiful lace-edged bed linen. Standing there in the nursery, holding his hand, she felt as filled with love and pride and hope as it was possible to be.

'I adore you. You must never forget that.' He held her face in his hands and looked right into her soul, and she was reassured.

When the carousing continued, she told herself she was being over-sensitive because she was heavily pregnant. As her due date arrived, he was shooting a small cameo role in a gangster movie, and several times in the papers there had been pictures of him out with Penny Porter, the leading lady.

'It's part of the job. You know that. See and be seen,' he protested.

Everyone on the film knew she was due any day. They wouldn't have thought it strange if he had ducked out of socialising. But she didn't say anything. When the baby was here . . .

Even Coco's birth turned into an excuse for revelry, as Raf and his mates hit the drinking dens of Soho, raising toast after toast to the little baby girl he had breathed fumes over in the hospital. Delilah was too exhausted to protest, the midwives were too starstruck to demur, and Raf crawled home at five o'clock the next morning. When the papers hit the doormat with photos of him out celebrating, he slumbered on, totally forgetting he was supposed to collect his wife and daughter from the hospital and bring them home later that afternoon. When the telephone finally drilled through and woke him up, he had to take a taxi to the hospital. And in his drunken stupor, he ordered armfuls and armfuls of flowers to be delivered, forgetting they would be left to languish in the regulation hospital vases just hours after their arrival because Delilah would no longer be there. The bemused nurses distributed them around the rest of the ward, knowing the other mums would be thrilled with a floral tribute from Raf Rafferty, even if it was by default.

Thus began fifteen years of accusation, recrimination, retribution and resolution. Every time Delilah confronted him, he eventually put his hands up, went down on his knees and begged forgiveness, promised to change. She spent fifteen exhausting years trying to hold it together while bringing up the three girls, wondering every time why she was prepared to have him back. They belonged together, he was the love of her life, and he was the father of her children. And, she suspected, he needed her. It was only because of his weakness that he fell prey to temptation.

Delilah often wondered what would have happened if the *Iliad* debacle hadn't happened. Would they have gone on like that for years, until eventually she couldn't take any more humiliation? As it was, the tables turned when he was thrown off the film.

Raf spent two days in the clinic before walking out. He recognised he had a problem, but he wasn't going to let somebody else profit from it. If he was going to be dry, he would do it himself. Luckily he had a fantastically sympathetic GP who was a huge fan of Delilah and had seen the girls through all their childhood ailments. He was able to provide Raf with support, and sleeping tablets, and encouragement.

Financially, the Raffertys hit crisis point. Raf had to pay his fee back to the film company, they had a huge tax-bill they hadn't saved for, the girls' school fees were due for the smart day school they attended. Delilah ploughed through the paper-work with mounting horror, added up their outgoings (huge) and their incomings (minimal) and realised they had to come up with over sixty thousand pounds cash on the spot if they weren't going to face total ruin, have the house sold from under them and the girls politely asked to leave school. And that was just to avert immediate crisis.

Raf wasn't going to be any help at all. If he was to stay on the straight and narrow he had to avoid any situation that involved temptation and, besides, no one would touch him with a shitty stick. She couldn't go back to modelling – she was nearly forty and had had three children. The only thing she could really do was entertain. Could she open a restaurant, perhaps? There were plenty of people in Richmond wanting somewhere good to eat. But of course she couldn't – how could she raise the capital for a venture like that when they were already hurtling towards bankruptcy?

She sat down at the kitchen table with a bulging file of recipes. Some were handed down from her family, others taken from friends, snipped out of magazines, or secrets she'd winkled out of restaurant chefs. She sorted them carefully into piles of starters, main courses, puddings, cakes, canapés, trying to establish some sort of order. There were certainly enough for a book.

There were plenty of serious cook books out there. Worthy tomes that demanded you make your own veal stock or rough puff pastry. But nothing that was carefree and simple and joyous, just dedicated to giving pleasure to your friends and family. So many women viewed cooking as torture, and were terrified of it. Delilah dreamed of taking the fear out of cooking and entertaining, and instead making it into a pleasure.

She invited three publishers to the house. While they were there, she sat them in the kitchen with a glass of very good wine, and talked to them while she cooked. Each of them sat, entranced, while she casually threw together a mouth-watering feast, making it look as easy as breathing, then served it up in the conservatory.

Two of them phoned back with the offer of a deal later that afternoon. The third called the next morning, begging her to hold off from making a decision just one more day. When he finally called the next day, she nearly fell off her chair. He didn't just want to do a book. He had phoned a production company. They wanted to sign her up to do a pilot television show, with a view to running a six-part series. The book would accompany it.

The fee and the advance were more than enough to keep the wolf from the door . . .

The rest was history. Over the next ten years, Delilah made cooking sexy. She wrote eight recipe books which between them sold millions. She won Television Personality of the Year, was top of the guest list at every party worth going to, was the darling of every chat show host and on the cover of every magazine. Her fans were legion and her detractors few and far between – there was nothing to dislike about Delilah Rafferty, and anyone who was sniffy about her was accused of being jealous. And Delilah fatigue didn't seem to have settled in by any means, mainly because she worked so hard at coming up with new ideas and always had something positive to say. She was popular because she was natural and uncontrived and made everything look easy. And she wasn't a hypocrite. In magazine articles she was always honest about the tough time she had had with Raf, and how she had doubted herself – even hated herself at times – and took the blame. Her self-effacing honesty endeared her even more to the nation.

Now Delilah was tired of being the nation's darling; the woman who inspired others. She was the goose that laid the golden eggs, but she'd reached stalemate. She just wanted to flop, to do all the things she longed to do but never had time for. Just simple pleasures, like reading a book because she wanted to read it, and not because she had been asked to give a quote. Or going horse riding in Richmond Park – it was on her doorstep, for heaven's sake. Or making jam that didn't have to be double-tested for inclusion in a book. And she wanted to spend more time with the girls. Now they weren't at home any longer, it was becoming impossible to fit them into her schedule as they had mad schedules of their own. She should be having lunch with Coco today – she'd sounded on edge, she really ought to get to the bottom of it. She should be going to Violet's gig tonight, but with all the people coming for lunch tomorrow she would be up till all hours preparing food. And she should find out what Tyger was up to. Silence from Tyger was unusual.

Yes, thought Delilah, with Raf taking this film, here was the ideal opportunity for her to take a back seat. But as she lay on the bed, the scent of wisteria curled in through the window, making her feel slightly nauseous. Why wasn't she giddy with relief, ecstatic with excitement, planning her new, relaxed lifestyle?

Because she wasn't going to be in control.

She sat up as the realisation hit her. She'd put her finger on it. She was no longer going to be the one calling the shots. That was how they had kept it together for the past ten years. She had been at the helm, making the decisions, earning the money, writing the cheques, dictating the pace. It was the only way they could have survived. If she hadn't fought, she might have gone down with Raf, watched him destroy first himself, then their marriage and finally their family. It was sheer determination and hard work that had kept them on course and made them one of Britain's most successful showbiz families. On the surface, at least. She'd been clever enough to hide the cracks, paper over them before they became a problem, steering the press in a different direction in order to deflect attention. But without Raf under her thumb, the dynamics were going to alter drastically.

She would just have to learn to let go.

She took a deep breath in and out again. For God's sake, Delilah, she told herself, Raf has been sober for ten years. He knows who he is. He will manage. You will manage. Don't be such a controlling bitch.

After his phone calls to Dickie and Delilah, Raf made his way to the car park in Soho, then headed out of London towards the motorway. Most people would do anything they could to avoid the M25 on a Friday afternoon, let alone drive there voluntarily if they didn't need to, but he wanted to put his foot down and clear his head. Delilah always chided him for driving into town: by the time he had paid the petrol, the congestion charge and the parking, it was ten times more expensive than jumping on the train. But he loved his car. It was his space. His vice. The pleasure that he refused to feel guilty about. A Maserati Quattroporte, it was a wolf in sheep's clothing, and he loved nothing better than opening it up. The thrill of its acceleration always made his blood tingle. He would sink back into the soft leather, turn up the music and glide through the traffic. It was one of the few good things about not drinking, being able to drive this car.

His pulse was still racing from the excitement. There was no going back now. Even though the terms of his contract hadn't actually been negotiated, Raf knew the film company would fall over themselves to meet whatever demands he made. Not that he was going to demand a ridiculous fee. How could he? He hadn't acted for ten years, his reputation was far from unsullied and he'd never been a greedy man. There would be plenty of time to increase his demands once he had proved himself – to himself as much as to anyone. He turned Aerosmith up full blast and hoped and prayed that this new venture was going to be the start of his becoming the person he really wanted to be.

Until now, his life had been divided into Jekyll and Hyde. The drinking years had unleashed the monster he hadn't wanted to be, the monster he had constantly battled against but couldn't restrain. The monster who filled him with disgust. He was able to bury the memory on a day-to-day basis, but there were always those times when a reminder brought him up short and took his breath away. His family were caring enough not to bring up his misdemeanours, but the press weren't as sensitive. And sometimes on the television there would be a movie that brought it all flooding back. Or even worse, a clip – like the time he had been on *Wogan* three sheets to the wind. They loved playing that one. It went down as television history, as well it might. He cringed when he

47

watched himself slurring and sliding off the sofa and trying to come on to the female guest, who did her very best to rebuff him as politely as she could. He couldn't believe what a total and utter tosser he had been. He couldn't imagine why Delilah had wanted to marry him. Unlike others, he was unable to see the charm. He made himself feel sick.

The problem was, he was no more enamoured of the flip side of this monster. For the past ten years he had been a sober, upright citizen who always knew that monster was capable of being unleashed, and had battled to keep it locked up. No one knew how hard that was. It never left you. Sometimes you could be distracted. Sometimes something took his mind off it and made him forget, perhaps for an hour. But then the needling feeling came back. He had found nothing to fill the vacuum. He knew other drinkers who had found solace in physical exercise, religion, fishing, charity work – and although he had found pastimes he enjoyed, none of them plugged the gap.

Maybe, just maybe, when he was driving in his car, this car, like he was right now, nudging the needle up past ninety, up towards a hundred – maybe then he got a sense of freedom, a sense of self, a sense of euphoria that made him almost complete. But he couldn't drive round the M25 for ever.

He really longed to find a happy medium. He longed to be free of the spectre of that monster, to be able to relax without fear of its reincarnation. But to keep it at bay he had to live a life of restraint. The real him wasn't either of those people. He wasn't the monster or the sober upright citizen, but someone in between. He wanted to be able to let his hair down, laugh and joke, relax with his friends and family with a bottle of wine. A bottle of wine, not four or six. But somebody up there had determined he was incapable of doing that. He was never going to be the person he wanted to be.

As a result, he wasn't happy. Not truly happy. He could pretend on the surface, but he felt as if he was acting out a role.

And he had to accept his lot. After all, that was his punishment. He had to atone for all that dreadful behaviour.

He didn't blame Delilah. Of course he didn't. Without her, they would have come apart at the seams, and God knows what mess their lives would have been in by now. But he had felt like half a person for the past ten years.

Mr Delilah Rafferty.

He wasn't the only man on the planet playing second fiddle to a successful wife. It was a modern way of life. But it still ate away at him. He knew Delilah loved what she did, thank God. But he still felt guilty that he had forced her into it.

He remembered a drunken man leaning across a dinner table one evening. 'Don't you feel emasculated?' he'd asked belligerently. 'Don't you feel as if she's chopped off your balls and used them for earrings? Don't you feel as if you should . . . contribute?' Raf had wanted to grab him by the tie and push his face into the tiramisu in the middle of the table.

And Delilah was as loyal as could be. She always said that she couldn't have done any of it without his support, and that he was as important to the Delilah Rafferty brand as she was. But he knew that wasn't true, that she could have done it without him – even better probably, because he wasn't easy. He knew he wasn't.

It was time to pay her back. He could take the pressure off. She could have a year off, recharge her batteries, do all the things she had been longing to do but never had time for. The things normal wives did.

Raf left the motorway, went round the roundabout and headed back in the opposite direction. He'd had his thinking time, and now he was going home. A light April shower fell as he drove, turning the tarmac from grey to black. He loved the sound of his tyres slicing through the wetness, the damp smell of spring through the half-open window.

Life was good.

*

Delilah jumped off her bed when she heard the low purr of the Maserati come through the gates. She ran down the stairs as Raf walked through the door and into the hallway, bringing with him the scent of blossom and fresh rain. She slid her arms round him, burying her face in his neck, the April droplets evaporating on the warmth of his skin. He smiled down at her, and when she saw the light in his eyes, the hope, the anticipation, her fears evaporated just as the rain was.

'Hey, movie star,' she murmured.

'Shit, Delilah,' he replied with a grin. 'I'm scared.'

'You'll be wonderful.'

Of course he'd be wonderful. He'd been wonderful in every film he'd ever made. Before now, that had been at too high a price. But this time round . . .

She took him by both hands, walking backwards towards the stairs, smiling.

Any normal couple would have cracked open a bottle of champagne, but that wasn't an option. And putting on the kettle for a cup of tea was hardly a way to mark today's triumph. There was only one way Delilah could think of to celebrate. They were on the bottom step, his warm hand on her hip, guiding her upwards, when the house phone starting ringing.

'Ignore it,' she muttered through slightly gritted teeth, but the ringing persisted. At the same time, the phone in his pocket started to chime. She pulled it out and dropped it into the vase of lilies on the hall table. He watched in horror as it sank slowly to the bottom, coming to rest amongst the stems.

'You mad bitch!' he said, more in wonder than ire.

She laughed and pulled him into her arms, just as Polly came into the hallway with the phone in her hand.

'Delilah, it's Tony on the phone. He needs to speak— Oh God, sorry.'

Polly blushed to the roots of her hair as she realised what they were doing. Delilah disentangled herself from Raf with a sigh and held out her hand.

'It's OK, Polly,' she sighed. 'I'll take it.'

Plus ça change.

'Hi, Tony,' Delilah said wearily, walking back through the hall towards the kitchen.

Polly looked at Raf and smiled, still feeling rather awkward.

'Congratulations. Delilah told me. About the movie . . .'

She watched his face light up as he smiled back. He looked like a small boy who has just been given his first bicycle. Her heart melted as she realised how much this deal meant to him. She rushed over and hugged him on impulse, her awkwardness forgotten.

'It's so exciting. You must be absolutely thrilled to bits . . .' Why did she always have to gush like an Enid Blyton schoolgirl?

Her heart turned over as he squeezed her to him. She was close enough to breathe in the scent of his cologne. Black Vetyver Café. She knew because Delilah had dispatched her to Jo Malone to buy it for his Christmas stocking. She'd gone through all the scents with the assistant until she found the one she thought suited him the best. It made her tummy flip, as it always did. She kept a stash of scented strips under her pillow, so she could breathe in its deep velvet muskiness as she drifted off to sleep. She thought she was probably insane.

'You'll look after Delilah for me, won't you, Poll?' he was saying. 'I'm going to be on location for a while. I don't know how she'll cope without me around.'

'Course I will,' she replied staunchly, not wanting to think about how *she* was going to cope without him around. Honestly, it was ludicrous having a crush at her age. Thirty-two years old, and she measured the success of her day by how often she had seen him, what they had spoken about, and whether she had been able to make him laugh.

She realised with a jolt that she was still clinging on to him. She stepped away, flustered.

'Do you know what would be really great?' he was asking, in

that low, slightly gruff voice that made her shiver. His hand was on her arm. He was looking into her eyes.

Oh God. He was going to ask her to come on location with him. He would need a PA, of course he would. All the top stars had their PAs with them when they did a film.

'What?' she asked, trembling, while visions of him stumbling into her room late one night and declaring undying love flashed through her mind.

He gazed at her, his cornflower-blue eyes crinkling up at the corners. She could feel them drawing her in. She felt quite helpless.

'What?' she repeated in a half whisper.

'A cup of tea.'

She stared at him, unable to speak. He looked back at her quizzically.

'I think we could all do with a cup of tea. Don't you?'

Five

Justine Amador-Fox turned on her heel and stormed out of her father's office, the heels of her Miu Miu whip-snake pumps sinking into the deep pile of the carpet. Tears stung the back of her eyelids, but she wasn't going to let them fall until she was out of his sight. They were tears of rage and frustration, not sorrow. Salty and scalding, they were going to ruin her perfect make-up. The perfect make-up that went with the perfect navy shift dress that showed she meant business.

It hadn't convinced him in the least.

She didn't have to look at her father to know the expression on his face. It would be slightly sardonic, a smile playing on the corner of his mouth. He would shake his head in fond exasperation at his daughter's outburst, but by the time she had reached the lift he would be onto something else, barking out instructions on his speaker phone or jabbing at his calculator.

She had tried so hard to play by his rules for the past couple of years. She knew better than to try and beat him at his own game. He was invincible. He always knew just which card to play to bring her down. Not because he wanted to beat her, but because he loved her. And he was moulding her in his own image.

It was so frustrating. She had been determined that this time he wasn't going to win, but he had her over a barrel.

What she didn't understand was why? She had done the poxy hospitality course he had asked her to do. Three bloody years of projects and essays and assessments and placements in hideous hotels that had nothing to teach her. And now he was expecting her to join the company and do its management course like any other graduate trainee. Did being his daughter count for nothing?

She had been fed the Amador philosophy from birth. It was in her blood. She had been to every single one of the hotels in the chain. She understood exactly what it was that made them stand out, why they were bastions of luxury and indulgence, why they rarely, if ever, received a complaint from one of their guests. She didn't *need* to have the company ethos drummed into her by joining the rest of the hopefuls that had been weeded out of the huge number of applications the company received on an annual basis. Who wouldn't want to work for Amador, with its super-luxurious hotels in stunning locations? They avoided the obvious – Vegas, Dubai, Miami – and went for the exotic and out of the way.

Justine didn't want to be a manager. She wanted to scout for new locations and be instrumental in the development of new hotels. She wanted to work with the architects and the designers, perfecting and finessing service and facilities for people who wanted the best but didn't feel the need to be surrounded by glitz and flash. Just pure understated quality and unrivalled comfort. 'Heaven on earth' was the Amador slogan. This meant the ultimate in bedding, superlative chefs, state-of-the-art sound and lighting, stunning artworks, and the best design in furniture. And none of the hotels was the same. Each was individually designed, drawing on inspiration from its location, utilising the best local resources and craftsmen.

She had brought her father a proposal that morning, to prove she was ready. She had found a run-down hotel in Berlin that was ripe for renovation. She had found an architect, drawn up plans, put together a detailed proposal complete with artist's impressions and, most importantly, a meticulous budget. Her father had just thrown the folder to one side and laughed.

'Don't you think I'd already have it, if it was any good?'

Bastard.

Justine had got the measure of Benedict Amador when she was fourteen and had deliberately engineered her expulsion from her exclusive boarding school. She was desperate to go to the London day school her friends went to. She couldn't see the difference, the results were the same, the facilities were the same, but for some inexplicable reason her father had refused to let her go there. He had insisted on her staying at Fortescue House. She'd stuck it out for as long as she could bear, but in the end had organised a prank phone call to the school office, announcing there was a bomb hidden in the gym. The school had been evacuated, the fire service swept every square inch of the building – and the swotty, spotty cow who Justine had made sure had overheard the call grassed her up. Her bags were packed and she was put on the train home before everyone had finished filing back in from the netball courts. A triumphant Justine was certain she would now get her way.

Her father just shrugged and enrolled her at the comprehensive adjoining the sink estate half a mile down the road. You were never far from slums in London, even if you lived in a six-million-pound mansion like the Amadors.

She had been outraged at first that he would let her go there. She had thrown tantrum after tantrum, but he had been to buy the uniform himself and driven her to the gates on the first day, giving her a measly two pounds lunch money.

To her surprise, she had thrived. She'd had to be tough to prove that she wasn't a snotty, spoilt rich kid. It had taken her six months to be accepted by the other pupils, but she did it eventually. And she was surprised to find they were fun. Far more self-sufficient than her other pampered friends. They could all look after themselves, looked out for each other. She learned to stand on her own two feet and became pretty streetwise. She learned how to get into a club without paying, how to tell good drugs from bad, and how to nick stuff from Selfridges without being caught. She lost her virginity to a drop-dead-gorgeous boy with waist-length dreadlocks and a cock the size of which she had never encountered since. It had been a more useful education than anything her father could have paid for. And it had made her tough. Tough enough to cope with most of his mind games. But not all . . .

Her father might be the one person who could reduce her to tears, but Justine composed herself in the lift and by the time she reached the street outside she was filled with resolve. She had to make a plan. Work out how the hell she was going to outmanoeuvre that lovable bastard. It wasn't going to be easy. But as he had pointed out to her on numerous occasions, nothing worth it ever is.

He'd been compared to a lot of entrepreneurs: Richard Branson, Alan Sugar, Rocco Forte. But Benedict Amador was one on his own. He was a renaissance man. Whatever he decided to turn his hand to was a success. He was sickeningly accomplished. He studied engineering at university, devised a barrier-breaking computer program, sold out for millions and spent the rest of his days and his money dabbling in projects for pleasure. Each of his hotels was there for his own personal use – he never built one in a place he had no intention of visiting. He had a vineyard in Australia which made wine to his specification. He spent a month every summer on a Greek island painting pictures that were sold through a gallery in Cork Street. He was an awesome golfer, horseman, sailor – he had sailed the Atlantic twice . . . The list of his achievements was endless.

They were all generated by his restlessness. He never truly relaxed. Not since his wife, Justine's mother, had died when Justine was three. He had never replaced her. No other woman held any interest for him. Jeanne Fox had been his soul-mate, the love of his life. He had adored her unreservedly. Now, he had women who would accompany him to social functions. And women with whom he had sex. They weren't paid professionals, but people he had met who knew the deal and were happy to accept it. No one had penetrated his heart. He had loved once, passionately, and that was it.

Justine knew that no matter what she did, he would never

cut her off, for she was the living embodiment of her mother. A living, breathing three-dimensional replica that he didn't want to lose. Everyone who knew Benedict knew that Justine was his Achilles heel, even though he gave her a hard time. And what he wanted more than anything was grandchildren. A grandson, to be precise. Someone he could leave his empire to. For all his maverick ways, a little bit of Benedict clung to tradition.

Although she had inherited her mother's looks – thick, dark eyebrows over wide, frank eyes and a full mouth – Justine had her father's spirit. She was a little fire-brand. Bossy, opinionated, but fun-loving, she breezed through life like a zephyr. Of course, she could have turned her back on her father when he didn't give in to her, and made her own way in the world. But it was his world she wanted to be part of. She just wasn't sure what she had to do to prove herself to him.

She walked along the pavement with her head down until she reached a little café with tables and chairs outside. She sat down and ordered a latte and a huge vanilla cupcake as she tried to think herself into her father's head. How could she outwit him and trap him into giving her what she wanted? There was no point in going head to head. He would win every time. She had to think of something leftfield, something that would give her the ultimate bargaining tool.

The cupcake arrived and she scooped the frosting off with her finger, enjoying the cloying sweetness. Then she crumbled the cake into little bite-size pieces, chewing as she thought.

Two men walked past and checked her out, admiring her tanned arms in the sleeveless shift dress, her long, bare legs, the thick dark hair smoothed back in a glossy ponytail. Never averse to being admired, she smiled back at them.

An unsuitable man? What if she found a boyfriend her father disapproved of? She could do a deal with him then – drop the bloke in return for the position she wanted. But Benedict was infuriatingly broad-minded. She couldn't for the life of her think of someone she could put up with and he would want her to drop. He had been immensely tolerant of all the skanky boys she had brought back from her comprehensive, knowing full well they were just a phase. He would feign approval for as long as it took, she knew he would. He had nerves of steel.

Her phone beeped to tell her she'd got a text. She crammed the rest of the cupcake in her mouth and pulled it out to look at it.

Hey babe – going to see Violet Rafferty at the Tinderbox tonight. Coming? Alex xxxxx

She hadn't thought as far as tonight yet. Alex was her dearest friend and her hairdresser and made everything fun, fun, fun. A night out with him and his pink pals was just the sort of evening that would help her forget her woes. They were outrageous, flamboyant and knew how to party. And they didn't take themselves too seriously, not like some of her other friends.

She texted back straight away: *Count me in xxxx*

Six

Violet Rafferty sat in front of the baby Bechstein her parents had given her for her twenty-first. Her back was straight, her hands poised over the keys, but her eyes were shut. She breathed deeply and evenly, trying to remember the notes that had played themselves to her while she was sleeping during her afternoon nap.

It happened so often. A snatch of some lilting melody that was hauntingly perfect would drift through her semi-conscious mind, teasing her. And no matter how hard she tried to catch it, it would elude her. She knew they were real and not imagined, but she still hadn't found a way of capturing the little wisps of sound.

It was ironic, really, when she only had to listen once to a piece of music composed by somebody else and she could play it. She had perfect pitch and a phonographic memory. Chopin, Rachmaninov, Coldplay, Gershwin – she could tinkle out anything anyone asked. Yet when it came to her own compositions, she froze.

How the hell did people do it? How did they manage to lose their self-consciousness? She knew she was a harsh critic – of other people's work but particularly of her own. She only had to string three notes together and she shuddered with distaste. As for lyrics, everything she wrote seemed trite and derivative.

She slammed the lid down in a fury, then immediately felt guilty. It wasn't the piano's fault that she was useless and untalented.

She was destined for a life of singing other people's songs.

She was, after all, very successful at it. Her shows were usually sell-outs. Not exactly Wembley, admittedly, but intimate little clubs and bars. Tonight, in a tight black dress and fishnet stockings, her hair slicked back and her lips ruby red, she would sing Piaf, Dietrich, Kurt Weill – burlesque mixed with jazz. She would become the ultimate seductress – a confident, sexual vamp who toyed with her audience, flirting, enticing. She knew she had power and presence, but to her it meant nothing. What was the point in performing something you hadn't composed? This was just a job. A way of getting a following.

She tried to shake off her gloom. She loved performing, of course she did. Why else would she do it? She had no other need. It wasn't as if the pay was that extraordinary – if she needed to work for her living she could make far more as a backing singer. She loved the dressing up, taking on another persona.

She left the piano and went into her bedroom to get herself ready. She let her red silk kimono drop to the floor, and began to put on the outfit she had laid out on the bed. She put on a black corset that squeezed her waist down to twenty-two inches. Black fishnet stockings with proper suspenders. Her favourite vintage dress – black moiré silk with a plunging neckline and a thigh-high slit. A black jet necklace. Skyscraper heels.

Then the make-up. Foundation paler than pale, her eyebrows a delicate arch. False eyelashes. And the famous red pout, which took ages to construct with lip-liner, lipstick and gloss, to achieve the perfect Cupid's bow.

To finish, she dabbed her pulse points with her signature perfume, breathing in its heady almond scent. She had to be the part completely, and to smell right was essential. She couldn't have gone on stage without perfume any more than she could have gone without a dress.

She picked up the phone and called for a cab, ignoring the winking light on her answer machine. Whatever it was she didn't want to know. She hated any sort of distraction when she was about to perform. Moments later she was gone, leaving behind the faintest trace of Le Baiser du Dragon.

The Tinderbox was tucked under an insignificant three-star hotel in Paddington. It was a well-kept secret, but it was always packed to capacity nevertheless, thanks to its manager's skill in creating an intimate but buzzy atmosphere and the incredible live music. It showcased performers from all over the world, a lot of it experimental and avant-garde, but time and again people who had debuted here went on to become huge stars, because what they all had in common was talent.

The décor was slightly decadent, with purple velvet banquettes, lamps trimmed with ostrich feathers and neon-pink lighting; it was camp but cosy. A small stage allowed as many tables as possible to be crammed in. By rights it should be smoky, but with the ban that was impossible, yet it still had the atmosphere of an intimate club from a bygone era.

Violet had a devoted following at the Tinderbox. She sang there twice a month to a full house and the audience had become her friends. They were a mixed crowd of arty middle-aged, flamboyant gays and younger people who enjoyed dressing up – gloves, basques, false eyelashes, fishnets and beauty spots abounded. She loved the venue because of the sense of self-expression it nurtured, but at the same time there was no pressure – if you turned up in jeans no one cared, as long as you appreciated the music. So she always made sure she put on her best show, and tried to introduce something new so her loyal followers wouldn't get bored.

She was in the tiny dressing room, gargling with warm water mixed with manuka honey to coat her throat. It was cramped and shabby, but she loved its familiarity, the huge foxed mirror she checked her make-up in, the postcards all over the wall from people who had played here over the years, the sofa spewing stuffing out of its cracked leather.

Sammy, who played the double bass for her, was standing in

the doorway. He was half Cuban, half French, the son of a wild *Parisienne* who had enjoyed a night of steamy passion in Havana and had come home with more than duty-free rum and a box of *cojibas*. Sammy was as poor as a church mouse, but he didn't care a jot, because he lived for his music. As well as playing for Violet, he sessioned for a number of other bands who played wild improvisational jazz, inaccessible to all but the most die-hard of aficionados. Sammy stayed up all night and slept all day, lived on his native *Moros y Christianos* – black beans and rice – and wore a rotation of faded jeans and worn granddad shirts, a selection of silver rings on his long, thin fingers. He spoke perfect English but his accent was indefinable – transatlantic tinged with French. Sometimes his crazy mother came to visit, with her wild black hair that Sammy had inherited now tinged with grey, and they would go out all night, partying till dawn, and Violet got an insight into how Sammy had grown up: a bohemian, nomadic life lived on a shoestring.

Violet had always kept Sammy away from her family. There was something so pure about him, ascetic almost. She knew he would be shocked by the opulence she lived in, and by the values her family held. Sammy lived for the moment, cared nothing for possessions apart from his double bass. He valued people above things, experience above everything else. She had learned a lot from him. He didn't crave fame – he wanted people to enjoy the music he played, but he didn't want a deal or to become a star. His existence was the polar opposite of what she was used to. The Rafferty ethic revolved around seeking the limelight, material gain, success, adulation. Violet sensed it was wrong, but it was what she had been brought up with and it was very hard to shake. She knew that no matter how much time she spent with Sammy, she could never be as pure as he was. The Rafferty drive to succeed was too engrained.

She stood up to hug him, winding her arms around his body.

He was as thin as a rake, not an ounce of meat on him, but so warm, his shirts always so soft.

'Hey, Violet,' his low, musical voice breathed into her ear. 'What's happening?'

She was tempted to tell him how she had been trying and trying to write a song, but couldn't do it. How it made her feel frustrated and claustrophobic. How it made her want to scream and throw things at the wall. But she wasn't sure he would understand. He and his friends found it so easy to create. They improvised together, throwing in ideas and running with them. Writing was like breathing to them. They had no trouble capturing their collective muse. Music trickled out of them freely. To admit her failing to Sammy was to admit weakness. She wanted him to have respect for her, not think she was a loser.

Instead, she handed him some sheet music: 'Wild Is The Wind', made famous by Nina Simone. She was going to try it tonight as her final song, hoping she would do its soul-baringly sensual lyrics justice. She'd worked hard to find a way to make it her own and bring something special to the composition – a lot of her audience would know the song, and she wanted to surprise them.

Sammy put the music on a stand and started moving his supple fingers over the strings. She adored the way he played. He seemed to know instinctively just how long she wanted him to hold a note, when to be silent, when to fill her silence. They were magic together. Like lovers. Even though they weren't. Violet knew that if they ever crossed that line, it would be very dangerous. Their partnership was too precious to be ruined by sex.

She began to sing, weaving her voice around the sonorous bass. It sent shivers down her spine.

At the end, Sammy looked at her in something bordering on astonishment.

'Hey, Violet – that was something special.'

It wasn't easy to impress Sammy. Everyone he worked with

had talent. Yet his words meant nothing to Violet. The magic was in the writing, not the performance. She felt her mood crash. What she was doing was pointless, masquerading behind other people's genius.

Why couldn't she write music like this?

Sammy could feel Violet's gloom. It enveloped the room, bringing with it a chill. He was used to bolstering her up. It was part of his role as her accompanist.

'Hey. Come on. We've got a full house tonight. Let's see that pretty smile.'

Violet rolled her eyes.

'What's the point, Sammy?'

It wasn't the first time she'd asked him this.

'The point is people love you. You bring them pleasure.'

'Great. I might as well strip for a living. It would amount to the same thing.'

'Don't give me that tortured-artist shit. You've got a talent most people would give their right finger for.'

'Arm.' Violet giggled despite herself. Even after all these years Sammy got his sayings muddled. 'Right arm.'

Sammy shook his head and held up his pinky, grinning.

'Right finger. Right finger is very important when you play bass.' He leaned in to her. 'So stop complaining and enjoy what you are good at.'

Violet shook her head, pouting. 'It's not fair, Sammy. I want to write. I want to write beautiful songs that tear people's hearts open. Songs that make them think, *That's exactly how I feel*. Songs that people want played at their weddings, their funerals . . .'

'You know what? You can't force it. So just enjoy what you can do and wait.'

She gave him a playful punch on the arm.

'You're an unsympathetic bastard, you know that?'

He took her chin in his fingers, turning her to face him.

'You know what? Maybe you haven't suffered enough to write songs like that.'

'You mean I'm a spoilt brat with nothing to say?'

Sammy shrugged. Violet scowled.

'Anyway, I have suffered.'

He nodded. 'Sure you have.'

Violet felt tears stinging the back of her eyelids. Why was it that just because you were the daughter of rich and famous parents, people thought you had it easy? She could still remember those terrible years. The shouting, the crying. The insecurity. The gnawing tightness in the pit of her stomach that she went to sleep with, woke up with and that didn't leave her all day. Violet remembered crying in bed one night and Delilah crawling in next to her, hugging her, and Violet realising that the tears on her cheeks weren't her own but her mother's.

OK, so now they lived a Sunday-supplement perfection. And she had her Grade Two listed flat, with its high ceilings and wooden floors. She wasn't exactly struggling like a lot of Sammy's friends. Not to live and eat, anyway. She was struggling in her own way.

Now wasn't the time to put her side of the argument. It was ten minutes until they were on. She needed to touch up her make-up, then go through the running order once more to see if she wanted to make any last-minute changes.

She didn't get nervous before a gig. Just excited. She supposed she should be grateful for that, at least. Some of her friends who were performers had crippling stage fright, to the extent that she wondered why on earth they put themselves through the ordeal. She wasn't afraid to sing. Ever since she had been tiny, she had loved performing. She remembered her parents standing her on the dining table when she was only three so she could sing 'There's A Worm At The Bottom Of My Garden', to the delight of the assembled guests. Of course she had moved on to more sophisticated renditions since then, but it never bothered her. She would perform at the drop of a hat, with no rehearsal, to anyone.

As soon as she smelled the audience she knew if they were on her side, if they wanted a good time or if they wanted to pick a fight. The Tinderbox audience was always a joy. She examined herself in the mirror one last time, smoothed down her perfectly arched eyebrows, and applied another slick of Chanel lipstick. She was ready.

Seven

Justine fought her way through the crowds in the Tinderbox, astonished that such an inconspicuous door could lead down to such a hot spot. The atmosphere was fantastic: laid-back, lively, people laughing, chattering, gossiping, drinking cocktails. She finally made it to Alex's table. He had the same one every week, to which he brought a selection of friends.

She adored Alex, who had been doing her hair since she was fifteen. He was a terrible gossip, a shocking flirt, a shameless tease, and what he didn't know about other people he made up. She had often bewailed his preference for his own sex, for she felt sure they would have made the perfect couple. They sometimes went shopping on a Saturday and ended up choosing the same things. Besides, being married to the man who made you look beautiful was surely the best move a girl could ever make?

He was dressed in skinny jeans, an immaculate white shirt and grey cashmere tank top, his hair backcombed into a messy black bob, his face white, his lips carmine, his eyelashes preposterously long. He looked perfect. A preppy geisha boy. He kissed Justine and she smelled Annick Goutal's Eau d'Hadrien.

'Darling, sit.' He gestured to a spare seat on the table, which was already filled with his eccentric and fashion-conscious friends. Justine suddenly felt dull in her jeans and tuxedo blazer. While she had probably paid more for her outfit than the whole table had paid for theirs combined, she favoured sharp, classic tailoring. Clothes for her were like armour; in a well-cut designer outfit, with killer heels and a sharp hairdo, she felt in control. Cream, navy, taupe and black were her palette. Alex often bemoaned her when she went to have her hair done.

'With that budget you could go crazy, darling. And that figure. You dress like an uptight New York businesswoman, not a twenty-three-year-old wild child.'

He'd tried to press her towards more outré designers, but she felt uncomfortable with anything remotely edgy or artistic. Tonight's outfit was as unstructured as it got. Anyway, she always looked good, and she knew how to do the look she favoured. She could never learn to let go like Alex and his friends – mix and match and experiment. But it certainly hadn't ever stopped her getting a man.

Alex ordered up the house cocktail, and soon she relaxed and forgot her slight self-consciousness. As the drink went down, the tension in her shoulders eased off, and the memory of her altercation with Benedict began to fade. Soon she was helpless with laughter as one of the other stylists from Alex's salon began describing the hideous behaviour of one of their clients – he was utterly outrageous, totally indiscreet and quite hilarious. She loved this bunch. They knew how to have fun, their anecdotes got increasingly preposterous, and she didn't have to worry about whether any of them fancied her or she them.

Being the daughter of an incredibly wealthy man was fraught with hazards. Justine never knew if men fancied her for herself or for her fortune. She'd had her fingers burned more than once with gold-diggers, and now she was very wary. It grieved her that it was unrealistic for her to socialise with the kids she'd been at school with. They'd made her part of who she was, and although she would never turn her back on them, their worlds were miles apart. She'd tried, of course she'd tried, but it was always awkward. Driving up to a grotty estate in a soft-top Mercedes was asking for trouble, but she didn't want to pretend she wasn't something she was, just as she didn't expect them to be pretend to be something they weren't.

Money was a pain in the arse, she'd long decided. But the making of it was her legacy. She wasn't going to turn her back on it. She was going to be as big a success as her father. If only he would let her prove to him that she was capable. Now.

Bollocks to Benedict. She wasn't going to let him spoil her evening. The compère had come on to introduce Violet Rafferty and the audience was settling down.

'You will absolutely adore her.' Alex leaned over and spoke in her ear. 'Honestly, she's enough to turn me straight.'

Smiling, Justine put down her drink and turned expectantly towards the stage.

As Violet walked out of the dressing room, the stage manager handed her a glass of incarnadine Campari. Moments later she was on the stage, greeted by raucous applause, whistles and whoops of joy.

She smiled over at Sammy who was tuning his double bass, then nodded at the pianist who had taken his position. As the introduction began, the piano and the bass entwining round each other, she scanned the faces in front of her. She always picked someone to sing to. Whether a man or woman, girl or boy, she sought out someone she could focus on, someone she could pour her heart and soul into. It wasn't a freaky declaration of love; it helped make her performance more personal and gave it some meaning.

Tonight she scanned the audience with an expert eye. A girl at one of the tables near the front caught her attention. She was striking, with dark eyebrows that gave definition to her heart-shaped face. She was on a table with a group of boys she recognised, her staunch gay fans. As she stepped up to the microphone she caught the girl's eye and stared right at her.

'Hello.'

Her voice was sultry, smokily suggestive, and commanded instant attention. The chatter subsided immediately.

'I hope you're all ready to have a good time. And welcome to the Tinderbox, if you haven't been before.'

She smiled again at the girl, who held her gaze. Good. She needed someone responsive, someone who could be her gauge.

Her pianist began the intro to her opening song. She took a small sip of her Campari, breathed in, and began.

'*I left a note on his dresser . . .*'

She began the melancholy lyrics, the story of a woman leaving her husband, and the audience were immediately under her spell as the narrative unfolded. She was very measured to begin with, holding back for the time being, but by keeping the words almost matter-of-fact the impact was somehow greater. She needed to build throughout the set. By the end she would let rip and let them have the full force of her emotions. Violet knew exactly how to take her audience on a journey. She chose the sequence of her songs very carefully, taking them up, then back down, then towards an earth-shattering climax that would leave them drained.

'*Remember, darling . . .*'

She fixed the girl with the sweetest of smiles.

'*Don't smoke in bed . . .*'

Justine watched, rapt, as the girl on the stage enchanted her audience, pulling them into her spell, her soft, smoky voice wrapping itself around them. One moment she would be sultry and seductive, the next wild and abandoned, then she came on like a dominatrix. Justine was transfixed.

At one point, Alex nudged her teasingly. 'Oi, stop drooling. I never knew you were that way inclined.'

Justine nudged him back with her elbow and rolled her eyes.

'I can think she's gorgeous without being a—'

'She certainly seems to like you.' He leaned in closer, whispering in her ear. 'She hasn't taken her eyes off you all evening.'

For some reason Justine found herself blushing. She thought

Violet had been catching her eye, and she found it flattering. The girl was utterly gorgeous, after all. Spellbinding, mysterious, but with a mischievous sense of humour that showed she didn't take herself too seriously, she interspersed her songs with little stories and anecdotes, some rather risqué.

She had to admit she'd felt a little peeved, a little spurned, when Violet had turned her attentions to the wild-haired bass player during the last song, draping herself around him, singing seductively in his ear, trailing her fingers down his cheek. He had smiled, as if he was used to her toying with him. Were they an item? Justine wondered. They were certainly both exotic and talented, living in a world far removed from most people's experience.

When Violet finally turned to look at her again, she felt her heart skip a beat. It was just vanity, she told herself. Who didn't like being the centre of someone's attention, especially someone so compelling? It didn't mean she was—

A sudden thought occurred to her.

Now that would shake her father in his shoes. If she announced she had a girlfriend. She grinned mischievously as she thought of the thunderous expression on his face. She felt a hundred per cent sure he wouldn't like it. For all his pretending to be broad-minded, that he wouldn't be able to handle. It would throw him completely.

And Violet Rafferty. There would be uproar. It would be all over the papers. The press would love it! Two beautiful girls, one rich, one rich and famous – the paparazzi would fall over themselves to get photos of them kissing. The fashion magazines would chronicle their every outfit. And they would look so good together. It was every red-top editor's wet dream. After all, wasn't it supposed to be every bloke's fantasy, two hot women together?

Saph-tastic, thought Justine with a grin. It was perfect. Benedict would be incandescent. He would rage and protest. She would defend herself. Then finally they would strike a deal. Justine would give up Violet if she got the position she wanted.

Justine took another sip of her cocktail. If Benedict Amador thought he could control his daughter, he had another thing coming. She could outmanoeuvre him any day. After all, hadn't she learned at the feet of a master?

She turned casually to Alex.

'So – has she got a boyfriend at the moment? Or a girl-friend?'

'Not that I know of.' He looked at her with a little smirk. 'Why – you interested?'

Justine felt a little stirring deep inside. She loved a challenge. And she hadn't met anyone she couldn't have if she wanted them.

Yet.

After her set, which included three encores, Violet always came and mixed with the audience. She liked to add the personal touch, and it wasn't as if she was in any danger. They were a sophisticated bunch, and far from starstruck – she chatted with them like old friends, which many of them were. Sammy refused to join her. He was too shy. He would pack up his bass and go home to the crazy house he shared with a bunch of musicians, despite Violet imploring him to stay on and have a drink.

'They don't want to talk to me,' he protested. 'You're the star.'

'Rubbish! You're part of the show. You're as important as I am. And look at all those adoring girls out there—'

He backed away in horror at that. Sammy didn't like the idea of being hit on by a fan one bit. Violet laughed and kissed him goodbye, then wove her way through the tables, greeting her fans, shaking hands, signing copies of her CD, posing for photographs. It was one of the advantages of not being a huge star. She would hate to be whisked off back-stage by security and driven off in a car with blacked-out windows or shoved onto a tour bus to the next destination.

By the time she reached the front, where her lucky mascot

had been sitting, she was feeling very mellow. The girl with the dark eyebrows stood up as she approached, held out a hand and drew her towards their table.

'Come and have a glass of champagne.'

There were two bottles of vintage Dom Perignon lolling in an ice bucket. Violet knew this crowd were wealthy, showy and sybaritic. They always bought the best. The girl pulled one of the bottles out of the bucket and poured the golden bubbles into a fresh glass. She handed it to Violet as she picked up her own, then went to clink her glass against hers.

'I'm Justine, by the way,' she informed her. 'And I loved your show. You're a complete star.'

'Thanks.' Violet was used to people heaping praise on her. 'You're a friend of these guys? They're my regulars.'

'Alex does my hair.' Justine ran a hand over her glossy mane. 'He knew I'd had a bad day so he asked me along to cheer me up. And it really did. I've never seen anything like it.'

Violet gave a self-deprecating shrug. 'It's just good old-fashioned entertainment. A little bit naughty, a little bit glamorous. Everyone wants a bit of escapism in their lives.'

Justine put her head on one side and surveyed Violet boldly.

'You were looking at me all the way through.'

Violet didn't look away. She smiled and took a sip of her champagne before she answered.

'Not *all* the way through.'

Her eyes were laughing.

Justine dropped her gaze down to Violet's mouth, and then back up again. She was trying to be cool, but her heart was beating very fast. This was a new game for her. She leaned in, until her lips were right by Violet's ear. She could feel her warmth, smell her scent – something expensive and exclusive.

'I'd love to talk to you about doing a showcase at some of our hotels.'

'Hotels?'

Justine nodded. 'It's my family business. We have a chain of luxury hotels. And we're always looking for top-class entertainment. You'd go down a storm. Maybe Moscow. Tokyo . . . definitely New York.'

'That sounds . . . wonderful.'

'Perhaps we could set up a tour? A week in each? You'd have five-star accommodation, first-class flights.'

Violet laughed. It was a wonderful sound, deep, musical, but filled with genuine mirth.

'Where do I sign? It sounds . . . too good to be true.'

Justine flicked a glance down to her Piaget watch. It was eleven thirty. Not too late. She could take Violet to the Ivy — they served until the early hours without complaint.

'Why don't we talk about it over dinner?'

Violet looked thoughtful. She loved the idea of what this girl was suggesting. She prided herself on not using her parents' contacts in her musical career. She hated the thought of Delilah or Raf pulling strings on her behalf. Every gig she had got she had got for herself. She knew the name Rafferty probably opened a few doors, but she couldn't help who she was. She just didn't approve of outright nepotism.

This was an exciting opportunity, a proposition she wanted to hear more about. She thought the girl was genuine. She only had to look at her clothes, her jewellery, the confident way she carried herself, to know she was successful. She wasn't stringing her a line.

She made up her mind in a split second.

'Give me a chance to freshen up and get my things. I'll meet you by the stage door in ten minutes.'

Justine watched her go, gliding through the crowds in her black dress, serene, elegant, stylish. She drained her champagne, and felt the bubbles hit her stomach, where they joined the ones that were already fizzing. She put her glass down on the table. She didn't want to have too much to drink. She wanted to go into this with a clear head.

She sidled over to Alex, slid her arm around his neck from behind, putting her hand over his mouth as she whispered in his ear.

'I'm taking Violet Rafferty out for dinner. Don't you dare breathe a word to anyone. I'll text you later.'

Alex's eyes were as round and wide with scandal as she had ever seen them, but he nodded his agreement to keep quiet and she took her hand away. Then she hurried to the cloak-room to touch up her make-up, pulling out her mobile as she went. She had the Ivy on speed-dial and the *maître d'* was on the waiting list for a job at Amador. She didn't usually call in favours, but this was an emergency.

Half an hour later, the two girls were led to a table for two in a discreet but well-positioned corner, which meant they were hidden from view but could see the rest of the room. The infamous restaurant was still buzzing with diners. Several well-known faces could be spotted – a newsreader, a best-selling author and a couple of racing drivers – so the two of them didn't stand out.

Justine waved away the menus and ordered from the waiter rapidly, pausing only to ascertain that Violet wasn't a veget-arian.

'We'll have the roast poulet des Landes for two with some pommes allumettes. And some creamed spinach. And a bottle of Pouilly Vinzelles.'

'Sounds lovely,' Violet murmured, suddenly realising she was ravenous. She rarely ate much before she performed, not because she was nervous but because it played havoc with her digestion. And she often found that by the time she was finished she was too far gone to eat.

The chicken arrived, and the two girls fell on it greedily. Justine realised she hadn't had anything since her cupcake earlier. They devoured the matchstick-thin fries with their fingers, hot and salty. As they ate, they chattered idly, filling each other in on their lives. They realised they were both very different, but at the same time they were under similar pres-sures. They each had ambition, and they each had things that were holding them back, though neither of them could exactly complain about their position in life. They were both very privileged, yet in some ways this made the frustrations even more difficult to deal with, because they could hardly expect sympathy.

'Everyone thinks you've got where you are because of who you are,' sighed Violet.

'Exactly,' sympathised Justine. 'But in fact my father is harder on me because I'm his daughter. If I was some random person who'd worked my way up through the ranks, I'd be where I wanted to be by now.'

'It's nice to talk to someone who understands.' Violet put her knife and fork together on the plate. 'I can't moan to my own family. And other people don't really get it. I mean, it's not exactly a sob story, is it? I'm really lucky to have got where I am. It's just . . . it's not enough. I want to be up there singing my own stuff, not churning out other people's. But I just can't seem to . . .'

She trailed off, realising with embarrassment that her voice had gone wobbly. What was the matter with her? It wasn't exactly a fucking tragedy. But it was to her. She knew she could do it. So what the hell was stopping her?

She put her hands on her eyelids to stop the tears that were threatening to leak out.

'Sorry . . .' She smiled, mortified that she was showing herself up in front of Justine, who had just offered her the opportunity of a lifetime. What a brat.

Justine took her hand, stroking the back of her knuckles with her thumb.

'It's OK,' she said softly. 'I know what it's like. You're expected to appreciate what you've got, and not want more.'

Violet nodded, grateful for the comfort, grateful for the fact that there was somebody who seemed to understand. She threaded her fingers through Justine's, not wanting the physical contact to stop. They sat in silence, staring at each other, both feeling a connection, but neither sure quite what to say, while the chaos of The Ivy carried on around them.

The waiter arrived with the dessert menu. Reluctantly, they let go of each other and looked down the list.

'I'm full,' declared Justine doubtfully.

'Me too. I think . . .'

'But I just fancy something sweet to finish off.'

'Mmm . . .'

'Let's share a chocolate mousse.'

'Perfect.'

The mousse arrived, wickedly dark and luscious. They both dug their spoons in, conscious that this sharing was intimate, sensual. They barely spoke until the unctuous mixture was finished.

Violet licked the last of the chocolate from her lips.

Justine was staring at her.

'Where now?' she asked huskily.

Violet stared back. They both knew how they were feeling. It was strange and new, but exciting. This was the moment when they could choose to step into forbidden territory, or to stay on familiar ground. It was up to her to make the choice.

'Come home with me.'

Justine put down her glass, her hand trembling slightly, and motioned to the waiter to bring the bill.

Justine was utterly enchanted by Violet's flat. It was a riot of girliness, but not twee in any way. Everywhere you looked there was something pretty to feast your eyes on. A gilt sofa covered in Cecil Beaton roses. A dainty writing desk. Nineteen twenties figurines on side tables. Hundreds of pictures in different frames. Lalique vases stuffed with freesias. A baby grand piano. Lace panels hung at the window, framed on either side by dusty hot-pink velvet curtains. A low coffee table was covered in books and magazines and a fruit bowl piled high with peaches and grapes. The mantelpiece was covered in invitations, thank-you letters, photographs, postcards.

It was a million miles from Justine's annexe in her father's house, which was sleek and minimalist and, she realised now, quite characterless.

Violet moved around the room, lighting scented candles that soon filled the room, flicking on a couple of lamps, turning on some music. Astrud Gilberto began to sing.

For a moment, time stood still as the two girls looked at each other.

Justine held out her arms.

'Dance with me,' she whispered.

Without demur, Violet slid into her embrace. For a few moments, the two of them moved to the music together. Justine could feel the warmth and softness of the other girl's breasts against hers. She moved in so that their cheeks were touching, their hair entangled. Their fingers were entwined again, just as they had been at the table in the restaurant.

They turned to look at each other, and began to kiss.

It was like meringues, marshmallows, cotton candy. It was soft and very, very sweet. And quite delicious. Justine was shocked at how easy it was, how natural it felt, how completely and utterly delectable.

She gave a little sigh and Violet stroked her cheek.

'Come on,' she whispered, and led her by the hand through to the bedroom.

Eight

Three thousand miles away, Tyger Rafferty was starting to tear her hair out.

She'd been in the bathroom for the past half-hour, furtively emailing the office on her iPhone while she left the shower running for cover. It wouldn't do to let her brand-new husband know she was in contact, but she didn't like to remain out of communication for long. She'd sent through some images she'd snapped – she was constantly looking for inspiration and there had been plenty of it in Vegas – and checked on sales figures for the last three days, as well as lining up several meetings for the following week. When you were a knicker magnate, you couldn't afford to stand still, not even on your honeymoon.

Now she was striding around the hotel room, naked and still damp from her shower. Louis was lying on the bed, again. It was all he seemed to have done these past few days, but as he pointed out the rest of the time he was constantly on the go. If he couldn't rest on his honeymoon . . .

'You're supposed to have packed,' she chided him. 'We're supposed to check in at nine.'

Louis Dagger shrugged. He was used to turning up late, catching planes by the skin of his teeth. Sometimes they waited, sometimes they didn't. He wasn't bothered. There was always another one.

'Mum will wig if we don't make it back in time for lunch tomorrow.'

He reached out and grabbed her, pulled her on top of him. She looked down at him indignantly.

'Seriously. You don't want to get on the wrong side of her.'

He patted out a drum beat with his hands on her bare arse.

'You belong to me now, baby,' he said, in his best slow Southern drawl. 'You don't have to do anything Momma says any more . . .'

'I so do,' Tyger corrected him. 'And if you don't get your ass off that bed right now and start packing, I'm filing for divorce.'

She scrambled off him and began to retrieve her clothes, peeling a stocking off a lampshade and a bra from under the bed, then stuffing them haphazardly into one of the cases. From time to time she stopped to admire the Theo Fennell ring on the third finger of her left hand – a ruby encrusted skull with a white diamond snake threading itself through the eye sockets. Not, it has to be said, everyone's taste in wedding jewellery, but a very appropriate gift from the baddest new kid on the rock 'n' roll block.

When you meet him, you'll know.

That's what their mother had always told the three girls when they were growing up. They had loved hearing her talk about the day she had met their father. It had almost become a fairy tale for the three of them. How Delilah had been a model, and had been asked to play a cameo role in a movie Raf was starring in, and how it had been love at first sight. They had met and married before the movie was even wrapped. It had become a showbiz legend.

And Tyger had held on to that legend throughout all the years of heartache. The rows, the shouting, the weeping. The door slamming. The headlines in the papers that her schoolfriends could never help pointing out. She knew Delilah and Raf loved each other passionately underneath all the drama, but it had been hard to live with all the same. Especially when your whole life was on show. Other people's parents had their problems, but they weren't splashed all over the news. Other people's fathers had affairs, but it wasn't public knowledge who their mistresses were. Almost every time Dad started a new film, the inevitable happened. The whispers began.

It had all calmed down now, of course. Their twenty-five-year marriage was held up as living proof that true love could exist and flourish. Delilah and Raf were the perfect showbiz couple. Time and again they were asked for the secret of their relationship. Raf would just smile his enigmatic smile, and Delilah would laugh her infamous, infectious laugh, and they would both shrug.

'You don't go through everything we've gone through and then give it up,' was the only clue Delilah would provide.

Raf wasn't as forthcoming. He played his cards very close to his chest. He always had. It was Delilah who was bubbly and effusive, who let slip intimate details, who let each journalist who interviewed her feel as if they had come away with a scoop.

Of course, it was all carefully orchestrated. Delilah never let anyone know anything she didn't want them to. But by opening her eyes wide, and dropping her voice to a whisper, like a schoolgirl divulging a piece of salacious gossip, she could turn the most inconsequential nugget of information into a story, thereby deflecting attention from the truth. Tyger had seen her do it on countless occasions. Delilah was the mistress of media manipulation. She got away with it because she was gorgeous and charming and everyone adored her, even the most hardened editor of the most scurrilous red top.

Time and again she had traded off photos of herself for covering up the girls' misdemeanours while they were growing up. Their publicist, Tony, spent his whole time horse-trading with the tabloids. A good photo of Delilah was usually worth more than a blurry snap of one of her daughters out on the town. The camera loved her and the public loved her, so it was valuable currency. Sexy, curvaceous, with that infamous cleavage and those tumbling chestnut curls, she worked a different look for every photo opportunity with the help of her tireless stylist. And no sooner was the look worked than it was copied by women all over the country. There had been a run on round-necked leopard-skin cardies, rope-soled wedges, multi-stranded strings of pearls, bandanas, berets, feather-trimmed evening bags – you name it, if Delilah Rafferty wore it, it would be sold out by the end of the week.

Thus Tyger had learned enough from her mother while growing up to know that she needed to order two limos for the trip to the airport, and that she and Louis should check in separately. The hotel had been discreet, because it had to be. But once they were outside, they were easy prey.

She looked over at her husband of three days and her tummy turned over. Delilah was right. You did know. Tyger remembered the feelings she had described and had felt them herself the moment she clapped eyes on Louis. Temporary inability to breathe, racing heart, butterflies in the stomach but at the same time a sense of incredible peace. A relief, almost, that the search was over.

That had been six days ago. Six days that now felt like a lifetime. And clearly he had felt the same, for here they were, Mr and Mrs Dagger. The thought still gave her a thrill. Tyger could feel desire bubbling up inside her even now. They hadn't left the room for a day and a half. But time was ticking by.

Louis grumbled as she forced him to pack up his clothes.

'Come on! You need to leave ahead of me. At least fifteen minutes.'

She didn't trust him to follow on behind. She had to see him into the limo.

'What's the big deal? Why all the skulduggery?'

'I don't want my family to find out about us from the papers.'

Louis frowned. 'We're both grown-ups, aren't we? You're over the age of consent.'

Tyger's phone went again. It was Polly. Chasing her about lunch tomorrow, no doubt. She let it go to voicemail, feeling a tiny bit guilty because she knew Polly would be stressed at not being able to get hold of her.

'One more day,' she pleaded. 'We can tell them tomorrow.'

'Do I get to sit next to you on the plane?'

He nuzzled his face into her neck and she felt her cheeks go pink as she thought of what he had done to her under the blanket on the way out.

'I've checked us in online. Two seats together. We'll have to board separately, though.'

They'd just have to hope and pray that there wasn't anyone sitting near them likely to sell their story. There probably wouldn't be. There was an unwritten code in First Class that most people seemed to adhere to.

The room phone went.

Tyger picked it up: their cars were waiting.

'We'll be down in twenty minutes,' she promised the receptionist, knowing full well it would be more like an hour. But that was her life all over. She was a busy girl. She always kept people waiting.

'Welcome aboard.'

The hostess smiled at Tyger as she took her boarding card, then directed her towards her seat. Louis was already in his, feet stretched out, eyes closed, earphones on.

Tyger glanced around the cabin before she sat down. No one seemed to have clocked her, and Louis wasn't properly famous on this side of the Atlantic yet, only if you were into underground music. But it was only a matter of time. And really, the way he dressed, there was only one thing he could be. He oozed the dissolute decadence of a rock star; he reeked of glamour and groupies.

No more groupies, Tyger hoped. She supposed that strictly speaking that was what she had been. Though your average groupie didn't have an Access All Areas pass that allowed you to barge straight into the lead singer's dressing room after a gig and tell him he was a genius, which is what she had done. Only last Saturday night, she realised.

She'd expected Louis to be disinterested. He had a

reputation as a moody, arrogant twat. He'd looked her up and down once, then twice, and she saw a flicker of recognition in his eyes.

'Your mum's the cookery bird,' was his reply.

Tyger rolled her eyes and sighed. Everywhere she went, men fancied her mother more than they did her. Delilah seemed to be the object of desire for every male in England from sixteen to sixty. Even, it seemed, the moody rebellious Louis Dagger.

'Yes . . .' She sighed.

He swaggered over to her. She could smell the post-gig sweat on him. It made her feel slightly faint.

'Great . . . gig,' she managed to murmur, feeling very self-conscious all of a sudden. Tyger was never tongue-tied. Never intimidated by anyone.

He surveyed her coolly for a few more moments.

'Let's get out of here.' He picked up his jacket. She looked at him quizzically. He jerked his head towards the door. 'You didn't just come here to make polite conversation, did you?'

Actually, she had. Not in a million years did she think Louis Dagger would be interested in her. She had just wanted to tell him how much she'd enjoyed his performance. His songs were melancholy, bitter-sweet, but had somehow struck a chord with her. She'd come away feeling as if he had laid his soul bare. It probably wasn't everyone's cup of tea, but Tyger wasn't one for mainstream.

'Aren't you supposed to be going to the after-show party . . . ?' she asked, but he took her arm, leading her out of the dressing room and down the gloomy corridors until they reached the fire exit. She struggled to keep up with his loping stride in her five-inch heels.

'Where are we going?' she asked breathlessly.

'My place.'

Outside the theatre a car was waiting. They jumped in the back. No paparazzi, thank God – the photographers were all inside, not thinking that any of the stars of the evening would be escaping yet. A wordless driver drove them through the streets of London, the tyres swishing through the puddles. Louis picked up her hand and held it, leaning his head back against the leather seat and shutting his eyes. Tyger didn't know what to think or do. He was running his thumb gently up and down hers. The hairs on her arms stood on end. She shivered. Was it the air conditioning, or . . . ?

He opened his eyes and looked straight at her.

'Sometimes you just know, you know?'

She gazed back at him, feeling like a rabbit trapped in the headlights. She nodded. She couldn't deny her attraction to him for a second – why else had she gone to seek him out in his dressing room? But what did he see in her? Until ten minutes ago he probably hadn't even known she had existed.

She wasn't going to argue. She wasn't going to break the spell. She leaned against him, snuggling in, breathing in his smell, relishing the warmth of his body.

His place blew her away. It was a warehouse apartment overlooking the Thames. Round the four walls of the main room ran a low shelf that held his collection of LPs. There must have been thousands, all pristine, all in alphabetical order.

'Wow,' breathed Tyger, pulling one out.

'What do you like?' he asked. 'I've got everything.'

Tyger felt her mind go blank. Tyger, who was never at a loss for words, suddenly felt under pressure to request something hiply obscure. All she could think of was Fleetwood Mac, for some reason, which was neither hip nor obscure.

'Surprise me,' she managed finally.

He pulled out an album and went and put it on a vintage record player. Mellow jazz oozed out of hidden speakers. She was surprised at his choice. She'd expected something radical and discordant, but in fact the gentle tinkling of the piano and the lazy saxophone were perfect.

He was fixing drinks at a bar. He handed her a chunky tumbler of Cointreau and ice. Again it was perfect. Damn, this boy was good.

*

The only thing in his bedroom was a bed. A black wrought-iron four-poster, seven foot wide. Oh, and hundreds of fat candles in an open fireplace, their dancing flames the only light in the room. As he carried her across the room, Tyger wondered dreamily if he left them burning all the time, or if he had somehow phoned ahead to get some mysterious house-keeper to light them.

He laid her gently in the middle of the bed, and she felt as if she was sinking into a cloud. He undressed her as carefully as a mother with a newborn baby, and she didn't resist. His fingertips glided over her skin. At times she couldn't be sure if he was really touching her. She felt his lips on her breasts, his tongue flickering over her nipples. It was almost imperceptible but sent the most incredible feeling shooting through her. As she arched her back in pleasure she reached out to touch him, eager to explore him too, but he pushed her hands away.

'Shhh . . . don't move,' he whispered, and she lay back obediently. She felt dizzy with the shock of it all.

When he finally slid inside her, she cried. And as they came together, she looked into his eyes, into his soul.

'Marry me,' he said.

How could she refuse?

It was insane. Of course it was insane. She didn't stop to think for a minute about the practicalities or the consequences. To deliberate would be to stop this incredible roller-coaster. Tyger was used to making her mind up quickly and trusting her gut. It was why she was such a successful businesswoman. Besides, she was twenty-one. She had her own money and she knew her own mind.

By the next day she had booked flights to Las Vegas and a hotel, dug out the necessary paperwork, and just found time to dive into her favourite vintage shop where she found a perfect Ossie Clark wedding dress. She said a word to no one, existing in a bubble of excitement that was unmatched by anything she had ever experienced before. The rest of the time she spent with Louis in his apartment. He seemed unruffled by the turn of events. When she'd commented on the whirlwind nature of their relationship, he just shrugged and smiled.

'Meant to be,' was all he would say.

It was only now, as the captain welcomed them on board and announced the flight time, that Tyger realised she was going to be back on English soil in less than ten hours and that reality would be waiting for her. She couldn't put off her family any longer. She couldn't put off work any longer – she'd told them she was on a 'research' trip talking to buyers. And she suspected that she couldn't put off the press any longer.

The butterflies fluttering at the bottom of her stomach weren't the same ones that had been there all week. These ones were churning up anxiety and apprehension. She took a big gulp of the Veuve Clicquot the hostess had handed her. Instead of soothing her, it burned. Louis was sipping his quite happily, drumming his fingers on the arm-rest, singing something softly to himself.

She wasn't going to say anything to him. Technically they were still on their honeymoon. She didn't want to spoil it. She leaned back and closed her eyes, trying to relive every single second of the past crazy week, starting with the moment she had first set eyes on Louis on stage. And gradually, as she worked her way down the glass of champagne, her anxiety subsided.

It was going to be fine, she told herself. After all, everyone loves a wedding. Don't they?

Three seats back, a delegate who had been attending a mind-numbingly dull conference peered with interest down the aisle. This was the highlight of his trip to Vegas. Everyone had told him the place would blow his mind, but it wasn't nearly as interesting as the couple he had been watching since take-off. The stewardess was emptying yet another bottle into their glasses, and they were getting careless.

You'd have to be dead not to recognise Tyger Rafferty. She or one or other of her sisters was in the papers constantly. And that was definitely Louis Dagger, who was being cited by the press as Pete Doherty's natural successor. It wasn't hard to figure out what they'd been doing in Vegas — not attending the monumentally tedious conference he'd been at, that's for sure. The way she kept looking at the hideous ring on her finger gave it away — it couldn't possibly be real diamonds, could it? — as did the way they were devouring each other in between gulping champagne. He took several photos very discreetly on his mobile, ready to email as soon as he landed. They wouldn't be printable quality, but good enough to guarantee a decent wedge.

It wasn't in his nature to blab to the press but someone was going to do it, so it might as well be him. And although his company paid him to travel First Class, he was only on a short-term contract. A few grand in the bank could come in very useful. He thought about picking up the in-flight phone and calling a newspaper, but he couldn't guarantee that he wouldn't be overheard, and besides the rates were astronomical. He'd wait till he landed. The pictures he'd already got were worth a mint.

Nine

It was half past ten on Saturday morning, and The Bower was already crawling with people. Raf stood at his bedroom window looking out onto the garden and stretched with a yawn. All he wanted to do was to go down to his own kitchen and enjoy a pot of freshly brewed coffee and leaf through the *Independent* in his boxers, but he knew there was no point. The kitchen would be a hive of activity. The bell had rung three times already with deliveries – flowers, organic vegetable box, wine and ice . . .

He could see Delilah gesticulating in the office adjacent to the house, talking to Tony, their publicist. He supposed he should be in there, as it was his new venture they would be discussing, but he wasn't bothered which bloody rag got the scoop or when. As far as he was concerned, he just wanted to get on with the job and bugger the hoo-ha that went with it, but that wasn't the deal in this house. No one in the Rafferty family could blow their nose without a press conference. That was the price of being successful, photogenic and high profile.

They were valuable, that was the problem. You couldn't just give your stories away. Each headline had a price, and it was Delilah who made sure that it went into the Rafferty coffers. She wasn't by nature particularly attention-seeking or money-grabbing, but she had cottoned on to the fact that there was money to be made for doing not much more than you were already doing. But it involved military precision and planning.

Every week was a constant trade-off. Interviews, photo-shoots, public appearances, guest slots. If it wasn't *Hello!*

rummaging around their knicker drawers then it was a personal appearance on some chat show or compèring a charity auction. They had to be seen at every glittering occasion in the social calendar, from Ascot to Glastonbury to the Serpentine summer party. Polo at Windsor. Harry Potter premieres. And none of them was ever seen in the same outfit. Admittedly they got a lot of the clobber for nothing – designers were desperate for their clothes to be seen on the back of celebrities – but Raf did find the nation's obsession with what they were wearing, well . . . wearing. He liked to look good, but he didn't want to be neurotic about wearing the same shirt twice. So he had favourite items of clothing – why shouldn't he get good use out of them?

There was a large lever-arch file in the office with Polaroids of what they had worn to every public event. Their stylist, Karen, completely freaked if they didn't keep it up to date. He liked Karen, he really did, and it was thanks to her that he had his Best Dressed Man accolades, but honestly . . . it was almost immoral, the time and attention and not least money that were spent agonising. At least today he could wear what the hell he wanted. Jeans, and a black-and-white floral Paul Smith shirt that should have looked ridiculous on a man of his age but somehow didn't.

He wished fervently that it was just the girls and close friends coming today. Although in theory it was a social occasion, they were all on parade. They couldn't just kick back and relax. Raf wanted to chill with his daughters, catch up on their gossip, make sure they were each all right. It was why they had established this monthly ritual, otherwise the weeks just slipped by and any one of them could have a serious problem that was overlooked because the wheels just kept on rolling. It was very difficult for the girls to be themselves with strangers in the camp. They wouldn't let their guards down.

He felt a flicker of annoyance at Delilah. Why did she have to turn everything into a bloody three-ring circus? After yesterday's momentous decision, they should have just relaxed amongst themselves, not least because they hadn't actually told the girls about the movie yet.

Oh well, he thought. Maybe the hangers-on would have the sensitivity to bugger off and leave them alone after lunch. Though Raf knew from experience that this was unlikely. Delilah's über-generous hospitality, the endless bottles of wine, the appearance of yet more food just when you thought you couldn't eat another thing, meant they were probably in it for the duration. Maybe he could persuade the girls to stay the night, and they could have brunch tomorrow, catch up, chew the fat. That was unlikely too – the chances of them not having to do something on a Saturday night were remote.

He thought wistfully back to when they were little. It was always a painful memory. He had wasted so much of their childhood in a drunken haze. He remembered Violet finding him crashed out on the trampoline one morning. He'd gone to sleep there the night before after a skinful, wanting to look at the stars. She'd been delighted to find him. She wanted him to bounce with her. He'd struggled to his feet reluctantly, managed three bounces, then thrown up spectacularly over the edge, to Violet's joint alarm and disgust. He remembered the look of horror on her face, and her concern – her sweet, innocent, childlike concern that her daddy was ill.

It had not been one of his finest moments.

Now he was dry, dry as a bone, and the trampoline had long been disposed of. But if he wished for anything it was to have that time back. He had tried to make it up to them since, but how could you compensate for all those years of self-indulgence? He'd been a selfish bastard, and he didn't deserve them. Or rather, they hadn't deserved him.

If any of his daughters fucked up their lives, it would be his fault. His fault and no one else's.

He shook himself out of his reminiscence. There was no point in looking backwards. He'd punished himself enough, and if he thought too much about his past, it sent him into a depression that could take days to recover from – a dark, black hole that was probably the reason he had turned to drink in the first place, because he'd always been prone to introspective self-doubt and gloom. The nation had only ever seen the flipside, the charismatic extravert party animal. They had no idea of the self-loathing, the lack of confidence, the fear . . .

He hadn't had any counselling or therapy to dig him out. He didn't want to be brainwashed into some other more sinister dependence. He'd seen other alcoholics spout shrink-speak, and it appalled him. He determined to figure it out for himself. If you couldn't fix yourself without the help of others, then you weren't really fixed, in his opinion. You were still using them as a crutch. Not for him weekly meetings in a draughty church hall. He valued his freedom too much. He wanted to be him, not a puppet on a string. He couldn't deny that it worked for some people, and he didn't diminish their achievement. It just wasn't his thing.

It had been a hideously rough ride – for him and for Delilah – but he'd made it. He didn't make it easy for himself, either. He didn't ban alcohol from the house or the dinner table or avoid friends who drank. What was the point? He had to train himself to keep off the booze with temptation right under his nose. It was the only way to be properly cured.

Though, of course, you never were. The urge never left you. Even now he could picture the bottles of white burgundy lined up in the fridge, dewy with condensation, the crystal jugs full of Pimm's – so innocuous, so deadly, so inviting – that would be served on arrival, the crate of beer chilling in the larder for the more casual guests. It would only take one sip . . .

He had his visualisation. He only had to remember the expression on Violet's face that day, and he was able to hold back. He had any number of pictures to choose from, and they all worked. In his bleakest moments, he replayed them to himself in chronological order: wasted at Sports Day, falling over in the dads' sack race while the horrified headmistress looked on; him and his mates taking over the bucking bronco at Coco's Wild West birthday party – they thought it was hilarious, but the children hadn't; making a pass at Tyger's best friend's mother in his own house – the mother hadn't minded, but her husband had put him up against the wall. Why the fuck had no one ever told him what a twat he was all that time?

They had. Of course they had. It was just that he had never listened.

Never mind. That incarnation had been banished for good. Today's Raf was clean, sober, bright-eyed and bushy-tailed. He looked in the mirror, decided on just two buttons undone on his shirt, and went downstairs to find his wife.

Delilah was back in the kitchen, putting the finishing touches to the food, talking on the phone, and all the while trying to keep her nails dry. The manicurist had arrived at half seven to reapply the pale pink varnish she favoured, and had finally got to her at ten. It wasn't that Delilah was a princess and couldn't paint her own nails; she just knew that unless she booked someone to come and do them she wouldn't bother and would let them chip. As a television chef, the state of her hands was important – she had to keep them looking as good as the rest of her.

Raf dropped a kiss on her neck and got one blown back at him in return as she patiently explained to the food editor of a national magazine why a particular photo could not be used in a recipe spread – 'No one's flaky pastry turns out like that in real life. It's giving the reader a false expectation. It should look rough and ready not perfect . . .' – and ran a blowtorch over some individual rhubarb meringue pies. Raf grinned and went to help himself to a coffee from the overworked Gaggia. No one did multi-tasking like Delilah. She was probably thinking about something completely different while she talked and worked, would hang up the phone and be onto the next thing. Would he merit a moment of her time? he wondered, piling two spoons of brown sugar into the inky depths of his espresso.

Finally, she was finished. She slung her iPhone onto the

worktop. Sometimes he thought she was surgically attached to it. He wondered what she thought would happen if she missed a call; did she fear the end of the world would come if someone was put through to voicemail? He imagined her reaction if he had dropped *her* phone into a vase of flowers. Complete meltdown, probably.

She came over and kissed him, holding her arms exaggeratedly out to the sides, still worried about smudging her nails. Their lips brushed, lingered. Raf felt the urge to pull her into him, to bury his face in her neck and smell her tangerine-scented hair. God, he was lucky. Even after twenty-five years he found her irresistible. It was rare they got the chance for any chandelier-swinging these days.

Doug the Pug scuttered in, his nails clattering across the limestone floor. He looked up at them anxiously, his eyes bulging, his breath coming fast. Raf let his wife go, laughing.

'Ok, little man. I'll let her go.'

'I've got to get on, anyway.' Delilah tested her nails against her top lip, and decided they were dry.

Raf rolled his eyes. 'Honestly, do I have to make an appointment?'

'Tomorrow,' promised Delilah. 'Tomorrow we have a clear diary, no guests, no commitments, phone off the hook. I promise.' Her eyes sparkled as she looked at him. 'What do you want to do? Anything. Absolutely anything.'

'Do you know what I want to do? Nothing. Absolutely nothing. With you.'

'Then nothing it is. I promise.'

'I'll believe it when I see it.' Raf smiled good-naturedly and opened the fridge, pulling out a large tub of natural yoghurt and some blueberries. 'Are the girls all coming?'

'I've got no idea. Polly hasn't been able to get hold of any of them. You know what they're like.'

'They'll turn up.' Raf was pretty certain, but he nevertheless felt the curdle of fear a parent gets when their offspring are out of their control. He had been devastated when Delilah had decided the three girls should move away from home. She had insisted they needed to stand on their own two feet, not least because she and Raf deserved their own space after all this time. He had protested volubly. It was cruel to push them out of the nest. He loved peering into their bedrooms at night when he couldn't sleep, watching them breathe, wondering what they were dreaming. He loved the energy they brought to every mealtime – maybe not breakfast, when they didn't usually appear, or if they did they were bleary-eyed and grumpy, but his favourite time was dinner, when they regaled him with scandal and anecdotes and asked for his opinion on matters of total insignificance to the world at large but which fascinated him, because they mattered to his girls. Two years on he had got used to the relative quiet and emptiness; it was unusual for him and Delilah to be totally alone at The Bower, but the decibel level had definitely gone down quite a few notches.

Never mind. In an hour or so they'd all be here, in a flurry of hair and perfume and sunglasses and laughter, and he could reassure himself that they were all right, his beautiful girls.

Delilah felt guilty, pushing her own husband away, but she needed to clear her head. Lunch for twelve, or however many it was, she could do with her eyes shut, but she had so many things whirling around her brain.

Her editor had phoned yesterday, to see if they could pull the publication of her next book forward. She was already up against it, but she knew they wouldn't have done it without good reason. The timing of a book was crucial – it depended on what marketing slots were available in the book stores and, even more importantly, the supermarkets, and what other books were scheduled to come out at the same time. She didn't want to run up against another Nigella or Delia and be competing for the same slots. And this one was going to be marketed as the ideal Christmas present: 'The Only Cookery Book You'll Ever Need.'

It had been conceived as Mrs Beeton for the twenty-first century – a cookery book for life, with everything from how to wean a three-month-old to preparing a funeral tea. It included detox plans, how to fill your freezer, how to stockpile for Christmas, nourishing recipes for students – in short, a recipe for every possible eventuality in life. It was nothing ground-breaking or new, but it was to be beautifully photographed, with spaces for the reader's own notes, and a link to Delilah's website where a shopping list for every recipe could be down-loaded and printed out. It was going to be a weighty tome, almost an encyclopaedia.

Compiling it was an arduous task. Delilah was a perfection-ist, and although she had a team of people who checked and double-checked each recipe, she still wanted to do it for her-self. She also hated repeating anything she had done in a previous book – it always annoyed her when other chefs did that – so unless a recipe was a classic, like Victoria sponge or *boeuf bourguignon*, everything had to be new. She never wanted to be accused of churning out the same old stuff under a different guise.

Pulling publication forward was going to put her under a lot more pressure. In theory it was only three weeks, but in reality it gave her less time to polish, to perfect, to go over what she had already done. So she knew promising Raf a day of undivided attention tomorrow was unfair. She would have to put in at least three hours' work, drafting out the final outline so her editor could go over it on Monday and then approve it. Maybe she could get up at five and fit it in then, before he surfaced. He wouldn't even know.

Her work was often a source of tension between them. He didn't understand why she had to drive herself so hard, but she had created an empire that wouldn't run itself. It was Brand Delilah, so everything had to have her stamp, her approval, her touch.

'You should delegate!' he would complain, but people were buying *her*, she would point out. How could she delegate?

Besides, she worked best when the pressure was on. The more she had to do the better she thrived. She knew that to anyone else it looked like an insane way of life, but the only way she kept going was through momentum. Which was why she was standing here now peeling the shells off three dozen quails' eggs. Just the top halves, so that each egg was sitting in a little jagged-edged cup. Of course she could have got someone else to do it, but while she was making sure that each egg was perfect, she could think about the next chapter. She loved the contrast of the pale blue speckled shell against the shiny white. And they would look gorgeous piled up on a platter with radishes and baby carrots, ready to dip into celery salt and home-made aioli.

A family day. Today was going to be a family day. And tomorrow was going to be Raf's. She walked past him with a handful of shells to put in the compost bin and dropped a kiss on his head. He looked up from his paper and smiled. As she planted the shells on top of the coffee grounds and banana skins, she thought to herself how lucky they were. They were a great team. That was how you made a showbiz marriage successful. Teamwork.

Ten

The April sun shone in through the window on a tangle of white linen and golden limbs. Its rays nudged gently at the eyelids of the bed's occupants. One girl slumbered on sweetly; the other drifted into consciousness, frowning slightly as she came to. It was her room, definitely, she could tell by the bough of cherry blossom outside the window. But something wasn't quite right . . . There was an unfamiliar arm around her waist and a scent she didn't recognise, sweetly delicious. As she breathed it in she found her head swimming, her heart beating faster. The memories were drifting back. And the body beside her told her it hadn't been a dream.

Violet looked down at the dark hair spread out on the pillow next to her. She was astonished to find that she didn't feel panic, regret, remorse . . . or disgust. She tried to analyse what she did feel and her mouth turned up at the corners into a secretive smile. Turned on. She felt totally, fizzily, meltingly horny. And she wanted more.

Violet had never even thought about sex with a girl until last night, but suddenly she wanted to touch Justine all over, bury herself in her softness. She reached out a tentative hand. If her recollections were correct, last night had been all about her. When Justine had finished, Violet had fallen asleep in her arms, exhausted. Now, she wanted to give Justine the same pleasure. She reached out to trace the outline of her breast, trailing her fingertips lightly over the skin, circling the nipple. Justine stirred slightly.

'Mmmm . . .' Her murmur of appreciation encouraged

Violet to be more adventurous. Her eyes opened, and they smiled at each other. Complicit. No embarrassment. Moments later they were in each other's arms, kissing languidly. Violet ran her hands over Justine's hips, slid it between her thighs, slightly unsure, then tentatively touched her. Justine gave a gasp, arched her back, pushing herself against Violet's fingers, definitely wanting more. She explored the wetness, found the little nub, began to rub it gently, circling it as it swelled. She watched, fascinated, as Justine drifted off, her eyes half closed, her breathing slightly shallow. Neither of them spoke as Violet stroked and teased, judging the pressure needed by Justine's reaction, sometimes barely touching her at all, her fingertips dancing with a pianist's grace.

Suddenly Justine reached out for Violet's other hand, clutching it as she pressed her thighs together and lifted her pelvis off the bed, her cries sounding like desperation but a wild look in her eyes and a smile on her lips assuring Violet this was far from the case. She lay back on the pillows, panting.

'Oh my God . . . Oh my God . . . !'

Violet rolled on top of her. She could feel Justine's body still trembling beneath her with post-coital aftershock.

'So, what do we do now?' she asked, with a mischievous smile.

Justine reached out and stroked her cheek.

'I don't know . . .' she whispered. 'I've never done this before.'

'Never?' Violet was surprised. Justine had been so assured. 'I thought . . . You seemed so . . .'

Justine laughed. 'Instinct, I guess. I just . . . did what I'd want someone to do to me.'

They stared into each other's eyes for a moment.

'I haven't either,' Violet admitted.

'Really? I thought maybe . . .'

'No. I think people think I have because I do all that decadent, vampy Marlene Dietrich gay icon stuff, but no.'

Violet felt moved by the softness of the body beneath hers. It was so alien but it felt so . . . right.

'This is so weird.'

She rolled off Justine and onto her back, staring at the ceiling. She didn't know what to think. What the hell had come over her? She'd never so much as looked at another girl before. And it wasn't as if she'd gone off men overnight either, she didn't think. The thought of a male touch certainly didn't repulse her, as far as she could make out.

It was, she supposed, about the person. About the chemistry. And boy, did they have chemistry. She'd never had an orgasm like it – it had seemed deeper, sweeter, longer than anything a man had ever given her. Though maybe it had just been the novelty of the situation. The naughtiness. Doing it with a girl.

Her eyes wandered over to the clock. Shit – it was nearly eleven o'clock. She was due in Richmond for lunch. She threw back the covers.

'I need to get going. I've got lunch at my parents'.'

Justine watched Violet slip into her kimono. Even now, she couldn't believe the girl had fallen into her hands quite so easily. It had been like picking the ripest plum from a tree – and things had moved faster than Justine could have predicted. What had started out as a calculated plan had turned into the most incredible night of . . . well, passion was pretty much the only word. As she watched Violet tie the silk sash of her kimono tight round her waist, pull her hair back and then shake it loose, the memory of what had happened between them made her throat tighten with desire.

'Come for lunch,' she could just hear Violet saying as the blood pounded in her head. 'My parents won't mind.'

Justine sat up. Lunch at the Raffertys'? Now that would be interesting.

'Really?' she managed in reply.

Violet looked over at her.

'The more the merrier, that's Mum's motto.'

Justine grinned. 'We're not going to mention anything, are we? About what's happened?'

Violet came and sat on the edge of the bed for a moment.

'I don't think so. Mum and Dad are pretty broad-minded, but it might be a bit of a shock even for them.' She bit her lip as she looked at Justine. 'Anyway, we don't know what's going to happen yet, do we?'

The two girls looked at each other. Justine swallowed.

'No,' she admitted. 'We don't. But . . . it was kind of fun. Right?'

She looked at Violet for reassurance. Her kimono had fallen open, revealing the curve of a perfect breast. Justine wanted to lean over, push away the silk, put her mouth around the cherry-pink nipple she knew lay underneath.

'Yes. Yes, it was fun.' Violet reached out and stroked Justine's hair, a swift, affectionate gesture that did nothing to reassure her. 'I'm going to jump in the shower.'

And suddenly she was gone, in a flash of red silk and dark hair.

Justine lay entwined in the sheets that smelled of Violet's perfume and salty, musky sex. She felt uncertainty fluttering in her stomach. She had to remind herself why she was doing this. Berlin. Or if not Berlin, then some other prime location. And so far, she'd achieved what she'd set out to do. She'd seduced Violet, secured an invitation to lunch chez Rafferty, got her feet under the proverbial table. When you looked at it, it was all going to plan. So why did she feel so unsure of herself?

She just had to focus. Justine was ambitious. She remembered her fury and her frustration when Benedict had rejected her proposal yesterday. This was all about her getting what she wanted, and if she had to use Violet to do that, so what? At no point in the evening had she held a gun to her head. The girl was fully compliant—

'Come on!' Violet bounded back in, still damp from her shower, covered in a white towel. Justine looked at her porcelain flesh and felt a sudden urge to reach out and touch it. 'Get your arse out of there and get dressed.'

Justine threw back the covers. She walked out of the bedroom, surprised to find that her legs were trembling. She wasn't used to feeling like this. She'd had plenty of one-night stands, nights of passion, but they'd never made her feel weak at the knees. She caught sight of herself in the mirror and gave herself a sheepish smile.

Yesterday she'd been a pragmatic, opinionated, heterosexual girl about town. A girl who never took no for an answer and had nerves of steel. And she never let anyone get to her. Well, apart from her father. Which was how this whole bloody thing had come about.

And here she was, turning to jelly. Get a grip, Justine, she told herself.

She found her clothes in the middle of the living room, crumpled, where she'd discarded them the night before. She wrinkled her nose in distaste. Justine never wore yesterday's clothes, ever. Everything went straight to the laundry or the drycleaner. She picked up her blazer and shook it, hoping the creases would fall out.

'Borrow something of mine. We're about the same size,' Violet offered. She was tidying up, opening the curtains and taking the empty glasses through to the kitchen. 'And help yourself to underwear. I've got truckloads. Tyger gives me all the samples.'

'Thanks.' Justine smiled at her. Violet smiled back. She breathed in her scent as she walked past and her stomach turned over. A cold shower, that's what she needed.

A few minutes later Justine stood under an icy deluge of freezing water that took her breath away. Soon her head cleared, and she felt able to concentrate on the task in hand. This was just an exercise in Justine Amador-Fox getting what she wanted.

While Justine was in the shower, Violet sat down at the piano. She practised every day without fail, even if it was just for ten minutes, and she knew she probably wouldn't get another chance – she'd be lucky to be back home from her parents by midnight.

She lifted the lid and caressed the ivory keys gently, wondering where to start. She felt rather light-headed, strangely dreamy. And hypersensitive to everything around her – she could feel the morning light on her skin; the freesias in the vase filled her head with their scent. She picked out three notes gently, seemingly at random, and the sound reverberated around the room, bright and clear. She added three more, then repeated the pattern. She stopped for a moment. Something was happening. Something or somebody somewhere was telling her what to play.

She watched in astonishment as her fingers danced across the piano keys, picking out a melody that was haunting in its simplicity. She barely dared to breathe until it was finished. As the last note died away, she sat very still.

Could she recapture it? Or was it going to tease her? Elude her? She tried not to think too hard. She let her fingers do as they wanted, allowing instinct to take over. Just as they had with Justine . . . And they did just as she had hoped. The song was there. Her own composition that had come from who knows where, but that moved her from somewhere deep inside.

She swallowed. She had to capture it. If she left the room and went away, by the time she came back it might be gone. She lifted the piano seat and pulled out her little tape recorder from the secret drawer that held her sheet music. Pressed the button to record, then shut her eyes and played the song again. It was as perfect as it had been the first time.

She felt elated. She wanted to dance and shout and laugh. She wanted to tell the world. She had written a song. A beautiful song. OK, it didn't have words yet, but she knew that it was special. She wasn't being arrogant. She just knew. She had spent so many years studying other people's work, she could recognise what made a song a work of art.

She sat very still for a moment, her head bowed. She wanted to savour the moment that she had spent so long waiting for. It was a mixture of relief and elation. Part of her wanted to lock the doors and windows and shut the rest of the world out, then spend the day trying to perfect her work, maybe add some lyrics. But she couldn't let her family down. She couldn't turn Justine away, now she had invited her.

Justine. Was it Justine, or her experience with her, that had unlocked her? She did feel different today, lighter of heart, almost feline – contented, sinuous, as if she could lie in a shaft of sunlight all day purring. She looked at her reflection in the Venetian mirror that hung over the piano. Did she look different?

Yes. Her eyes were sparkling. Her lips were curled into a satisfied, secretive smile.

Bloody hell. She'd had no idea that a girl was what it would take.

Justine came out of the shower and started to look through Violet's clothes to find something to wear. She wanted to look good. She wanted to make an impression on Raf and Delilah, for a start. Not to mention Violet's sisters. Even though they wouldn't know the details of their relationship, she would still be under scrutiny.

She ran her hand over the rack of Violet's dresses, mostly vintage, an enticing collection of silk and lace, a million miles from the sharp, tailored clothing she wore – stuff that said 'Don't mess with me'. These clothes said, 'Look at me, feast on me, fall in love with me.' She pulled out a button-through dress in sage-green chiffon spattered with tiny white dots, which would work well with the four-inch courts she'd had on the night before. It was a whole new look for her – softer, more feminine.

Putting on Violet's underwear was an experience in itself, just knowing that her breasts had been inside the bra, that the knickers had touched her in the most intimate of places. Her heart was pitter-pattering, a little pulse between her legs mirrored its pace. No man had ever made her feel like this. Fizzy and bubbly and helpless. As she slid the dress over her head, felt the sensual fabric that had been so close to Violet, she had to sit down on the bed.

Eventually she managed to stand and look at herself in the cheval mirror. She was astonished at what she saw. A softer, prettier version of herself. The fabric clung in all the right places. Usually her clothes gave her angles, but this dress gave her curves.

'Wow.' Violet was in the doorway. 'That looks amazing. You'd better have it.'

Justine laughed. 'This is so not my look. But I quite like it.'

'It really suits you. Here.' Violet scooped back her hair and tied it with a white silk camellia. Justine shivered at the touch of her fingers on her neck.

They looked at themselves in the mirror, their arms round each other's waists.

'Butter wouldn't melt,' murmured Violet.

Butter wouldn't melt, thought Justine, but I might . . .

Genevieve Duke paid even more attention than usual to her wardrobe that morning.

She had been delighted with the invitation when it came through from her agent. Lunch at the Raffertys', in that infamous orangery. It was just a shame that it was going to be a private function, and the cameras wouldn't be there. There would be plenty of time for that, she told herself.

The problem was how to look chic and fashionable without looking like mutton. Or frumpy. Short was out. Sleeveless was out. Black was out because it was April, and was very draining without heavy make-up, which was inappropriate for daytime.

She'd finally chosen a Bottega Veneta chinoiserie silk dress in a coppery-tea colour. Pretty, elegant and chic, and suitably spring like. Not too formal. To the knee and with little capped sleeves, which removed the upper-arm problem. Genevieve hadn't descended into bingo wings yet, but there was no denying that women of a certain age should not go sleeveless. And the sleeves had raw edges, which made it a little bit – well, edgy, because the last thing she wanted·to look was matronly.

She was seven years older than Delilah, though only three on paper. That had been a tricky one to circle around while she wrote her autobiography – how did you lose four years without some clever clogs working out from what you were wearing when you were fourteen exactly what age you must now be? She thought she'd excised them successfully. However, there was nothing like sitting next to someone supposedly close to your own age for showing you up. A dewy complexion soon showed up against open pores and a crêpey neckline.

Her hairdresser had painstakingly painted cool ash tones into her graduated bob the night before. Her make-up artist had been through her make-up bag only last week, and had been out with her to purchase new foundation and powder. Your skin tone changed all the time when you were ageing. And it was definitely a question of less is more. There was nothing worse than the sight of foundation settling into wrinkles.

A tinted moisturiser, a little judicious highlighter around the eyes, a sweep of pink on the cheeks, a light coating of mascara and some neutral lipstick. She had the bone structure, and her neck was holding up well.

She gave herself the renowned Genevieve Duke icy smile. She hadn't met a man yet who had been able to resist the gauntlet it threw down. But none of them had interested her for more than a year, which was why she had never married. She had been the subject of much speculation over the years, not least the rumour that she was having a long-running affair with one of the nation's best-loved newsreaders. The truth was she simply preferred her own company – although she and Jeremy did meet up regularly for long lunches. Very long lunches. Yet Genevieve preferred waking up alone in her own bed. Not having to confer with anyone else about what to have for supper. Not listening to someone's protests if you decided not to go to the theatre or to a party.

Pleasing yourself.

That was the title of her autobiography. *Pleasing Myself.* She liked the slightly naughty connotations. It was going to be explosive, revealing intimate details about her leading men over the years. The publishers had given her a substantial advance on the basis that she would pretty much spill all, because over the years she had bedded a startling number of heart-throbs and pin-ups. Genevieve knew she was selling out, but so what? She had spent so many years keeping these secrets that they were now worth a fortune, and she was ready to cash in on her discretion. She had no loyalty to any of her paramours. And as the saying goes, it takes two.

This book was her pension plan. It was obvious that the roles were going to start drying up as she hurtled towards sixty. A best seller would give her enough publicity to ensure a few plum parts over the next couple of years, and then she could retire gracefully. She longed to be at peace mentally and put her career to bed. She wanted to tell her agent 'no more'. Then she could get up in the morning and not sit and wait for the phone to ring, or leaf through the papers to search for reviews either of her own work or of her competitors.

Doing a movie with Raf Rafferty was just the boost she needed. Media interest in how the movie was going would be constant, as the press seemed to be obsessed with the Raffertys: there wasn't a week went by without one or other of the family in the news – whether it was Tyger's inappropriate attire, Coco on the arm of some super-hunk, or Delilah charming a member of the royal family. It would multiply her own column inches tenfold, guarantee her bum on the sofa of every chat show – they would all want to know what it was like working with Raf. So much easier than tedious book tours, pressing the flesh and talking to the WI, which was what she was in danger of facing if she didn't raise her game.

With any luck, she could time the publication of her book to coincide with the release of *Something For the Weekend*. Genevieve had always handled her career with a businesslike precision, choosing her parts carefully and strategically. She had never done something she wasn't proud of. She wouldn't have accepted this film if the script hadn't been razor sharp and uplifting but at the same time thought-provoking – there were few pieces around that reflected the love and sex lives of those in advanced middle age. And she was proud of her book, too. She wrote well, with a waspish pithiness and a wicked wit. She'd been trained to observe, and this came out in her anecdotes. Yes, decided Genevieve, she deserved to have a best seller on her hands, and she was determined to do whatever she could to make sure that happened.

The phone rang. She picked it up, in case it was the cab firm wondering where her house was.

'I'm thinking a walk round the new exhibition at the Serpentine, and lunch at Café Anglais?'

It was Jeremy, with that rich, creamy voice he used to deliver the headlines to the nation. It usually made her feel warm. But today she felt slightly irritated. He was interrupting her train of thought.

'Sorry. I've got a lunch. A work thing. Maybe next weekend . . . ?'

She heard the taxi driver ring the doorbell.

'I've got to go. My cab's here.'

She hung up, gave herself a little spritz of Guerlain, and ran down the stairs, not feeling guilty that she'd been a bit curt. She had never made Jeremy any promises. And her final move was coming into play. After this, it was a life of lolling by the Italian lakes without a care in the world.

The flight from Vegas landed at Heathrow at eleven twenty-five local time.

For a moment Tyger was tempted to throw caution to the wind and walk out with Louis. The Veuve Clicquot had given her a false confidence.

No, she told herself. It was quite likely there would be some stray paps stalking the arrivals hall. They often met the flights from the US, usually the ones from LA, to see who they could catch unawares stumbling off the red-eye not looking their best. They'd leave the airport separately, get two cabs. It wasn't far from Heathrow to Richmond. They would be at The Bower in perfect time for lunch.

She headed for Baggage Reclaim. On the other side of the carousel, Louis was waiting, arms folded. He stared at her, playing the game, not a hint of recognition in his eyes. She stuck out her tongue. He didn't bat an eyelid. She felt a sudden lurch of fear. What if he was getting second thoughts about what they had done?

She looked at him again and he gave an almost imperceptible wink, reached out for the battered Gladstone bag that had held the few clothes he had brought, then strode towards Customs without a backward glance.

'Excuse me, sir?' The customs officer beckoned the tall young man in the top hat to one side.

Louis Dagger looked at him with an easy smile.

'Did you pack this bag yourself?'

'I certainly did, sir.'

'Would you mind if I took a look inside?'

'No problem at all, sir.'

The officer zipped open the bag with an accomplished flourish and began to extricate Louis' belongings, pawing through them and scrutinising each item with an expert eye.

'What was the reason for your journey?'

'I got married, sir.'

The officer flicked him a doubtful glance.

'So where's your wife?'

'She's following on behind. We couldn't get on the same flight.'

The officer didn't comment or offer congratulations. That

wasn't his job. Instead he turned his attention to the inside of Louis' bag, undoing the zip on the inner pocket.

In the queue behind, Tyger saw what was happening and felt her stomach fall into her boots. Louis was being searched. Shit, what if he had taken something with him? Or what if he'd left something in there from a previous trip that he'd forgotten about? Surely he wouldn't be that stupid, or take such a risk? Would he?

As she waited in line, her heart hammering, she realised she had no idea whether he would or not. When it came down to it, she knew absolutely nothing about her husband or what his habits were. She had a horrible feeling he was a very big risk-taker indeed. She thought back to the few hours they had spent in the casino – he'd been reckless, cavalier, ready to gamble everything on the roll of the dice. Luck had been with him, he'd won a few grand, but he'd just as soon have lost. The thrill for him was in the risk, not the winning, she could see that.

So it was perfectly possible he could have something stashed away in his bag.

Tyger looked at the ground. She couldn't bear to watch. Was she going to have to turn up to lunch at her parents' and admit that her husband of three days had been arrested? What had she done? She'd hardly known him a week. She suddenly felt filled with uncertainty. Love at first sight was all very well, but maybe she should have waited. Why the big hurry to hitch herself to a man she hardly knew, and then only by ill repute?

The ink was barely dry on her wedding certificate and she was already having doubts. Why couldn't she have thought twice before he'd led her into that bloody chapel in her vintage Ossie Clark?

She forced herself to look up. The officer was handing Louis back his bag. Sweet relief zinged through her. She wanted to rush over and throw her arms around him, but this was the most dangerous part of the journey; the leg they were most likely to be spotted on. Just another hour and she could hug him all she liked. She shifted up another place in the queue and smiled at a man in a grey suit who was busy texting on his BlackBerry. Couldn't the poor guy give himself a break? What was so important that he couldn't even wait before he'd cleared Customs?

The taxi pulled up to the gates of The Bower. She saw Louis' taxi pull up behind. She checked around for cameras. You never knew. Sometimes they turned up on the off-chance.

There were none.

She slipped out and paid the driver, just as Louis came up.

'Can I have your bag?'

'Sure.'

She beamed, charmed by his chivalry, then frowned as he put it on the floor, bent down and started to rummage through it.

'What are you doing?'

He didn't reply, just pulled out her wedding shoes – vintage YSL – and slipped a hand inside, pulling out a small bag.

'What the fuck?' Tyger exploded. 'What the hell is that?'

She went to grab it off him, but he stood up and held it in the air. She was six inches shorter than him. She had no hope of reaching. He was killing himself laughing.

'It's not fucking funny. Did you plant that on me? What is it?'

'You don't need to know.' He tucked it into his pocket.

'You used me to take your shit through Customs? What kind of a stunt is that?'

She started to punch him. He was laughing. She was furious. Finally he grabbed her wrists.

'Tyger, Tyger – hold on. Stop.'

'You bastard! How could you do that to me?'

He pinned her wrists behind her and looked into her eyes.

'Tyger – they're hay fever tablets.'

She stared back at him.

'What?'

'I got them in the pharmacy. American antihistamines are way better.' He nodded at the row of cherry trees on the road outside, heavy with blossom. 'And this stuff makes me sneeze like crazy. I don't want to meet everyone with my nose running and my eyes streaming.'

Tyger was speechless. He reached out and stroked her cheek. Inside she melted.

'Did you wind me up on purpose?'

'You wind yourself up,' he told her. 'Come on.'

He picked up their bags and loped towards the gate. She followed him, not sure what to think. She was suddenly incredibly nervous. She cleared her throat.

'Um – we'll wait till everyone gets here before we announce what we've done. Is that OK?'

'Sure.' He curled an arm round her shoulders as she typed in the security code. 'Whatever you think's best.'

Coco negotiated the Richmond traffic expertly. She'd grown up here. She knew all the rat runs. She stopped to let a pair of boys cross the road in front of her, then gave them a little wave as they recognised her through the open car window. She could see them in the rear-view mirror, open-mouthed. She giggled. In a couple of weeks' time, when Emily Farraday hit the screens, she would be even more famous.

She felt happier than she had done for months. She had spent the morning on her tiny balcony overlooking the Thames, a pot of peppermint tea at her side, her scripts on her lap. She had gone through them meticulously, plotting her story arc, making sure she understood what her mind-set was in every scene, jotting down notes to ask the director or script editor. And coming up with suggestions to make the scene better. Making television was a collaborative process. The script was being finessed at every stage of the game. What ended up on the screen would be a million miles from what had been delivered by the writer at first draft. And Coco knew it was the actor's job to lift the script even higher.

Before, she had been too nervous to risk suggesting any changes. She learned what was there in black and white. But now she had found a way to conquer her fear, she felt brave enough to contribute. And the more time she spent in Emily's skin, the more the part would become hers.

Turning the corner made her feel triumphant. At long last she could hold her head up at home. She had felt like a fraud of late, convinced she was going to fail. It was hard being in a family of success stories. Tyger was coining it in with her knicker empire and was always being interviewed in her role as a young female entrepreneur. Violet had endless glowing reviews and articles written about her in the weekend supplements and a huge following on MySpace and Facebook. Coco felt inconsequential in comparison. She was often in the papers, but not for *doing* anything.

Her parents had always done their best to treat them all equally, but it was very hard not to judge yourself against your own siblings, even more so when the press were happy to do it for you. Coco, despite being the eldest, was the least confident of the Rafferty sisters. Perhaps it was because she had borne the brunt of those years of turbulence. She had always felt the need to protect the other two, taking them up to her bedroom to play loud music when the rows got heated, reassuring them, telling them it was going to be fine. Which it always was, until the next time . . .

Now, of course, it was hunky-dory. Though how damaged any of them were it was hard to say. Perhaps not at all. Raf and Delilah had smothered them in love, if not each other. Maybe it had made them better equipped to deal with life. None of them expected it to be a fairy tale. So the only way was up.

As she reached the bottom of Richmond Hill, she felt her heart soar. A beautiful sunny day, lunch with her family, lines learned, and the answer to all her troubles in the bottom of her handbag.

'Woo hoo!' she whooped, and put her foot right down, to the disapproval of two old ladies tottering out of their mansion block.

As she pulled up outside The Bower, she saw an elegant blonde getting out of a taxi. On closer inspection the woman was older than she looked, but she was very striking. Confident. Elegant.

Coco frowned. It was Genevieve Duke. She was certain of it. She was one of her heroines. A proper actress, of the old school. One of those women who oozed sex appeal but without feeling the need to have it all out on display. She had spent many hours watching DVDs of her films, watching how she took on a role, managing to make the part her own, remaining true to herself but creating an entirely believable character.

What on earth was she doing here?

As the woman approached the gates, Coco pressed the button to roll down her car window and leaned out with a smile, holding out her hand.

'Miss Duke? Coco Rafferty. It's lovely to meet you. Have you come for lunch?'

Eleven

Delilah knew she shouldn't read her press cuttings. She especially shouldn't read her press cuttings before Tony had been through them and taken out anything remotely derogatory. She could never resist it, though. She picked up the sheaf of clippings that had come in overnight from the cuttings agency.

Nothing much. A nice picture of her at a charity lunch. An interview she had done for a women's magazine about her skincare routine. A picture of her in Julien MacDonald next to an actress wearing the same dress – she came off more favourably, thank goodness, thanks to Karen's impeccable accessorising and dexterity with the tit tape that made her look comely, not slutty.

The last clipping was a piece from Wednesday's *Daily Mail*. It was a profile of Thomasina Brown, a winsome twenty-six-year-old with a gardening slot on daytime television. She wore dungarees with not a lot on underneath, and was, apparently, the latest object of lust for the nation at large. She was currently on the cover of a leading lads' mag with nothing more than a trug covering her decency and the hideous strapline, *'putting the "ard" into gardening'*. Delilah rolled her eyes, then narrowed them when she spotted her name towards the end of the rather fawning article.

There are rumours that Thomasina aspires to a cookery programme, utilising the fresh produce coaxed out of the ground by her green fingers. And judging by her popularity, she could be the logical successor to

Delilah Rafferty, who has graced our screens for long enough now. Surely it's time for a change?

Delilah felt slightly sick as she read the article again. Was that what everyone thought? That she had been around for too long?

That was it. Her time was over. Once the press turned on you, it was only a matter of time before the public followed. An article like this could be hugely influential, not to mention damaging. Everyone would jump on the bandwagon and start Delilah-bashing. She'd been lucky to make it this far, to be honest. She knew in her heart of hearts that she was past her sell-by date – ironically, something she told her viewers and readers to be scrupulous about.

Then she told herself not to be so ridiculous. It was one tiny line in a single article tucked away in the women's section of the paper. And it was probably Thomasina's publicist who had planted the idea in the journalist's head. It was a throw-away remark that no one would notice. She was just being paranoid.

She screwed up the clipping and threw it in the bin, determined not to give it a second thought.

Tony Allan had been the Raffertys' publicist for nine years, and he knew them better than they knew themselves. He was baby-faced, clean-shaven and box fresh, his uniform of striped shirt and jeans always crisply ironed, his shoes polished, his cuff-links gleaming. He looked like an off-duty banker and talked like a barrow boy. He was quick-witted, one step ahead of the game and a fierce negotiator. He understood exactly the value of every story and every photo he had at his disposal. Working with the press was a delicate operation. You had to build up relationships, and be careful not to destroy them. Letting one paper or magazine have an exclusive inevitably pissed off one you might need another day. He was constantly calling in favours, doing trades, building bridges, making contacts. He had three mobiles – one for clients, one for photographers and one for the press. On a bad day – or good, because Tony thrived on chaos – all three phones would be going at once.

He was devoted to the Raffertys. They were his most important clients, because there were so many of them, and over the years he had almost become one of the family. He didn't have one of his own. He was married to the job, on call twenty-four hours a day. Delilah had tried to match-make on several occasions, but he insisted he was happy on his own.

'Why do I want a bird around? She'll just bitch about me being on the blower all the time. And ask me what time I'm going to be home.'

He had a point. The hours he kept weren't conducive to a healthy relationship. So Delilah spoiled him whenever he came over, fussing over him, feeding him, giving him food parcels to take home because she was convinced he lived on Marks and Spencer sandwiches. She always had him and his old mother, whom he adored, over on Christmas Day, and spent as long choosing his Christmas present as she did Raf's.

Today Tony was on a high. He was blown away by Raf's new venture, and was salivating at the thought of all the coverage the movie was going to bring. He had already put a new white board up in the office and started charting out a campaign. They would announce the film at the beginning of next week, then line up interviews, starting with the heavyweight Sunday supplements, moving on to the glossy monthlies, then the daily papers. Raf was too old to target the celeb magazines just yet. None of their readers would remember his first incarnation, but once the movie was a hit he would become prime fodder. He still had the looks. Bastard, thought Tony fondly.

He was sitting at the island in the kitchen with a coffee, drafting out a press release. Polly's MacBook was open on the other side. She'd been going through all the emails that had come in overnight – even on a Saturday there would be hundreds to deal with. Poll was a diamond, he thought. Having a relationship with her would be ideal – she understood the nature of his job, wouldn't start bitching if he had to drop everything. It was just a pity he didn't fancy her, but she was too 'jolly hockey-sticks' for him. She was the type to put on another jumper instead of turning on the heating in winter. He was very fond of her, nevertheless. She was a grafter, and Tony respected grafters. There weren't many around in this day and age. Everyone seemed to want a free lunch and a party bag to go with it. ·

As he worked through his press release, he heard the front door slam and voices in the hall. The bell hadn't gone, so it must be one of the girls. He looked up as Tyger bounded in. Trailing behind her was a lanky figure in skinny jeans and a top hat. His heart sank.

Louis Dagger. He hoped to God this was a one-night stand. He knew Dagger's reputation. The guy was a nightmare. Shot his mouth off about all the wrong things and wouldn't dish the dirt on what everyone really wanted to know. He turned up to press conferences late or drunk or both. Working for a client like Dagger was all about damage limitation. Tony certainly didn't want any of his shit rubbing off on Tyger, who was already the most controversial of the sisters, being outspoken, gregarious and impulsive. He was always having to tell her off for being indiscreet.

'Tony-babes!' Tyger threw her arms round him and gave him a big kiss. 'This is Louis. He's a *rock-star* . . .'

'I know who he is,' Tony replied slightly stiffly.

'Tony only likes Bruce Springsteen,' Tyger explained to Louis, who was looking shifty in the doorway. 'He won't have heard any of your stuff.'

'Tyger's not being fair. I like the Rolling Stones, too,' Tony defended himself. 'And actually, I loved that track you did – the zombie one.'

One of Louis' hits had been the soundtrack to a cult television show – the one every kid in the country wanted to see and every parent wanted banned.

'Hey, Tony – be careful,' teased Tyger. 'You're getting dangerously close to entering the twenty-first century.'

Tony ignored the jibe. He was used to Tyger calling him an old fart.

'I don't know where your mum and dad are. Help yourselves to a drink . . .'

But Tyger wasn't listening. She was already throwing her arms around Polly, who was coming back in from the office.

'Polly Wolly! I want you to meet Louis. My . . . new best friend.'

'Hello, Louis. Lovely to meet you.'

Tony smothered a smile as the unlikely pair shook hands: Polly beaming and blushing, Louis cool and aloof. The wholesome Polly and the dissolute Mr Dagger. Polar opposites.

Tyger pulled open the fridge.

'Louis – what do you want to drink? We're already completely tanked,' she announced to the room at large. 'We had two bottles of champagne on the . . .' She trailed off. 'On the balcony at breakfast,' she finished brightly.

Tony tensed. She was lying. What was Tyger trying to hide?

'I'll have a beer,' said Louis.

So he can speak, thought Tony darkly, when he wanted something.

Tyger pulled out a bottle of Peroni.

'Tony?' She smiled at him innocently. He knew her well enough by now to know she was up to something.

'I'm fine with my coffee, thanks,' he said, staring her out. She blushed, turned back to the fridge.

Guilty, guilty, guilty. But of what?

Before he had time to enquire further, Coco floated in. With Genevieve Duke two paces behind her.

'Hey, guys, look who I found at the gate.'

Everyone turned to stare. Genevieve smiled, quite unflustered. Tony hurried forward, hand outstretched.

'Miss Duke. I can't tell you how thrilled we are. Raf is so excited.'

'About what?' demanded Tyger.

'Dad's doing a movie. With Genevieve. A romantic comedy,' Coco told her.

'No shit!'

'*Hope*fully not shit.' Genevieve chuckled in her famous throaty drawl, immediately getting them all on side.

'Well, it's got to be more champagne, then,' said Tyger, pulling a bottle of Piper-Heidsieck out of the fridge door. 'That really is something to celebrate.'

Tony didn't miss her catching Louis' eye. He was trained to observe. They were definitely complicit in something. He just hoped it wasn't what he thought it was.

As Tyger poured the champagne, getting more of it over the work surface on the island than in the glasses, Violet arrived with a tall, tanned, glossy-haired brunette in tow.

'Everyone, this is my friend Justine.'

'Isn't that Violet's dress?' Tyger asked, handing her a brimming glass.

Justine felt a blush creeping over her cheeks.

'She crashed at my place last night,' explained Violet airily. 'I lent it to her.'

'Suits Justine better than it does you.'

Violet thumped Tyger's arm.

'Are you in the music business?' Tony asked. He liked to keep track of exactly who the girls were friends with so he wasn't caught unawares. Like he had been this morning.

'I'm in the hotel business,' Justine replied. 'I work for Amador.'

Tony looked impressed. 'Nice. They're a great chain. Have you been with them long?'

'Well, kind of all my life.' She might as well tell him now. There was no point in hiding the fact. 'My father's Benedict Amador.'

He surveyed her thoughtfully. 'You're Justine Amador-Fox?'

Justine looked startled that he knew her full name. 'Yes . . .'

'Don't worry,' Tony reassured her. 'It's my job to know who all the movers and shakers are in London. And I do quite a lot of business in your father's hotels. Anyway, welcome to the madhouse.'

He grinned at her and raised his glass. Justine started to relax. She was going to be accepted as one of Violet's friends. She didn't have to explain herself. Nobody suspected anything. Why would they?

She looked over at Violet, in a white Grecian dress with gladiator sandals, leaning up against the fridge, talking to Louis Dagger. She was listening intently to what he was saying, running her finger around the rim of her glass, her eyes fixed on his. She felt a sudden rush of jealousy. Was Violet interested in him? They'd have a lot in common, both being singers, musicians . . . He would probably have more in common with her than Justine did. And he was devastatingly attractive. She took another sip of her drink, feeling slightly self-conscious. It wasn't like Justine to feel out of place, but she'd never slept with a girl and been brought home to meet her family before. And this was one high-profile family.

Justine was used to wealth and glamour. She'd been brought up with the world's elite. Not showbiz types, but powerbrokers and oligarchs and entrepreneurs, most of them infinitely wealthier than this lot. But the kitchen was crammed with more than its fair share of A-listers. It was as if the pages of a magazine had come to life. For the first time in her life she felt slightly awkward.

But then it was all right, because Violet left Louis Dagger and came over to her and dropped a kiss on her shoulder, unnoticed by anyone else.

'You OK?'

'Fine,' replied Justine. Wild horses wouldn't get her to admit that she was just the tiniest bit starstruck.

'That Louis Dagger's hard work,' Violet confided. 'I was just being polite and asking about his music, but I could hardly get a word out of him.'

Justine smiled. 'He's probably shy. It's quite scary, being thrown in at the deep end with you lot.'

'Don't be silly.' Violet shot her a quizzical glance. 'We're just the same as anyone else. Dad!'

And just to prove that her last statement was entirely preposterous, she put down her glass and threw open her arms as the living legend that was Raf Rafferty walked into the room.

Wow, thought Justine. No photo she had ever seen did him justice. He had to be – what? – fifty-five? As old as her father, for sure. But that chiselled face, the blue eyes that were glacial yet kind and pulled you right in when they looked at you, the laughter lines that softened the perfect bone structure that could otherwise have been harsh. And his body – it was slight, yet there was power in his shoulders, a feline grace to the way he walked. Not feminine – far from it. Despite his floral shirt, his beauty and his elegance, he was overwhelmingly male.

He seemed unaffected, too – very laid-back and down-to-earth. He hugged his daughters, greeted his guests, grabbed himself a bottle of soda from the refrigerator. And when Delilah arrived, it was obvious he only had eyes for her. It made Justine feel sad for a moment. She knew her father had worshipped her mother. Not from Benedict – he never spoke about Jeanne – but from snippets she had gleaned from other people over the years. He had worshipped her so much so that he had never replaced her.

Had her father looked at her mother the way Raf looked at Delilah?

'Penny for them,' Violet whispered in her ear, and she shivered. She caught her hand, holding it tight.

'Mum – this is my friend Justine.' Violet drew her forward and introduced her to Delilah.

It was funny how different people looked in real life. With her wild tortoiseshell curls, her heart-shaped faced and doe eyes, Delilah was instantly recognisable, yet she was far tinier than she seemed on the television, and her skin had a lustre to it that didn't come across on the small screen. Justine felt cumbersome and ordinary in comparison as she shook Delilah's hand.

'Isn't that Violet's dress?' Delilah asked, her eyes dancing. 'It really suits you – she should give it to you. Violet – you should give that dress to Justine . . . It looks amazing on her.'

In a split second, Justine felt gorgeous again. Delilah did that to people. She had a way of handing out compliments, boosting their confidence, so they didn't feel as if they were in her shadow.

'Why does everyone keep saying that?' Violet complained, but she was laughing as she said it. 'OK, you'd better have it, since you look so fabulous in it and I look so awful.'

She slid her arm around Justine's waist as she spoke, and Justine felt a sharp stab of lust. She gripped the stem of her glass and tried to look demure. She didn't know how long she was going to keep up this act.

By one o'clock the kitchen was getting crowded and everyone moved through into the orangery.

Nearly everyone in the country knew and lusted after this room, although 'room' was understating it, really. One and a half storeys high, with twelve floor-to-ceiling arched windows, it was flooded with natural light. The ceiling was painted a deep cobalt blue and studded with hundreds of tiny pin-prick lights, so that when the sun went down it looked like the most heavenly night sky. Down the centre was a long, narrow refectory table reclaimed from a nunnery – the sisters would be turning in their graves if they could see and hear what went on around it now. The places were set with mismatched china plates, floppy lace-trimmed napkins, chunky wineglasses and bone-handled cutlery. Two vases stuffed with peonies, sweet peas and masses of frothy greenery filled the air with a heady scent. Rodrigo y Gabriela played softly in the background, with no hope of being heard over the excited babble.

Raf was desperately trying to play down being the centre of attention, but it was difficult. He had wanted to wait for Dickie to arrive before he announced the film to them all, but Genevieve had inadvertently let it slip to Coco, who had then spilled the beans to Tyger, and, frankly, the minute Tyger got hold of something that was supposed to be played down, she played it right up.

'I want to read the script. Can I read the script?' Coco was demanding.

'Who's doing the soundtrack?' He knew Violet wasn't hustling, just interested.

'Make sure they all wear my underwear.' Tyger was definitely hustling.

'For goodness' sake,' Raf laughed. 'I know it's a novelty, me having a job. But calm down.'

'We're just proud, Dad.' Coco put her arms around his neck and squeezed him tight.

For a moment, Raf thought he was going to burst with pride. He'd almost forgotten what it was like, to have the limelight. And it was wonderful having the girls cooing over him. He sometimes thought he'd been a terrible father figure to them – drunk all those years, and then pretty useless for the next ten, taking a back seat. Now he was going to have the chance to show them what he was made of, that he was talented, not just an old soak or a slacker.

Delilah had brought in more champagne and a tray of glasses. For one moment, he was tempted to reach out and take one. Surely he'd be able to handle one glass? He was a different man now to the one who had never known when to stop. He had self-control, self-awareness—

Stop right there, he told himself. You're getting above yourself. Euphoria was a dangerous emotion – it swept you along in its wake, egging you on. Raf knew the coming months were going to be tough, that temptation was going to be put in his way repeatedly. He couldn't fall at the first fence just because his circumstances had changed. He turned and picked up his soda and lime.

One thing was for sure, he was never going to get scurvy.

In the midst of the commotion, Tony's phone went. It was the one he never ignored. He snatched it up, moved to the edge of the room. A few moments later his voice rang out, the anger in it making everyone turn and stare.

'What the hell are you talking about?'

His face was red with fury.

'You've got absolutely no evidence to stand this story up. It's just conjecture, totally spurious.' He listened patiently for a few more moments. His face drained from red to white. When he spoke again, his voice was calm, controlled, deadly. 'Let me call you back.'

He hung up the phone and stared at Tyger.

Everyone else turned to look at her.

She had the grace to look a little abashed, then stepped forward.

'Um . . . Mum, Dad. And everyone . . .' She gave an awkward smile. 'Louis and I have got something to tell you.' She pulled the skull ring out of her pocket and slipped it onto her finger. 'We . . . um . . . got married!'

There was instant uproar. Coco and Violet both leapt to their feet, squealing, and came round to hug their sister. Tony threw his phone onto the table, thunderous. Raf suddenly wished very badly that he did have a proper drink in his hand.

And Delilah – Delilah felt a myriad emotions wash over her. Terror, that her youngest daughter had got herself in a situation that wasn't going to be so easy to get out of. Disappointment, that she hadn't been able to include her in the most exciting event of her life so far. Curiosity, as to what made Louis so different – no man before had turned Tyger's head. And fury, that Tyger had managed to overshadow Raf. She knew how much uproar this was going to cause. Could she not have had the common sense to give them all the heads up? She supposed that would have made it so much less exciting. The whole point of eloping with someone was the secrecy, the clandestine nature of the adventure, and Tyger, who lived life to the full, would have got off on that.

She should expect nothing less.

She came round the table to Louis, who was standing rather awkwardly next to Tyger, obviously wishing the floor would swallow him up. She took his hand in both of hers, looked him in the eye and gave him her best heartbreaking smile.

'You're very brave. I hope you realise what you've let yourself in for. She's an absolute monkey. But welcome to the family.'

There was no point whatsoever in making a huge fuss. The damage was done. She leaned in and gave him a kiss, just as the doorbell drilled through the commotion. Delilah sighed.

'Who left the gates open?'

'That'll be the first of the scum . . .' The press were always scum when they weren't doing as Tony wanted.

'I'll get rid of them,' Polly said firmly. She'd worked with the Raffertys long enough to deal with the situation. And her ringing Downe House tones usually sent them packing.

Polly opened the door to a lanky man blinking behind horn-rimmed glasses. He was wearing a scruffy green jumper and jeans. He scratched his head awkwardly, his hair tufting up.

'Um – I'm awfully sorry. I think I'm late. I overslept. I forgot to go to bed. Then I fell asleep . . . The cat woke me up in the end.'

Polly stared at him, puzzled. He was definitely not the usual door-stepping journalist.

'I'm Dickie. Dickie Rushe? Raf said . . . come for lunch? Have I missed it?'

Polly's face broke into a broad beam. 'Dickie – hi! I'm so sorry. No, we haven't even started eating yet. Usual chaos. Actually, even more than usual. Come on in. I'm Polly. Delilah and Raf's assistant.'

Dickie loped in through the door and looked around the hall, unashamedly taking it all in with his director's eye. His hands were in his pockets and he grinned at Polly.

'I'm so rude – I haven't even brought a bottle. But when I realised what the time was I jumped in the nearest taxi.'

'How did you forget to go to bed?'

'Nothing exciting, I can assure you. Reading through the script.'

He looked rueful. Polly wondered if he'd actually had a shave, or even a cup of coffee, before he had left the house. His shirt collar was still stuck inside his jumper. She pulled it out for him and patted it into place wordlessly. He didn't seem to mind.

'Never mind,' she consoled him. 'It's fun and games here, I can tell you. Come and have a drink.'

With the arrival of Dickie, Delilah decided it was time everyone got some food inside them. The drink had been flowing rather fast, and maybe some carbohydrates would calm everyone down.

She brought out tarragon chicken, mashed potato with finely diced leeks stirred through, and zesty carrots and green beans. Soon everyone was helping themselves, passing the gravy, pouring each other wine, diets forgotten in the face of such temptation. She sat down at the foot of the table, feeling slightly calmer. She was always happy when people were eating. She felt totally drained by the morning's events. It was just another prime example of never knowing what life was going to throw at you. No matter how carefully you planned things, no matter how vigilant you were, there was always something to trip you up.

She looked down the table at Tyger, chattering nineteen to the dozen, totally oblivious to the trouble her latest announcement was going to cause. And Louis next to her – he played his cards very close to his chest. He wasn't saying much. Probably wise. She wondered what his motive was in marrying her daughter. Whose idea had it been? A drunken impulse, no doubt. They probably both had low boredom thresholds.

Tony was missing from the table. He was already on the phone, fire-fighting. She should go and get him, tell him not to worry for the time being, but he would insist. And he was right. The tabloids weren't going to stop just because the Raffertys wanted to have their lunch in peace.

She helped herself to some chicken wearily. At the end of the day, it would be her decision what game plan they made. She wished someone else would take responsibility. Raf wouldn't – his attitude was things would sort themselves out. He was old school. He didn't really understand the power of the press. When he had been at the height of his fame, the press hadn't been so vicious, so celebrity obsessed. It caused a lot of friction between them, what he called her obsession and she called his disregard.

'Isn't there some middle ground?' he would ask plaintively, and she would laugh hollowly.

'No,' she would counter. 'That's the whole point. You can't pick and choose. If you're in the fame game, you have to play it all the time.'

Everyone was devouring their mini rhubarb meringue pies when Tony came back. He put his notebook down at the head of the table next to Delilah. He looked drained and serious, like a police chief about to brief his top men on a murder inquiry.

'OK. Here's our story. We knew all about the wedding. We are having a private family party here to celebrate, and we'll throw a proper reception next week to which all the press will be invited as long as they respect our privacy over the weekend.'

'No.' Tyger looked mutinous. 'That's a lie, and I don't want a bloody wedding reception. The whole point was it was secret and private—'

'Tyger.' Raf's warning tone was not to be ignored.

'No, Dad, I'm not having some scummy fake party with a load of people I don't know and care even less about, because I know that's what will happen.' She threw a glance at Tony who was looking very unhappy. He knew exactly what Tyger was like when she dug her heels in.

'If you don't comply then they're just going to hound you,' he objected. 'Come on, Tyger. You know the deal.'

'This is my wedding!'

'And you knew damn well when you went off and did it that there would be hell to pay.'

Tyger crossed her arms and stuck out her bottom lip. Her parents knew the look well from childhood.

Delilah decided to pull rank.

'Tyger, I'm sorry, but that is what is going to happen. Otherwise we're going to get no peace whatsoever, any of us. And frankly, we've got enough to worry about—'

'That's right, just worry about yourselves. Never mind what I want.'

'Your father's about to start on this film. It's a big deal for him. He doesn't need the stress.'

'OK. Have your reception. But you needn't think Louis and I are coming. Are we?'

She looked at her husband for support. He shifted in his seat uncomfortably and shrugged. 'Could be a laugh.'

Tyger looked at him, dumbfounded.

'Great. Even my husband won't support me. You're just as bad as the rest of them. I suppose you want the publicity—'

'Tyger, that's enough!'

'Maybe that's why you married me!' Tyger slammed her glass down on the table.

Louis sat back in his chair, looking pissed off.

Violet grinned at him sympathetically from the other side of the table.

'Welcome to Tyger-world. You've got no idea what you've let yourself in for, have you?'

She was the second person to say that to him.

Tyger burst into tears.

Delilah took a deep breath in. She knew the routine. Tears were what Tyger used when she knew she was fighting a losing battle.

'You can have the party where you want, how you want,' she soothed.

'Yeah, right, Mum. As long as I invite everyone you and Tony want.'

Delilah was getting exasperated. This could go on all afternoon. And, frankly, it was embarrassing. Scenes like this were common enough in the Rafferty household, but there was no need to subject their guests to the full horror. Genevieve and Dickie were both looking on in polite fascination.

'OK, let's get this into perspective. This was supposed to be a lunch to celebrate *Something for the Weekend*. Maybe we should park this conversation until later? I'd like to raise a glass and say here's to a fantastic film.'

Everyone picked up on the diversion eagerly and grabbed their glasses.

Tyger wiped away her tears sulkily and lifted hers too.

At the other end of the table, Genevieve caught Dickie's eye and raised an eyebrow. He gave her a little grimace in return. They were both fish out of water, and slightly embarrassed by the turn of events. Dickie cleared his throat, and got to his feet to respond to the toast.

'I'd just like to say how thrilled I am to have two British icons working together on this movie. It's going to be . . . stupendous. So let's have a toast . . . to Genevieve and Raf.'

Everyone raised their glasses again. Then Raf stood up. Tyger rolled her eyes.

'Oh for God's sake. This is *worse* than a bloody wedding reception.'

Delilah fixed her daughter with a steely glare. Raf ignored the interruption.

'There are probably only two people who could have persuaded me to get back on the horse, and they're both here in this room. I'm incredibly excited about working with them, and I just hope they bear with me if I'm a bit rusty. It's been a while . . .' He held up his sparkling mineral water and watched the ice catch the light. 'To Dickie and Genevieve.'

'Dickie and Genevieve,' everyone chorused, and Delilah breathed a sigh of relief. Crisis averted. For the time being, at least.

Twelve

After pudding, Delilah poured coffee for everyone and came to sit next to Genevieve. She was conscious that her guests had been somewhat sidelined during the earlier drama. Genevieve had been very polite throughout the entire meal, dividing her attention equally between the other guests. She was charm itself, and didn't spend the whole time talking about herself. Delilah was relieved. She had read a lot in the past about Genevieve being rather aloof and self-absorbed, so was pleasantly surprised to find her quite the reverse.

She drew up her chair.

'Thanks for chatting to Coco. I know she values your advice. *Critical but Stable* is her first big job . . .'

'I think she's going to be a star.'

Being one already, Genevieve could afford to say that.

'Raf and I are so thrilled about the film, and about you. It's going to be wonderful.'

'Well, it's an honour to be playing his wife. I'm a huge admirer of his work.'

'He is of yours, too. We both are.'

The two women looked at each other, then laughed. They both sounded as sycophantic as each other.

'Well, that's the mutual appreciation over,' said Genevieve. 'But seriously – Dickie was a genius to bring him on board. It's going to be the most fabulous film. We're going to have a ball.'

Delilah leaned in with an air of confidentiality. Those who knew her well would recognise it as one of her weapons – she had a way of drawing people in, getting them on her side, so as to make sure they were an ally. She took them into her confidence, made them feel special.

'I think he's quite nervous. After all, it's been ten years. Though I wouldn't expect him to admit it.'

Genevieve looked sympathetic.

'It's always frightening. No matter how often you've done it. We all get the jitters.'

'Do you?'

'Anyone who says they don't is lying.'

Delilah looked thoughtful.

'Would you do me a favour?'

Genevieve raised an eyebrow. What sort of a favour could Delilah want?

'Of course.'

Delilah looked round the table to check no one else was listening.

'I know I shouldn't be worried. It was all years ago, and of course he's given up the drink since. But . . . well, you must know that Raf had a terrible reputation for affairs with his leading ladies . . .'

Genevieve started to smile. She was about to reassure Delilah when she carried on.

'. . . but, well, have you seen Pandora Hammond?'

Genevieve had. The first thing she had done when she had heard who was playing the mistress was Google Pandora and look at as many clips of her as she could. She was stunning, with porcelain skin and violet eyes. The last couple of films she had done had received both critical acclaim and the thumbs-up from the public at large. She was currently on the cover of *Vogue*, dressed in a wispy chiffon dress and a garland of spring flowers. She was the darling of the gossip magazines, who were all falling over themselves to find positive role models in these testing times. Pandora was the perfect English rose, who preferred cucumber sandwiches to caviar, knitting to nightclubs and charity shops to Chloe – or so she said. Genevieve knew spin when she saw it.

'She is absolutely gorgeous,' Delilah went on. 'No man in his right mind could resist her. Obviously you'll all be working closely together. And I know how intense things can get on a film-set. Could you . . . keep an eye on him for me?'

Genevieve just about managed a gracious smile. Inside, she was seething.

Delilah obviously considered Genevieve no threat to her marriage whatsoever. Whereas Pandora Hammond was . . . Delilah couldn't have insulted her more if she'd recommended a good plastic surgeon. Didn't she realise that every man Genevieve had ever worked with had fallen under her spell? She'd had affairs with a lot of them, but for every one she had romanced, there were three who had declared undying love but had found it unrequited. She could pick and choose her paramours, and Delilah needn't think that just because she was only four years off drawing her pension she didn't still have the powers of attraction.

She didn't show that she was rattled. 'Don't worry. He won't put a foot wrong with my beady eye on him,' she reassured Delilah. 'I'm used to being Mother Hen these days.'

Delilah pushed back her hair with a nervous laugh. At close quarters, Genevieve noticed a few fine lines around her eyes that didn't show up on camera. She'd also spotted that Delilah seemed jumpy and nervy, unable to relax. Was the pressure getting to her?

Genevieve could play ingenuous to perfection. She picked Delilah's hand up and held it in hers.

'Darling, you need to give yourself a break. You look exhausted.'

Delilah snatched her hand away.

'I'm fine,' she snapped, then seemed to remember who she was talking to. 'I'm fine,' she repeated with an unconvincing smile. 'It's just been a bit of a mad day, that's all.'

'Of course it has. You are only human. You've got a hell of a lot on your plate.'

Genevieve cast an eye around the room. She certainly had –

those three little madams, for a start. Totally self-interested, not remotely concerned about their mother. Not for the first time Genevieve blessed her own foresight in not having children. A thankless task, if ever there was one.

For one awful moment, Delilah thought she was going to cry. It was seldom she let her guard down, seldom she elicited sympathy from anyone. She was used to being the strong one. Genevieve's sympathy suddenly made her feel vulnerable.

She stood up.

'Excuse me. I must get the cheese . . .'

She walked out of the orangery, through the kitchen and into the larder where a huge maple board was waiting, laden with a towering chunk of craggy, sharp English cheddar and a chalky wheel of Brie. She poured water from the butler's sink into a glass, pressing its coolness against her forehead before drinking it down. Why had Genevieve Duke rattled her? She had merely been showing concern.

Damn. She'd let the woman see a chink in her armour. Delilah usually kept her true feelings in check – whilst coming across as soft and warm and emotionally honest, of course. It was important the public thought she was human, like them, because that was why they watched her on television and bought her books – they honestly believed they could live just like she did. But of course, they couldn't. Far from it. It was a constant battle to keep all the balls in the air.

Usually she was on top. Of everything. Work, family, marriage. But suddenly she was starting to feel it all slipping away. She was relinquishing control, and not willingly. She'd been delighted at first about Raf's new venture, but now doubts were starting to creep in. And Tyger – bloody Tyger . . .

She wasn't going to go under. This was a blip. She'd just have to get back on top.

Delilah put down the glass, picked up the cheese and walked back through to the orangery. The perfect hostess.

*

Polly surreptitiously sneaked a glance at her watch and sighed.

There was no way she was going to get away from The Bower before six o'clock. Whenever there was a crisis in the Rafferty household, they sucked the life out of her. She supposed she should be flattered that they relied on her, Polly Fry, a mere mortal, to give them moral support. She knew if she made to leave that Delilah would suddenly find a thousand things for her to do – even though it was a Saturday. There would be lists, phone calls, people to chase.

It was ironic. Most people in the country would give their right arm to be sitting at this table, eating a Delilah Rafferty meal. The last thing Polly wanted was food. She had promised herself that she would go to the swimming baths this afternoon and do at least twenty lengths. There was fat chance of that now.

She turned to put a hand over her glass. Dickie Rushe was next to her, and was chivalrously filling it.

'No – thank you. I need to keep a clear head.'

'Whatever for? It's a glorious Saturday afternoon.'

'I'll probably have to work later.'

He looked surprised. 'You have to switch off every now and again. Trust me, I know. I'm the world's worst for giving myself a break.'

Polly giggled. 'Reading scripts till four o'clock in the morning?'

'As if I hadn't read it seventy-four times already. But every time I read it I think of something new I could do.'

Polly cupped her chin in her hand and looked at him. He was sweet. Shy, but smiley.

'So – how do you prepare for a film? I mean, I wouldn't know where to start.'

As she said it, she thought this was probably the most banal question in the world. She should be chatting knowledgeably about recent art-house films she'd seen. The last time she'd been to the pictures – she still called it the pictures, for heaven's sake – had been when she had taken her two nieces to see *High School Musical 3*. Not exactly highbrow.

Dickie didn't seem bothered.

'I'm not sure I do. Sometimes it just . . . overwhelms me, thinking about the logistics. And the budget.' He winced. 'That's the tricky bit. It would be easy as pie if you didn't have to worry about the numbers adding up. And I'm not awfully good at numbers.'

'Don't you have people looking after them for you?'

'Yes. But their favourite word is "no". And I've already gone over my limit with the casting.' He looked meaningfully at Genevieve and Raf. 'The cream of British talent doesn't come cheap.'

'Yes, but surely they'll mean the film's a success?'

Dickie sighed. 'If only it was that simple.'

'You'll have to cut back somewhere else, then.' Genius, Poll. He'll be offering you a job as a consultant any minute.

'I know. But the trouble is with stars like this on board, expectation is high. The supporting cast have got to measure up. I need great locations so it looks good. I'm trying to find the perfect manor house to shoot in at the moment. If we're going to crack the American market, we need to make it look quintessentially English. Chocolate box.'

'It sounds like fun to me.'

'When you get it right, there's nothing better.' He grinned at her. His smile was wonky, but his eyes were kind behind his glasses. Polly thought he was the nicest person she had met in ages. 'You should come and visit when we start shooting.'

'I'd love to.'

'Let me know.'

'You won't want any distractions, surely—'

'Room for a small one?' A silvery voice cut through their conversation, as Coco sidled up and pulled her chair in the other side of Dickie. Polly's heart sank. Dickie wouldn't pay her any attention now. Coco was ravishing, and an actress, and she wouldn't bombard him with inanities.

Dickie turned to her with a polite smile.

Polly pushed back her chair.

'Excuse me. I must . . .'

Go and look at my three chins in the mirror? Go and think of some more spectacularly stupid questions to ask? Stuff in another piece of cake in the kitchen while nobody's looking?

She tried to slip out of the room unnoticed, but as she walked past Delilah she put out her hand to stop her.

'You're not going, are you, darling?'

'Not yet . . .' Bugger.

'Good. Only I need you for half an hour before you slip off.' Half an hour? Rafferty speak for two hours, at least. 'We need to make a list of possible venues for Tyger's reception. And get on to Karen about clothes. And do a guest list – shit, do you think we should email invitations, or courier them? Or maybe there's something more interesting we could do?'

Get them hand-delivered by white doves? wondered Polly sourly, but she didn't dare suggest this for fear of being taken seriously.

'I'll think about it,' she reassured Delilah, then made her escape. Oh well. Richmond swimming baths probably didn't want their water displaced by a great big whale of a thing anyway.

Halfway through the afternoon, Justine felt the need for some fresh air. She had eaten ten times more than she had meant to, and drunk more than she was used to drinking during the day. Add to that the fact she'd had barely any sleep, and it was no surprise she felt her eyelids closing.

Violet was busy gossiping with Polly, so she pushed the door of the orangery open and made her way out into the garden. A light breeze caressed her face. She made her way past the still, dark pools and down a set of wide, deep steps to a bench made up of intertwined serpents. She sat back and shut her eyes, relishing being alone with her thoughts for a few moments.

It had been a wonderful afternoon. After her initial

reticence, she now felt completely comfortable – with Violet, with the Raffertys. By the end of lunch, she had been made to feel one of the family, unusual for her, for she usually felt such an outsider in other people's homes. She wasn't used to the concept of family.

There had only ever been her and Benedict.

Her childhood hadn't been a conventional one. Of course it had been marred by the tragedy of her mother's death, but afterwards it hadn't been unhappy as such. Just unusual. She had been like a little companion to her father, who had taken her with him everywhere on his travels, made her part of his life. She had become used to dining in the grandest of hotels, choosing from the grown-up menu. Her father had never asked the waiter to ask the chef to rustle up something suitable for a child. She could swallow oysters raw from the age of five. She was used to sitting at tables, listening to adult conversations. Going to art galleries, race meetings, plays, cocktail parties – there wasn't much he left her out of. They were very close. She had all the love and attention she needed. But it was a strangely formal and slightly claustrophobic relationship. Rather intense.

She'd seen other families interact, of course she had. She'd been back to girls' houses for the weekend from school. She'd never been all that envious. Other people's mothers were slightly alien to her, creatures who seemed to fuss about the most insignificant of things. And other people's fathers were never as handsome or interesting as her own. She had never envied anyone their family.

But the Raffertys were something else. For a moment she imagined being one of the sisters. They were like a crazy club. It must have been wonderful growing up together, always having someone to do your make-up and tell your problems to, tell you whether you looked fat. Delilah was wonderful – warm and caring without being mumsy. And Raf – how could you not fall in love with Raf on the spot? He wasn't as voluble as the distaff side of the family, but he had made her feel welcome nevertheless. Justine had felt completely at home; the whole experience made her feel warm inside. She didn't want to leave.

She was sitting in the sunshine, her eyes closed, her face turned to the light, basking in the memory of the last twelve hours and trying to make some sense of it, when she heard someone on the path.

It was Violet. She came and sat on the bench next to her.

'Are you OK?'

'I'm just enjoying the sunshine.'

'Are they all too much for you? I know my family's mad.'

'Your family's wonderful,' Justine told her honestly.

Violet rolled her eyes fondly. 'There's always some drama.'

She looked at Justine and Justine's heart skittered. She put up a hand and stroked Violet's hair tentatively. Neither of them took their eyes from the other's face. It was still there. It hadn't been a crazy, drunken moment of impulse. The attraction hovered in the air between them, like a bee heavy with pollen, buzzing with languid contentment.

If last night's first kiss had been heavenly, this afternoon's took it into another dimension. As their lips met, Justine felt herself almost swooning with the most delicious lust, her insides looping and coiling into honeycomb. Not just lust – an ardent desire to possess another being, make them hers.

'My God,' she breathed.

'I know,' replied Violet, pulling her even closer.

'Don't mind me,' said a voice, and the two girls' heads snapped round.

Louis Dagger was observing them wryly through a haze of smoke.

'You carry on.'

'Shit,' Violet said softly. 'I don't think Mum and Dad can take another shock. Not today.'

Louis took another drag on his cigarette.

'Don't worry,' he assured them. 'I won't say a word.'

'Not even to Tyger?'

'No.'

Justine stood up. She marched over to Louis.

'You better not,' she threatened, 'or you'll have me to deal with.'

He looked at her, his eyes laughing.

'Whoooah,' he remarked. 'Feisty. You must be the bloke in the relationship.'

Justine felt an overwhelming urge to slap him, then realised that, if things were going to carry on as they were, this was probably the sort of remark she was going to have to get used to.

Thirteen

Louis wandered back up to the house after his interesting discovery in the garden, walking through the French windows that led into the living room rather than the orangery. He stood for a few moments admiring the room – like the rest of the house, it was cool and stylish but still managed to feel homely. Windows dressed in crushed pale gold velvet and stone-coloured walls gave a neutral backdrop to the stunning collection of seaside paintings that provided bright splashes of colour – jolly fishing boats bobbing in harbours, children shrimping in rock pools, gaily painted beach huts, they harked back to another, happier age. An age of innocence. Even Louis was charmed.

He turned when he heard a step behind him. It was Raf.

'It's always easy to know what to get Delilah for a present. She's got quite a collection.'

Louis stood in front of the one that took his eye. A seascape executed in bold, colourful strokes, it depicted coral pink waves crashing onto red rocks. Why he liked it best he wasn't sure.

'Irish impressionist – Roderic O'Conor,' approved Raf. 'Probably one of the most valuable paintings here.'

Louis surveyed the painting critically. 'It's not about how much it's worth, is it? It's about how it makes you feel.'

'Quite.'

Raf was standing next to him now, arms crossed. The two men stood side by side. Louis felt uncomfortable. He sensed he was being judged. Well, of course he was. He'd just married this bloke's daughter.

'Can we have a chat?'

Louis tensed.

'What about? My prospects? I've got half a million quid in the bank,' he replied.

'I don't give a toss about how much money you've got.'

Louis clenched his jaw. He hated confrontation. He usually avoided it by being so antagonistic that no one dared make him answerable. The problem was this time he cared about the outcome. He wanted to defend himself. To prove himself. But how to do this without tarnishing his image?. If he was going to live up to his reputation, he should stick two fingers up at Raf, then go and sit down with a bottle of Southern Comfort somewhere until he was sick in the pond outside.

'Shall we go into my study?'

Louis nodded cautiously, then followed Raf out of the room, feeling rather like a small boy being led to see the head-master. It wasn't a feeling he was used to.

Raf's study – although study was a misnomer; he never did any studying in it, he never spent much time in it at all, but it was his space, his masculine bit of space – was the ultimate in what every man dreamed of. It was monochromatic, with pale grey walls, charcoal eggshell shelving, and charcoal and grey ticking blinds. There was an iMac, a plasma screen and a Bang and Olufsen sound system. One wall was lined with paperbacks, everything from Amis (Kingsley and Martin) to Wilbur Smith, which he was unashamed about enjoying. The other was lined with his DVD collection, which included copies of every film he had ever been in. Raf wasn't vain; the girls had clubbed together and given them to him for Christmas one year, not realising that he would have been happier forgetting those times. He had feigned delight, of course he had, but not once had he taken one of the films out of its cover and watched it.

He waved a hand at one of the club chairs in front of his

desk for Louis to sit down, then sat down behind his desk. He was aware that he had an unfair advantage and that he was asserting his authority, which wasn't Raf's usual way, but on this occasion he thought it was fair enough. If Louis hadn't done him the courtesy of asking for Tyger's hand, he could bloody well fight for it now.

He surveyed his son-in-law critically. Louis was handsome, in a villainous, dissolute way. His dark eyes glittered, his mouth was cruel, his lean physique suited the tight black jeans and skinny T-shirt. Raf could see the attraction all right. A thousand hits had been launched off the back of this look – Keith Richards, Steve Tyler, Phil Lynott. It was a cliché, but it worked. It was inevitable that one of his daughters would fall for such a cliché. It was also inevitable that it would be Tyger, the one who had pushed the barriers the most, the one who wasn't afraid to take risks. It was this lack of fear that had made her such a success, but also made her vulnerable. Fear rose in his belly. Instinct told him Louis could be trouble. He was at a dangerous stage: rising to the top of his game, used to getting his own way but without the maturity that experience brought. Potentially explosive. And destructive. He should know. He'd been there.

Raf wasn't too worried about the fact that Louis and Tyger had tied the knot. It was only a bit of paper. If it all went wrong, it could be dealt with swiftly. His concern was what would happen to Tyger if it *did* all go wrong. He didn't want her hurt. He didn't want her to make a fool of herself, either. From this point on, all eyes would be on the newly-weds, gleefully counting down to disaster. Their marriage would be under pressure, almost predestined to collapse. All the papers would want was a decree absolute, and they wouldn't much care how they got it. How long had Peaches Geldof's marriage lasted? Six weeks? They would be out to beat that, and he couldn't bear the thought of his funny, feisty daughter being the victim of their manipulation. So whatever he could do to limit the damage on this marriage, he would do.

'So,' said Raf pleasantly – he wasn't on the attack, there was no point. 'What do your parents think about you getting married?'

Louis leaned back in his chair and looked at Raf levelly. Raf gave him one point for eye contact.

'I'm not in touch with my parents.'

'Any particular reason?'

A bitter smile. 'Mutual disinterest.'

'I'm sorry to hear that.'

'Don't be. There's no love lost on either side.'

'And what do your management think?'

Louis shrugged. 'They can think what they like.'

Raf raised an eyebrow.

'Isn't that a bit . . . naive?'

The boy shot him a glance. Raf detected a glimmer of anxiety, which pleased him. Mr Dagger wasn't as tough and sorted as he liked to make out. He leaned forward.

'Look, Louis – I'm not on your case. But Tyger's my daughter and I love her probably more than anyone could realise. So I want to make sure she's going to be OK. I want to make sure you're going to look after her. It's my duty as a father. You might find yourself in the same situation one day. So . . . is there anything I should know? You might as well tell me, because I'll find out in the end. I'm not going to go all Don Corleone on you, but . . .'

The message was pretty clear. He had people who could rake up the dirt if need be.

There was silence for a few moments. Louis stared at a Damien Hirst skull print on the wall while he considered his reply. All the while he could feel Raf's blue eyes boring into him. He wished he could be somewhere else. Anywhere else.

The problem was he respected Raf. If he had been some blundering, blustering Victorian father figure, he'd have called his bluff. But Raf was cool. Louis had never wanted anyone's approval in his life, but there was something about the guy . . . Maybe it was because he knew that in his time Raf had been wilder than he could ever hope to be, and was now comfortable in his own skin, with no need to prove himself.

He suddenly felt very uncomfortable. What the hell could he do to reassure Raf, and make sure he didn't go digging about in his past?

To add to his conundrum, he genuinely liked Tyger. In the short time he'd known her, she made him feel good about himself. She didn't know it, but she was the only girl Louis had ever chosen to wake up with. Sure, he'd slept with pretty girl after pretty girl, but he always threw them out before he went to sleep. But he'd wanted to curl his arms round Tyger and fall asleep with her.

The snarling bad boy image was so easy to put on. And who wouldn't enjoy the lifestyle that went with it? Sex and drugs and rock 'n' roll. But he'd been getting bored with it recently. Get up late, write a song, sound check, gig, get lashed, get laid. It became totally meaningless after a while. A pattern that repeated itself day after day, but there was nothing to get hold of. Tyger had made him realise there was more to life. She had drive. Ambition. Go. And a sense of fun. The last person he wanted to end up with was some crazy Courtney Love wannabe hell-bent on self-destruction. He wanted someone who understood what he was doing. Who understood him. And who wasn't going to drag him under.

He needed Tyger. So he couldn't blow it with her father. He'd pretend to come clean. He'd give him the sanitised version, and hope that would put him off the scent.

He sighed heavily, as if he was about to embark on a confession.

'My dad fucked off when I was three. I haven't met him since, so he doesn't know Louis Dagger is me – there's no way he'd recognise me. My mum went off with another bloke, a total bastard who didn't want me around. He wasn't averse to lamping me one every now and then when he knew I wasn't looking. I ran away to London when I was fifteen, before I hit him back, because I knew I would kill him. I got a job on a building site, lived in the site manager's Portakabin, worked in a few clubs in the evenings collecting glasses so I could listen to live music. Then I moved to a squat in Camden. The guys there had a band – they taught me to play guitar. You probably know the rest.'

There wasn't a newspaper or magazine that hadn't followed his meteoric rise. There wasn't a person who didn't know the jangling, stomach-wrenching power ballad with a twist – the twist of a knife – that had been such a huge underground hit last summer. The song had become the most downloaded track that year, and now Louis was a star. He played it right down. He wouldn't do stadiums. He wanted to see people's eyes when he sang. So tickets to his gigs were like gold-dust, allocated through his website via a complicated system of loyalty points that his followers could collect – basically by downloading other stuff his record company wanted to shift. He couldn't get away with it for ever. Everyone knew that big tours were where the big money was, so Louis was going to have to bite the bullet eventually.

Of course Raf knew all this. And none of it interested him – he was media savvy. He knew all about creating myths and manufacturing stardom, reinvention, disinformation. What he was interested in was Louis' past. Why was there nothing about that in the papers?

'Welsh.'

'Sorry?'

'I spent years studying dialect. I can hear Welsh in your voice. Even though you've got the generic rock 'n' roll art college accent.'

'Very good.' Louis nodded, indicating that Raf's hunch was correct. 'I never go back there.'

Louis made it pretty clear the subject of Wales was closed.

Raf could tell this conversation was going nowhere. Unless he tied Louis up and applied nipple clamps to his balls, he wasn't going to get anything out of him.

'Louis – the last thing I want to do is patronise you. The

only thing that matters to me is that Tyger is happy. I'm willing to support you as long as I think you are genuine and you aren't messing her around. Which at the moment I do. So don't ever be afraid to come to me – for advice, or guidance. On anything. You probably know that my copybook isn't exactly unblemished, so I'm not going to judge. And I understand temptation, of every kind.'

'Thank you.' Louis felt the sudden urge to call him 'sir'.

Raf stretched out his hand to shake. Louis took it in a grip that was reassuringly firm.

Half of him felt secure and happy that he'd passed some sort of test. The other half was absolutely terrified that he was going to be found out, and it would all come crashing down around his ears.

Fourteen

By seven o'clock that evening, the party had started to break up.

'I need to learn my lines for next week,' Coco said. 'Does anyone need a lift back into town?'

Both Dickie and Genevieve accepted her offer eagerly.

In the orangery, Tyger had kicked off her shoes and put her feet in Louis' lap. Raf was nursing a coffee. Tony and Delilah had gone into the office.

'So – whose place are we going to live in?' Tyger demanded. 'You realise you haven't even seen my flat yet? I bet you've got no proper cooking stuff in yours, have you?'

'Nope,' Louis admitted. 'But there's a great Chinese down the road.'

Tyger wrinkled her nose.

'I suppose we should think about selling and getting a place together. A little mews house – I've always wanted a mews house.'

Raf raised an eyebrow. He hoped they would wait a bit and see how things worked out before they did anything too drastic, but he didn't say anything. Tyger would go mad if he started pouring cold water on her ideas.

Tyger scooped up Doug the Pug and plonked him in her lap. 'Then I can have you living with me, can't I, my darling?' She picked up his front paws and waggled them.

'Yes,' said Raf meaningfully. 'It was only supposed to be a temporary stay.'

'Don't say that. You love him.'

'Of course we do. But he is your responsibility.'

'Is he yours, then?' asked Louis.

'Tyger went to open a Rescue Centre in Surrey. She came back with Doug. The Rescue Centre were delighted. They got loads of publicity. But Tyger had forgotten her flat doesn't allow pets.' Raf's tone was dry. 'So guess where he ended up?'

'Poor darling. He'd been totally neglected. His coat was covered in sores. We soon put him right, didn't we?' She ruffled the little dog's ears.

'We . . . ?' interjected Raf.

'I spent hundreds of pounds on stuff from the vet!'

'Who feeds him? Who walks him?'

'OK, OK. As soon as we have a place . . .' She lifted Doug up and put him on Louis' lap. 'Say hello to your new daddy.'

Louis put out a tentative hand and stroked him. It was obvious Doug wasn't sure.

'He'll get used to you,' Tyger assured him.

Louis scratched him behind the ears. 'At least you don't dress him up. Or keep him in your handbag.'

Raf snorted. Tyger looked bolshy.

'He has got the coolest Christian Audigier skull tee. But Mum won't let me put it on him while he's living here.'

'Quite right,' said Louis. 'Not while he's living under my roof either.'

Raf smothered a smile. He was warming to his son-in-law more and more by the minute.

Tony came back in. He fell into a chair and poured himself a coffee.

'You look knackered,' observed Tyger.

Tony shot her a filthy look. 'Do you ever think about the consequences of what you do?'

'If I stayed in all the time and didn't put a foot wrong,' replied Tyger sweetly, 'you'd be out of a job.'

Tony lobbed two sugar-lumps into his cup.

'I've been trying to get in touch with your people,' he told Louis. 'I expect they'll want some say in how we handle this. I don't suppose they'll be too pleased you've gone and got yourself married. It doesn't exactly go with the image.'

Louis shrugged. 'It's my life.'

'Ah, but it isn't, is it?' Tony pointed out. 'In this game, you're the last person who gets a say in what happens.'

Once they were in town, Dickie got Coco to drop him at the tube station, so he could get the District line round to his flat. He had spent the journey clinging on to the passenger strap in the back of the car. He was a nervous passenger at the best of times, and Coco drove like a maniac, with little regard for the speed limit, cheerfully cutting people up and roaring off at traffic lights. And all the time she was chattering away to Genevieve in the front seat. He felt much safer once he was in the bowels of the underground.

He got back home just as the light was starting to fade. A first-floor flat with a balcony in a period conversion in Paddington, it was Dickie's only real possession, apart from his MacBook. He didn't go in for stuff in a big way. He didn't have a car, or even a watch. The furnishings were minimal, scrounged from parents and friends, a mismatched assortment of unwanted sofas and chairs he had purloined. The floor was covered with scripts, the pages torn out and laid into different piles. The walls were covered in Post-It notes, copies of face-shots taken from *Spotlight*, the actors' directory, estate agent's details and photos of locations. As well as this were images torn from magazines. All of these together were Dickie's fragmented vision of his film.

Dickie didn't really have a life outside whichever film he had in progress. Going out today had been unusual, but it had been important to him to see Raf and Genevieve together. And now he had, he felt inspired. He wanted to get back to his script and work in all the ideas he'd had. He was pleased that they had seemed of a similar age, and believable as a couple. Sometimes when you got a man and a woman together they just didn't gel.

This was a momentous project for him. He had a huge

emotional investment in the script. He had written the treatment himself, and then commissioned one of his favourite screenwriters to flesh it out and add sparkling dialogue, and he was still finding ways to improve it. As far as he was concerned, a script was always a work in progress and could alter right up to the very last minute.

As well as emotional investment, however, he had put a good chunk of his own money into the project – extended the mortgage on his flat by quite a bit, in fact. It was the only way he could guarantee getting the cast he wanted. It just wouldn't work without the best – the script was good, but it was light, and he needed class actors to give it weight. He knew that once they got together, once they got to work, they would bring it to life, add colour and depth and breadth and nuance.

He was sure it was going to be a hit. He was sure it was going to be a sleeper, one of those low-budget films that grossed high. Just to prove that you didn't need CGI and multi-million-pound special effects to make a memorable film. That story and character were what mattered.

If it bombed – which it wouldn't, it simply couldn't – Dickie was going to be in big trouble. He would be in hock to the tune of half a million quid, with no hope of picking up any new work. People didn't tend to employ directors responsible for turkeys. So he was using all his mental energy thinking up ways to make the film wittier, more stylish, more moving, more memorable. Feeding in all the little quirks that would make it stand out from the next romantic comedy. Making it accessible to a wide age range – the big stars were middle-aged, so he had to make sure it appealed to a younger audience as well, which meant great clothes and even greater music. Soundtracks were vitally important to the success of a film. His iPod was crammed with possible tracks to include. He'd already decided on the theme tune: 'You're Having My Baby' by Paul Anka. A big blast of nostalgia always did the trick.

He picked up his script. He didn't even bother to go into the kitchen to fix a drink. The sink was piled high with two or three days' washing-up, and there was bound to be no milk. He'd had enough to eat today to keep him going for a while, anyway. Food wasn't high on Dickie's list of priorities. Nor was sleep. Or any of the usual things that preoccupied anyone normal on a daily basis. In fact, given Dickie's lack of interest in anything that motivated the average human being, it was astonishing that he made films that touched people and made them walk out of the cinema with smiles on their faces.

Making people happy. That's what made him happy.

'Listen,' said Violet, 'don't take this the wrong way, but I need to go home. Sort stuff out. Sort my head out. I need to be on my own.'

She and Justine were waiting in the hall for a taxi.

Justine was surprised at how disappointed she felt. She was being given the brush-off. Violet didn't want to know. She'd decided last night had been a mistake. A bit of fun. An experiment. Or maybe she did this sort of thing all the time, and Justine hadn't been her first after all? Maybe she was just a one-night stand.

Bugger. That was her plan blown. Although actually, it wasn't so much that she now wasn't going to have a bargaining tool with Benedict. She'd been looking forward to seeing where this encounter was going to lead. She'd been looking forward to spending the evening with Violet. But if Violet wasn't into it . . .

'No problem,' she said. 'Thanks for a lovely day.'

'Hey, it doesn't mean I don't want to be with you. I'm just . . . used to my own space. It's how I am.' Violet wrapped her arms around the other girl. Justine breathed in her perfume. 'Let's meet for lunch tomorrow. I'll call you.'

'OK . . .' Justine was hardly going to beg. That wasn't how she worked. If Violet called, she called. If she didn't, then they'd had fun. When the cabdriver rang the buzzer, she gathered up her bag, put on a smile and said goodbye. Then left the house without a backward glance.

Well, one backward glance. Violet was still in the doorway, waving. She blew her a kiss. Justine shut her eyes and imagined catching it, as light and soft as a dandelion clock. Then wondered what on earth had got into her. Kisses like dandelion clocks? Until now, she hadn't had a romantic bone in her body. This was the girl who'd started reading Harold Robbins at the age of ten. She'd never had a Mills and Boon moment. Ever.

'Where to, love?'

She gave him the address in Little Venice. Impressed, the taxi driver pulled away, thinking his passenger could look a bit happier, considering she'd just left one mansion and was heading off to another. Some people didn't know they were born.

As the taxi pulled up outside the gracious white Georgian house she shared with her father, Justine saw his car was there, and there were lights on inside. She wasn't surprised. Benedict rarely went out on a Saturday night. His socialising was mostly business, conducted during the week. Saturday was his night off. The housekeeper would leave him his favourite dinner, and he would re-run all the TV shows he had missed during the week on SkyPlus, reading the weekend papers at the same time: the *FT*, *The Times*, and the *Mail*, which together told him the mood and the economic state of the world and the nation. She realised she hadn't seen him since their disagreement the day before. It felt like a lifetime ago.

She walked across the gravel drive and up the stone steps, pausing for a moment before she opened the door. Until this evening, she had known exactly who she was. She had never been one for self-examination, because she had self-belief. Now, everything had been thrown to the winds. Tough, smart, wise, unbreakable Justine Amador-Fox had turned to putty in another woman's hands. Why? Had this helpless, vulnerable creature been lurking inside all along? Who the hell was she?

As predicted, Benedict was in the living room, an elegant room that took up the whole of the first floor, furnished in simple luxury with sleek furniture and some stunning pieces of art. He was stretched out on the U-shaped Roche Bobois sofa in front of the television. His supper things were still on the coffee table, the papers were spread round him, and he was nursing the last third of a very good bottle of red wine.

Benedict was healthy and handsome, if a little stockier and a lot balder than he would otherwise have liked, but put him in a well-cut suit and he was a very attractive proposition. A year-round tan helped – acquired from visiting his further-flung hotels – and he only drank at weekends. He looked fit, prosperous and discerning.

'Hey!' He looked up and smiled as his daughter came in. As far as he was concerned, their argument was forgotten. They might spar, in a healthy way, but they never fell out for long, and he certainly didn't bear grudges. 'Where've you been?'

He wasn't interrogating her, just being politely curious.

She put her bag down, and he frowned. She was in a strange dress. Strange both because he didn't recognise it and because it was a million miles from what she usually wore. It suited her. It was more feminine than her usual garb.

'Nice dress,' he commented. 'Change of image?'

'I borrowed it . . . from a friend,' she told him. 'Violet Rafferty?'

He rolled through his mental Rolodex. 'Violet Rafferty as in Delilah Rafferty?'

'Yeah. I've been to their house for lunch.'

'I didn't know you knew them.'

'I didn't, till today.'

Benedict flicked off the telly. He'd rather talk to Justine than watch reruns of *CSI Miami*. She was standing in front of the drinks cabinet, surveying the bottles, deciding what to have.

'You're not out tonight then?'

'Um . . . no. Bit of a mad one last night. I could do with a quiet night in.'

Benedict looked at his daughter askance. He couldn't remember the last time she'd stayed in on a Saturday. He wondered if she was going to use the opportunity to have another go about Berlin. Justine never gave in until she got what she wanted.

As soon as they had finished their conversation yesterday, he had got straight on to the agent about the derelict hotel and put in an offer. He knew his daughter would have done her homework. Now, she just had to prove to him that she really was hungry enough to take on the project. He was sure she had the wherewithal to make it a success – he'd been through her proposal and was favourably impressed. Of course, he expected nothing less. She'd learned at the feet of a master.

But to his surprise, she didn't bring it up. She poured herself a glass of elderflower cordial, kicked off her shoes, sprawled on the sofa – and fell asleep.

'Cheers,' said Benedict, raising his glass to his comatose daughter.

Violet flew in through the door of her flat, not even pausing to take off her jacket before throwing open the lid of her piano. All day long she had been longing to get home and start writing. She had felt the music bubbling up inside her, but she knew she couldn't make her escape until it was polite. Tearing herself away from Justine had been hard, but she couldn't risk her inspiration drying up. She needed to be alone.

Thank God the man who lived upstairs was away for the weekend. He would have had every right to come storming down as she pounded out the notes, her fingers flying. Black dots danced across the pages of her manuscript paper as phrases occurred to her – she couldn't get it all down fast enough. She was terrified it would disappear into the ether.

By four o'clock in the morning she had three songs. Not perfect, not finished, but she had captured their essence on paper. They couldn't get away from her now. She wanted to phone Sammy. He would understand her euphoria. She wanted to play her songs to him, to start arranging them, working out what instruments she would need – whether to go for stripped-back and bare, or big, brave over-the-top lushness with a full orchestra. But even nocturnal Sammy probably wouldn't appreciate a call at this hour of the morning. She would ring him tomorrow.

This was the moment she had been waiting for all her life. She knew she could write. She had never given up hope. All the time she had spent analysing other people's music, picking it apart to see how it worked, how it was structured. She had the tools. She'd just needed the catalyst – the life-changing moment that unlocked her.

She dragged herself to the bedroom and fell onto the bed. She couldn't be bothered to get undressed. She pulled the sheets to her and breathed in. The scent of Justine lingered, and the memory made her insides flutter. She would see her again tomorrow. They'd go for lunch somewhere, sit outside in the sunshine, drink strawberry Bellinis, go shopping . . . she pictured the two of them trying on dresses, spraying perfume onto each other's wrists, teetering around shoe shops in impossibly high heels, laughing. The images floated in and out of her head, becoming faster, then becoming fuzzy, as sweet sleep eventually overtook her.

Delilah couldn't sleep at all that night.

She tried separating all the anxieties out and examining them. Individually, she could cope. It was when they all melded into one that she began to panic, tossing and turning, flipping her pillow over when it became overheated. More than anything right now she needed her sleep. She couldn't cope with the smallest of problems if she was tired.

Maybe she should get up and try to get a couple of hours' work done? That would tire her out – she could slip back into bed later and sleep. It was Sunday. She didn't need to get up.

But the thought of tackling the book only increased her panic. It was an unwieldy beast – a mammoth task but somehow uninspiring. She didn't feel her usual enthusiasm. It was merely a chore.

She gave a huge sigh, and Raf opened one eye, drowsy but concerned.

'What's the matter?'

'I don't know. Everything and nothing.'

'You worry too much.' He closed his eyes and patted her consolingly, clearly eager to fall back to sleep.

Delilah gritted her teeth. Of all the platitudes, she hated this one the most. How dare he patronise her? It was her bloody worrying that had got them where they were: on top. If she hadn't worried, where would they be? Surrounded by lawsuits and bankruptcy charges, no doubt.

'It's all right for you to say that,' she said, her voice tight with anger. 'It's OK for you. There's always someone there to pick up the pieces.'

Her. She was always there, two steps behind, protecting him from the world, making sure that nothing happened to knock him off his perch and send him back to the bottle. All anyone did when she was feeling the pressure was belittle her and imply that she brought it on herself.

She'd tried not worrying. Of course she had, but the moment she took her foot off the gas and tried to relax, there was a crisis. So she was permanently coiled, waiting for things to go wrong, ready to take on the world and start trouble-shooting. No wonder her stress levels were sky high. No wonder she felt exhausted.

Raf stroked her arm.

'You need a break.'

That was another platitude she hated. Of course she needed a break, but she wasn't going to get one. She was on a never-ending roller-coaster ride that didn't stop to let anyone off. Even if she had managed to take time off from her schedule, she would only worry about the workload that was building up while she was away. It wasn't worth it.

'Roll over. I'll give you a massage. It might help you sleep.'

Gratefully, she turned onto her stomach, and leaned her head on her arms. Raf drizzled a lavender-scented massage oil onto her bare skin, and started rubbing it in gently, working at the knots in her muscles. After a few minutes, she realised that his hands were straying, that he was stroking her bare arse. He wasn't interested in making her relax at all. It was pure self-interest.

She rolled over and sat up.

'For God's sake,' she shouted. 'All anyone ever wants from me is money, sex or reassurance. I've had enough of it. Why can't you leave me alone?'

She scrambled out of bed, half-crying. She fled the room without looking back, knowing that Raf would have an expression of hurt and shock on his face that she wouldn't be able to bear. She ran down the stairs, into the kitchen and fell onto the small sofa she kept in there, for visiting guests to sit in sipping wine while she cooked. Doug the Pug flopped out of his basket and waddled over to her, his eyes wide with alarm at this unaccustomed interruption. She scooped him up and held his fat, warm body. Already guilt was creeping over her. She had behaved appallingly. She'd been totally unreasonable. Raf had been trying to help in the only way he knew how.

That was what was so frustrating. She wanted more than murmured reassurance and a massage. She wanted someone to take the pressure off. She was overworked, overwrought, overwound. She was just so sick of the *responsibility* . . .

And she didn't like the person she was becoming. She was a million miles from her public persona. Glamorous, fun-loving, laid-back Delilah Rafferty? The woman who had got it right? People would be shocked if they knew the truth. Everyone thought that her life was one happy social gathering after another, that she just wafted from one to another with a smile on her face. No one knew the graft, the angst, the juggling, the mental energy that went into it all. Not to mention the fear that it was all going to go wrong, that the nation would get bored with her, that her books would be consigned to the remainder bin.

That was what was really bothering her, she decided. That bloody article in the paper this morning. She had told herself to ignore it, but she couldn't. Somehow it summed up everything she was afraid of. The comments had hurt, and they had knocked her confidence.

She tried to curl herself up and lie down on the sofa, but it was annoyingly small, and Doug was snuffling. She should go back upstairs and apologise to Raf, but she couldn't help feeling resentful. In the end she plopped Doug back into his basket, went into the office and turned on the computer, where she stared at her work-in-progress for a good half-hour before falling asleep with her head in her arms.

Louis had the dream again that night. It had been several months since the last one, and he had thought he was free of the curse and turned a corner. But no. This time, if anything, it was worse than ever.

The sight. A pair of melting brown eyes pleading with him. How the hell could he ignore the sheer terror manifest in the being that had once trusted him?

The sound. The pathetic whimper, the only sound that could be managed, but in his head it was amplified to a desperate keening that echoed around his head.

And the smell. The stifling stench. He didn't know you could dream smells, but the odour was suffocating him, acrid, putrid, unforgettable. He gasped for breath, crying out, knowing the ending before it even happened, because it happened the same every time—

'Hey, hey! Louis! Baby, what's the matter?'

Tyger's arms were round him, but he fought them away. He had to get away. Tears were streaming down his face, sweat was pouring from his brow.

'Louis!'

At last he surfaced, the vestiges of the dream slipping away. He saw Tyger looking at him, her eyes wide with anxiety. He slumped onto her. She held him, her voice soothing as she stroked his back.

'Shh – it's OK. You're all right.'

'Oh God . . .' he groaned. He held onto her tightly, not wanting to let her go, relishing the comfort of her warmth. Eventually his heart rate subsided and his breathing eased. He felt calm.

Tyger frowned, her little face screwed up with concern. 'What were you dreaming about, anyway?'

'I don't know. Just . . . weird shit.' He got out of bed. 'I'm going to take a shower.'

His T-shirt was drenched in sour-smelling perspiration. Not the sweat that poured out of him when he did a gig, but sweat that stank of fear. And cowardice.

He was nothing but a fucking coward. But it was too late. There was nothing he could do now. The stakes were too high.

He looked over at Tyger. She had fallen back onto the pillows. He gazed at her mussed-up blonde crop, the bright pink camisole and boy pants she was wearing. She was a jewel. She totally got him – or at least the 'him' he was prepared to show her. She was one in a million, but there was no way he could confide in her. She would never understand. And he wasn't going to mess up the one properly good thing that had happened to him.

Millions of people could only dream of the rock 'n' roll life that had been foisted on him. But it had never given him a moment's happiness. Performing for him wasn't a high, it was more of an exorcism. Writing songs was a purging process, excruciatingly painful. And all the shit that went with it: the riders, the limos, the ass-kissing – it only made him feel more of a fraud. He was playing a role. The snarling, capricious, arrogant Louis Dagger was completely at odds with the real person inside him, but now he was trapped. He was never going to be at peace with himself until he'd confronted the past. If he had done it at the beginning, it would be all right by now, but every day that went past only increased the severity of his crime.

He came out of the shower feeling clean, on the outside at least. He slipped on another white T-shirt and boxers, but he didn't want to get back into bed. His side was still soaked in sour sweat, and he dreaded falling asleep. Instead, he sat by the window, and lit a cigarette, knowing he'd still be sitting there when the dawn broke, trying to find a way out.

Fifteen

Coco was finally settling into a routine at the studios. Her self-esteem had risen tenfold, although she was very strict with herself about how she administered her illicit confidence booster. She never took it more than once a day. Luckily, most of her scenes seemed to be scheduled for the mornings, which meant a cruelly early start, but she could leave the studios by mid-afternoon, then get home and have a nap before the evening began. And if she had a precious day off, she didn't touch it. There was absolutely no need. She could deal with everyday life. It was just the horrible fear of exposure, of letting her colleagues down, the nerves, the lack of self-belief in her own ability that was her Achilles heel. Why did actors do it to themselves? she wondered.

Because of the thrill of getting it right. Because of the satisfaction of nailing a really good scene, and knowing that at some point in the future an audience would be drawn into the world you had created. Because it was completely and utterly addictive. That was why.

She supposed she could have talked to her father about her fears. After all, Raf must have experienced something similar himself, else why had he become such a drunken wreck? He probably started just the same – a little nip from the flask to blur the edges before going on stage – but he hadn't had the will-power to keep it in check like she had. Besides, drinking was more socially acceptable, especially in those days. Actors were always rolling around drunk and causing havoc, only some were drunker than others. And Raf had been the drunkest of them all . . .

She didn't confide in him, firstly because he had always been ambivalent about her going into acting, and secondly because she was quite a private person. She found it hard to share. And she liked to solve her problems for herself. Talking to Raf would only make him worry, and then he would divulge her secrets to Delilah, and once Mum got wind of her insecurity that would be it – hypnotherapy, Bach's rescue remedy, constant phone calls . . .

She was talking to Delilah far less these days, Coco realised. When she started on the show she used to need to ring her constantly, but now she felt able to stand on her own two feet. Besides, she had her colleagues. The team on *Critical but Stable* were great. There was always someone to have a coffee with, or someone to go to the gym up the road with if you had time off between scenes. Someone to lend you a book or a magazine, someone to recommend a new fake tan or a great new band to download. Without turning it into a cliché, they *were* like one big happy family. She knew that wasn't always the case on a long-running show. With gruelling hours and immense pressure to perform, it was all too easy for disillusionment to set in. And once it started it spread. Actors became disgruntled, paranoid and uncooperative, and it wasn't long before that showed in their performances. There would be complaints about the scripts, which would knock the confidence of the script team, and before you knew it anyone with any talent jumped ship and the whole show started to fall apart. *Critical but Stable*, however, was just getting better and better. Morale was at an all time high.

The only fly in the ointment was Neal. He seemed to think that the fact they were onscreen lovers gave them a special bond – a special bond that Coco definitely didn't feel.

Neal was one of those people who seemed like a great guy on first meeting. It helped that he was incredibly good-looking, with his tanned skin, ripped body, tousled shoulder-length locks and green eyes. But it had soon become apparent that there wasn't much more to him than that. He was vain, superficial, self-centred and cocky, strutting around the lot like a cockerel. It was hard to keep out of his way as they had so many scenes together, but Coco did her best. He was incredibly thick-skinned and didn't seem able to take no for an answer. Twice he had barged into her dressing room without knocking. She didn't keep it locked usually, to avoid undue suspicion.

'For heaven's sake,' she snapped at him the second time. 'Haven't you heard of knocking?'

'Why? What were you doing?' he looked at her lasciviously. 'Something you shouldn't?'

Lecherous as well. It wasn't long before the rest of the cast and crew were trying to avoid him, especially the younger girls. One day Coco found him pinning one of the runners up against the wall in the green room. The poor girl was nearly in tears.

'Can't you take no for an answer?' Coco hissed at him as she pulled him away. The runner escaped gratefully and the two of them were left facing each other. An ugly expression came into his eyes: hostile and dangerous.

'I don't know who you think you are,' he replied. 'But you're no better than the rest of us mere mortals. And let's face it – you certainly weren't hired for your acting ability.'

Coco paled. 'What did you say?'

'Haven't you heard your nickname? Pinocchio – because you're so wooden? They're trying to figure out how to write you out of the script as we speak.' He flashed her a smile of evil triumph and walked out of the door.

Coco sat down in the nearest chair. She felt winded. No one could have hurt her more if they tried. She had been working so hard over the past few weeks, and had been pleased with her performances. The feedback she had got from the directors had seemed positive. She knew jolly well that on a show like this if you weren't cutting the mustard you soon knew about it. Everyone had to do their best in the limited time they were given. The producers didn't tolerate anything less than a hundred per cent.

She put her head in her hands, tears pricking her eyelids. Perhaps she should go straight away and offer her resignation? There might still be time to find someone else to take over her part, and reshoot everything she had done so far before the episodes were due to be transmitted. She didn't want to be responsible for the show going down the pan. She would rather bow out now than be publicly humiliated. She didn't want the whole nation to have proof of the fact that she couldn't act for toffee.

She looked at her watch. There was half an hour before she was due back on set. She ran up the four flights of steps that led to the production offices. She walked through the main area, where the script co-ordinators were busy collating that week's changes and getting them copied onto coloured paper – there was a different colour for each draft, so they could be easily differentiated. Off the central area were other areas, for scheduling, finance, research, then finally a long corridor where the producers and script team reigned. It looked like any ordinary set of offices. They could all have been accountants or market researchers. There was nothing glamorous about it, just the usual coffee machines and water coolers and a lot of white boards.

The executive producer, Lisa Gray, was a plump, blunt girl from Pontefract, well respected in the television industry for having a vision and getting it onto the screen on time and within budget. She looked up as Coco knocked tentatively and beckoned her in.

The two of them sat facing each other on the red L-shaped sofa Lisa kept for meetings. Lisa kicked off her shoes and curled her feet up under her. She liked to keep things as informal as possible. She hadn't had an awful lot of dealings with Coco – they'd had dinner when the team had first approached her, and she had welcomed her on her first day, and she was usually around at the weekly read-through, but Lisa spent most of the time in her office dealing with scripts. It was her forte, and it showed in the high standard the team achieved. She wondered what the actress wanted: a bigger dressing room, probably, or time off that would throw the schedule into total disarray.

'So . . . ?' she started, prompting her.

Coco decided not to beat about the bush.

'Lisa. Listen. I know it's not working.'

Lisa looked at her with polite puzzlement. Coco carried on.

'I know you took a risk when you took me on, and I'm really grateful to you for the break, but . . . I don't want to jeopardise the success of *Critical but Stable*. I want the show to be something you can be proud of, not something you're embarrassed by. And I just want to say – I'd rather you axed me sooner rather than later. I don't even expect you to honour my contract—'

'Coco.' Lisa cut across her smoothly. 'What the fuck are you talking about?'

Coco blinked. Did she have to spell it out to her?

'Pinocchio,' she replied. 'Isn't that what they call me?'

Lisa sighed. She had three first-draft scripts to read, two show reels to look at, a storyline to approve and a character breakdown to write for the casting director. By three o'clock. But this was part of the job. Massaging egos, soothing ruffled feathers. She did it all the time. Only this morning she'd had a producer and lighting director slugging it out in front of her, and she'd had to intervene. The problem was there were an infinite number of ways of doing things in television, and people didn't always see eye to eye. The executive producer had to be the adjudicator and the nanny.

She put on her most reassuring smile, careful not to show any sign of irritation.

'Coco, we are completely thrilled with everything you've done so far. You've exceeded our expectations. You've brought something to Emily that we can really build on now the character is bedded in. I don't understand why you think otherwise.'

'I was told . . . you were going to write me out.'

Lisa folded her arms. The trouble with actors was they got very bored when they weren't actually in the studio, and tended to cause mischief. Idle gossip was an occupational hazard. And it could be very damaging.

'Who told you that?' she demanded.

Coco remained silent. She wasn't a grass.

'Let me guess,' said Lisa drily. 'The towering talent that is Neal.'

Coco's lack of reply confirmed her suspicions.

Lisa gritted her teeth. She couldn't afford to let Coco have a crisis of confidence. She rapidly assessed whether to divulge the information she was party to, and decided it was worth the risk. It was the only way to boost the girl's self-esteem and convince her she wasn't on her way out.

'You tell anybody this, and I'll rip your contract up right in front of you,' she told Coco. 'It's not you we want to get rid of. It's Neal. He's absolutely fine when he's lying there in a coma. He looks great. But when he comes to life in those dream sequences? Laurence Olivier he is not.'

Coco smothered a giggle. And thought how incandescent Neal would be if he could hear Lisa talking.

'The minute his contract is up he is out. We're already looking at ways of getting rid of his character. At the moment we're favouring Emily turning off his life support machine in a fit of remorse.'

'Please!' Coco's eyes were shining. 'Please let me do it!'

Lisa looked reproachful.

'This isn't about revenge, Coco. It's about what's best for the show.'

'Sorry. Yes, of course.' Coco tried to seem penitent.

'Now bugger off and let me get on with my work. And carry on doing what you do.'

'Thanks. And sorry. I just . . .'

'Bugger *off*!'

Lisa watched Coco leave her office, making sure she was really gone before going back to her desk. Bloody actors. They were all the same. They could walk off stage holding an Oscar in their hand and still need reassurance.

Coco felt mildly vindicated after her meeting with Lisa, but she was still riddled with doubt. What if the production team thought she was great, but the actors thought she was rubbish? It wouldn't be the first time. And it was almost more important what your peers thought of you than the production team. You had to have their respect.

She was horrified to find that her legs were trembling at the thought of going back to the studio in ten minutes. She couldn't face the imagined slights. It was exactly the same feeling she used to have in the classroom – too afraid to put up her hand for fear of ridicule, even though she knew the answer. Sometimes it was hard to believe she was from the same family as Violet, who didn't much care what anyone thought and jumped on stage at the drop of a hat. Or Tyger, who would knock you over in her rush to get to the top. She longed for an ounce of their chutzpah.

Well, she was just going to have to get her chutzpah from somewhere else.

She grabbed her bag, pulled out the little plastic pouch. OK, so she'd sworn she would only do one line a day, and she'd had her ration this morning, but this was an emergency. She'd had a shock. She couldn't be expected to bounce back from that straight away. She realised she only had enough for one last line. Damn – how had that happened? She'd been careful to ration it out. Never mind, she'd text Harley, get him to meet her later. He'd sort her out.

She chopped out a line, bent her head and sniffed. Thank God. Almost within moments she felt on top of the world. Ready to face anyone and anything. With her head held high and a smile on her face, she glided out of her dressing room and down to the studio.

They were shooting part of a dream sequence that afternoon, when Emily imagines Zak has come back to life and they kiss. Neal was looking cockier than ever, obviously relishing the prospect. Coco felt her stomach churn with distaste. She shut her eyes and thought of the big, fat fee she had been paid as she took her place on the set.

'Act,' she told herself sternly. 'You've got to act. This guy is the love of your life. His lips on yours is your *raison d'être*.'

If she could do this she could do anything.

The director was brilliant. He talked to the two of them, exploring the feelings of the characters. Coco was almost, *almost*, convinced she was Emily.

'This is momentous,' the director enthused. 'Zak has been in a coma for three months, and now here he is in front of her, living, breathing. It's a miracle. A dream come true. I want the audience to feel her relief, her elation, her passion . . .'

Coco sneaked a look at Neal, who was smirking. She *could* do this.

After several awkward rehearsals, they were ready for a take.

'I want you to hold that moment just before the kiss. Really crank up the sense of anticipation, so when your lips finally do meet, it's electric.' The director was determined to milk this for all he was worth.

Please God we do this in one, thought Coco, as the cameras started rolling.

She could feel a collective holding of breath as the crew watched the two young lovers rediscover themselves. She let her fingers trail over Neal's face in wonder, and he looked down at her in adoration. They held each other's gaze for a moment longer, then another, before their lips finally locked. It was going to be an epic television moment, the sort of moment awards were made of. Coco felt an overwhelming sense of elation.

Then Neal put his tongue in her mouth.

She tried not to gag. She gave an urgent grunt of disgust, hoping he would get the message, but he plunged it in further. She tried pinching him, grabbing some of the taut flesh on his side to give him a warning, but nothing doing. She tried to pull away, but he had her head in one of his hands, running his fingers through her hair. To the onlooker, it seemed as if they were getting really passionate.

There was nothing for it. She bit down hard.

'Aaaargh!' He leapt back. 'You bitch! You fucking bitch! What the hell did you do that for?'

He looked round the studio in outrage, then spat onto the floor. There was blood.

Shit, thought Coco.

'Sorry,' she said, eyes wide with innocence. 'I got carried away.'

'You fucking bit me!'

'I'm really sorry. I'm a little tiger when I get aroused. You're just lucky it was only your tongue in my mouth.'

The crew collapsed laughing. Neal looked to the director, furious.

'You're not going to let her get away with that, surely?'

The director just looked at the clock.

'I need this in the can by half past. Unless it's actually hanging off by a thread, can we get on with it?'

'I'm going to Lisa!'

'Fine. But after, please?'

For a moment it looked as though Neal was going to storm out. Coco stared down at the floor, biting the inside of her cheeks to stop herself from laughing. She didn't dare catch anyone's eye.

'Guys, that was totally great. You were on fire. More of the same, please. Without the biting . . .' The director tried to keep the panic out of his voice. If they over-ran it would mean bringing everyone in at the weekend.

Neal turned his back with his hands in his pockets, tossing

up whether to be difficult or not. Eventually he turned back, his expression sulky. He had the sense to realise that no one was on his side – if he kicked up the only person he would be making trouble for was himself.

'Let's do it.'

When they finally went for the clinch again, there were no tongues.

Coco recounted the day's events to Harley that evening in a little bar in Soho.

'I'll be lucky if he doesn't sue me,' she gurgled, 'but I don't care if he does. It was worth it.'

'So it's all going OK now?'

She put a hand on his arm.

'Thanks to your genius idea. It's made all the difference.' She paused for a moment. 'I could do with some more.'

'You've used it all already?' Harley looked alarmed. 'Jesus, Coco. I only gave you more last Saturday.'

'Some of it spilt in my bag,' she lied.

'Crap.' Harley's expression was stony.

'I don't know why you're coming over all judgemental. It was your idea in the first place.' Coco thought she had every right to be indignant.

'It was a present. I'm not a bloody dealer.'

'Why are you taking the moral high ground all of a sudden?'

'Coco – I wanted to help you. I don't want you to fuck up. I didn't realise you were going to hoover it up. I thought you had more sense.'

'I know what I'm doing.'

'Yeah, right. So why are you looking so panicky?'

'I'm not. I'm just pissed off that you dish it out with one hand and take it away with the other.'

'I made a mistake. It was just supposed to be a little something to give you confidence, not a crutch.'

Coco fell silent. She was furious with Harley. But the more she protested that she could handle it, the more desperate she would seem. Well, it wasn't as though Harley was the only person in the world she could get cocaine from.

'I'm sorry,' she said, her voice sweet. 'You're right. I should do without it.'

He nodded, not remotely convinced by her turnaround.

'You wouldn't be the first actress to blow it. Coke's a fickle friend. Before you know it you'll have a five-hundred-quid-a-week habit and you won't be able to operate without it.'

'Save the lecture, Harley,' Coco retorted. 'You're a fucking hypocrite.'

'Well, aren't you glad? If I wasn't, I'd be slipping you another few grams under the table and watching you go off to destroy yourself.'

He was being completely melodramatic, thought Coco. She was a million miles away from having a proper habit. After all, she was out now, perfectly happy without it. She didn't feel the need to rush to the toilet for a line. It was just a tool, that's all. She had her rules and her limits and she stuck to them.

She kept quiet. Harley wasn't playing ball. Five minutes later, she finished her drink and kissed him goodbye. He watched her go with a sense of disquiet. He liked Coco, he really did, but he knew she had problems. He hoped she'd taken everything he had said on board.

It didn't take Coco long to find another source. She was doing a shoot for a magazine – a feature on four young British actresses and their style secrets. The photographer's assistant, a podgy, pasty self-important emo called Gavin, made it pretty clear that his wages weren't enough to keep him in the lifestyle to which he had become accustomed, and he had ways of supplementing his income. He had put his number in her mobile at the end of the shoot.

'You never know,' he'd said to her with a flick of his long, black fringe.

Half an hour later, Coco had another stash of coke.

'Keep me on speed-dial. I'm available twenty-four seven,' he said as he pocketed the cash outside a pub in Soho.

Coco hoped he was discreet. Well, of course he was. He wouldn't do much business if he wasn't. And he certainly wouldn't give her a lecture every time she asked for more.

Sixteen

Louis waved the eighth scented stick under his nose, and recoiled in disgust.

'I'm sorry, but it just smells like Toilet Block to me. Why would anyone want to smell like this?'

'You do need to give it a moment to settle.'

The girl from the perfume company looked anxious.

Next to Louis, Tyger got to her feet.

'I'm sorry, but I agree with Louis. If we're going to license a perfume that represents us, it needs to be top quality. I love the designs for the bottle . . .'

She picked up the heavy glass flagon with a silver dagger through the stopper that had been mocked up.

'. . . but the samples you've given us just don't match up to it.'

Since the world at large had heard about their wedding, Tyger and Louis had been inundated with offers to endorse various different products. Tyger had taken control, marching Louis along to any number of meetings to discuss Brand Dagger.

The girl nodded, clearly disappointed.

'I'll get onto it straight away.'

Tyger picked up her bag and nodded to Louis that it was time to leave.

'Give us a call as soon as you've got some new samples.'

The two of them left the room, arm in arm.

'We'll do it ourselves,' declared Tyger. 'We'll market it through the Knickers To It website. I don't know why I didn't think of it before. Oh, bollocks,' she groaned, as they hit the street to find it lined with paparazzi. 'How did they know we were in there?'

Instinctively, she stood closer to Louis on the pavement and smiled.

'Hey – Mrs Dagger, over here!'

'When do we get to hear the pitter-patter of tiny Converse?'

'Show us your ring, Tyger!'

Louis pulled her to him and took her face in his hands lovingly. She was pint-size, reaching up to him even in her five-inch peep-toe stilettos. As their lips met, the flashbulbs exploded. The picture would be all over this week's gossip columns.

They were each used to the paparazzi, of course. The fashion magazines had always loved Tyger, with her kooky style, and had snapped her at every social event, every restaurant and bar, every shop she went into, so their readers could share her world and see what she was wearing. And Louis had been a target for months, though until now he hadn't been as cooperative – that hadn't been his image.

Now Louis and Tyger were married, their value had more than doubled. They were the celebrity couple of the moment. They were both photogenic, both style icons, and their picture told a story – the newly-weds, fresh from their elopement. And the fact that they looked blissfully happy in every photo that had been taken so far was something of a novelty in this age of marital breakdown and disharmony.

They played up to it, enjoying the attention, laying it on thick. Holding hands wherever they went, wearing matching Ray-Bans, kissing passionately on every street corner. They teased their stalkers by going into MacDonald's one minute, Cartier the next; waiting in a queue for a movie like any other young couple, then dashing into the Dorchester.

Of course, while the nation revelled in this ostensibly perfect marriage what the paps were really waiting for was the money shot: the disagreement, the drunken row, or the photo of one of them with someone else. The clock was ticking on their marriage. When would the novelty wear off and the whole thing go horribly wrong?

Tyger was thriving on the attention, and milked it for all it was worth. At the faux reception party they had been forced into by Tony, she wore a microscopic wedding dress, and bent over to show her knickers – white with *Mrs Dagger* embroidered in pink across her bottom – thereby earning invaluable publicity for Knickers To It. And off the back of that she persuaded Louis to endorse a line of male underwear she had designed – snug, raunchy boxers embellished with a digital print of barbed wire and gold chains. They sold like hot cakes after he modelled them on her website.

The nation loved her. They loved that she worked hard and played hard, was cheeky, with a sense of humour and a strong opinion, and that she was so clearly head over heels in love. She might only have become famous because of her lineage, but she didn't expect things to fall into her lap. She went out and made them happen. She wasn't some spoilt brat who believed the world owed her a living and free entry to every fashionable nightclub in the city. She was lauded as a great role model for young women.

They were more wary of Louis. He was yet to prove himself. They were poised ready to spring to Tyger's defence if he hurt her. He had spent so long nurturing his snarling, love-'em-and-leave-'em image that they found it hard to believe he had it in him to be loyal to her. Surely he would run true to type and be tempted to stray?

Nothing could be further from the truth. Although he was surrounded from dawn till dusk by stunning women who made it perfectly clear they were available, he only had eyes for one person. Louis Dagger was falling, hook, line and sinker, for the girl he had married on impulse.

He couldn't deny he'd been attracted to her on sight. Somehow he'd known in his gut that she was the only person on the planet who could handle him. Or who he wanted to handle him. He knew she admired him, but wasn't unduly impressed by him. He knew she was unshockable, yet had the potential to shock him.

What he wasn't ready for was that the more he got to know her, the more he fell under her spell. She had given him hope. It was astonishing to think that someone like Louis, who was living a dream, needed hope, but actually his world was very bleak. Tyger made him see the beauty. He felt as if he was coming to life, unfurling like a flower, a green shoot in the heart that had been black for so long.

What was lucky was his fans hadn't turned against him, or her, since the wedding. At the first gig he did, they all threw rice and confetti onto the stage. He felt as if his songs had more meaning. Instead of being fuelled by anger, they were fuelled by passion, and his performance went up a notch.

His management were delighted, having initially been royally pissed off that he had gone behind their backs. They'd hauled him into the office and carpeted him, even though they knew it was a pointless exercise. The thing about Louis Dagger was that he didn't seem to care about anyone or anything.

Only now he did.

The photographers appeased, he and Tyger turned and went down into the basement depths of Hakkasan, her favourite Chinese restaurant. His head was still spinning from the noxious samples the perfume company had waved under their noses – frankly, he wouldn't have put his name to any of it. And he felt the sick stone of dread in his chest. There had been hundreds, literally hundreds of articles written about the two of them since their marriage hit the headlines. It was only a matter of time before someone took the trouble to do some real digging.

Each day that went by took him closer to the day he would have to tell her. And he would have to. If he didn't, he would be living a lie. Every time he thought he had plucked up the courage, he couldn't do it. He wanted one more day with her, one day when he was still her hero. Once she knew, he was pretty certain it would all be over. How could she still love him, after what he had done?

He barely spoke as they ordered cocktails and dim sum in the crepuscular Shanghai chic. When the food arrived, he could barely touch it.

'Hey . . .' Tyger leaned over the table and spoke to him softly. 'What's up?'

'Let's go home,' he said.

'We've only just started eating,' she protested, but he stood up.

'Let's go home,' he repeated obstinately.

Tyger took her napkin off her lap and put it on the table.

'OK.' She sighed wearily.

As they stood up to leave, the waiter came over anxiously to see what was wrong.

'It's all fine,' Tyger reassured him, thrusting her credit card at him. 'Can we just pay for what we've had so far? My husband doesn't feel very well.'

Five minutes later they were on the pavement, calling a cab. As Tyger got into the seat next to Louis, he grabbed her, pulled her to him. He was squeezing her so hard she could barely breathe.

'You are such a nightmare,' she chided him. 'I was looking forward to that. What is it with you?'

He didn't answer.

'Well, I'm starving,' she went on, wriggling out of his grasp and leaning forward to tap on the glass. 'I'll get the driver to stop. We'll have to get something on the way home—'

'Tell me you love me.' He cut straight through her words.

Tyger started to laugh. He scowled.

'Don't bloody laugh at me. Just tell me you love me.'

'Of course I love you. You crazy messed-up son of a bitch.'

He sat back in his seat sulkily, stretching his legs out and resting them on the flip-down chair opposite. Crazy messed-up son of a bitch. She'd got that right for sure.

*

Tyger looked at her husband sideways, chewing her lip. His dark brows were furrowed, his lip curled in a sulky snarl. She was getting used to these mood swings. He would be carefree and sunny one minute, then suddenly his mood would plummet, and there would be nothing she could do to cajole him back. She hated it. It made her feel unsettled. She wanted to make him happy.

Maybe he regretted marrying her? Maybe the novelty was wearing off, and as he got to know her he was gradually realising he had made a huge mistake? If that was the case she wanted to know sooner rather than later. Tyger didn't want to be around someone who didn't want to be around her.

She grabbed his shirt and pulled him round to face her.

'You're not sorry, are you?' she demanded. 'Sorry you married me? Because if you are, tell me now and we can sort it.'

'Sorry?' He seemed genuinely shocked by her question. 'Are you joking? Marrying you is the best thing I have ever done.'

'Then what is it? Why do you get so . . . black?'

He gazed straight past her, into the middle distance.

'Louis?'

He turned back to her. She could see tears in his eyes.

'I'm terrified of losing you,' he told her. 'I've never cared about anyone before, and it's freaking me out.'

'You're not going to lose me,' she assured him. 'There's nothing you can do to stop me loving you. Nothing.'

He seemed to be considering whether to tell her something.

'Louis,' she persisted. 'What is it?'

The cab pulled up outside her apartment block. He jumped up and opened the door, leaping onto the pavement. Sighing, she scrambled after him.

'Oi!' called the cabdriver. 'That's seventeen quid.'

She scrabbled in her bag for a twenty-pound note and thrust it at him through the window, then ran to catch up with her husband as he unlocked the door.

'You go and sit down,' he told her. 'I'll go to the shop to get some food. What would you like?'

It was as if nothing had happened. As if he hadn't just demanded they walk out of a restaurant mid-meal, as if he hadn't been on the verge of tears in the taxi. Tyger wondered whether to press him but Louis wasn't the sort of person who responded to pressure. It hadn't taken her long to work that bit of him out.

'I don't care. Just get a pizza from the freezer section,' she told him with a sigh, and wondered how long she was going to be able to keep this game up before it drove her crazy.

Seventeen

It was the perfect day for the Portobello Road. The sun was shining. Tourists and locals jostled together amongst the stalls. Music blared from the shop fronts, the notes melding together seamlessly. A man on a bike with an enormous ghetto-blaster drove his way through the crowds, the bass-line of his reggae trailing after him.

Violet and Justine were doing what girls do best: shopping. They'd bought vintage dresses trimmed with lace, bejewelled hair slides, sequinned flip-flops. Violet found an antique evening bag in the shape of a frog, his mouth opening wide ready to accept whatever contents its new owner cared to insert – a lipstick, a powder compact, a packet of cigarettes.

Justine wasn't used to rummaging and picking over and bargaining. She was used to being waited on while she shopped, and having her purchases wrapped in monogrammed tissue paper and delivered to her house. Uncertain at first, she had hung back, but now she was getting the hang of it. The thrill of searching through a rack of dresses and finding one that caught your eye. Diving into the make-shift changing room to try it on, and then haggling with the stallholder. She'd even bought a wicker bag decorated with raffia flowers for all her purchases.

'I'm exhausted,' she told Violet, but her eyes were sparkling.

They went to the Electric Cinema for eggs Benedict and mimosas. As she sat amongst the crowd of like-minded Notting Hill hedonists, sipping cocktails, reading the papers, placating hungry children with chips, she felt a burst of happiness. She wasn't sure how to identify the feeling, and then realised what it was – she was relaxed. Usually her life was so ordered, timetabled down to the last nanosecond, with no room for spontaneity. Violet had taught her that spontaneity was what mattered. That if you hadn't booked a table at your favourite restaurant in advance, so what? Something would turn up.

It had been a whirlwind, their affair. Sweetly intense. They had barely been apart since that first night. They spent most of the time at Violet's flat, as Justine lived with her father. They did everything a young couple who were falling in love did. They went to see bands, went out for meals, went dancing. Justine had bought a whole new wardrobe. Out went her structured Armani and Prada, in came pretty dresses by Twenty8Twelve and Sass & Bide. And jewellery. Justine had always stuck to a plain Cartier tank and diamond earrings. Now she was draped in strings of beads and jingly charm bracelets.

In such a small space of time, she had changed. And she knew her father was suspicious. She was neglecting her work. Nothing was left undone, but she wasn't ferociously conscientious, obsessive about detail, working all the hours God sends in an effort to prove herself. She was clocking off when everyone else did, sailing out of the door without a backward glance. She was happy to delegate things to other people, and didn't breathe down their necks.

And, she had to admit, she was loving it.

She stroked Violet's hand across the table.

'What shall we do tonight?' she asked.

A cloud drifted across Violet's face.

'I've got to go and do some recording,' she replied. 'Sammy's organised the guys to come round later this afternoon . . .'

'Can I come?'

Violet didn't reply straight away.

'I won't be any trouble. I won't get in the way.'

Violet drew her hand away and picked up her glass.

'Honestly, you'll be so bored. Why don't you pick up a DVD and have a night in? I'll be back later.'

Justine opened her mouth to protest, but she could see by the look on Violet's face that she didn't want an argument. And she felt a hot torrent rise up inside her.

Jealousy. It was jealousy. She tried to swallow it down with a sip of her mimosa, but it was burning her throat. She picked up the menu and studied it, so that Violet wouldn't see the tears that were threatening to spill. She blinked hard. For God's sake, Justine, pull yourself together.

She put down the menu.

'I'll have supper with Dad,' she said. 'He's been complaining that he hasn't seen me.'

Violet smiled back at her gratefully. 'Good idea.'

Later that afternoon, Violet lay back on the cushions enjoying the warmth of the early-evening sun as it began its descent. She was sprawled on a rug with Sammy as he strummed on a guitar. The courtyard was lit up by candles in jam-jars and fairy-lights. She was eating roasted figs out of tin foil that had been cooked on the dying embers of the barbecue, then drizzled with mascarpone and honey.

They had spent the afternoon recording. She had wanted to get the songs she had written recorded as quickly as she could: the ink was barely dry on the manuscript paper. She had such a clear idea of how she wanted them to sound – stripped back, acoustic, with as few effects as possible. Violet didn't believe in trickery. She loved rawness and talent to shine through, and she only worked with people who believed the same, people who had confidence in their musicality and weren't afraid to expose themselves. They had laid down three tracks in the basement studio that afternoon, she and Sammy together with a drummer and a pianist, and now they were basking in post-recording euphoria.

Inevitably the session turned into a party, with someone cooking spicy chicken drumsticks on the makeshift barbecue in the tiny courtyard garden, and someone else making a huge mound of couscous, and a crate of beer appearing from nowhere, and dreamy soulful music blaring out rather too loudly than was neighbourly, but it was such great music that no one complained, but instead drifted round to the house with their own contributions.

Violet realised rather guiltily that she was glad Justine wasn't there. She wanted to chill out and be herself, not have to think about someone else. She chewed on her thumbnail, worrying about what this meant. It wasn't good, was it, being glad about not being with someone? Or did everyone need time out? The problem was their relationship was so intense, so all-consuming, especially as it was clandestine. Not that Violet wasn't enjoying it. Violet had enjoyed dressing Justine up, encouraging her to change her image, but she thought perhaps this made her a bit kinky. Having a girlfriend was a bit like having a dolly. She knew she was just playing. Or was she? When they made love, when they lay in each other's arms, it was magical. Just thinking about it made her inside fizz. But there was something – something just a tiny bit . . . claustrophobic about it all, that made Violet feel uncomfortable. And guilty.

'Sammy,' she said, 'I need to talk to someone.'

He didn't stop strumming. His fingers moved deftly across the guitar strings. But he was listening.

'I'm having an affair. A really, really hot affair.' She paused. 'With a girl.'

He still didn't falter. Just nodded.

'Uh huh.'

'You're not shocked.'

Sammy gave a small shrug. Of course he wasn't shocked. He'd seen it all, even if he hadn't actually done it.

'I guessed something was going on. Those songs you wrote, they came out of somewhere.'

He gave her a knowing smile.

'I'm not really sure where I'm going with it, that's the problem,' she confided, garrulous after three of his knock-out mojitos. 'And I keep feeling guilty. Not because I'm ashamed of what I'm doing. But because I think I'm doing it for the wrong reasons.'

'So – what are your reasons?'

'It's fun, it's flattering, it's naughty. It's something new – you know how bored I get.'

Sammy knew only too well. Violet was always trying to change her set, throw in new songs, and got impatient when her accompanists grumbled. She hated getting stale, but as Sammy pointed out she never stuck with a set-list long enough for it to get stale. So he was hardly surprised to find she got bored in her love life.

'I feel as if I'm . . . toying with her. I mean, I love being with her, we have an amazing time and the sex is . . . mind-blowing . . . and . . . I don't know, I kind of love her but I don't *love* love her, if you know what I mean . . . I don't want to spend the rest of my life with her or have some kind of weird marriage thing.'

'You're using her,' said Sammy simply.

'Do you think?'

'Definitely. Men do it all the time – string women along just because they are having a good time, but they have no intentions . . .'

'Do you do that, Sammy?' Violet poked him with her foot playfully. 'Do you string women along?'

'Of course not.' He looked at her in mock hurt at her suggestion. 'I have integrity.'

Violet sat up in indignation.

'Are you saying I haven't?'

'I'm just saying . . . don't play with people's hearts. It's cruel.'

Violet sat back. He wasn't really telling her anything she didn't already know, but hearing it spoken out loud drove it home. It wasn't fair on Justine, making this seem like something it wasn't. For Violet it was a novelty. She couldn't pretend it hadn't affected her – it was the first thing that had even made her write a decent song, for a start – but this wasn't a forever thing. She could quite easily imagine a future without Justine in it.

Which meant that, really and truly, to be fair, she had to break it off.

She took another sip of her mojito, thoughtful.

As the sun finally went down, Violet shivered. She only had on a thin dress.

'Here.' Sammy took off his jumper and slipped it on over her head. It was warm and smelled of him. Of a man. She felt a sudden frisson. Startled, she looked at him surreptitiously. Did she have feelings for Sammy? She'd never felt this for him before. They worked so closely together. They were almost like brother and sister.

He looked up and caught her staring.

'What?' he asked her with a smile, and she swallowed. No, she thought. It had just been a moment. She'd been seduced by his chivalry. Of course she didn't fancy Sammy. She was confused, that's all. Clutching at straws to find an escape from a situation that made her feel awkward, uncomfortable, guilty.

Except when she was actually with Justine, of course. Now the end of the evening was approaching, she found herself longing for her soft warmth. She wanted to kiss her, run her fingers through her hair, feel Justine's lips on her skin . . .

She threw back the rest of the mojito. What the hell. She should stop feeling guilty, and enjoy the relationship for what it was.

Benedict Amador knew there was something wrong with his daughter.

Not that she seemed to be suffering. On the contrary, she was blooming. He knew he was biased, but she looked more beautiful than ever these days. She had changed her image completely. Justine had always been tailored, understated, reined in. Now she drifted into the office in brightly coloured silk maxi dresses that showed off her cleavage, set off with eye-catching jewellery, her dark hair loose and flowing. She even smelled different, an exotic scent redolent of frangipani that was a million miles from the classic Chanel No. 5 she had worn since she was sixteen.

And she was dreamy. She had a cat-that-got-the-cream smile on her face. She was still efficient and motivated, but she had lost her headstrong bullishness. Once, she would have been in his office every day, badgering him for what she wanted, bombarding him with ideas. Now, she did everything she was asked, and with impressive results, but that was it.

He decided to call her bluff.

They were at the oyster bar in Bibendum, just the two of them. Sharing a bottle of champagne and a tiny pot of sevruga caviar. She was wearing a Melissa Odabash kaftan, linen Capri pants and flip-flops, her hair piled on top of her head in a messy topknot, and big hooped earrings. She looked as if she should be in some glitzy beach bar in Ibiza, not in Knightsbridge.

He watched as she spooned a tiny mound of glistening black pearls onto a piece of toast. His beautiful daughter, who made him so proud. His beautiful daughter, who was keeping a secret from him.

He thought about the file lying on his desk. The file that she had brought him with all the details of the hotel in Berlin she had discovered. The file which now contained a final contract ready for him to sign. His daughter's hunch had been correct, unsurprisingly. As soon as he had put in the offer, he sent a surveyor and an architect out on the next plane. His team had reported back to him with their findings – pleasingly close to the conclusions Justine had drawn.

'I've got some exciting news for you,' he told her now.

She looked wary as she bit into her toast.

'Berlin,' he said. 'I was wrong not to listen to you. It was a very good idea. I've got an offer in on the property – we're about to exchange contracts. I want you out there as soon as. I want the hotel up and running by Christmas.'

He flashed her a smile, an ill-disguised gauntlet.

For a moment, she looked completely horrified. She put down her caviar spoon. Then she composed herself.

'Why the sudden change of heart?' she asked. 'I thought you weren't interested?'

'Well, I changed my mind. And I think you're ready for the challenge. I think you'd bring a certain energy to the project.'

Justine stared at him in disbelief.

'I've got an apartment lined up,' he went on. 'I'm sending back the contract next week. You can be on site as soon as we complete.'

Justine picked up her champagne. Her stomach was churning. He couldn't do this to her. He couldn't. It was bloody typical Benedict, moving the goalposts.

'I don't know if I'm ready for it.'

'Hang on a moment. You were begging me. You told me it was your dream. You told me you could make this place the jewel in Amador's crown—'

'Well, I was wrong. I was being unrealistic. Over-confident. I was trying to run before I could walk. I've got so much to learn. I'm not ready for a challenge like this.'

'You'd cope. You know you would. You've got back-up. I can always be on the next flight if there is a problem. I trust you.'

Their gazes locked.

'I can't just drop everything.'

'Whyever not? There's nothing spoiling, is there?'

Justine realised in a flash just what this was all about. Her father was testing her. He wanted to know what was going on. But she wasn't ready. She thought quickly.

Berlin was perfect for Violet. She would thrive on its edgy, decadent ambience. She could get any number of gigs out there, make a name for herself. A six-month break while Justine set up the hotel.

'Can I have some time to think about it?'

Benedict surveyed her coolly.

'What exactly is there to think about?'

She didn't answer.

'Is it a man? Who is he? Maybe we can get him a role—'

'It's not a man.'

'Well, what then?' He was completely mystified. Something or someone had got hold of his daughter and made her unrecognisable. Not in a bad way. She was just . . . different.

'I need to sort my head out. I'm not sure who I am or where I'm going right now.'

Benedict frowned. Justine had never wavered about her identity or her direction in life.

'Let me know,' he told her, and passed her the tiny pot of caviar. 'Here – you finish it.'

But Justine shook her head. She felt sick.

'And remember: I've got plenty of employees who would jump at the chance of a lifetime.'

He couldn't resist a dig. He hated the way she was shutting him out. He was desperate for her to come clean, but it was obvious she wasn't going to. There was, after all, only one thing he cared about in the world. He cared not a jot for his empire, his millions, his magnificent home, his art collection, his cars. He cared not a jot for any of his staff beyond a vaguely paternalistic concern for their well-being. Or any other human being he came into contact with during his business or personal life. But Justine – Justine was the centre of his universe. He would walk over burning coals to ensure her happiness. Not that he thought she was unhappy at the moment. He just sensed that she was slipping away from him, in which case he wanted to know exactly who, what, why, when and where.

On Sunday morning, after a sleepless night apart from Violet, Justine turned up at her flat with a posy of sweet-smelling freesias and a box of macaroons. They ate them cross-legged on the carpet, dipped into huge cups of milky coffee.

'I've got a proposal,' said Justine, her eyes shining. She'd thought of nothing else for the past twelve hours, and she was sure it could work. 'My father wants me to go to Berlin, to open a new hotel. Why don't you come with me? It would just be for six months, till the place is up and running—'

'Berlin?' said Violet. 'Are you crazy?'

'But it's perfect for you! They love your sort of music over there. You could sing every night of the week if you wanted. Get a new following. It's the coolest city – you'd love it.'

Violet put her cup down, frowning.

'Justine, I can't. It's all about to happen for me here, I can feel it. I'm finally writing my own stuff. I'm getting together a demo. I need to see about getting a deal—'

'They've got recording studios in Berlin. Come on – it's an amazing opportunity. Just think of the art, and the restaurants, and the clubs. You've told me more than once you're bored of London.'

'Yes, but it's my home.'

'This isn't for ever. Six months. Where's your sense of adventure?' Justine put her hands on her hips. 'I thought you had more about you than that.'

'If it's what you want to do, Justine, you go. I can come and visit you.'

Justine looked down at the floor. She pressed her finger into a few macaroon crumbs while she thought. Eventually she looked up.

'No,' she said softly. 'You're too important to me. I've spent my life putting my career first, and now I've found someone who matters. So you come first.' She smiled, a little uncertain. 'I'll tell my father to send someone else. There'll be other opportunities.'

Violet wondered if she should insist that Justine go. She thought that would take the pressure off the relationship. She didn't want to end it, but it was a little intense. And there was so much she needed to do. There wasn't room in her head for song-writing and recording *and* Justine. But she couldn't bring herself to do it. There was something in her that wanted Justine around. Something in her presence that she found both comforting and stimulating.

'I'm glad,' she said, and the next moment they were kissing. Justine tasted of coffee and sugar and strawberry-scented lip-gloss.

She couldn't get enough . . .

Later in the week, Violet took the first few songs she had recorded round for Delilah and Raf to listen to.

'No Dad?' she asked, as she put her iPod into the docking station in the kitchen.

Delilah sighed. 'Lunch with a journalist or a publicist or a columnist or some sort of –ist.'

Violet looked at her mother. There was an edge to her voice that wasn't usually there. She hesitated for a moment.

'Come on,' said Delilah, 'let's have a listen.'

Violet decided she must have imagined it, and pressed Play. As her voice filled the room, accompanied by piano and Sammy on the double bass, she felt a surge of pride. It was exactly as she wanted it to sound. Sammy was a genius. He understood her so completely. Anyone else would have felt the urge to have layer upon layer of different sounds, but Sammy was as brave as she was.

'Darling, it's completely fantastic,' declared Delilah. 'Get me a copy and I'll send it round to Max Ridley straight away. If he doesn't sign you on the spot I'll eat my hat.'

Max Ridley was an old friend, the head of Locomotion Records, a hit factory with a talent for spotting the next big thing. Delilah had recently catered Max's sixtieth birthday, on a huge yacht moored in St Catherine's Dock.

'No,' said Violet. 'I've told you before. I don't want you to pull any strings.'

'Don't be silly. It's not pulling strings. I'd be doing him a favour. He'd be furious if I didn't make sure he had first refusal.'

'Mum, I want to make my own way. I don't want people to think I only got a contract with Locomotion because you know him.'

'He wouldn't sign you if you didn't have talent.'

'You don't get it, do you?'

'I don't get why you want to make life hard for yourself, no. It's tough enough, Violet. If you've got contacts, you should use them. Everyone else on the planet does.'

'Well, they're not me, are they? Success off the back of someone else's string-pulling is meaningless.'

'So why don't you change your name? Then no one could ever accuse you of nepotism.'

'I'm not going to pretend to be someone else either.'

Delilah shook her head in bewilderment. Her middle daughter had always been obstinate, and managed to find ways of making life difficult.

'Look,' she tried to cajole her, 'being the daughter of famous people has its drawbacks as well as its advantages. You might as well take the advantages, because the drawbacks will kick in some day. It all evens itself out in the end.'

Violet snatched her iPod out of the docking station.

'I wish I'd never played them to you now. I wanted your opinion, not a lecture.'

'I think you're being childish.'

'Because I won't play things your way?' Violet demanded. 'Admit it, Mum. If I make it on my own, then you don't have control. That's what you're afraid of, isn't it? I won't be part of the Rafferty franchise.'

Delilah choked on her peppermint tea.

'How dare you?'

'It's true. You might not like it, but it's true. Everything's tickety-boo as long as we're doing what you want. The minute we step out of line, you start playing your face . . .'

Delilah put down her teacup with a shaking hand.

'If that's what you really think, you might as well go now. I don't have to listen to your spiteful bile. I was trying to help.'

'You were trying to interfere.'

Violet shoved her iPod back in her handbag and stormed out of the house, tearful and angry. Delilah had infuriated her. Of course, she should have known that by playing her the demo Delilah would want to get involved. She should have seen it coming. And she hadn't meant to say what she had said. Delilah only wanted to do the best for all of them, which technically did make her a control freak, but for all the right reasons.

She paused at the gate. She should go back and apologise. Her mother had looked genuinely shocked at her outburst, and Violet knew she had over-reacted. She knew why, too: because her relationship with Justine was playing on her conscience. Half of her wanted to talk to Delilah about it, because she trusted her mother's opinion and she wanted her advice. But the other half of her knew that once the cat was out of the bag, she would have to make a decision, when all she really wanted to do was keep things going as they were. No real commitment, just a delicious secret between the two of them. Once it was out in the open then real life would kick in.

Was she selfish to want to keep things as they were? Violet hadn't ever needed anyone's advice before on affairs of the heart. She was very definite about where she stood. This time, she was thoroughly confused.

The pragmatist in her said she was living a lie, and exploiting someone she was supposed to love. The hedonist in her said stop worrying and enjoy it. The hedonist in her had no conscience.

The hedonist won.

She shut the gate behind her and walked off down Richmond Hill without a backward glance.

'Delilah?'

Delilah turned her attention back to Polly wearily. They were going through the sample menus the venue had sent over for her party, and she hadn't felt inspired by any of the suggestions so far. But then, she didn't feel much like having a party at all. Why on earth had she even thought of it?

Violet's words had stung Delilah more than she could realise. Is that really how her family saw her? As some megalomaniac matriarch, manipulating them all to her own advantage? It was incredibly hurtful to imagine that might be so.

She tried to analyse the past ten years. She had been nothing but supportive and encouraging. Or so she thought. Perhaps she had been smothering? Maybe they couldn't wait to get away and carve their own futures?

She thought about Coco and Tyger. Coco was definitely standing on her own two feet. She scarcely heard a peep from her during the week. When she had remarked upon it, Coco had explained her work schedule had nearly tripled – she was in so many more scenes, there was barely time to take a breath between takes, let alone phone. And Tyger – well, Tyger hadn't just flown the nest, she'd jumped out of it without a parachute.

It was a terrible moment, realising you hadn't been the wonderful mother you thought you had. And what about wife? Did Raf think the same? He'd certainly jumped at the chance of *Something for the Weekend.* Even if he had pretended to discuss it with her, maybe he had made his mind up from the start. Had he seen it as a chance to escape her clutches?

Delilah put her face in her hands, pressing her fingers into her eyeballs to staunch the tears. She was being silly. It must be the wrong time of the month or something – she always got tearful before a period these days, more than she ever had done in the past. They were probably just reminding her of their presence before they disappeared altogether.

Fuck it, she thought. There was absolutely nothing glamorous about being about to turn fifty. Dried up, barren, unloved, surrounded by ungrateful offspring—

'Are you OK?' Polly asked her.

'Do you think it's too late to cancel?' she asked in reply.

'Don't be silly. You can't cancel. It's going to be wonderful,'

Polly told her stoutly. 'Now come on. We haven't even chosen the cocktails yet. I think raspberry Bellinis sound just the thing . . .'

Delilah picked up the cocktail list with a sigh, wanting to snap that you couldn't have raspberry Bellinis, the whole point about Bellinis was they were made with peaches. But she didn't, because the last person who deserved her ill temper was Polly.

'Polly, why don't you choose for me? It all looks fine, and I trust your judgement. Just bring me the final menu for approval . . .' And she drifted out of the kitchen.

Polly looked after her, concerned. It was very unlike Delilah not to be interested, but she had picked up on a certain tension in the house of late. Ever since Raf had agreed to be in the film, in fact.

She picked up the menus with a sigh. It was all very well asking her to choose, but Polly had a lot on her plate. The admin was through the roof with the film coming up, Delilah's editor was chasing for material which Polly had to double-check, she wasn't getting home before eight most nights . . .

She supposed it would calm down once Raf was on location. Though she didn't like the thought of that one bit. She was going to miss him horribly.

She turned her attention back to the menus to distract herself. Japanese egg custard with shitake mushrooms, lotus root and soy. Yuk! Who thought up these things? What people really wanted was some really good sausages on sticks to soak up the booze. But this party was a showcase. The nation's culinary sweetheart was going to be fifty. It had to be perfect.

Eighteen

Benedict was striding around The Melksham, the latest of his projects. It was a small, three-storey town house on the edge of Covent Garden that had been a rather run-down and unimaginative pub. Benedict had transformed it into a small but perfectly formed hotel-cum-members' club that felt almost like home on the surface, but with discreet facilities that made it luxurious, convenient and utterly irresistible for anyone who wanted a little place in town. There were twelve bedrooms, a delightfully intimate restaurant, a screening room, and even a facility for members to leave their favourite items so they could be installed each time they stayed. The long-term rates were very favourable, so as to appeal to anyone who had been considering renting a flat but who didn't want to be bothered with the maintenance.

His brief to the designer had been 'restrained flamboyance' – which sounded impossible but the designer had worked with him on many other projects and understood what Benedict meant by this apparent contradiction in terms. One still had the sense of being in a Regency house but with a modern take.

Adjoining the main hotel was a delicatessen, with exposed rough brick walls, a stone floor, and a wood-burning pizza oven. In the basement was an intimate bar with a slightly clubby feel – again the exposed brick, but with industrial chrome fittings and violet down-lighters. To save it from starkness there were plush white velvet sofas, while canvases printed with iconic London symbols – taxi cabs, a policeman's helmet, Big Ben – gave it a witty edge.

It had been open a month, and Benedict was concerned that it wasn't yet as busy as he would have liked, hence the visit. He always kept his staff on their toes, as he was fond of impromptu visits to make sure they were keeping up his incredibly high standards. Woe betide the manager if things weren't up to scratch. In fact, where the hell was the manager? Benedict had been here nearly ten minutes and no one had bothered to approach him . . .

He finally caught sight of him, escorting someone back up the stairs from the bar area, giving her the spiel. He recognised her immediately: Coco Rafferty. She was just the sort of person they needed as a member. She had a great pedigree, a high profile; she was beautiful, fashionable, intelligent, and people would flock to follow in her footsteps. That was how London worked these days. In the current economic climate, being too discreet could mean disappearing altogether. Benedict needed bright young things who liked the idea of belonging to something exclusive. Once one joined, the others would follow.

And he had another reason for being interested in Coco. Justine was spending a lot of time with the Raffertys these days. Maybe Coco could shed some light on what had made her change so dramatically? He was still waiting for Justine to tell him whether she wanted to go to Berlin. She'd definitely been avoiding him for the past few days. And a month or so ago, she'd have had his hand off at the offer. He needed to get to the bottom of what was going on with his daughter.

He stepped forward, cutting in between the manager and Coco.

'I'll show Miss Rafferty round. Thank you.'

The manager knew better than to protest. He melted discreetly away into the background. Benedict turned to Coco with a charming smile and an outstretched hand.

'Benedict Amador. Are you interested in becoming a member?'

'Actually, I'm looking for somewhere to have a private

screening. Just family and close friends. And maybe dinner afterwards?'

'Well, you've definitely come to the right place.'

She was elegant, in a chocolate-brown silk safari dress, her hair in a smooth ponytail, large Mark Jacobs sunglasses and wedges so high she was nearly as tall as Benedict, who was over six foot. His first impression was that she smelled delicious and it threw him slightly. He was used to beautiful women, but not used to being affected by them.

'I'll show you our screening room. It seats twenty – would that be big enough?'

He led her swiftly through the building and opened the double doors into the cinema, where five rows of four seats covered in pony skin were ranged in front of a huge screen.

'It's intimate . . .'

'It looks perfect.' She smiled. 'I want somewhere to watch my first transmission. I don't want to make a huge deal of it, but I know the family want to see it.'

She didn't tell him what she was going to be appearing in. She didn't need to.

'We can do you champagne and canapés in here. Then dinner in the private dining room?'

He held open the door and ushered her through, leading her back down the corridor.

'In the meantime, if you were thinking of joining . . . We could offer you complimentary membership for a year.'

'Why?' Her smile was polite, her stare frank.

'I'll be honest. It would be great publicity for me. And in return, if you have a meeting, or want to throw a little party, or take someone for dinner, you do it here.'

Coco didn't reply straight away. She stopped and looked at a painting with interest. It was a small Ben Nicholson. She obviously had a good eye. Or else she was very good at pretending, which was, of course, a possibility. She was an actress, after all.

She turned to him and again he was struck by her beauty – it was almost an old-fashioned look, proper film-star glamour.

'That's very generous. Thank you. It's a really lovely place.'

She smiled. It lit up her face and made her eyes sparkle. Benedict swallowed. She really was unnervingly attractive. He felt drawn to her in a way he hadn't felt for years. Women had so little mystery these days. They gave away all their cards at the beginning. There was usually nothing to beguile a man like him.

Coco intrigued him. He'd expected a slightly vacuous and rather brittle creature with the self-important self-confidence that came from one brought up in the public eye. But Coco was reserved, polite, thoughtful – he didn't want to let her go without finding out more. He wondered what would emerge if she was allowed to relax, if things moved on to a less business-like footing. With a start, he realised he had almost forgotten his original purpose. His real intent, he recalled, had been to pump her for information that might lead him to find out what was pre-occupying Justine.

That could wait for the time being, he decided. Or he could kill two birds with one stone.

'Would you have lunch with me?' Benedict asked, grasping the nettle. 'I'd be interested to know what you think of the menu.'

Coco hesitated. She'd been thinking of going shopping, but in fact she was hungry. She realised she hadn't eaten the night before, nor had she had breakfast. And there were delicious smells wafting from the dining room. It was a better offer than picking up a sandwich from Marks and Spencer in Longacre.

'That would be lovely.'

Benedict found himself taking her arm, in an old-fashioned and chivalrous gesture. She made him feel debonair, gallant – and strangely protective. As they walked through the reception area and through the brick arch that led to the restaurant, he realised there was only one other woman who had ever made him feel that way before.

His wife.

*

Two hours later, they were still sitting at the table window the waiter had led them to, an almost empty bottle of Puligny-Montrachet between them. They'd had seasonal asparagus risotto with creamy pecorino, and corn-fed chicken with chorizo, chickpeas and razor clams. For dessert, Coco had unashamedly ordered the house speciality – a triple-chocolate brownie with vanilla ice cream.

'I hardly get a chance to eat properly these days,' she confided. 'The studio caterers are great, but you know that if it's Tuesday it's pasta tricolore with Mediterranean vegetables. And by supper I'm so tired I just want to fall into bed when I get home.'

She didn't mention that her appetite had been somewhat killed of late.

Benedict poured the last of the wine into her glass. He didn't want her to go. They had chatted about everything and nothing. They both knew a little bit about each other's worlds – Coco because she had stayed in lots of luxury hotels in her time, Benedict because he found television the quickest way to relax in the evening if he wasn't doing business – so they each found the trade secrets and inside information fascinating.

Once she had relaxed, Coco was highly amusing. Her drive to perform made her a natural raconteur and she knew how to tell a story. Benedict, too, could paint pictures with words. They gossiped and laughed and outdid each other's anecdotes as the meal progressed, and each felt as if they had known the other for years.

Eventually, the meal came to a natural conclusion. The plates were cleared, the wine finished, the coffee drunk. The dining room was empty. Slightly flushed from the unaccustomed lunchtime drinking, Coco picked up her handbag.

'I should get home, learn my lines for tomorrow. Though I know I'll just fall asleep. That was so delicious. Thank you. And I'm really looking forward to coming here. It's going to be . . .' She trailed off, unable to find a suitable adjective, knowing she was gabbling. She felt incredibly self-conscious all of a sudden.

She wanted to see this man again. It was two years since she had dated. She had made a conscious decision to concentrate on her career. Being in a relationship so often sapped your energy and made you make bad decisions.

Benedict was in a different league from her other boy-friends. Confident without being arrogant. Suave without being slimy. Witty without being frivolous. And handsome. He was as old as her father, she was sure, but there was something so distinguished and sexy about him. She found her heartbeat tripling as she motioned to the waiter to bring her coat.

'Would you like to join us for my screening?' she heard herself saying. 'It'll just be my parents, and my sisters, and a few friends . . . I know Violet and Justine have been hanging out together lately. They'll probably come . . .'

'I'd love to.' Benedict's voice was warm with enthusiasm. He put out his hand to hold hers. He squeezed it tight, just for one moment.

Then he watched her walk away. It was as if the wine they had been drinking had been anti-freeze, and had de-frosted the ice in his veins. Suddenly, after all these years, he could feel again. He picked up her napkin and breathed in her scent. His heart skipped a beat, he felt his cock stir involuntarily. And he realised he had completely and utterly forgotten to bring up the subject of Justine.

Nineteen

So when Justine told him, the night after Coco's screening, that she wasn't going to go to Berlin, Benedict cursed himself yet again for taking his eye off the ball. He had been so wrapped up in the prospect of seeing Coco again that any other concerns had paled into insignificance. The fact that Coco had agreed to go out for dinner with him the following weekend had overshadowed everything. All he was thinking about was where to take her, how to behave – even what to wear, for heaven's sake.

And now his daughter had as good as told him she was jacking in her career, without a satisfactory explanation. He felt rising panic.

'Is it a man?' he asked her as she poured them both a nightcap in the living room.

'No,' she assured him, 'it's not a man. I just need to . . . get my head around some stuff. Figure out where I'm going in life.'

Benedict frowned. Justine had always known exactly where she was going: full steam ahead. She had been incandescent when he had first refused her the Berlin gig. What the hell was going on? Was she trying to outmanoeuvre him? Did she have some wily master plan? And if so, what? Surely he had given her what she wanted?

'Dad.' Justine was standing in front of him, holding out a glass of Courvoisier XO, the liquid glowing amber. 'Tell me about my mother.'

She couldn't have shocked him more if she'd turned round

with a gun in her hand. Benedict took the glass and took a swig of the fiery liquid as Justine sat next to him, curling her legs up underneath her.

'I need to know,' she told him. 'I need to know about her.'

Benedict and Justine had never ever spoken about Jeanne Fox. There had seemed no need. Justine had been barely three when her mother had died. Too young to have it explained. And after that, there had been no reason to bring the subject up. And Justine had never asked. She had seemed happy to accept that it was just the two of them. That was how it always had been, and still was. There were probably some shrinks who would say it was unhealthy, but they were full of shit. Benedict and Justine were a team. They lived together, worked together, fought, argued, and enjoyed the fruits of their success. She admired him and he adored her. And it wasn't as if he had ever stood in the way of her having a relationship. She'd had boyfriends, whom he had welcomed and entertained. He'd never scared any of them off. He didn't need to. She bored of every one of them in the end. They never lived up to him.

The only relic Justine had of Jeanne was her maiden name – Fox – which Benedict and Jeanne had agreed to add on to Amador the day she was born. The name had a ring to it, and made Justine an individual in her own right. After all, they reasoned, she was a product of both of them. That had been in the days when they still got on. Before . . . well, before.

Benedict always told himself that on the day Justine asked what had happened to her mother, he would be honest. That he would tell her everything. He wouldn't leave out a single detail. It wasn't a pretty tale, and he knew he wouldn't come out of it well. He had to risk being judged by his daughter, but he owed her the truth.

Now that moment had arrived, he felt nervous. Even when faced with a fifty-foot wave in the middle of the Atlantic, or sitting on a sixteen-hand horse with very different ideas about where they should be going, or trying to charm millions out of an international bank, he hadn't felt his stomach churn like this.

'She was American,' he began slowly. 'You know that. She came over here one summer with a bunch of students. To "do" England. Strat*ford*, Bucking*ham* Palace – you know the deal . . . We met, and that was kind of it. We had a strange, transatlantic romance for four years, then she agreed to come and live in England. And marry me . . .'

It was the jealousy he hadn't bargained for. It had never been there to start with – at first he had been proud of the fact that she was magnetically attractive to men. Jeanne wasn't strictly beautiful, but she had . . . something, something that drew men to her, something immensely powerful that was hard to resist. Maybe it was the way everything she said sounded like a tease, maybe it was the way she seemed to understand everything about whoever she was talking to, maybe it was as basic as the dark eyebrows and the full mouth and the cleavage, but men flocked to her side.

It didn't bother him at first, but once they were married Benedict wanted to murder every last one of them. It was the source of much tension between the couple. Jeanne was incensed that he suspected her of leading men on, and refused not to speak to them. She enjoyed men's company. It didn't mean she was going to be unfaithful. Benedict could never conquer that fear.

It grew and grew. Hot, white and destructive, uncontrollable. If she spoke to a waiter, his hands gripped the side of the table until the conversation was finished. If she chatted to another man at a party, it was all he could do not to drag him outside by the tie. He phoned her six, ten, twelve times a day to check what she was doing. He knew it was going to destroy them. He tried to be rational. When they were together, alone, they were so happy. There were no threats. But there were rafts of time when they weren't together, when she was left to her own devices. He worked long hours, and during those long hours the jealousy gnawed away at him.

He was constantly looking for clues. He never found any proof, but then he knew she would be clever. He tortured himself, thinking of all the people she could have come into contact with during the day. All the opportunities she might have had for a liaison. Or liaisons – why should she stop at one? His questions, his traps, grew more feverish, and she grew more resentful.

'Why is it so hard for you to believe I'm faithful? Do you really think so little of me? Or think I think so little of you?'

Eventually, his mistrust wore her down so much that she began to drink more and more. By the time he got home at night, she had already started on the wine, to inure herself to his line of questioning. He saw only one possible reason for that: she was guilty. She was having an affair. She protested her innocence, then gave him an ultimatum. Back off, or she would leave. He was appalled. He begged forgiveness. In the end, she had to give in to him.

She was pregnant.

The year Justine was born was their happiest. Benedict could relax, because while Jeanne was pregnant she was out of bounds to other men. And the first six months after the baby was born were bliss. Jeanne was so involved in being a mother she scarcely left the house. Eventually, however, she emerged from the post natal fuddle and ventured out into the world. His paranoia re-emerged. He was aware that motherhood had made her even more attractive – riper, more rounded, womanly. She drove him crazy with desire, so she must have the same effect on every other red-blooded male she came into contact with.

She wanted to have a thirtieth birthday party. Benedict was reluctant. It was his worst scenario, her being the hostess, skipping from guest to guest. How could he reasonably prevent her from circulating? He tried everything to dissuade her from the idea, but she was adamant, even refusing the offer of a week in Bora Bora as an alternative.

'We haven't had a party since Justine was born,' she insisted. 'I've got my figure back. I want to be me again. I want to let my hair down.'

In the run-up to the party things were tense between them. He couldn't help it. He kept reading signs into what she was doing. When she showed him the emerald silk dress she had chosen, he couldn't help feeling she had picked it with some-one else in mind. Repeatedly he told himself he was being irrational, that he would lose her if he didn't get a grip on his emotions. He promised himself he wouldn't let it spoil the party. She was right – she deserved to have fun. She was doing such a wonderful job of bringing up their daughter. He was immensely proud of them. If he didn't get a grip, he would lose them both. This was a sobering thought indeed, and Benedict resolved to relax. If she spoke to another man, so what? It was his bed she would climb into at the end of the night.

He knew the moment he set eyes on them talking. The man was leaning casually up against the wall, looking at her sleepily, his hand curled around his glass. There was a familiarity between them that didn't just come from having had a few cocktails. And as Jeanne walked away, he watched the man watching her, proprietorial lust in his eyes.

He could scarcely wait until the last guest was gone before he hurled accusations at her. She hurled back denials.

'Do you know what? I wish I was fucking him. Because I'm being punished enough for it. I might as well.'

She left the room. Benedict lay back on the bed, exhausted. It was too late to call her back and apologise. He knew he should. He had behaved disgracefully, but it was only because he loved her so much. Maybe he should see a shrink. Other husbands didn't seem to have this overwhelming possessive-ness. He pulled the covers over his head and sought refuge in sleep, hating himself for his temper. He would make it up to her tomorrow, he thought drowsily. They would go some-where lovely for lunch with the baby. He thought of his little family with a warm glow as he drifted off into un-consciousness.

At this point in the story, Benedict halted. It was as vivid as if it had happened yesterday. He wasn't leaving any detail out. Justine had the right to know everything. He wanted her to know exactly how guilty he had been for everything that had followed. He could have given her the sanitised version, but what was the point?

She was staring at him, sitting upright, her arms clasped around her knees. She knew it wasn't going to be a happy ending.

'Go on,' she whispered.

He took a final slug of brandy. He wasn't going to white-wash himself, but he wasn't going to whitewash Jeanne either. The truth had been festering inside him for years, and he was ready to be judged. He had been judging himself for long enough, after all.

Someone came to wake him at half past five that morning. He couldn't remember who. A member of staff, a policeman, a paramedic – he had no idea. No recall. Jeanne had been found floating face down in the swimming pool, still in her green dress. There was a glass by a chair on the side of the pool smeared with her lipstick, next to her discarded shoes.

The post mortem showed that she had died with an excessive level of alcohol in her body. And that she had had sex several hours before she drowned.

Benedict looked at his daughter as he revealed the last piece of the puzzle. The piece that he could have held back, if he had wanted to, but it was the piece of information that redeemed him.

Jeanne and Benedict had not made love for three weeks.

It had been a double-edged sword, that piece of information. It made him realise that his fears hadn't been irrational, but the fact that his suspicions weren't unfounded, that she had been unfaithful, were hardly a consolation. And now he would never know if her drowning had simply been a terrible accident, or if she had tried to take her life because she was embroiled in a passionate but unrequited love affair, or if indeed he had driven her to seek solace in someone else's arms because of his paranoia. He never found out who the man at the party had been.

His way of dealing with it was to wipe Jeanne out of his life. He excised all trace of her. He changed all of his staff. He no longer mixed with the same friends. He paid someone very well to keep as much of the detail out of the press as possible. Even now, he paid someone a retainer to comb the Internet on a regular basis, erasing any mention of her, so that even if Justine chose to do some digging, she would never find anything.

Benedict finished his story, and waited for his daughter's judgement. If his confession meant losing her, then so be it. It was all he deserved.

For several moments, Justine didn't speak. She looked around her, bewildered, as if someone was going to come forward and tell her what to think. Then she turned to face Benedict, and he saw the tears glittering in her eyes.

'Oh Dad,' she said softly. 'That's so sad . . .'

And she reached out and held his face in her hands, and stroked his cheeks with her thumbs, and he realised she was wiping away his tears, tears that had remained unshed for all this time.

'It was an accident,' she told him. 'A terrible, tragic accident. There was no one to blame.'

There was everyone to blame. Him. Jeanne. They were all culpable. He'd been over it often enough in his head.

And then she pulled him into her arms as he wept, all the

grief and regret and sorrow pouring out of him at long last. And along with those emotions was an overwhelming sense of relief, that at last he had confessed, and that she wasn't going to punish him, his beautiful daughter. She understood.

Of course she understood.

She understood completely. The only thing he was guilty of was loving too much, with a passion that had engulfed him and driven him to near madness.

By asking Benedict about her mother, she had hoped to find a clue about the new person she had become. She had assumed that what she was going through was courtesy of character-istics she had inherited from Jeanne. Now she realised that she was replicating her father – the man she had thought so strong, so self-sufficient.

Her father's story was a lesson to her. She was going to have to tread carefully on her journey with Violet. Already she had felt the emotions he described – the sense of wanting to possess someone entirely, the sickening dread when they spoke to someone else, the desperation when they were out of sight and all the time questions: how did they feel, what were they doing, would they come back . . . ?

Benedict had stopped weeping now. He sat back on the sofa, drained.

'Sorry . . .' he muttered, then gave an embarrassed laugh as he wiped away the last of his tears with his sleeve. It was a moving gesture, almost childlike, and Justine felt tears catch again at the back of her throat.

He put his hand over hers and gave it a tight squeeze, gathering strength as much as giving it.

'Why today?' he asked curiously. 'What made you ask me today?'

She opened her mouth to tell him, then decided against it. Something told her now was not the time to deliver such a shock, when she had no real idea where she stood or where she was going.

'I don't know,' she replied eventually. 'Maybe it was . . . seeing Delilah with all her daughters. It just made me wonder . . .'

They sat for a while in silence, Justine curled under the crook of his arm.

Benedict sensed she was lying. Something had happened to change his daughter. He could tell. He hoped she hadn't been hurt, or wasn't going to be. He felt a flash of protectiveness – that familiar searing pain in his gut, different from the one he had felt for his wife, but all-consuming nevertheless.

He wasn't going to let any harm come to Justine. He wasn't going to let any bastard harm a single hair on her head. She might not be forthcoming, but Benedict had ways of finding things out. If there was someone out there with the power to hurt his daughter, he would know soon enough.

Twenty

It was the day Raf was due to decamp to Bath to start work on *Something for the Weekend*, and for the first time in her life, Delilah thought that perhaps today she just wouldn't get up. Her limbs felt heavy, and every thought that made its way into her head was unwelcome. She didn't feel ill. Just overwhelmed. She genuinely didn't see the point in throwing back the duvet. She wanted to snuggle back under the protective cloak of white linen and goose-down and float away to oblivion.

There had been a hideous, horrible piece in one of the papers after Coco's screening. An immensely unflattering photo of Delilah coming out of The Melksham looking puffy and bloated. She wasn't puffy and bloated, not at all, but the camera angle, and the fact that she had had her head down, made her look as jowly as Doug the Pug. The long grey silk cardigan over wide-legged trousers that looked chicly sleek in the mirror transformed her into a ship in full sail when seen through a lens.

The strap-line had read: *Who Ate All the Pies?*

She knew she should brush it off. She knew she didn't look old and fat but had been caught unawares by a photographer determined to make her look her worst, and that no effort had been made to improve her appearance. And she knew what this meant.

The tide was turning. They were out to get her. This was the start. Whereas once she had been revered as a national treasure, now she was going to be an easy target, over-shadowed by her ravishing daughters. The spiteful copy would increase tenfold. There would be competition as to who could photograph her at her worst. There would be speculation about her state of mind, her marriage, her health. They wouldn't be happy until they had destroyed her. She'd seen it so many times before. While you were a success, you thought you were immune. But nobody was immune. She didn't know who decided it was your turn for a downfall. It happened almost as if by osmosis. But it was her turn. She could feel it in her bones.

And once *they* – whoever *they* were, those nameless, faceless arbiters of destiny – had decided your card was marked, you began to fulfil their prophecy. Loss of confidence, paranoia, ill-chosen decisions all combined to hasten your fall from grace.

She tried to breathe deeply to suppress her rising panic. There was no one she could turn to for reassurance. Everyone around her was paid to be nice. Polly, Tony, Miriam – they all had a huge vested interest in her continued success. If she voiced her fears, their response would be biased.

And Raf. She couldn't turn to him either, even though she had steered him through the most spectacular downfall. The difference was that he had engineered that downfall – it had been entirely of his own making. The press at the time hadn't decided to de-throne him; he had done it for himself. They had recorded it all, of course, but they hadn't actually brought it about. And now they were preparing themselves for his resurrection.

Maybe there wasn't room for two on the throne? Maybe she had to sacrifice herself to make way for him? There was already a sea-change in Raf that she found difficult to cope with. He had a new energy to him. Where once her phone had rung all day, now it was his. Production assistants, wardrobe girls, people asking about dates, accommodation, costumes, his dietary preferences. The production company had sent him a welcome hamper from Daylesford Organic, stuffed with all sorts of culinary delights to take with him on location. Couriers with updated scripts arrived at all hours. A photographer came to do a portrait shot for the publicity. And he seemed to be out for lunch or dinner every day of the week. Not that Delilah wasn't able to go if she wanted, but she knew how dull it was sitting in on someone else's gig. The old adage don't mix business with pleasure always hit home.

Her phone, in the meantime, was suspiciously quiet. She had finished shooting her latest series, and was battling to finish the next book. So she was in a fallow period. People should still be ringing her, though. She was on everyone's wish list. Wasn't she?

There was no doubt that the focus at The Bower had shifted.

Delilah hated herself for minding. She wasn't so shallow and self-centred that she had to be the star of the show all the time. Or was she? Maybe all those years of being top bitch, the one that ruled the roost, had affected her. Made her think that she was the one the world revolved around.

And the resonance of Violet's words were still stinging. Her daughter hadn't phoned to apologise, or even defend her slur. In fact, none of them had phoned for days. They were wrapped up in their own worlds. She was no longer needed.

Until they needed a handout, or a favour, she told herself bitterly. One or other of them would be on the phone sooner or later.

She stared up at the Abigail Ahern chandelier that swung over her bed. On her feet lay Doug the Pug, a dead weight, wheezing gently.

Come on, she told herself. Get up and go into the gym. Do a workout, eat some fruit, drink some water, have a shower, get dressed. You'll feel better.

She still didn't move. She could hear Polly and Tony talking to Raf downstairs in the kitchen. She didn't want to know about what. She was pretty sure it wouldn't be her. Laughter floated up the stairwell. There's nothing worse than other people's laughter when you are feeling below par. She felt a nasty twitch in her gut; a slightly burning sensation. Was she ill? Had she eaten something, or caught a bug? Maybe that would explain her lassitude. As she ran over what she had had for dinner last night, a slow realisation hit her. The boiling acid in her stomach wasn't food-related.

It was jealousy.

Once more she felt the overwhelming urge to throw the duvet over her head. But she couldn't. This was Raf's big day. She didn't want to look like a sour-faced old bag, even if that was what she felt like. With a Herculean effort, she extricated her feet from underneath Doug and got out of bed.

Delilah waited until Raf was lining his cases up in the hall ready to put into the boot of the Maserati before presenting him with her farewell gift. She dangled it in front of him with a grin.

He took it from her, puzzled.

'What this?'

'The key to the most gorgeous bachelor pad in the Royal Crescent. You will absolutely love it.'

'But Dickie's sorted the accommodation. He's rented a house on the outskirts of Bath.'

'It looks horrible. Didn't you see the details he emailed?' Delilah was disparaging. 'Half the rooms haven't even got their own bathroom, for heaven's sake.'

'I don't mind—'

'What if I want to come and stay?'

'It's perfectly good enough.'

'And you're going to have to share the kitchen with everyone else.'

'So? It's me that's got to stay there. If I'm happy with it, what's the problem?'

'If you're going to be away from home for three months then you need decent accommodation. And your own space. This is perfect. It's got all the mod cons; there's even a mini-gym in the spare room.'

'No.' Raf shook his head, his lips tight. 'We're on a strict budget. Of course Dickie would love to put us all up in some Regency shag palace, but he can't afford to—'

'I'm not expecting him to pay. I've dealt with it.'

Raf knew this tone in Delilah's voice. It meant she had made up her mind. Well, this time he was going to dig his heels in. He had become used to her making all the decisions over the past few years. He'd been happy to go along with it – she had such firm opinions about things, and he usually wasn't bothered about details. This, however, was a point of principle.

'I'm sorry, but I'm staying with the rest of the guys. It'll look bad if I don't. Besides, I don't want to be stuck in some flat on my own.'

'But I've paid for it up front.'

'Tough.' They stared each other out for a moment. They rarely argued like this, but Raf knew that if he didn't stand his ground, she would get her way. He felt very strongly about this. He'd be seen as an absolute wanker if he distanced himself from the others. Surely she could see that? 'It's out of the question. I'm sorry.'

He gave the key back to her. She threw it down on the hall table and he could see there were tears in her eyes.

'I thought you'd be pleased.'

'It was a really nice thought. But I'm not doing it.'

'So what do I do with an empty flat in Bath for three months?'

He was itching to say she should have asked him before she booked it.

'You could probably sublet it.'

She put her face in her hands. She was crying. Raf felt unsettled. Delilah rarely cried like this. She cried at happy things, and when something moved her, but not over day-to-day trivia.

'What's the matter?'

'Why won't anyone let me help any more?' she sobbed.

'What do you mean?'

'All of you. You're just pushing me away.'

'Rubbish.'

'You are! Coco used to call me all the time – every day – but she never does any more. Violet won't let me help her with her music. And Tyger's totally wrapped up in Louis.' Even as she said it, Delilah realised she sounded self-pitying.

'Delilah, they're grown-ups. They don't need you any more. Not so much, anyway.'

She looked up at him.

'They'll need me when it all goes wrong. You watch.'

Raf looked at her evenly.

'Well, let's hope it doesn't. You should be happy you've brought up three independent, free-spirited girls.'

'I know, I know, but it's hard.' She sniffed. 'And . . . I'm going to miss you.'

There. She'd said it. That was what was really bothering her. What on earth was she going to do without Raf around?

'Hey, come on.' He drew her into his arms. 'We all love you, you know we do.' He started to kiss her. Her hair, her cheek, then her mouth. As he became more ardent, she pushed him away with a nervous laugh.

'That's enough. I've got to go and do some work. I want to finish another chapter by lunchtime . . .'

And she edged out of the room.

Raf watched her go, then turned back to his suitcases with a sigh. He didn't know what was the matter with her at the moment. Pressure of work, he supposed, but she didn't have to keep pushing him away like that. She'd never been one of those wives who was too tired, or had a headache. He always felt sorry for men who complained about not getting any action. He'd never had that problem with Delilah – there was a time when she couldn't go more than a couple of hours without seeking him out, luring him up to the bedroom. Or not even bothering with that – the island in the kitchen had sufficed on many an occasion. Just recently, however, she almost seemed to recoil.

He carried his cases out to the car, stacking them neatly in the boot. It was difficult to know how much to take, but he could always pick up more stuff when he came home at weekends. If he came home . . .

Raf would never have said anything to Delilah, but he was really looking forward to three months away. Three whole months of being his own person, with his own identity. Able to make decisions that wouldn't be over-ruled, plans that wouldn't be changed. He could do what he liked without having to check Delilah's diary. He could wear what he liked, without her suggesting a different shirt or another pair of shoes.

He still adored his wife. Of course he did. But he couldn't deny he was relishing the prospect of no longer being Mr Delilah Rafferty.

Polly sat in the office, fiddling with the stapler. She had just finished collating all the paperwork that Raf would have to take with him. She'd waded through all the stuff that had been sent by the production company, chucking out all the boring bits about health and safety, and putting all the relevant information in the smart, leather-bound file she had got him.

She felt immensely tearful. She couldn't pin down why. Whether it was over-work. Or general exhaustion. Or PMT. Or the fact that she had got on the scales this morning and had put on two pounds.

Or was it just the simple fact that today Raf was going? The day she had been dreading for weeks. It was going to be so strange without him. Whatever else was going on, Polly knew that she could always chill out with him in the kitchen over a cup of coffee. That he was always calm and kind and considerate, and managed to cheer her up if she was feeling a bit glum. Delilah and the girls were sweet, but they did take her for granted a little bit. In their eyes, she was good old Polly Wolly, whereas Raf treated her like a human being.

She picked up the file. And the good luck card she had bought him in Paperchase, which now seemed a little bit silly.

If she found him now, she could rush straight off to the post office with that day's mail, before she made a fool of herself and started crying. Which she could well do.

Raf was in the hall. He'd just come in from packing his stuff in the car.

She handed him the file.

'This is everything important that you need,' she told him. 'Shooting schedules, maps, travel arrangements, contact details. And the script.'

'Thanks, Polly. What would I do without you?'

'And here.' She handed him the card with a shy smile.

He opened it and read it. She hadn't been sure how many kisses to put. If any. In the end she had put two.

'That's lovely,' he told her, tucking it into his jacket pocket. 'I'll put it up in my bedroom.'

He held out his arms and she gave him a huge hug, breathing in his smell for the last time.

Not for the last time, she told herself. Don't be so melodramatic.

'Look after everyone for me, Poll,' he told her, and she nodded. That was what she was here for, after all. To look after everyone.

'Don't do anything I wouldn't do,' she croaked, thinking that wouldn't restrict him in the least. After all, what mischief did podgy, plain old dumpling Polly Fry ever get up to?

Delilah was hiding in the downstairs cloakroom. Where else could she go in her own home and have a good howl? She couldn't go back up to the bedroom, because Raf was running in and out for things he had forgotten. She couldn't go into the office — Polly and Tony would wonder what on earth the matter was. She could hear the housekeeper clattering about in the kitchen. The gardener was jet-washing the terrace. She put her head down, tears plopping onto the black and white tiles.

She had the world at her feet and nowhere to cry.

'Dee!' Raf was shouting from the hall. 'Delilah – I'm almost ready to go. Where are you?'

She looked in the mirror over the sink. She didn't think she looked much different to the day she had met him twenty-five years ago. A few lines around the eyes, the skin slightly less luminous. But inside, she felt totally changed. She felt as if a light had been turned off. As if it was all over, somehow. Nothing to look forward to. Everything had been achieved. The lustre had gone from her life. It was all her heart could do to keep beating, it felt so heavy. It was as though it was asking what was the point of pushing her blood round her body any longer. She'd served her purpose.

She picked up the lipstick she kept on the shelf and painted on a smile. Fluffed up her hair. Straightened her shoulders. She better make an effort for Raf, or he might not come back.

Twenty-One

Raf felt his heart soar as he drove from the motorway towards Bath, looking down into the deep green bowl studded with pale ginger houses. If you were going to be stranded anywhere for three months, Bath was as good a place as any, he reckoned. As the steep, winding hill dropped down into the city, and he began to negotiate the traffic-filled streets, he marvelled at the architecture, the splendour, the grandeur of the place. It must have been breath-taking in the days before cars, when all the stone was mellow yellow and not stained grey by pollution. It still looked magnificent even now, the handsome Georgian façades and the more ornate Victorian villas interspersed with the necessities of modern life – garage forecourts, blocks of flats, traffic lights. He spied interesting shops he would take time to visit, little restaurants that looked inviting, and he felt a flutter of excitement – the same feeling he got on the first day of a holiday, with the prospect of so many places to discover and get to know.

The sat-nav guided him calmly through the streets and up a steep hill, then past the magnificent splendour of the Royal Crescent, the curved row of four-storey houses facing the immaculate green. For a moment Raf wondered if he was mad to turn down Delilah's offer. It would be wonderful to live there, if only for a short time, to be part of the history of this architectural masterpiece. No, he told himself. The decision he had made had been the right one. He was part of a team. They were all going to pull together to make this movie a resounding success.

Eventually he was told he had reached his destination. It might not be as grand as the Royal Crescent, but Collingwood was still pleasing to the eye. Set squarely in its own grounds, Raf warmed to the house at once. He drove in through the sturdy stone pillars, crunched over the pale yellow chippings and parked.

A pleasant woman of around thirty came out and introduced herself as the housekeeper.

'You're the first to arrive,' she beamed, 'so you get first dibs.'

Raf explored the house with a childlike excitement so he could choose his room. It was an easy decision to make in the end, and it didn't make him look as if he had bagged the best. He didn't want the biggest, or either of the ones with their own en-suite. He wanted the attic room at the top of the house, the one with a tiny castellated balcony that looked out over the garden and the roofs of the city beyond, so he could sit there at night and wonder what people were doing under those roofs, and what the people who had lived there before had done. He put his suitcases on the bed, threw open the window and breathed in, as the housekeeper brought him a cup of tea and two shortbread biscuits on a tray.

'You won't be getting this every day, I'm afraid,' she told him. 'I'll just be in twice a week to clear up after you.'

Raf took the tea gratefully, thinking that actually it would be wonderful not to have people underfoot all the time. You couldn't put a cup down in The Bower without it being whisked away and put in the dishwasher – only at the week-ends, when the staff didn't come in unless there was a special occasion. He'd always relished the peace and quiet and the reassuring clutter that built up over those two days. He liked finding yesterday's newspaper where he had left it, not folded away and put in the recycling before he'd had a chance to finish it.

He put his tea down on the bedside table, stretched out on the bed with his arms behind his head.

The peace and quiet was wonderful. He supposed the

housekeeper was somewhere about, but he couldn't hear her. There were no phones ringing, no hoovers, no dog barking, no chatter. He could actually hear himself think.

He took out his copy of the script. It was well thumbed and tattered by now. He had scrawled notes all over it. On the back, he had drawn the arc of Hugo's journey throughout the story – his high points and low points. He'd written down ideas about what books and films he might like, what hobbies he might have, a little biography of his past – stuff that might never actually be seen on screen, but helped him get a broader picture of who this man was.

He'd been shopping with the wardrobe girl the week before, to assemble Hugo's wardrobe, and had enjoyed arguing with her over the finer points. Raf was a perfectionist who believed that the devil was in the detail – everything, down to the last button, had to be right. He was adamant that Hugo was the sort of man who would always get things slightly wrong – as a result he knew that he wouldn't be taking home any of the clothes they ended up buying after the shoot was over. They'd had a real laugh, collapsing into giggles in various shops in Covent Garden as Raf emerged from the changing rooms looking like a middle-aged raver – trousers slightly too tight, shirts a bit too garish. By the end of the day Raf felt confident that he had nailed the character down sartorially – though the hardest bit was yet to come. The day before they started actual filming, he was going to have to have his hair cut in a suitably Hugo-esque style. He'd been growing out his trademark crop in anticipation, but wasn't relishing three months looking like an idiot. Such was the price of fame, he thought to himself.

Mind you, it was going to be worth it. He couldn't believe how much he was looking forward to working again. At last his life would have some momentum. He would have satisfaction at the end of the day, and anticipation at the beginning, neither of which he had really felt for years. He had been existing in a vacuum. There had been times when he couldn't see the point of getting up in the morning. The world certainly wouldn't have stopped turning if he hadn't. Only through a monumental effort of will, and the realisation that he had already put Delilah and the girls through enough hell, did he manage to drag himself out from between the sheets.

This time around, he was going to be fully aware of what he was doing. In the past, he hadn't bothered with researching his characters, and looking back now he couldn't believe how arrogant he had been, just winging it, and how lucky he had been to get away with it. He must have been a nightmare to work with. He remembered resolutely refusing to discuss motivation with the directors. 'I'll just do it,' he used to say, and he did, and to be fair his performances had always been right on the button, but it had been a huge risk.

The thought of doing it that way now made him shudder. This film was going to be all about teamwork, he decided, as if in some way he could atone for his previous neglect.

Raf felt his toes starting to curl, as they always did when he burrowed about in the past. He leapt up off the bed. He wasn't going to look back. He was going to look forward. He had even, momentarily, toyed with the idea of changing his name for his on-screen credit, dropping the Raf and going with his real name, Richard, the name no one ever called him, just to make it clear to both himself and the world that he and that other despicable person were poles apart. Miriam had persuaded him otherwise – it looked cowardly, and although he might harbour strong feelings of resentment towards the old Raf, he still had a lot of admirers out there.

'Don't turn your back on who you were,' she told him. 'That person has made you who you are today.'

He remembered with distaste his ritual on arriving for a shoot in the old days. By now he would have been propping up the bar, or stocking up on vodka to stash in his digs. He would have worked out where the nearest pub was, and sniffed out the fellow cast members whom he could lead astray so he wouldn't feel alone, feeding on their weakness to mask his own.

Today, by contrast, he was going to take a stroll into Bath, get the feel of the place where his character lived, see if he could work out where he shopped, where he took his wife for their anniversary meal. And it was a far, far better feeling than the drunken oblivion he would have been heading for in the past.

Dickie Rushe was throwing a first-night dinner for the cast and crew at Bablake House. He was paying for it himself, because the budget they were on didn't run to luxuries like dinner in five-star establishments, but he felt it was important to make his team feel important. And there was nothing like getting drunk together for bonding.

Not that they were all going to get drunk. He was very conscious of protecting Raf's sensibilities, and had rung him before booking it.

'Look, I want to give everyone the chance to let their hair down and get to know each other. But if it's going to make you feel uncomfortable . . .' He gave a nervous laugh. 'There will be drinking involved.'

Raf just laughed.

'Dickie, I'm used to it. And I actually enjoy watching everyone fall apart on these occasions. It's great people-watching. You go for it. And I'd like to cover the bar bill. Anonymously, of course.'

Dickie hung up the phone, relieved and touched by Raf's generous gesture. He was going to be wonderful to work with. He couldn't wait.

Bablake House was a Palladian mansion set in the Somerset countryside five miles outside Bath. It had established itself as an out-of-town playground for the city's elite, with a country club atmosphere that was decidedly unstuffy. It was going to be used as one of the locations in the film so they gave Dickie a great rate on their ballroom, and worked him out a menu that was delicious but wasn't going to break the bank – huge platters of antipasti (mozzarella, figs, prosciutto, char-grilled peppers and olives), herby roast chicken and baked peaches with amaretti. The barman created a special '*Something for the Weekend*' cocktail, with elderflower and prosecco. It was far more important, Dickie always thought, to have a great kick-off than a wrap party. Once you had wrapped, the damage had been done, but a memorable morale-booster at the beginning worked wonders.

At seven o'clock that evening, he was standing in the room he had booked for himself. As the director he had to stay until the bitter end, and he wanted to be able to crawl upstairs, not wait for a taxi to take him back to their digs. His stomach was churning. He went into the bathroom, threw up neatly into the gleaming white porcelain of the state-of-the-art toilet, flushed and did his teeth. This was it – this was really it. His film was about to start taking shape.

For a moment he wished he had someone to share his anxiety with. There had been a girl once, a very special girl, but he had blown it, with his obsession, his introspection, his inability to think about anything much apart from work. He had paid a high price all right. He thought back to that face he had loved, and the last time he had seen it, streaked with tears, as she had walked away.

He put the lid back on his toothpaste and squared his shoulders. Of course he had regrets, but he had made his choice. For the time being, *Something for the Weekend* was the love of his life.

He pulled a white shirt out of his suitcase. He'd actually made the effort to go and buy something new. He owed his team that much at least. He took it out of his cellophane wrapping, shook out the creases as best he could and slipped it over his head, tucking it into the waistband of his jeans. He ruffled his hair with his fingers, slipped on his glasses and headed for the door. Then stopped. He needed to be sick again. Once tonight was over, he'd be fine. It was just first-night nerves.

*

In a room down the corridor, Genevieve was rubbing Laura Mercier primer into her skin before applying her foundation. She too had booked a room. She was jolly glad she had. The accommodation at Bablake House was charming. Stripped back, fresh and luxurious – the best linen sheets, brightly coloured mohair blankets, a wonderful claw-footed bath by the window that looked out onto the rolling hills. A mini-bar stuffed with all sorts of enticing witticisms – designer jelly babies, for heaven's sake. And any number of gorgeous toiletries, including, she noticed sensual massage oil. And a very discreet pack of condoms in the bedside table. Not that she had much use for those these days – the risk of her reproducing was pretty much nil – but she supposed sex, if she were to have it, should be safe.

She needed to make sure she looked her best tonight. The character she was playing in the film was supposed to have gone to seed, which was the reason for her husband having an affair, but that didn't mean she had to look like a thick-waisted frump all the time. Hair, make-up, dowdy clothes and a bit of padding would transform her when she was filming, but off camera she was determined to look her radiant best. She didn't want anyone wondering why on earth she had been cast as Raf Rafferty's wife.

Even she felt rather tingly when she thought about Raf. Genevieve Duke, who had dallied with more of the nation's heart-throbs than anyone could count, found him mesmerising. He had a calm and laid-back manner that belied his former reputation, yet there was still a flash of the rebel in him – the way he laughed at something, a dry and off-the-cuff remark, a gleam in his eye.

Raf Rafferty was definitely a challenge. She wanted to prove to herself that she could still cut it. She didn't want to wreck his marriage. Far from it. She just wanted irrefutable proof that she was irresistible. Delilah's blithe assumption that he wouldn't be tempted had spurred her on. Besides, there was nothing Genevieve liked more than seducing attractive men.

The ensuing affairs were usually brief but intense, and they gave her a renewed vigour for life. Until the next one.

She'd seen Raf Rafferty look at his wife adoringly. But she could also see he was kept on a pretty tight rein. It was screamingly obvious that Delilah wore the trousers in The Bower. And Genevieve had done her research. This was going to be Raf's first time away from home for years. And once an infidel, always an infidel. In her experience – which was, by anyone's standards, pretty vast.

She didn't feel guilty about Jeremy. She wasn't being unfaithful, because she'd never promised him fidelity. She'd never promised anyone fidelity. They were just . . . what was the term? Fuck buddies. Friends, good friends, who enjoyed each other's company and sometimes found solace in each other's bodies, with no strings.

She stood in front of the mirror. Dressing was a layering process. First, her underwear. Kiki de Montparnasse. The bra boosted her cleavage to inviting rather than obscene, the briefs covered her arse in a perfect fit, nothing digging in or spilling over the edges. Over that she slipped on a sexy, pinstriped Vivienne Westwood skirt: she loved Vivienne's clothes, they had a twist to them that the more mature woman could get away with because they were so fabulously cut. She teamed it with a scoop-necked black cashmere sweater with short sleeves, and a towering pair of Terry de Havilland snakeskin wedges that made her legs seem endless. She finished the look with smoky-grey eyes and a swipe of red lipstick.

She examined herself critically in the mirror. Yep. Sophisticated, alluring, knowing. She hadn't lost her touch.

Pandora Hammond made people realise that any woman they had considered beautiful in the past was merely pretty. A cloud of dark hair hung just past her shoulders, and her face peeped out from amidst the curls, her skin paler than pale, the whites of her eyes dazzling, her irises the colour of violets. She seemed fragile, yet she had perfectly proportioned breasts and hips, making her feminine, not just a coat-hanger. She was the sort of girl who made men want to throw their cloaks over the merest puddle. She should have been in a low-slung sports-car hurtling along a perilous road in the Pyrenees, or in the casino of a hotel in Monaco, or sipping cocktails on the terrace of a Cape Cod beach house.

She knew this film was her turning-point. She was already being fêted as the one to watch. The quality magazines – *Vogue*, *Tatler*, *Vanity Fair* – had all done features on her, fawning over her beauty and her potential. Pandora knew that this sort of puff was all very well, but you could fade into oblivion pretty quickly if you didn't make your mark. She was banking on *Something for the Weekend* to send her into the stratosphere.

'It's such a wonderful script,' she had told the press, 'and the chance to work with Genevieve Duke and Raf Rafferty? It's a dream come true. I know I'm going to learn so much from them.'

She was standing awkwardly now at the edge of the ball-room at Bablake House, glass in hand. Her dress was a simple silk shift, purple shot through with gold, that she'd had made up in Hong Kong while shooting her most recent film. Apart from Dickie and the casting director, she knew no one. A lot of the crew had worked together before, so there were shouts of recognition and people clapping each other on the back. It was often like this at the beginning of a shoot. You felt conspicuous, the new girl that no one wanted to talk to, but by the end of the evening they would all be best friends. It took everyone a few drinks to start mingling, but it would happen. She took another sip of her elderflower cocktail, reminding herself not to drink *too* much in case she let her guard down. It might be fun, but it was enormously damaging. The paps were always after pictures of stars looking worse for wear, flashing their gussets as they got into a cab. Pandora wanted to look as fresh at the end of the evening as she did at the beginning. Not for her spider-web eyes and blotchy skin.

She checked out her surroundings while she waited for

Dickie to arrive. She loved the bar, which was covered in quilted white leather, the tongue-in-cheek papier mâché hunting trophies on the walls, the funky Italian bar stools. She wished she could have booked a room here for the duration of the shoot, but the main cast had been billeted in a house in the city. She'd checked in there earlier. There hadn't been anyone else around, and she'd had a moment of homesickness as she unpacked her clothes and hung them up. She hadn't had the nerve to knock on any of the other doors, so she'd got changed quickly and called a taxi to take her to the party.

It was going to be fine, she told herself. Everyone else was probably as nervous as she was.

'You must be Pandora.'

Someone touched her on the arm and she nearly jumped out of her skin. She turned, and looked into a pair of the bluest eyes she had ever seen. They crinkled at her in a smile of greeting.

'Sorry – I didn't mean to make you jump. I'm Raf. I don't know a soul here,' he said as he leaned in confidentially, 'so can I talk to you?'

It was one thing seeing a person on television or in a magazine and imagining what they were like in real life. It was another when they were there in front of you, living and breathing, exuding a charisma and sexuality that you could almost smell, yet so totally understated, dressed in black linen jeans and a pale blue shirt.

Pandora felt quite giddy as she took his hand.

'Yes, of course. Yes, I'm Pandora. Hammond. It's lovely to meet you. Can I get you a cocktail . . . ?' Fuck. He didn't drink. What a complete idiot. How could she have forgotten? It was always the first thing that was mentioned in articles about him. 'I mean, can I get you something to drink? A soft drink . . .'

Shut up, Pandora! She was making it worse. She blushed beetroot at her faux pas. How totally uncool. Just because he didn't do alcohol didn't mean she couldn't offer him a drink. He didn't seem bothered, though. Just grinned.

'I've got my own jug of elderflower cordial behind the bar,' he replied.

Pandora took another glug of her cocktail to calm her nerves and racked her brain for something to say next. She wasn't a stupid girl, she'd got a first-class honours degree in drama from Bristol University, but she felt completely starstruck and tongue-tied. She'd better get over it. Tomorrow she was going to be working with this man. Playing his mistress.

'It's always nerve-racking, isn't it? The first night? I always feel so self-conscious. Of course, what I used to do is get totally and utterly bladdered, but I can't any more,' Raf confided.

Pandora found herself melting even more. What a lovely man. Self-deprecating, unstarry, down-to-earth. She managed to find her tongue.

'Have you been to the house we're staying in?' she asked. 'It's not bad.'

He nodded. 'It's going to be great. Like being students. I hope you've put your name on your Marmite.'

Pandora giggled, and felt a huge wave of relief. This wasn't going to be so difficult after all. Raf was going to be a joy to work with.

'Darling.' There was a low, sexy growl behind them. Pandora turned to see Genevieve Duke. She radiated stardom and effortless glamour as she kissed Raf on both cheeks. 'Have you been to the house yet? Is it grim? I've checked in here for tonight – I want one last night of luxury.'

She ignored Pandora completely.

'The house is lovely. Pandora and I were just saying what fun it's going to be . . .' Raf chivalrously brought her into the conversation. 'Pandora, this is Genevieve. Genevieve, Pandora.'

Genevieve turned and held out her hand. She smiled, but her eyes didn't. As lovely and easy-going as Raf was, Pandora instinctively knew she was going to have her work cut out with Genevieve.

'I'm so thrilled to be working with you, Miss Duke,' she breathed.

It was the subtlest of slights. Referring to her as Miss Duke was respectful on the surface, but was a thinly disguised dig at the fact that Genevieve was twice her age. Pandora met her icy gaze with a beguiling smile, safe in the knowledge that she had scored the first point in the battle that was inevitable.

Luckily at that moment Dickie bumbled up.

'Oh good, you've all found each other. Now listen, you're going to hate me for this but I'm not going to allow you to stick together in a clique just because you're the stars . . .'

Pandora didn't miss Genevieve looking at her askance.

'. . . I'm going to force you all to circulate. There's going to be no hierarchy on this set. Everyone's equal.'

Pandora raised her glass to her lips.

'Only some are more equal than others,' she murmured, and heard Raf give a little snort beside her. She felt a thrill at this gesture of solidarity. She wasn't going to let Genevieve Duke put her in her place.

Genevieve wasn't taken in by Pandora Hammond for a second. That naive, fragile, haven't-a-clue-what's-happening thing she had going on? It was utter bollocks. She was as disingenuous as they come, totally calculating, ruthlessly ambitious.

How did she know? Because she recognised herself, that was how. That trick of catching someone's eye, smiling bashfully, then looking away, slightly distracted, as if you had something of vital importance on your mind? Genevieve had perfected that look more than thirty years ago. The trick of leaning into a man as he spoke to you, nodding thoughtfully, lashes lowered? That was the best way to get him to notice your cleavage that she knew of. That dress that looked so demure on the surface, but was surprisingly revealing if one knew where to peer, so a man felt he had sneaked a free glimpse of your breast or your thigh? Genevieve had worked that look for years. Still did. She knew that subtle worked far better than overt. She knew that Pandora knew that if you stood behind her, in a certain light, her frock was entirely see-through, but no one could accuse her of choosing it for that reason, as it looked perfectly respectable in a normal light. That walk, the slightly aimless drift with the little-girl-lost look? The wide-eyed expression of slight surprise? Oh please.

As they say, it takes one to know one.

What she also recognised, however, was that Pandora was more dangerous than she had ever been, because she was needy. She had it rolling off her. That was one thing Genevieve had never been. Too far the other way, some would have said. Frighteningly independent. Time and again men were shocked at how easily she accepted the end of an affair, and moved on to the next. She never allowed herself to get emotionally involved.

As soon as she had walked into the room she had seen them together. They were laughing, and they looked so right. In that split second she realised that she had no chance whatsoever with Raf while Pandora was around. She might be a revered actress with a raft of awards on her mantelpiece, she might still have a great pair of legs and an impressive embonpoint, she might still be upheld as a sex symbol by the press, but in the cold light of day she was no competition against youth and beauty.

It hurt. Oh how it hurt. It ripped through her in a savage swipe, eviscerating her. In one moment, her magic had gone. She would still be respected, but she no longer held men in her thrall. She had walked over some invisible finishing line and there was no going back.

She realised with a jolt that this was life imitating art. That this was how her character was supposed to feel, on seeing her husband with his mistress. Sour bile filled her mouth. She caught sight of her face in the mirrored backdrop of the bar.

How on earth could she have thought she was God's gift, or that she was in with a chance? She looked over-made-up, her skirt was too short, her heels were too high, her cleavage too exposed. She wanted to rush upstairs and change, wipe off her lipstick, come back down in something more fitting to a woman of her age.

As she stood in the middle of the room she suddenly felt invisible. Apart from Raf, she was probably the oldest person there by about twenty years. She looked around and the place was buzzing, full of people chattering and laughing – sound guys in their jeans and band T-shirts, girls from costume and make-up in gregarious huddles, people in black with trendy thick-rimmed glasses looking earnest, a gaggle of rebels on the terrace sharing cigarettes. Once she would have been surrounded, unable to move without someone asking if she wanted another drink.

What on earth was happening to her? She had never lacked confidence, never in her life. Not even when she was starting out. She had been a cocky, bolshy little madam from the very beginning. Now she felt frozen. She watched as Raf and Pandora worked the room independently. She felt petrified. Who was she going to walk up to? What was she supposed to say?

To her horror, she thought she might cry. She turned hastily to the bar before anyone could notice, and busied herself looking at the cocktail menu.

There was a tap on her shoulder.

'Genevieve?' It was Raf, looking at her, concerned. 'Come and join us.'

'We're not supposed to gang together,' she joked, just managing to keep the tremor out of her voice.

'Rubbish. Safety in numbers. Come on.'

He took her by the arm and led her into the throng. Genevieve didn't protest, but she felt mortified that Raf had obviously spotted her discomfort.

In that moment she vowed that she wouldn't let Pandora

Hammond get her claws into him. She knew exactly how the little puss would operate. She would use her affair with Raf Rafferty to push herself into the limelight and get into the gossip columns. It wouldn't do her any harm, but it would harm Raf. This was his chance to turn over a new leaf and prove himself. A sordid affair with a girl half his age would be great copy, but terrible for his reputation. As a happily married man, it could destroy him.

And it would certainly destroy Delilah.

For the first time in her life, Genevieve felt a strong urge of protectiveness for another woman. It was up to her to make sure that Delilah didn't get hurt. It wasn't just a question of sour grapes. Maybe she was trying to atone for all those years of affairs with married men? She may never have caused a marriage break-up, but there was no way her paramours hadn't gone home unchanged. Looking back on it now, she felt grubby. How could she have been so smug? Stealing someone else's husband for the duration of a film shoot, for her own personal pleasure and gratification, was selfish and shallow. And where had it left her?

Alone. That's where it had left her. Alone, with a clutch of sordid conquests as memories. She felt her head throb. How tempting it was to excuse herself, slip away back up to the luxury of her bedroom and get into bed.

Then she caught sight of Pandora. She was looking across the room at Raf. She caught his eye, and gave him a little smile, together with a slight roll of the eyes, as if to say, *When can we get out of here?*

No way, baby, thought Genevieve. You're not going to get him that easily, not if I've got anything to do with it. She grabbed a full glass off the tray of a passing waiter, took in a deep breath and introduced herself to a group of young men huddled in a corner.

Moments later, she was gratified. Far from ignoring her, they fawned over her, competing with each other to name their favourite Genevieve Duke film. And when Raf passed nearby, she reached out a hand to draw him into the circle, and very quickly felt like her old self again.

It had been a momentary crisis of confidence, she told herself.

Nerves and shyness and being totally overwhelmed by meeting Raf, combined with having had little for lunch and less for supper, meant that Pandora had more to drink than she had intended. The problem with prosecco and elderflower was that it tasted so innocuous; before she knew it she had drunk five. Once you'd drunk five, all caution went to the winds. And of course, once you realised that, it was far, far too late to do anything about it.

She was standing by a tall palm by the French window leading out onto the terrace. Her head was swimming. She had met so many people; she was never going to remember all of their names. She put out a hand to steady herself against the wall. Her vision was a bit blurry. She really should try to get to the bar and get some water . . .

Moments later all she could hear was a babble of voices. One in particular cut through the rest.

'Take her up to my room. No, I insist. I can go back to the digs. It's no problem at all. Poor girl – nerves, I expect.'

Genevieve Duke? Wasn't that Genevieve Duke talking? Pandora opened her eyes and realised she was looking at the ceiling. Four of the crew were standing over her, about to lift her to her feet. Dickie was crouched by her, concerned.

'Can you speak, Pandora? Can you hear me?'

'Yes. Yes . . .' She could hear him, but really she just wanted to go back into the safe, warm tunnel she had been in a minute ago.

'Shit,' Dickie muttered to the first assistant director who was next to him. 'That's all I need, to lose one of my leading ladies on the first night.'

'She'll be fine. She's just had a skinful. Bit rough tomorrow, though.'

Were they talking about her? Pandora wondered dreamily as she felt herself being lifted up and carried across the ballroom.

Genevieve bit her lip to stop herself from smirking. She couldn't have stage-managed it better if she'd spiked the girl's drink herself. Raf appeared, concerned and anxious.

'You know what actresses are like these days. They don't eat, they're all on slimming tablets and anti-depressants, and they wonder why they keel over at the first sniff of a cork.'

'It was good of you to give her your room.'

Genevieve shrugged. 'Can't have her getting in a taxi in that state. She'll only throw up everywhere.'

Raf nodded agreement, and Genevieve felt pleased. If Raf didn't drink he was hardly going to be attracted to someone who'd shown herself up in public like that, and Pandora had certainly lost her charm. She hadn't looked such an enticing prospect, sprawled on the floor, her eyes rolling round in the back of her head.

The next morning Pandora crept into the rehearsal room in jeans, sneakers and a hoody, wearing Maui Jim sunglasses to shield her eyes from the bright light and hide the fact that they were hideously bloodshot. She had been in two minds whether to do a runner when she had woken up. She had put in a call to her agent and sobbed down the phone, then run away to be sick. Her agent called her back.

'You won't be the first and you won't be the last. And you're working with Raf Rafferty, for heaven's sake – he made Oliver Reed look positively abstemious.'

'I know, but he's so lovely and he doesn't drink at all now. He'll think I'm awful.'

'He'll think you're a bit silly, and by tomorrow it will all be forgotten. Get back on the horse, Pandora. Phone room service – get paracetamol, poached eggs on toast and a taxi to the rehearsal room. They'll be more pissed off if you're late than because you overdid it last night.'

She obeyed, of course, because the alternative – total humiliation at the hands of the press – was worse. But only just. She tried to sneak into a seat unnoticed, but Raf spotted her straight away. He came and gave her a huge hug.

'I'm so embarrassed. I'm so sorry . . .'

'Don't be. I've got three daughters. I've seen worse, let me tell you.'

He handed her a can of Coke and a bag of jam doughnuts.

'My secret cure. Trust me – you'll feel better in an hour. You're talking to an expert.'

When Genevieve arrived, she found Pandora and Raf sitting together. Pandora jumped up straight away.

'Miss Duke – I just want to say thank you for letting me have your room last night. And apologise – I feel such an idiot—'

'Darling, we've all done it. Got over-excited on the first night. Haven't we?' She looked at Raf for affirmation.

'Yes, we have and I bloody well miss it,' he admitted, and Pandora hugged him.

'You're just saying that to be nice. Oh God, there's Dickie. I'd better go and apologise.'

She ran across the room. Genevieve watched after her, eyes narrowed. It was going to be harder than she thought, keeping this girl in her place. She had a magical charm that worked on everyone, it seemed, except her. Raf was watching after her soupily.

'It's good of you to keep an eye on her,' she remarked, hating herself for sounding waspish. 'You must be missing your daughters.'

By lunchtime, it was apparent to everyone that the chemistry between Raf and Pandora was spectacular. As they read through the script, they barely needed to act. The seduction of Hugo by Pandora's character Saskia was scorching hot and entirely believable. And Genevieve didn't have to try hard to portray the wronged wife. She was genuinely tight-lipped and boot-faced.

At the end of the day, Dickie thanked everyone with the broadest of smiles on his face.

'This is going to be a winner,' he proclaimed to them all. 'I am so proud of everyone. We're going to have a hit on our hands. I can feel it in my bones.'

Twenty-Two

The waiter from Wild Honey nodded as Coco gave him her name, and gestured for her to follow him without even checking the reservations.

'This way, madam.'

Coco smiled, tucked a stray hair behind her ear, and followed him through the restaurant to a discreet booth at the back, where she could see Benedict was already waiting. Thank goodness. She hated being first, sitting waiting for a date to arrive, feeling like a lemon – yet she hadn't wanted to be late. She had arrived bang on time, so to find him already here was a relief.

He stood up and kissed her lightly on one cheek, then sat down and poured a glass of champagne from the bottle chilling on the table while she sat down on the chocolate suede banquette. He discreetly ushered the waiter away – he was perfectly capable of pouring it himself. Benedict wasn't the sort of man who needed staff grovelling round him to make him feel good about himself.

'Have you been here before?' he asked as she picked up the menu.

'No. But I've heard great things.' She cast a glance around the room. It was buzzy, but not over-full, the clientele sufficiently self-interested not to notice her. She had kept a fairly low profile since her first transmission, but she knew that intrusion was going to be inevitable. Not, however, in Michelin-starred Mayfair restaurants.

She picked up the menu and started to study it intently, but she found she couldn't focus. She felt fidgety, on edge. She took a gulp of the champagne, but to her it tasted of bitter almonds.

She was desperate for this evening to go well. But she couldn't relax.

The waiter arrived to take their order.

'What are you going to have?' Benedict put his menu down with the air of one who had already decided.

'Um . . .' Coco ran her eye down the delicious-sounding selection of dishes. She didn't have a clue what she wanted. She couldn't think about food.

'I'll have the heritage beetroot with ricotta,' she told the waiter at last. 'And the sea bream with artichokes.'

Benedict nodded his approval and went on to give his order. She barely heard what he was saying. She knew what she needed. But she didn't have any more. And she'd promised herself. She didn't need it any longer. She'd proved herself – to several million people. She had the reviews to back it up – overall, the television critics had given her performance the seal of approval. And a mature, sophisticated man like Benedict wouldn't be interested in someone who dabbled in class-A drugs.

The trouble was she didn't know if she could get through the evening without it. It was all she could think about.

All she needed was a little lift. Just to get her through the early stages of this relationship. It wasn't unlike stage fright, after all – the nerves of a first date. Once they were established; once she was more confident . . .

She took her napkin off her lap and put it on the table.

'Excuse me.' She smiled charmingly, and of course he didn't demur. She made her way to the Ladies. It was downstairs, and she prayed she would get a signal. Two bars – thank goodness. She dialled Gavin, and he answered after three rings.

'It's Coco. Where are you? I need a delivery. Urgently.'

Relief flooded through her. He was five minutes away, in the West End. Of course he was. Where else did your average scuzzy wannabe drug dealer hang out on a Saturday night? She told him to make it over as quickly as he could, then text her. She'd meet him outside the restaurant.

The minutes before Gavin's arrival seemed like hours. The conversation with Benedict was stilted – she was groping for answers to his questions. The starter arrived, but she barely ate. It was as dry as dust in her mouth.

She was staring at her half-eaten sea bream when her phone chirruped at her. A text.

'I'm so sorry; it's my producer,' she said to Benedict. 'I need to call her back. Probably some script changes for tomorrow.'

Benedict smiled his lack of concern over her leaving the table. He was used to the reliance of the young on mobiles, thanks to Justine. Coco bolted outside. Gavin was lurking down the pavement, looking as much like what he was as anyone possibly could. She grabbed her stash off him and thrust a wad of notes in his hand.

'Thank-you wouldn't hurt,' grumbled Gavin. They were always so desperate to see him, and then could barely give him the time of day. He was used to it.

As soon as he had gone, she looked up and down the street, then walked smartly to the nearest shop doorway. She knew she was being reckless, but she couldn't wait for the next opportune moment to go to the loo. She didn't want Benedict to think she had a weak bladder. Besides, she was fairly certain she was safe. With her back turned away from the street, she administered herself a line of the precious powder as discreetly as she could.

Moments later she slid gracefully back into her seat. She had barely been gone five minutes. The waiter was hovering with the dessert menu.

Now she could focus. Now she could respond. She felt confident. All her nerves had melted away; the butterflies had flown.

'I'm so sorry,' she said to Benedict. 'When you're on a show like *Critical*, your life's not your own.'

'It must be enormous pressure,' he agreed. 'I admire you.'

'Please don't,' Coco begged him. 'It's hardly rocket science.'

'No, but it's entertainment. And we all need some light relief in our lives.'

'I suppose so . . .' She looked down at the menu. The cocaine had killed what little appetite she'd had, but she didn't want to be a bore, like so many showbiz people, and refuse pudding. 'I'll have the wild honey ice cream.'

She could force that down if she had to.

'And so will I.' Benedict handed his menu back to the waiter, then leaned forward. 'Tell me, what have my daughter and your sister been getting up to? They seem as thick as thieves.'

'Justine and Violet?' Coco looked at him, startled, then shook her head. 'Just . . . whatever it is girls do, I think.' She frowned. 'Why?'

'Nothing in particular. It's only that Justine seems a little . . . distracted at the moment.'

Coco surveyed him coolly. Was that why he'd asked her out? To grill her about her sister? She hated it when people started quizzing her about her family, even when there was nothing to hide.

'Violet knows how to have fun.' She shrugged. 'In fact, we all do. Maybe Justine's enjoying being a part of that?'

Benedict sensed her unease.

'I'm sorry,' said Benedict. 'That's not what this meal is about.'

He poured her another glass of wine. There was an awkward silence. Coco worried that she'd been a little too defensive, but it was her default setting when it came to her family. She quickly changed the subject.

'Tell me about your hotels. I was thinking of booking Mum and Dad a weekend away somewhere amazing – it's her fiftieth birthday soon. Where would you recommend?'

Benedict warmed to his subject straight away. Soon, they were debating the benefits of Marrakesh versus Montenegro, and the honey ice cream arrived and was sublime, and they had a glass of Tokay to complement its luscious sweetness, and they were laughing and . . .

It was time to go. The bill was dealt with discreetly. The waiter slipped Coco's suede Jil Sander jacket on; a driver appeared outside with the Bentley.

'Let me run you home,' offered Benedict.

Coco relaxed in the comfort of the back seat. They were close, but he didn't make a move to put an arm around her. When they arrived at her flat, he got out to open her door. Before she could even think about offering him a liqueur, or a coffee, he had kissed her goodbye on the cheek.

'I enjoyed our evening,' he told her. 'I'll see you again soon.'

He slipped into the back of the car without another word, and it slid away.

Coco shivered in the cold night air as she watched the tail-lights fade. She'd blown it. He'd got the measure of her. He'd seen how agitated she was at the beginning of the evening, then how animated she was when she came back. He was on to her. And he didn't want a cokehead for a girlfriend. He had given her the most polite of brush-offs.

With a sinking heart she went up the stairs to her flat and threw herself onto the bed without getting undressed. How the hell had she got herself into this mess? She'd thrown away the chance of a relationship with a man she found devastatingly attractive, because she was self-medicating. Dabbling in something she should never have started, because of her lack of confidence. She hadn't meant to let it take a hold like this . . .

But of course it had. She should have known that. Cocaine was addictive. Addiction ran in her family. If she wasn't careful she was going to lose everything. Hadn't her father's experience taught her anything?

She lay there, her heart pounding, cursing herself for her stupidity. Why had she taken the easy way out, like her dad? Why couldn't she have just faced up to her fears, like a normal person? Only a coward took refuge in something that gave them false confidence. She was a fool, a failure—

Her phone beeped. She sat up. Who would send her a text at this time of night? Maybe Tyger. She grabbed it and stared at the screen.

Meant to say, have tickets for the opera next Thursday. If you fancy it. B

Joy flooded through her. She'd been given a reprieve. She had a second chance. She flopped back onto the pillows with a huge smile on her face, then quickly typed her response.

Definitely. Thank you for a lovely evening. C

Next week, she would be as clean as a whistle. She would make sure of it. Yes, thought Coco with a sudden burst of happiness.

It was goodbye Charlie, hello Benedict.

Twenty-Three

Less than two weeks after the opening party, Raf and Pandora were in bed together.

They were huddled under the duvet, waiting to shoot the first time Hugo and Saskia make love. As usual the set-up was taking ages. The lighting director wasn't happy. It could mean hours of adjustment, but there was no point in them getting out again, just in case.

Pandora was shivering. It wasn't cold in the room, so it must be fear. Raf stroked her reassuringly, as if she was a frightened animal.

'This is worse than the first real time,' said Pandora, her teeth chattering.

Raf pulled her into him, snuggling her.

'Just take yourself somewhere else. Think of somewhere you'd like to be.'

Pandora gazed at him, her eyes huge.

'That's the problem,' she confided. 'This is exactly where I'd like to be. It's just . . . I'd rather we didn't have the world and his wife watching.'

She didn't take her eyes away from his.

Raf fell silent. That was a pretty big confession. Was she winding him up?

'OK, we're ready when you are.'

They both slithered out of their dressing gowns and handed them to the floor manager, then pulled the duvet up to shoulder height.

'And . . . action!'

Raf put his hands out to touch Pandora. He could do this. It was what he did best, acting. He could pretend to be someone else. He was Hugo, not Raf. His fingers tingled as he touched her warm skin. So soft but so firm. He had forgotten what youth felt like. He went to slide his hand down her leg then leapt back.

Jesus Christ! She didn't have a stitch on underneath. Most actresses kept their knickers on at least for sex scenes. He snatched his hand away as if he had been electrocuted, but it was too late. She caught his eye. She knew that he knew, and she gave him a secretive, minxy little smile. She stretched sensually, pressed herself up against him. He could feel her breasts, perfectly round, her nipples erect.

She was totally turned on by this, not nervous at all. And now he was going to have to kiss her. That's what was in the script.

Then next thing he knew she had wrapped her legs around his and pushed herself against him. He could feel her warm wetness on his thigh. Raf groaned involuntarily. There was no way she couldn't feel the desire on him. He had never been so hard. His whole being, his whole raison d'être, was in his cock.

'I dare you,' she whispered in his ear, and every hair on the back of his neck rippled.

He couldn't. He couldn't fuck Pandora in front of an entire camera crew. He was a happily married man who loved his wife.

A happily married man who hadn't had sex for two months.

Raf assessed the situation. He couldn't deny he found the girl attractive. She was totally stunning. And they had become quite close over the past couple of weeks, rehearsing together during the day, working on the script at night, sharing the same house. He might have fantasised about her in the odd quiet moment, but he hadn't really thought about it seriously. There had never really been an opportunity. Genevieve seemed to be with them most of the time, after all, acting as his conscience, like some bloody chaperone.

She wasn't here now, though. And he was only bloody human. Pandora was kissing him, slow, sensual, deliberately provocative, sliding her tongue over his lips. With one hand she slid down the waistband of his boxer shorts.

He rolled on top of her. Instinctively she parted her legs.

It was so easy. Two seconds and he was inside her. He barely had to move. He could feel her body respond to the slightest thrust. She was starting to moan, her head tilted back, and he kissed her throat, knowing this would look good for the camera. She threw her arms open wide, arching her back, pushing herself against him, and he clenched his jaw to stop himself from coming. They needed a good few minutes of this. He didn't dare look around him to get the crew's reaction. The fact that the cameras were still rolling said it all.

'Oh my God! Oh my Jesus fucking God Christ fuck.'

She was pulsing round him, so tight. He couldn't hold back any longer. Raf didn't cry out, or swear, like Pandora. He had never been particularly vocal during sex. All he wanted was to look in her eyes. It was all about the eye contact for him. And as they locked gazes, he found himself falling. Maybe if he hadn't looked, he could have saved himself, but that soul-sharing moment sealed his fate.

Raf came up for air, panting, sweating. He knew he had to hold the moment until the director shouted, 'Cut!' He bent his head and kissed Pandora's forehead. She was laughing, exhilarated, pupils huge, her breath ragged with the exertion.

'Oh my God, that was the best ever. Oh my God – do it again . . . !'

She pulled his head down to her, kissing him over and over in a frenzy, a demented lover. Was she acting? Was she? He didn't think so. Her orgasm had been real all right. And to his surprise, he found himself responding, kissing her back, not wanting this to end.

Eventually they fell back onto the pillows tangled in each other's arms, laughing, exhausted.

The crew broke into spontaneous applause and the pair of

them looked round in surprise. They had all but forgotten they were being filmed.

Dickie came over, beaming and blushing.

'Guys – that was amazing. You were on fire. There's some serious on-screen chemistry going on there.'

He fanned the air in front of him to indicate fanning flames.

'Just don't ask me to do it again,' pleaded Raf. 'There's no way I could repeat that performance.'

'Not just yet, anyway,' he heard Pandora murmur wickedly.

The crew teased them incessantly for the rest of the day. There were constant references to Julie Christie and Donald Sutherland, who were rumoured to have done their sex scene for real in *Don't Look Now*.

It was a testament to their acting skills that it didn't seem to occur to anyone that perhaps Raf and Pandora *had* done it for real.

Raf's mouth was dry and his legs felt shaky. How the hell had he let himself do that? Was he mad? He'd screwed another woman and it was all on camera. Once they looked back at the rushes, it would be bloody obvious. They were both great actors, but not that good. He felt slightly feverish. The exertion, the adrenalin, and now the panic were getting to him.

Pandora was as cool as a cucumber. She was wandering around in that bloody robe, looking dishevelled and divine, blagging a cigarette off one of the crew.

'I always need a post-coital cigarette,' he heard her joking, and everyone laughed. He felt a chill descend on him. The whole incident didn't seem to have fazed her in the least.

Well, of course it hadn't. She wasn't the one with a twenty-five-year marriage at stake.

The thing is, once you've fucked someone in front of a room full of people, there really isn't any excuse not to carry on doing it.

Pandora came to Raf in his room that night. A bunch of them had been out for dinner. She had – deliberately, he realised now — not sat next to him, but had spent all night chatting to one of the sound guys. A cheap trick, and an obvious one, but it had worked. He'd spent all evening casting glances at her to check what she was up to. All he could think about was her velvet-soft skin on his. And the scent of her body. He hadn't showered. He could still smell her on him, where her wetness had dried on his limbs. What a pervert, he thought, disgusted with himself, but not disgusted enough to wash her away.

He had tried phoning Delilah to get Pandora out of his system. He thought perhaps the sound of his wife's voice would instil such guilt in him that any thoughts he had of a repeat performance would be quashed. But no. When he heard her, he felt nothing. No little needles of doubt or pinpricks of remorse. No desire to rush home and take her in his arms. No need to confess and then atone.

What did that say about the state of his marriage? Raf was a little bit shocked. He hadn't realised things were so bad. If you'd asked him even yesterday whether he would cheat on Delilah, he would have said a resounding no. Things weren't perfect, but there was no such thing as a perfect marriage. They were under a lot of strain, he supposed. Then he scoffed. Not real strain. Not husband-properly-out-of-work, disabled-wife-needing-full-time-care, up-to-your-eyes-in-debt and living-on-a-sink-estate sort of strain.

As for the lack of sex in the past couple of months, if you read the statistics it wasn't so unusual. It certainly didn't excuse what he had done. Which was, essentially, succumb to lust. He wasn't in love with Pandora Hammond. He didn't even have that excuse.

So when she stood in his doorway, in the same silky robe she had worn on set earlier that day, he just smiled and stood to one side to let her in.

'You know this doesn't mean anything,' he said, sliding his hands over her shoulders, pushing back the silk to expose that porcelain skin he'd been thinking about all afternoon.

'Course it doesn't,' she countered. 'You've got a stunningly beautiful, talented wife who you adore. This is just sex. And anyway,' she continued, tracing her fingers gently across his lips, 'what goes on tour, stays on tour.'

'It bloody better,' said Raf, a slightly threatening tone to his voice. 'No one finds out about this. OK?'

'Course not,' replied Pandora, thinking that for a one-time alcoholic serial adulterer who still lived in the public eye, he was pretty naive.

Twenty-Four

'Delilah.'

It was Miriam. Delilah's agent. And when she said Delilah's name like that, she knew it was bad news. If it was good news, she burbled on for a few minutes about nonsense.

'As you know, I've been talking about renegotiating your contract with the production company.'

'Are they baulking at my fee?' They shouldn't be. In the light of the current climate, Delilah hadn't been unreasonable in what she was asking.

'No.'

'Then . . . what?' Shit. They wanted her to have a co-host. Well, that would depend very much on who it was—

'Dee – they're not renewing your contract. They're . . . dropping the show.'

Delilah sat down on a nearby stool.

Not in a million years had she considered this possibility. The ratings for the last show had been great. She was easy to work with. She turned it in every time. She did all the publicity they needed and more. She'd given that programme a hundred and ten per cent, and they had the audience share to prove it.

'Wh . . . why?' she stammered, truly shocked.

'You know how it is. They've got a new Head of Programming. He wants to put his stamp on the schedule. He thinks the show's . . . done everything it can.'

This was, to a certain extent, true. She'd done everything from avocado mousse to zabaglione.

'What's replacing me?'

Miriam cleared her throat.

'He wants to do a show about self-sufficiency. Making your own bread and jam. Growing your own veg. *The Good Life* for the twenty-first century.'

'I can do that.'

'Delilah – he's made his mind up. There's nothing I can do.'

'He thinks I'm too old.' Age paranoia. It was inevitable, with fifty staring her in the face.

Miriam didn't reply. Which was as good as saying yes, she was too old.

'Who's presenting it?' Delilah persisted, even though she didn't really want the answer.

'Thomasina Brown.'

Thomasina Brown. Her nemesis. Delilah could just imagine how she had gone about getting the job.

'I'm sorry.' Of course Miriam was sorry. Fifteen per cent of a lot was a lot.

Delilah's mouth was dry. She didn't want to carry on the conversation. There wasn't much to be said.

'Let me take it on board,' she managed. 'I'll speak to you later.'

She put the phone down. Her hands were trembling.

She'd been stupid to think she was invincible. She had believed her own publicity. She had thought she was a national treasure. Why hadn't she seen this coming?

She had a sudden rush of hope. Surely one of the other channels would be glad to have her? She was always being approached. Why hadn't Miriam thought of that? She put out her hand to pick up the phone, then stopped. Other channels were happy to poach you while you were still a success. They probably weren't so keen on picking you up when you'd been dropped.

She sat down, trying to gather her thoughts. It was only a television show, she told herself. She had plenty of other irons in the fire. She had offers to do things every week that she turned down because she was too busy. There was no need to panic yet.

It had been her way of life for so long. It dictated the pace in the house. It governed everything she and everyone else did. It was the engine.

Why hadn't the producer had the courtesy to call her himself? Wouldn't that have been the polite thing to do? But no – he was too busy wielding his new broom, building himself an empire. And, no doubt, fucking Thomasina Brown. She hadn't got the job because of her green fingers. What did green fingers have to do with presenting a cookery show?

Rage and hurt boiled up inside her. Years of loyal service and fantastic viewing figures and they could dump you just like that.

And then another even more terrible thought occurred to her, and her veins turned to ice.

When the phone rang again half an hour later, she knew who it would be.

'Delilah.'

She was right. It was her editor.

'Delilah, I am so, so sorry.'

They were dropping the book. Without the television show to boost its sales, they couldn't justify the massive print run they had planned. And without a massive print run, they couldn't justify the massive production costs. It was a hugely ambitious project. Without the exposure, the figures just didn't add up. The publishers were pulling the plug.

'That's not to say we won't try something less ambitious at a later date.' The editor tried to soothe her, but both of them knew it was bullshit.

She was yesterday's news. Tomorrow's fish and chip wrappers.

It was not a good feeling.

She lay in bed all afternoon and on into the evening. She'd spent more and more time there lately. If you lay in bed, you didn't have to make decisions. You could let everything wash over you, drift off to sleep if the reality became too painful.

She didn't want to cry. Or scream. Or throw plates.

She wanted Raf.

Raf would reassure her. Raf would bolster her up. Raf would make sure she didn't feel like a washed-up old harridan.

She dialled his mobile, looking at the clock. It was nearly nine o'clock. Perhaps he could nip home? He could be back in under two hours in the Maserati. She just wanted to feel his arms around her, hear his soothing voice.

But the phone went straight to voicemail.

She imagined him in some trendy restaurant in Bath, Pandora Hammond hanging on his every word, Genevieve Duke regaling him with tales of her lurid past. The three of them wrapped up in that bubble of closeness that working on a film always brings.

Maybe she should drive down there? She wouldn't know where to find him. She supposed she could go to his digs. Hang out in his room till he got back. They wouldn't be madly late, would they? Film sets were pretty puritanical these days. Everyone was paranoid about getting a decent night's sleep so they didn't look their age.

She decided not to leave a message. She'd probably break down in the middle of it and start blubbing. She ran upstairs and threw a few things into a bag, phoning Polly and asking her to come and collect Doug the Pug – she couldn't take him with her. She searched through the file in the office until she found the address of where Raf was staying, wrote down the postcode so she could programme it into the sat-nav, found her car-keys and locked up the house.

Twenty minutes later she was on the M4.

Genevieve only slept about five hours a night these days. She tended to doze off eventually at about one, then woke up at six. She was a voracious reader, and she did the crossword every day.

So when she heard the crunch of tyres on the gravel outside, her curiosity was roused. Any distraction was welcome at this time of night. Anything to break the tedium of sixteen across. She walked over to the window and pulled back the curtain.

As a figure stepped out of the car and into the light thrown by the front door, she saw it was Delilah.

Shit.

She knew as well as the next person that, despite their best efforts to keep it quiet, Raf was shagging the arse off Pandora. It was an open secret that had so far been kept from the press. She had come to terms with it, though she made it clear she didn't approve. She certainly wasn't going to stand by now and watch Raf's marriage go down the pan. She wasn't going to let Pandora have that privilege.

There was no time to go up to Raf's room and warn him. She'd have to go downstairs and ward Delilah off. Without stopping to put on a dressing gown, she opened the door, shot down the corridor and down the stairs just as Delilah came in through the front door. They'd long decided it was easier to leave it on the latch than keep remembering their keys.

'Delilah!' she beamed radiantly. 'Thank God. Another human being to talk to. Everyone else is snoring their heads off. I was just going to make myself a cup of tea. Say you'll have one with me.'

Delilah looked at her dully. Genevieve saw that she looked dreadful. Her face was drawn and pinched, and she looked as if she might have been crying.

'Is everything all right?'

'Fine. Well, not fine. But nobody's ill or dead or anything.'

'Oh. Good.' Genevieve indicated the kitchen. 'Well, come and have a cup of char and tell me about it. You won't get anything out of Raf – he went off hours ago.'

Delilah followed her reluctantly into the kitchen. Genevieve busied herself putting the kettle on, wondering how she was going to get upstairs to warn the others without arousing Delilah's suspicion.

'Bugger,' she exclaimed. 'I've left my herbal teabags up in my room. If I have the real McCoy I really won't sleep. Keep an eye on the kettle, would you? I'll just go and fetch them.'

Delilah smiled wanly in acquiescence. Genevieve padded up the stairs, then turned right instead of left until she reached Raf's room at the end. She knocked as loudly as she dared. It had to be hard enough to wake them.

There was no reply. She rattled the knob. Eventually she heard footsteps. She put her finger to her lips so that whoever answered the door would know to be quiet. It was Raf.

'Shh!' Genevieve's eyes were wide with alarm as she stepped past him into the room. 'Delilah's downstairs. I'm making her a cup of tea, but I don't know how long I can distract her. Get rid of Pandora!'

She could see the girl's inky black hair spread out on the pillow. She was fast asleep. Raf rushed over and shook her awake.

'Pandora, Pandora – quick. Wake up!'

She was one of those irritating people who don't respond well to being roused out of their slumber. She sat up, sleepy and confused.

'What is it?' She saw Genevieve and smiled. 'A threesome?'

'For Christ's sake—'

A panic-stricken Raf was practically dragging her by the arm. 'Ow! Let go.'

'Delilah's here,' he hissed.

Pandora swung her legs over the edge of the bed, stretched up her arms and yawned. It was almost as if she was trying to be annoying. Genevieve felt the urge to slap her, but couldn't risk the noise.

'Hurry up!'

'OK, OK.'

Pandora stumbled sleepily across the room, stark naked, making no effort to cover herself, her long, dark hair tumbling over her shoulders.

Thank God, thought Genevieve. Just in time.

And turned to see Delilah behind her, taking in every bit of the scene.

'Oh God, am I sleepwalking again?' attempted Pandora valiantly, then pretended to realise she had no clothes on. She gave a little squeal and tried to cover herself up. 'I'm so sorry . . . oh my God, how embarrassing . . .'

'Save it for the director.' Delilah gave her a withering look, then turned to Raf. 'A leopard never changes its spots, does it?'

Twenty-Five

Delilah wasn't sure what was blurring her vision: her tears or the torrential early summer rain that was falling in heavy sheets. As she drove blindly through the streets of Bath, her sat-nav became increasingly hysterical.

'Turn around where possible! Turn around where possible!'

'Shut up! Shut up!' screamed Delilah in reply, stabbing wildly at the buttons to turn it off, then peering through the windscreen for any clue as to where she was. Eventually she saw a blue motorway sign for the M4.

Bastard. Bastard bastard bastard. All those years she had put up with his infidelity, and she had excused him, thinking it was the drink. Time and again she had smiled bravely, even though her heart was crackle-glazed with tiny fissures, and taken him back, because she loved him – and she thought he loved her, despite his errant ways. Incredulous journalists used to ask how she could find it in her heart to forgive him when he had betrayed her so publicly. She would shrug and say the affairs meant nothing, because she didn't think they did. She thought the only thing that was truly important to Raf was his family, and that somehow their love was stronger for all his betrayal. And besides, the Raf who was unfaithful to her wasn't the real Raf – it was the Raf who had been taken over by the demon drink. She never held him accountable – it was always the fault of Mr Gordon or Mr Bailey or Mr Hennessey. She didn't care that some women derided her for her loyalty, and accused her of enabling men to think it was all right to take a lover or a mistress just because they were drunk.

When you found a love like hers, you didn't let it go that easily.

And once he had fought his final battle against alcohol and won, she thought she had at last been vindicated. Raf had shown no signs of straying in his sober years. She had been right to stand by him. He wasn't the guilty party. The booze was.

Only now, she was faced with the truth. Booze had nothing to do with it.

She'd seen the evidence for herself. A stunning, inky-haired, milky-skinned floozy in his bed. And he was stone-cold sober. She would know if he'd been drinking. The signs were engrained in her. She only had to look at his eyes to know if he'd hit the bottle. The look he had given her was one of shock mixed with sorrow. And fear. But not alcohol.

As she drove away from Collingwood, she could feel all the fissures she'd acquired over the years start to join up, and a giant crack formed in her heart. It almost took her breath away, but she had to keep driving. He would be following her, she was sure of it, and there was no way she was going to keep ahead of him for long.

She couldn't face him. She quite simply couldn't face him. What on earth could he say to her that would make it all right? Excuses, platitudes, justifications, denial? Or worse, the revelation that he was in love with whoever-she-was. Pandora bloody Hammond. She remembered her conversation with Genevieve, how she'd asked her to keep an eye open. She'd been half-joking at the time; she hadn't really viewed Pandora as a threat.

She slowed the car down as she reached the motorway roundabout. How long would it take her to get home? How far behind her would he be? She looked nervously over her shoulder, as if expecting to see him flashing his lights behind her. If she beat him back, she could bolt lock the doors from the inside. It wasn't what she wanted, to barricade herself inside her own home, and he'd find a way in eventually, but she really wasn't ready for what lay ahead. God, it was so sordid. There was no way of making her immediate future anything other than high-octane, hysterical melodrama.

An impatient beep behind her made her realise she had been sitting at the roundabout for quite a while, staring through her tears and the relentless rain.

Without really thinking about it, Delilah indicated left and pulled out onto the roundabout, then took the slip-road leading to the motorway. Gradually a plan formed in her mind. She had a change of clothes in the boot in her overnight bag. She kept her passport in her handbag. And at the end of this road was Fishguard, and the ferry to Ireland.

In the kitchen at Collingwood, Pandora was sobbing uncontrollably. She wasn't such an attractive proposition with a bubble of snot protruding from one nostril. Genevieve looked at her with distaste.

'For God's sake,' she snapped. 'If you want to play with the grown-ups . . .'

Pandora glared at her through swollen eyes.

'You say that as if you never did it.'

'I never got caught.'

Raf came in with his car keys. He looked pale, but resolved.

'I'm going after her.'

'I'll come with you.' Genevieve stood up decisively. 'You've had a shock. You shouldn't drive on your own.'

'What about me?' wailed Pandora.

'What about you?' asked Genevieve. 'You've got nothing to lose. Except your reputation.'

She couldn't resist this last snipe. She was exasperated. The whole debacle was so predictable. She'd seen it coming a mile off, and had tried to prevent it, but how could you prevent the inevitable? Now she felt like the form captain, trouble-shooting for a bunch of naughty pupils who'd been caught out.

The door opened and Dickie came in, his hair sticking up at all angles, looking like a little mole without his glasses.

'What's going on?'

Everyone looked at each other.

'Pandora's just . . . a little upset about something,' said Genevieve brightly. 'No need to worry. Off you go back to bed.'

The last thing they wanted was for Dickie to get a whiff of the scandal. He'd only panic. He didn't show any sign of going back to bed. He sat down at the kitchen table.

'If there's any tea going, I'll have a cup. Can't sleep. Bit keyed up about tomorrow.'

Tomorrow they were shooting the big scene where Hugo's wife discovers he's been having an affair with Saskia.

Raf started to laugh hollowly. Dickie blinked up at him.

'You might as well know,' said Raf, as Pandora desperately signalled to him to keep quiet. 'Delilah's just caught me in the sack with Pandora.'

Dickie went pale.

'Shit.'

'Shit indeed,' replied Raf gravely. 'Sorry, mate, but I've got to go after her.'

'I'll make sure he's back in time for the shoot tomorrow,' Genevieve added helpfully.

Dickie slumped until his forehead rested on the kitchen table.

'I knew it was going too well,' he groaned. For a moment, he said nothing, then he looked up, remembering that he was the director, he was in charge. 'Right. Off you two go. Be back here by eleven tomorrow – we can have a late start. The important thing is none of this gets out to the press. We don't want them crawling all over the set like a rash.'

'Too right,' agreed Raf. 'And I don't want the girls getting wind of this.'

For some reason, everyone was looking at Pandora.

'Why are you looking at me?' she demanded.

'You wouldn't be the first person to use a bit of star-fucking to further their career.'

Dickie and Raf both flinched at Genevieve's bluntness. Pandora fought back.

'You never did, I suppose?'

'Nope,' said Genevieve. 'I didn't. Come on.' She nodded towards the door. 'I'll share the driving with you.'

Raf stopped in front of Dickie.

'I'll be back. I won't screw things up for you, I promise.'

Dickie nodded wearily.

Genevieve wanted one last shot at Pandora.

'I'd go to bed if I were you. And put cold-water compresses on your eyes, or you'll look like death in the morning.'

A few moments later Dickie and Pandora heard the throaty roar of the Maserati start up in the car park.

'Oh dear,' sighed Pandora. 'I feel awful about all this.'

Dickie gave her a withering look and left the room.

Delilah just managed to get on the midnight boat to Ireland.

She parked her car in the bowels of the ferry, inhaling the smell of diesel, and made her way up onto the deck. She leaned her arms on the side, shivering in the cold night air and watching the lights of Fishguard slip away. She felt drained, unable to focus her mind on what had just happened, but grateful for the distance being put between her and reality.

She could feel her phone go in the pocket of her jeans. Raf, of course. And before long it would be the world and his wife, feigning concern. They'd all be on, wondering where she was, what was going on. It would be full-scale panic. Tony would wig as soon as he found out. There would be lectures, contingency plans, press releases, publicity stunts to ensure the press didn't get any sniff of what had happened.

She didn't want to go through it. She didn't want to sit in the bloody office having her private life picked over yet again. It was humiliating. She'd done it for long enough. They could all figure it out for themselves. She was going to worry about herself for once.

Her phone went again. She took it out and looked at it.

She'd been a slave to it for years. She was never without it. It ruled her life from dawn until dusk. She ignored it at her peril. Without thinking twice, she held it out over the side and dropped it into the churning sea below.

As the rain started to fall again she realised she was the only person mad enough to be out on deck, and she made her way to her cabin. She passed the purser, who told her cheerfully it was going to be the roughest crossing for weeks. She lay on her bunk, her stomach churning, her mind whirling, tears running down her cheeks as she pitched and rolled with the ship.

Her only consolation was things couldn't possibly get any worse.

Raf and Genevieve arrived at The Bower to find the house in darkness.

'Maybe she's not here yet. We must have overtaken her on the motorway. '

Raf was prowling around, opening doors, as if he might find his wife cowering in the downstairs loo or the coat cupboard.

They sat down in the kitchen to wait. Genevieve thought about making tea, but decided that apart from the ritual it would be no help whatsoever.

By two o'clock, Delilah still hadn't arrived.

'I'm calling the police,' said Raf. 'She might have had an accident. And why isn't she answering her phone?'

'Because she doesn't want to talk to you?' suggested Genevieve. 'And don't phone the police. That's the quickest way to get the press on the case.'

Raf paced the kitchen, then stopped.

'Where's Doug? Where's Doug the Pug?' He looked in the corner where Doug's basket usually lay.

'She must have him with her.'

'But all his stuff's gone: his bowls, his food.'

Raf was opening cupboards frantically.

'Delilah must have it,' reasoned Genevieve.

Raf picked up the phone.

'I'm calling Polly.'

'You can't call her at this time of night.'

'She'll know what's happened—'

'Raf, it's half past two in the morning. The poor girl—'

'We pay her more than enough to be entitled to wake her up.'

Genevieve raised an eyebrow but didn't comment any further. Raf was obviously under pressure. That wasn't his usual attitude, thank goodness.

'Polly! It's Raf. Have you got any idea what's going on?'

Polly sat up, her heart racing. She hated being woken by the phone in the middle of the night. Doug was dozing at the bottom of the bed. He opened one eye in recognition of the interruption, then went back to sleep.

'Delilah called me at about nine,' Polly told Raf. 'She asked if I'd come and collect Doug. She didn't say where she was going – I thought she was with you?'

'No.' Raf's reply was curt. 'Call me if you hear from her, will you?'

'Of course. Has something happened?'

But Raf had already rung off.

Polly sank back onto the pillow. What on earth was going on? She sensed a Rafferty crisis. The dust had only just settled since Tyger's wedding fiasco. As she snuggled back under the duvet, she knew she wouldn't get back to sleep.

'Come here, you.' She scooped Doug up and tucked him under her arm, comforted by his warm, velvety presence.

Sometimes she wished she'd gone and done the teacher training course she'd meant to go on all those years ago. She'd be at some primary school by now, supervising finger painting and stick insects and times tables. She might have a normal life, then. Instead of a vicarious A-list whirlwind, when you were at someone else's beck and call at all hours of the day and night with no hope of a life of your own. Every time she booked a day off, something would happen and she would be called in to the office. And she was expected to be in on all their social occasions. Of course it was lovely being considered one of the family, but actually, what she would really like was . . .

A family of her own?

Fat chance, thought Polly gloomily. While she was mixing with stars and celebs she would never get a look-in. No one she met was ever potential husband material. They were always well out of her reach. As long as she was fat she had no hope. While she was working for the Raffertys she could never lose weight. Delilah had told her to use the gym any time she liked, but there was never a minute.

She was never going to move forward until she had the courage to break free. And while they were paying her what they paid her, and she was working for people she cared about and loved, and while she still got a little bit of a kick out of the glamour, she was never going to find that courage.

The ferry arrived in Rosslare just after dawn. A watery sun smiled down upon the town as Delilah drove her car down the ramp. She felt light-headed with fatigue, but strangely exhilarated.

She didn't need any of them. Her feckless husband, her selfish children, her bloodsucking agent, publicist, editor, producer . . . the list was endless. She felt a tiny prick of guilt about Polly. Polly, who was resolutely loyal and never asked anything of her. She shrugged it off. Polly was still going to get paid. At the end of the day, looking after the Raffertys was just a job to her.

She pulled into a petrol station to fill up her car and buy a decent map, a sandwich and a bottle of water. Her stomach had just about settled, and she sat in the driver's seat chewing on slightly stale bread and ham as she looked at where she was. And decided where she might like to go.

Where exactly did a woman who had been sacked, dumped, cuckolded and ignored head for?

Twenty-Six

'*The tragic thing is, Hugo, I'm really not surprised. You are such an astounding cliché. It was the cowboy boots that gave it away. Any man over fifty who wears pointy crocodile-skin cowboy boots is in denial about his age.*'

Genevieve's performance was magnificent. She was towering over the end of her marital bed, in which she had just caught her husband and mistress in flagrante delicto. She was unrecognisable. Clad in comfortable slacks, Clarks sandals, a pie-crust collar and sporting an iron-grey perm, she was the personification of a stalwart of the WI. Her diatribe would have made any errant husband quiver with fear and trepidation.

Raf and Pandora were each finding shooting this scene almost unbearable. It was too close to the truth for comfort. As the floor manager called cut, they both lay back on the pillows, drained and exhausted. Neither of them had had any sleep.

'You OK?' Raf turned to look at Pandora, who had dark purple rings under her eyes that were already starting to show through her make-up.

'I'm fine,' she assured him. 'I'm just wondering . . . what happens next?'

'I suppose we'll do a couple more takes then break for lunch—'

'I mean . . . about us?'

'Us?'

Oh shit, thought Raf. Hadn't he spelled it out to her at the

267

very beginning? He thought she'd understood. He really, really didn't need this – a clingy, needy actress who imagined that just because they'd been fucking like snakes for the past fortnight that they were some sort of item.

He'd have to tread very carefully.

He stroked her hair in a tender gesture he didn't mean.

'We're just going to have to play it all right down. Until I can find Delilah. In fact, it's probably best if I move out of the house, to stop any tongues from wagging.'

He pulled out his phone and called Polly.

'Poll – it's Raf. Can you call Bablake House and get me a room for the next few days? Try to knock them down a bit if you can, but it doesn't really matter. Starting tonight.'

He hung up.

Pandora grabbed his arm.

'Can I come and see you there?'

'Of course you bloody can't.' His tone was sharper than he meant it to be, but she really wasn't making things easy.

Genevieve came and sat on the edge of the bed while the crew looked back over what they had shot.

'Any news from Delilah?'

Raf looked glum. 'Not a squeak.'

He rubbed his face with both hands and ran his fingers through his hair, the picture of despair. 'I'm going to have to tell the girls.'

'Ready for another take?' The assistant floor manager came up to them politely, as the make-up girls descended to retouch their powder.

Dickie bounded up.

'OK, guys, that's just great. We're going to shoot it all from Genevieve's POV now, so we'll be on you. Just imagine how you're both feeling. Wrapped in each other's arms one minute, faced with the wrath of the wronged wife the next . . .'

There was an uncomfortable silence.

'Just imagine,' said Raf drily.

*

There was a horrible atmosphere hanging over The Bower, and it was unsettling Polly. She wasn't used to this silence. There was always something going on in the office, but today even the phone wasn't ringing. Except when Raf called to bark out some curt order. It wasn't like him to be rude. There was definitely something wrong.

Where had Delilah gone, for a start? Her mind turned over all the options, until she hit on the most likely possibility.

She'd gone to get some 'work' done. She was sneaking off for a quick face lift, or maybe an eye job. Polly knew that Delilah was feeling increasingly sensitive about her age, with her fiftieth birthday looming, and although of course she didn't need a thing doing, it was hard to convince a woman of a certain age that she didn't need to turn back the clock.

And Raf had obviously got wind of what she was doing, and was furious. Although that didn't explain why he wanted to stay at Bablake House. Maybe the communal living was getting to him? Raf was quite a private person, after all.

Polly sighed. She eyed the pile of invitations to Delilah's party that had arrived from the printers yesterday. They were very simple, on thick square card with a lilac bow threaded through the top. That would be the perfect task to take her mind off it all. She'd work her way through the guest list and get them all in the post this afternoon, with a bit of luck. There were over three hundred, and she was already dreading the replies, with their ridiculous dietary requests and the travel arrangements and the demands for suggestions for presents that it would be up to Polly to sort out.

She took out the thick-nibbed fountain pen that she'd had since school, and a pot of deep purple ink. She'd done a calligraphy course at the local college, and she couldn't wait. It was going to take her hours to make them look perfect, but it would be worth it. She imagined the invitations perched on A-list mantelpieces all over the country. It was what the Raffertys needed, a good party . . .

The one thing she didn't want to think about was what she

was going to wear. Delilah had very sweetly given her a cheque to buy whatever she wanted, but Polly had looked and looked online and although she'd seen plenty of dresses she liked, there wasn't one she'd be able to fit into. And now it was too late to lose all the weight she had been planning to lose when the party was first mentioned.

As if it mattered, she thought glumly, putting an elaborate flourish on the end of the first guest's name. No one was going to notice her anyway. Dickie Rushe had virtually ignored her at Coco's screening. Not that she had expected him to sweep her off her feet, but he had been very nice to her when he had come round to lunch, invited her down to watch the filming, and it would have been nice to have been . . . well, at least acknowledged . . .

Underneath the desk, Doug the Pug broke wind and gazed up at her, unrepentant.

In a small town, Delilah stopped at a shop that was clearly aimed at tourists: all linen handkerchiefs with shamrocks in the corner. She bought two capacious Arran sweaters – it might be June, but Ireland was running true to form, wet, windy and chilly – a pair of cords, some stout walking boots and a grey tweed flat cap that made her look about twelve. She added a pair of plain sunglasses, a million miles from the large, blingy Loewe pair she usually wore. With her hair tied back she hoped she was unrecognisable – like an outward-bound tourist about to stride up the nearest mountain. She didn't want people assailing her, asking for her autograph or tips on how to get their cupcakes the same size. Usually she didn't mind chatting to members of the public in the least, but right now she just wanted to be alone.

Dressed in her new guise, she carried on her journey. At four o'clock that afternoon, she drove over the hump-backed bridge over the river Laune into the market town of Killorglin. Grey stone buildings with gaily painted doors lined the wide street – mostly pubs, bookmakers, hotels and funny little supermarkets. She found a parking place and headed for the tourist office.

'I want somewhere to stay for a couple of weeks,' she told the girls behind the desk. 'Somewhere nice and quiet, but pretty. Which preferably does food, so I don't have to go out. I'm . . .' She searched around in her brain for a plausible explanation. 'I'm going to be writing my family history. They came from round here.'

The girls nodded. They heard this often enough. Plenty of people came to Kerry in search of their roots. Usually Americans.

'Your best bet would be Mrs Glass's place out on the lake,' said one helpfully, in her singsong lilt. 'She usually only opens at the weekends out of high season, but seeing as there's just the one of you . . .' She handed her a slim brochure. 'Will I call her?'

Delilah turned the brochure over in her hands. Gortnaflor, the place was called, which apparently meant Garden of Flowers. It promised traditional accommodation in a splendid lakeside setting, and home-cooked food.

'Please do.'

'Will I take your name?'

She hesitated for a moment. She hadn't thought about a name. Giving her real one was going to be a complete give-away, if they hadn't recognised her in her disguise.

She'd give her maiden name, and her childhood nickname.

'Dee,' she told her. 'Dee MacBride.'

Half an hour later, she was on her way, with a garbled set of instructions, and a hastily drawn map.

'Sure, if you don't find it, just ask anyone for Gortnaflor,' the girls told her, and she set off out of Killorglin following the finger sign posts to Caragh Lake.

The scenery was spectacular. Knowing that her journey was soon going to be at an end meant Delilah was more inclined to take in her surroundings. The sky was grey against the bruised purple of the hills, the colours smudged in as if a painter had been over it with a wet brush. The hedges were low and tangled with fuchsia, hot pink amidst the lush greenery. Every now and again she would pass the entrance to a bungalow, often painted a dirty yellow with gateposts proudly displaying a set of eagles or horse heads. She could see scars in the fields where the peat had been cut out. It felt like a very foreign land indeed.

Eventually she turned into a road that followed the curve of the lake, which she couldn't yet see as it was lined with thick rows of pine trees protecting it from the onlooker's gaze, as if a glimpse was only the privilege of those who lived on its shores. She slowed down so as not to miss her destination. So many of the gates had no name, it was a guessing game.

Finally she spotted an old wooden sign with painted letters telling her this was Gortnaflor. The drive didn't look very promising: it was pitted and overgrown. To her surprise it was a good quarter of a mile long, with the trees overhanging – although the rain had stopped the drops collecting on the leaves still fell with a pitter patter. It was eerie, silent but for the raindrops, and from time to time an ethereal wisp of cloud drifted across her path. She felt an increasing sense of unease, not sure what to expect.

Then she rounded the corner and her breath was taken away. The lake loomed before her, the late-afternoon mist rising off it as the sun broke through. It was the most extraordinary colour – a deep emerald green that seemed to glow with phosphorescence. And just by its shores, a grey stone house nestled amongst the trees, its windows winking a coy welcome in the sunlight. The garden surrounding it was a riot of deep pinks and blues and reds, unashamedly glorious and clashing, unrestrained in its ebullience.

She parked the car in the gravelled semi-circle in front of the house and stepped out. All around her she could hear joyous birdsong, the kind you get after heavy rain has just stopped.

She breathed in: the air smelled peaty and damp, but so fresh. She couldn't fill her lungs with enough of it.

The dark red front door was wide open, leading into a porch area stuffed with wellingtons, fishing tackle, trugs and walking sticks, then on into a large, cool hallway with a stone floor and several doors leading off. There were a few good paintings, and fish in glass cases, a fine grandfather clock, and a vase of carelessly arranged flowers that had obviously been picked from the garden.

'Hello!' Delilah called, wondering if there was a reception desk, or a bell. Before she could explore any further, a woman strode out of the kitchen. She must have been in her late seventies, tall, with a cloud of white hair and clothes that had once been expensive – mostly Jaeger, Delilah suspected – but were now rather worn and out of date. But they suited her – tweed and silk and lambswool, and sensible brogues.

She had the gentle Irish accent of one who had spent a lot of time with English people.

'You found us. Grand. You wouldn't believe how many people miss the sign. If they're particularly gullible Americans I tell them the leprechauns have been up to their tricks.' She gave a wonderfully rich laugh, then looked at Delilah anxiously. 'You're not a gullible American, are you? The girls would have said.'

'No.' Delilah laughed, warming to her hostess immediately. 'I'm perfectly English.'

The woman held out a large hand.

'Elizabeth Glass. Welcome to Gortnaflor. I hope they explained, I only really open at weekends at the moment. So you'll have to take me as you find me.'

'Dee MacBride,' equivocated Delilah smoothly, getting used to her new identity. 'The house looks wonderful. And I won't be much trouble.'

Elizabeth peered at her and she suddenly felt the need to validate her reason for being here.

'I'm going to be writing a history of my family. They're

supposed to be from round here.' She could go and buy notebooks and pens to back this up tomorrow.

'Ach, half the world comes from County Kerry, on account of so many people trying to get out of it.'

'I don't know why. It looks beautiful.'

'It's beautiful all right. But you won't be getting any Michelin-starred restaurants or nightclubs.'

'Good,' said Delilah. 'I'm delighted to hear it.'

Elizabeth led her up the staircase with its faded rich red carpet to a large bedroom on the first floor. The furniture was antique and well-polished. A vase of sweet peas sat on the bedside table. The bed was wide and high, and made up with proper sheets, thick Irish blankets and a mound of pillows. Best of all was the view of the lake from the window, in front of which was a little writing desk. Perfect for her fictional oeuvre.

'Will I bring you a cup of tea? And something to eat?'

'That would be lovely,' said Delilah gratefully, realising she'd had nothing since her unappetising sandwich early that morning.

Ten minutes later a tray arrived. A silver tea pot, a proper cup and saucer, a plate of thickly buttered soda bread, a glass dish of raspberry jam and another plate with a wedge of sponge cake and a date slice.

'You're welcome to have your dinner with me tonight,' Elizabeth told her. 'It'll be nothing fancy. Lamb chops and potatoes, and some vegetables from the garden.'

'Sounds wonderful.'

Elizabeth left her in peace. Delilah opened her bag and unpacked the few items she'd brought with her, as well as her purchases. She put her toothpaste and toothbrush in the little en-suite bathroom, and carefully positioned her skincare products on the wooden shelf over the sink.

Then she sat on the bed.

Right. So. What was she going to do with the rest of her life?

There was no sound in the room but the ticking of a carriage clock on top of the dressing table. It was just over twenty-four hours since she'd been dropped from her show and her book had been dumped. Coming up to a day since she'd found her husband in bed with another woman. Until now she had got by on the adrenalin of running away. Now she had stopped, she wasn't sure what to do. She felt a tiny swoop of panic in her chest as her maternal instinct kicked in. She really should phone the girls and see if they were each all right.

Of course they were, she told herself, and decided to run herself a bath before going down to supper. The bath was scarred with rust stains, and the water came out in juddering spurts, but it was boiling hot and the lavender salts provided soon filled the air with their pungent scent. As she slid into the warmth, Delilah felt comforted and cleansed, and she lay there for almost an hour before finally pulling out the plug.

She went down to supper in her new cords and a jumper, her face free of make-up and her hair in a long plait. She felt like an impostor, but she quite enjoyed her new role. It was certainly quicker to get ready.

Elizabeth had laid supper for them in the dining room, and lit a peat fire. They sat at a round mahogany table set with well-worn Irish silver, crystal and linen, all of which had obviously been in the family for generations. Around the dark red walls were ancestral portraits and hunting scenes.

'All my husband's mad relatives.' Elizabeth explained them away with a wave of her hand.

Her husband had been the local doctor, taking over from his father before him. He had retired fifteen years ago, and died five. She hadn't wanted to leave Gortnaflor.

'Of course not!' exclaimed Delilah. 'Why would you?'

She'd been running it as a bed and breakfast ever since.

'Though I do dinner for guests I like.' She smiled, then her face became sad. 'It's a struggle. The garden's a mind of its own. There's just me and Johnny Roche keep it in hand. But I love it. I'm seventy-eight next birthday, but I'd rather die here struggling than bored to tears in one of those terrible homes. I've a girl who comes in from the village to help with the cleaning. Regine.' She poured Delilah a tiny glass of her raspberry liqueur. 'It's a magical place, Gortnaflor. It helps people forget.'

'Then maybe I was meant to come here.'

Elizabeth's wise blue eyes gazed at her. Delilah blushed, wondering if she'd given too much away.

'It was the Tourist Board sent you here, not the leprechauns,' said Elizabeth gently. 'But we'll do our best.'

At ten o'clock, Delilah climbed the stairs. She was exhausted. She opened the window in the bedroom and leaned out into the velvety blackness, relishing the silence, and the cool night air on her face.

She climbed into bed. The sheets were heavy Irish linen, cold at first, and rather scratchy, but somehow they moulded themselves to her body and the blankets soon warmed her up and before she knew it she had drifted off into the most deliciously healing sleep.

The next morning she woke with a lump of dread in her throat and a sudden sense of panic at what she had done.

She had spent so much of her life being responsible that suddenly doing something rather reckless didn't sit easily with her. She started to run through all the people who would be affected by her disappearance, and felt increasingly uncomfortable. What would the girls think? Did they even know? And poor Polly would be getting the brunt of the drama, running round like a headless chicken. Tony, too, would be pulling his hair out.

She didn't care how Raf was feeling. Not one jot. In fact, she hoped he hadn't slept a wink all night.

However, she did feel she ought to do something to stop everyone panicking. She had effectively disappeared without trace. What if police had been called? They would be combing the country now, trying to track her down. And she supposed they would, eventually – they would find her details on the ferry booking system, and where she had spent money.

The last thing she wanted was to be found. She knew the police wouldn't do anything until she had been missing for twenty-four hours – it was just coming up to thirty since she had left Bath – so if she got in contact any search would be called off.

She got up and dressed quickly, and went down for breakfast. She could only manage a piece of toasted soda bread and some thick-cut marmalade.

'I don't suppose you've got a computer here?' she asked Elizabeth, not holding out much hope. There wasn't even a television as far as she could see.

'I have not,' replied Elizabeth. 'My son's always on at me to get one. And a mobile phone. But I can honestly say I have never felt the need for either.'

'You lucky thing,' said Delilah. 'My whole life is ruled by emails and text messages.'

'The girls in the tourist office will let you use theirs. I'll ring them.'

An hour later, Delilah was opening her Hotmail account on the Tourist Board computer system. She chewed the side of her finger as she composed a suitable missive. She'd send it to Polly, who was at the centre of operations.

Dear Polly, she wrote. *Just a note to tell you not to panic. I expect you've heard what's happened by now. I've gone away for a while to get my head together. Please look after Doug for me, or if you can't get Tyger to move into The Bower. I'm safe and well. Love to the girls. And to you. Delilah*

She didn't put a kiss. She wasn't in a kissy mood. She pressed Send, then felt a sense of relief. She'd done the responsible thing – nobody could accuse her of a melodramatic disappearance – and the police wouldn't be interested. She was safe in her little bubble for the time being.

Twenty-Seven

Polly put her hands over her ears while Tony exploded.

He had turned up at The Bower that morning to find Delilah missing, and quickly put together the missing pieces of the jigsaw, finding out from Miriam that both Delilah's show and her book had been dropped. He got straight on the phone to Raf.

'Why the hell didn't she tell me?' Tony thundered. 'She knows the bloody rules. It would be pretty embarrassing if the press started phoning for comments and I didn't even know. What's she thinking of?'

'Um . . .' Raf said awkwardly. 'There might be something else on her mind.'

'What? What else could be more important?'

Raf told him about Pandora.

Tony hit the roof.

'For God's sake, haven't you learned from your mistakes? You've got the chance for a clean slate, a new beginning, and you go and fuck it up. Royally.'

'Nobody knows. We were very discreet.'

'For fuck's sake, don't be so naive. Pandora might as well be walking around with an *I've shagged Raf Rafferty* T-shirt on. Where is she? I need to talk to her.'

'Calm down, Tony. It's all cool. Pandora knows to keep her mouth shut.'

'She's an *actress*. If she thinks she can get some good publicity out of this, she'll squeal. I need to make sure she knows exactly what this all means. I'll come down. Take her out for lunch. Put her in the picture.'

'OK.' Raf knew there was no point in trying to stop Tony when he was on a roll. After all, this was what he was being paid for. And he did have a point.

'We need a game plan. We don't want the press finding out Delilah's done a runner. If we're going to salvage anything from this fiasco, we've got to be watertight. I'll draft a press release about her being dumped and get it sent out. It's better they find out from us than someone leaks it.' He paused momentarily for breath. 'Tell Pandora I'll be there by one o'clock.' And he slammed the phone down.

Polly looked at him.

'Raf and Pandora Hammond,' Tony told her. 'Caught in delicto by Delilah. Full marks to him for a monumental cock-up. I knew this would happen. I warned him to be careful. I must admit, I had my money on Genevieve Duke, but at least she would have had the sense not to get caught. Not like some publicity-hungry little slut—'

'Tony . . .' Polly was staring at her inbox. The email from Delilah had just appeared. She printed it off and handed it to Tony, who read it with an impassive expression.

'Well, at least we know she hasn't jumped off Beachy Head.' He crumpled the message up and fired it across the kitchen. He feigned fury, but Polly privately thought that Tony was rather enjoying the drama. He got terribly bored if there wasn't anything cooking, and this was brewing up nicely.

'You don't know where she's gone, do you?' His eyes bored into Polly. 'Only I know how much she trusts you.'

'No, I don't!' Polly protested.

Disgruntled, Tony sat down and compiled a press release. After fifteen minutes huffing and puffing, he read it out: '*Delilah Rafferty and her production company have decided that the time has come for her to take a well-earned break from her television commitments so she can concentrate on her other projects.* What the fuck they are I've got no idea, but it sounds good. *She is on holiday at the moment, recharging her batteries, but she has lots of ideas for the future, and is welcoming the opportunity for a change of direction. Watch this space!'* He looked at Polly. 'All PR speak for *she's been fired and had a nervous breakdown*, but you've got to go through the motions. What do you think?'

Polly looked upset. 'I think we should call the police.'

'That's the last thing we should do. We know she's all right. Send that off to all the appropriate people. I'm off to Bath. Book me somewhere for lunch with the fragrant Miss Hammond, will you? Text me the details.'

And he was gone.

Polly looked after him with her mouth open. How rude could you get? She was employed by the Raffertys, not him – she wasn't his personal assistant. But it wasn't in Polly's remit to rock the boat, and so she went online to find a restaurant and booked him a table, then dutifully sent off the press release.

Then she went out into the garden and sat on the bench. She started to peel an orange – she was trying to be good, and only snack on fruit – but she had barely got the skin off before big, fat tears began trickling down her cheeks.

She'd put Raf on a pedestal for all those years. Of course, she knew about his womanising in the old days, but she thought that was all in the past. She thought he was devoted to Delilah. To think she had wasted all that time worshipping him, when he was no better than all the other low-rent celebrities who couldn't keep it in their trousers.

Raf Rafferty, her god, her hero, was nothing but a sleaze.

Three hours later, Tony sat Pandora down for a discreet lunch in the Queensberry Hotel in Bath. He made it clear he wasn't going to spend much time on small talk.

'We'll have the *menu rapide*,' he told the waiter.

That was fine by Pandora, who didn't feel much like eating.

'I'll cut straight to the chase,' Tony said as soon as their food arrived. 'I can't impress on you quite how important it is that this doesn't get out. We're rebuilding Raf's brand from womanising pisshead to style-icon and family man, so we don't want anyone getting wind of him getting his leg over.'

Pandora looked at him, her violet eyes wide and brimming with unshed tears.

'I'd never do anything to hurt Raf or his reputation. I feel terrible about what's happened.'

Not so terrible you couldn't keep your legs shut in the first place, thought Tony viciously. He leaned forward.

'The thing is, if it does come out, then it won't look good for you. The press are never very keen on the "other woman". They'll rake up all sorts of dirt about you, and what they don't rake up they'll make up. So best just to keep schtum in the first place, eh?'

His message was pretty clear. What the press didn't dig up, he would provide.

'Of course,' Pandora agreed, but her chin was wobbling. 'I can't believe this has happened. I don't know what to do. I've got no one I can talk to about it. I . . .'

She took in a deep breath, ready to unburden herself. Tony rolled his eyes.

'Don't tell me. You love him.'

She nodded, weeping into her tuna carpaccio. Tony looked at his watch and heaved a sigh. He really didn't have time for this. Bloody women. They were all the same. One orgasm and they thought they were in love.

Raf put a kindly arm around a red-eyed Pandora when she came back to the shoot after her lunch with Tony.

'He wasn't too tough on you, was he?'

'He was a pig,' she blurted out. 'I don't know why you have someone like that working for you.'

'Because he's good at his job,' said Raf. 'I'm sorry if he was harsh.'

'Don't be nice to me,' pleaded Pandora. 'I'll start crying again.'

Genevieve came over with a cup of tea and a vial of Optrex. Dickie was looking increasingly stressed, and the crew were looking curious. They sensed that something was up.

'Go and put some of these in before people start asking questions.' Genevieve handed Pandora the eye-drops, then turned to Raf with a rueful smile.

'I feel like bloody Brown Owl,' she told him. 'Tea and sympathy. It's really not my thing, you know.'

'You've been a star,' he said gratefully. 'I don't know where I'd be without you.'

'On the front page of the *News of the World*, probably. Any word from Delilah?'

'No. Not since her enigmatic email to Polly.' Tony had given him the details. In the meantime, Raf had given up trying to phone Delilah. It was obvious she wasn't going to answer. 'I'm going to have to go home tonight. Tell the girls in the morning.'

Genevieve winced. She imagined the news would go down with those three like a cup of cold sick.

'Do you want me to come with you? Give you a bit of moral support? Or should that be immoral support?'

'Would you?' Raf was really starting to value Genevieve's friendship. She'd proved a stalwart throughout the whole thing. 'It's really going beyond the call of duty.'

'There but for the grace of God,' she told him with a shrug. 'And it keeps my mind off the fact that *I'm* too old to see any action.'

The next morning, Polly eyed up the island in the centre of the kitchen and decided that if there was anything missing it was tough. She'd laid out blueberry muffins, maple and pecan Danish pastries and a huge white platter of fruit – slices of mango, pineapple, peaches and nectarines and a mound of cherries. Coffee was brewing, and there were jugs of blood orange juice and bottles of water.

It was Saturday morning, and she should have been going to

meet her parents for lunch. But Tony had called her the afternoon before and told her that Coco, Violet and Tyger had been gathered together for a 'breakfast meeting'. Her parents had been disappointed, but she had explained to them that there was a crisis.

Sometimes she wondered what the Raffertys would do if *she* had a crisis. She never did. She had barely had any time off, even for illness, since she started working for them. She was too soft, that was the truth of it. She knew she was a fool to be at their beck and call, but even now her loyalty meant that she had cancelled her own commitments on a Saturday to make sure that everything was perfect, because she couldn't bear the thought of the girls hearing the news, and she wanted to be there for them. Plus she felt guilty about Delilah's disappearance, because Polly felt guilty about everything, even if it wasn't her fault. And she missed her. The house was desolate without her.

Doug the Pug was pining, too. He wasn't eating, and he was starting to tuck at the ribs already. He was listless and could barely heave himself out of his basket. She'd let him sleep in her bed with her every night and lavished as much affection on him as she could, but she wasn't Delilah.

She looked at the clock. The council of war was due to start at eleven, but it would be a miracle if anyone was here before midday on a Saturday morning, so she wasn't going to hold her breath. She covered everything with cling-film and decided to try to coax Doug out for a walk.

He just looked up at her as if to say, *What's the point?*

She sighed, and went to check her computer again in case Delilah had got in touch. She kept sending emails through to her Hotmail account, and texting her phone, but nothing. Delilah didn't want anyone to know where she had gone.

The alarm clock went off for the third time that morning, and this time it wasn't taking any nonsense.

'It's no good, we're going to have to get up.' Tyger's voice was muffled. She had her head buried in the pillows, the duvet over her head. She began prodding Louis playfully, digging him in the ribs with her finger. 'Make me coffee.'

'You make *me* coffee. You're the wife.' He poked her back good-naturedly, and she pretended to gasp in outrage. Moments later they were play-fighting, which inevitably led to frenzied love-making. As he pretended to pin her down with both his arms, then spread her legs with his knees, Tyger made a half-hearted effort to protest.

'Dad's going to be furious if we're late. He said it was really important. And Dad never – oh! Oh God. Oh fuck it, who cares?'

She gave in as Louis slid in and out of her with sadistically slow and deliberate strokes, a mischievous smile on his face. She tried to make him move faster, urging him with her hips.

'Ah ah,' he chided. 'My game. My speed.'

Tyger knew better than to argue, and anyway, the feeling building up inside her was so delicious she had lost the will to resist.

They'd been out to a club the night before – a swanky new venue where they had been invited to be guest DJs. And they'd rocked the place. No one had left until four, when they had to be forcibly ejected by security. They would all still be there now given half the chance. It hadn't been a tacky rent-a-crowd event either. It had been a long time since Tyger had seen so many famous faces in one room. It just went to show how much pulling power she and Louis now had. They were making the most of being the king and queen of the London scene while it lasted, and cashing in on their notoriety. *Knickers to It* sales had rocketed. As fast as Tyger thought up new designs, they sold out. Tickets for Louis' upcoming tour in the summer had sold out in minutes. They were on the cover of every magazine.

Tyger knew it wouldn't last for ever. You were only ever flavour of the month for a limited time.

'We've got to make hay while the sun shines,' she told Louis, who never failed to be awed by Tyger's energy, her enthusiasm, her ability to work her socks off all day and then party all night. He did his best to keep up. Secretly, all he ever wanted was to be alone with her, to have her to himself. Make love to her all day and all night, if he could. There was nothing like a bit of morning nookie to get your adrenalin going, he thought, as Tyger exploded in yet another mind-blowing climax.

'Fuck me, you're good,' she breathed in Louis' ear.

'I know.' He grinned. They both lay back for a moment, as their heartbeats subsided. Then Tyger threw back the sheets.

'We really, really, really have to get ready,' she told him, striding across the room and pulling open the wardrobe. Yesterday's clothes were strewn on the floor, but she just stepped over them.

'What's it all about?' he asked.

'I dunno. Probably something to do with Mum's birthday. It's her fiftieth soon – Dad might be planning a surprise.'

Louis felt the familiar claw of panic. Maybe he'd been found out? Maybe the Raffertys were going to interrogate him? Maybe this was it? Maybe that was the last time he would be allowed to make love to his gorgeous, funny, crazy, sexy wife? She wouldn't want him once she found out.

Subdued, he clambered out of his side of the bed. He couldn't put up with this much longer. Whatever happened, he was going to come clean to Tyger tonight.

Violet came to, drowsily, as she felt a velvet pair of lips skittering over her skin. She stretched out languorously, enjoying the sensation. She could never get used to the powdery softness of Justine's skin against hers, the silkiness of her hair, her delicate perfume. It never ceased to make her head swim and her senses tingle. Only a girl could really know what another girl wanted. She cried out in pleasure, clutching at the empty air with her fists, as Justine teased her to climax yet again, the tip of her tongue flickering oh-so-lightly, almost not there. A man would never have the knowledge or the patience to be so subtle, so elusive, so confident of the right moment to finally apply pressure. It was heavenly.

As Justine laughed in delight at the success of her perseverance, Violet pulled her face up to meet hers and kissed her own juices away, wrapping her tongue around her lover's.

Moments later, however, as the last waves of her orgasm ebbed away, she felt her usual sense of discomfort. What she was doing was wrong. Not morally – she had no problem with same-sex relationships. What was wrong was that Justine meant nothing to her emotionally, not really. Violet was ashamed to admit that for her it was just a game, and she knew it wasn't for Justine. The fact that she'd given up the opportunity to go to Berlin proved it, and she could also tell by the intensity, by the way she looked at her, by the way she held her, that Justine was properly in love. Whereas for Violet this was . . . well, a novelty, a distraction.

She certainly couldn't imagine being with a girl for ever. For a start, she couldn't deny what she was missing: maleness. Hard muscles, a broad chest. Stubble. Sweat. Strength. Being overpowered. The contrast. She would swap subtlety for masculinity any day of the week. When she was in Justine's arms, she certainly enjoyed the pleasure she gave her, but she was starting to hunger for something different. It was almost like eating too much chocolate – irresistible at the time, but afterwards it left her feeling slightly sick, unable to face another bite, and craving something savoury.

'Violet?'

Justine was next to her, staring at the ceiling thoughtfully. Violet knew she wasn't going to like what was coming.

'Mmm?' she managed.

Justine rolled over to face her.

'Maybe . . . you should tell everyone today. About us. As your whole family's going to be together.'

Violet tensed. She had deliberately been avoiding this conversation. She knew it was bothering Justine that their affair was clandestine. Deliberately so.

'I don't know,' she replied. 'I don't know if I'm ready.'

For heaven's sake, she told herself. Just tell her it's over. Why couldn't she do that? If she wasn't emotionally attached, it should be easy. One swift blow. Finished. Job done.

'I really think I should tell my dad,' Justine was saying. 'I know he suspects something. He just can't understand why I didn't want to go to Berlin. I've got to tell him soon.'

Violet thought quickly. She reached out and stroked Justine's shoulder.

'Can we wait a couple of weeks?' she pleaded. 'I'm doing so well with my writing at the moment.' This was true. She'd written three more songs, and she and Sammy were working on them in preparation for a big gig they had coming up. Violet was going to sing her own stuff for the first time. She was going to ask some industry people to come and watch. 'Once we make an announcement, our lives won't be our own,' she went on. 'It'll be mega stressful. I don't want to mess up my chances for the sake of waiting a little longer.'

'I just feel like I'm living a lie, not telling people.'

For a long time, Violet didn't answer. She was the one living a lie. She was a spineless coward, using someone else for her own pleasure, with no intention of making a commitment whatsoever. A blood-sucking vampire who was exploiting the novelty of a deliciously naughty situation to her own end. If she had any moral fibre at all, she would end it now.

She looked at the clock. Shit. She had less than half an hour to get to The Bower. If she finished with Justine now, there would be tears, recriminations, heartbreak. She didn't have time.

Tonight. She'd sit her down and tell her tonight.

Coco woke up feeling like death. Fluey, and thick in the head. She'd been feeling like this on and off for the past week. When you looked at her schedule, it wasn't surprising – she had been in almost every scene, even if it was just carrying a bedpan.

And that was great, because it meant she would have lots of exposure, but she really felt like she needed a break.

What she didn't need was a trip over to Richmond for a family pow-wow. She wondered what it was all about. Raf had sounded mysterious on the phone. It wasn't like him to summon them all like that – it was much more Delilah's style. She couldn't just ignore it, though. Hopefully they would be finished by lunchtime, then the rest of the day would be her own. She'd go over to The Melksham, get a couple of spa treatments, chill out and relax. Get their amazing chicken and butternut squash salad sprinkled with pumpkin seeds – that should boost her energy levels. Then get ready for her evening out.

Benedict Amador had phoned and asked her out for dinner. They had been to the opera the week before, and Coco was starting to realise that she liked him. Really, really liked him. OK, so he was as old as her father, but neither Raf nor Benedict looked or acted over fifty. He was sophisticated without being stuffy; very witty and erudite, without being superior. And he had an underlying sense of power that Coco found incredibly attractive. You got the feeling when you were with him that he could make anything happen with a discreet click of his fingers. Doors opened, staff were attentive, bottles of champagne arrived seamlessly, there was never anything so vulgar as a bill to be paid. It was far more discreet than the showy, showbiz way of life she was used to – of course she got attention wherever she went, but at a price. With Benedict, everything was understated.

But he hadn't made a move on her yet. He was the perfect gentleman. Just like the first night, he had his driver take her home at the end of the evening, kissing her politely on both cheeks before he drove off again in the Bentley. Which meant, of course, that Coco was getting quietly desperate. She longed to feel his long, tanned fingers on her skin. She knew he would be masterful in bed. He was a man who paid attention to detail, who liked the best things in life, and that ethos would be carried through into the bedroom.

She went over to her wardrobe to choose a couple of outfits to take with her. She quickly picked out a tan silk Chloe skirt that skimmed her thighs – it would be perfect teemed with a pair of Tabitha Simmons wedges and a white tee, with some statement jewellery. She packed them up in a large bag together with a selection of underwear. Then she pulled on her cashmere yoga pants and hooded top, together with her MBTs. She still felt under the weather. She swallowed down a cup of tea and picked at some toast, but ended up chucking it in the bin.

Her hand hovered over her handbag.

What the hell was she thinking? She never usually indulged on a day off. And she had been doing so well to keep off it over the past week. But this morning she felt a bit under the weather, as if everything was a huge effort. Maybe one line would kick start her into action . . .

No. There wasn't any need for it any more, she reminded herself. She had got over her initial fears. She had got to know all her colleagues at the studio – she was part of the gang. And she certainly knew her part well enough by now. She had worked hard on the role of Emily, brought little characteristics and quirks to her. Playing her had become second nature – she and Emily were one.

She had to learn to face the world without it.

Raf arrived at The Bower before the girls. His stomach was in knots. How was he going to tell them what had happened? He went over and over different explanations in his mind, but no matter how he said it, he came out of it the bad guy. Which, of course, he was.

Polly could barely look him in the eye. He went to give her a peck on the cheek but she bolted out of the kitchen, muttering about getting something from the office.

'Darling, you're just going to have to bite the bullet.'

Genevieve was brisk and frank. 'You've been a total cock, and now you have to face the music. God, how many more clichés can I pop out?'

'I am a cliché,' observed Raf ruefully. 'I've run true to type, haven't I?'

'For God's sake, everyone does it, given half the chance. Don't beat yourself up about it. Your only crime was getting caught.'

'Delilah wouldn't do it. I know she wouldn't. Never.' He poured some fresh coffee beans into the grinder, and winced as the machine pulped them into fine powder with seconds. It should be his dick in there, he thought. That was the punishment he deserved.

Doug the Pug stared at him from his basket, his eyes glassy.

'Even the bloody dog knows.'

'Don't be so stupid.' Genevieve couldn't be doing with sentimentality over animals.

'He does. He's lying there looking at me accusingly.'

'He's lying there because he's too fat to get up. He needs to lose some weight.'

'He is losing weight. He's pining—'

The security buzzer went, which meant someone had driven in through the gates. Raf's stomach lurched. He had no idea how they were going to react. Which one of them would judge him, and which one would forgive?

The first to arrive was Coco. She looked around the kitchen suspiciously. 'What's the story? Where's Mum?'

Raf cleared his throat nervously. 'Sit down,' he said. 'I'll make you a coffee.'

'No thanks.' Coco was fiddling with the trio of slim gold bangles she wore on her wrist. She looked at Genevieve suspiciously.

'How's the show going?' asked Genevieve. 'We've been watching it when we can.'

Coco looked backwards and forwards between her and Raf. 'We?'

'All of us. In the digs. I love the guy who plays your boyfriend—'

'He's a twat.'

Raf put a cup of coffee down in front of her.

'Dad – I said no to coffee. What is all this about?'

'Let's wait till the others get here. I don't want to go through it all twice.'

He didn't want to go through it all once, for that matter.

Finally, they were all lined up in front of him, sitting at the island. His beautiful daughters: Coco, cool and classic, slightly haughty, the most suspicious and hostile; Violet, exotic with her short, sharp bob and her cherry-red lips, and Tyger, fizzy, kooky and lovable. How was he going confess he had betrayed not just Delilah but the three of them?

Genevieve had tactfully asked Louis to come out into the garden with her, for which he was grateful. And Polly had scuttled back into the office yet again, only appearing to kiss all three girls hello before vanishing with yet another reproachful glance.

'I'm not proud of what I'm about to tell you,' Raf began. 'I've been a selfish, foolish, uncaring, self-indulgent—'

'Cut to the chase, Dad,' said Violet, rolling her eyes. 'We can decide what you've been when you tell us.'

'OK. Your mum caught me in bed with another woman.'

There was a stunned silence.

Coco banged her hand down on the island.

'I knew it,' she exclaimed. 'Fucking Genevieve Duke. How dare she even show her face here? Get her out of here now.'

'No, no. It's not Genevieve,' Raf assured them all hastily. 'Believe me; she's given me a harder time than anyone over it. No, it was . . . Pandora Hammond.'

'Pandora Hammond!' sputtered Tyger. 'She's young enough to be—'

'I know. I know.'

'So hang on. Where *is* Mum? What happened when she found out?' Violet demanded.

'I don't know,' admitted Raf. 'She's . . . done a runner. She just drove off into the night, and I haven't heard from her since.'

'So she could be dead? She might have had an accident.'

'For God's sake, Dad!'

'Have you called the police?'

They were all talking at him at once. He held up his hand.

'Hold on. She's sent an email to Polly saying she's perfectly fine, but she doesn't want anyone to know where she is.'

'So she's safe?'

'As far as I know.' Raf ran his fingers through his hair. 'But she's not answering her phone or her emails. And we've got no way of finding out where she's gone.'

'What about the police? Surely they can help?'

He shook his head. 'She's not officially missing, because she's contacted us. There's nothing they can do.'

'Everyone can do something for the right price,' Violet pointed out.

'Well, we could contact the papers. Ask for the public's help. But I don't think that's what your mother would want.'

'Or you,' said Coco, harsh to the end. 'They'd soon get to the bottom of what has happened.'

'Yep,' agreed Violet. 'The Raffertys' dirty linen all over the headlines. Again.' She stared stonily at her father. 'Why? I don't get it.'

'Yeah, Dad,' chipped in Tyger. 'Why are you shagging some-one half your age?'

Raf flinched. It sounded so cheap, coming from the lips of his beloved youngest daughter. Well, it was cheap. There was nothing honourable about it at all. It wasn't as if he'd gone and fallen madly in love with Pandora. There was no defence for it at all.

'I don't know,' he said bleakly. 'All I know is we need to try to track down your mother. So if anyone can come up with any ideas . . .'

Justine stood uncertainly in Violet's kitchen, peering in through the glass of the oven door, wondering how her asparagus quiche would turn out. Would it be like the picture, or would it be a total disaster? It certainly smelled delicious, but she wanted it to look perfect too. Just like the photo in Delilah's cookery book, which was lying open on the work surface.

In the past, she had never spent any more time in the kitchen than was necessary, but since she had turned her back on her career, there was a whole new world opening up for her. And she was astonished how relaxing and therapeutic she found it. Normally on a Saturday she'd be at the gym or the pool undertaking one of her punishing regimes, or meeting Alex and his gang for a late lunch at the Bluebird Café, or calling into one of her favourite boutiques to check out their new stock.

Instead, she'd had the radio on while she chopped and stirred, humming happily with an apron on! Not stalking Sloane Street in her killer heels. It was strange. Men had always found her intimidating and slightly aggressive. It had taken another woman to soften her. She felt as if she was turning from a predatory puma into a fluffy kitten. And she loved it. She was purring her way through life, discovering things about herself that she never knew.

She tried to analyse it. What did she have to prove? Was she trying to show that she was as good as Delilah in order to win Violet's affections? Or maybe it was simply that she was happy and relaxed, and therefore content to indulge herself in something she had previously considered mundane, not to mention messy. Her philosophy had always been why get your hands dirty when there was usually someone else around to do it for you?

The timer pinged and she opened the oven door tentatively.

As she pulled the quiche towards her, she felt an immense glow of satisfaction. It didn't look bad at all. OK, so she hadn't made the pastry herself – hadn't even rolled it, in fact, but had bought a ready-made shell – but there was no point in trying to run before she could walk. This was her first culinary triumph, and she couldn't wait to share it. It bubbled golden, the spears of asparagus perfectly spaced. Her mouth watered.

When she heard Violet at the door, she rushed to greet her, hardly able to wait to show off her achievement.

She stopped in her tracks when she saw her. Violet's face was blotchy from crying. As soon as she saw Justine, she fell into her arms, sobbing.

'Bastard,' she sobbed. 'What a complete and utter bastard. I can't believe it. After everything he put us through, he goes and does it again.'

Justine could barely make out what she was saying. She put her arms round Violet, stroking her back, shushing her until she had calmed down enough to explain what Raf had told them.

'I just feel so guilty,' she wailed. 'I had that stupid row with Mum and I didn't phone her. I left Coco's screening without making it up to her properly. And now she's vanished off the face of the earth. Who knows what she's going to do?'

'Now come on.' Justine was the voice of reason. 'Your mum's not stupid. She probably just needs a bit of time out. Some space to think.'

Violet calmed down eventually.

'I'm so angry with him. Why does he have to do it? Mum is so gorgeous – why does he feel the need to be unfaithful to her?'

'Why does anybody?' asked Justine. 'People do it all the time.'

'I thought he'd changed. He was so awful when we were young. It was unbelievable, what Mum had to put up with. Every week his name was linked with some actress or starlet. He had the most terrible reputation. And he was always drunk.

I don't think I had a proper conversation with him until I was fifteen. Some of the time he didn't even recognise us, he was so out of it. We could never ask friends back, even though they were always dying to meet him.' She wiped her nose with the back of her hand. 'Then he turned into Mr Nice. For ten years he was the perfect father. Always there, completely reliable, supportive. And now he's reverted to type. But he can't blame the booze this time. He's obviously just a bastard through and through.'

Justine made no judgements, just murmured soothing phrases as Violet talked. Which she did. She poured her heart and soul out about their childhood and how difficult it had all been. How she used to feel sick because she was so worried that one day her mother would have had enough and would kick her father out. And in the end how she would pray that she would, just to bring an end to the terrible cycle.

'It's obviously engrained in him. Some terrible need to feel irresistible. He needs some bloody counselling. All those smug articles where he said he didn't need help to kick the booze? Took the credit for sorting himself out? Well, what about the sex addiction? He hasn't addressed that, has he?'

She started crying again.

'And I feel so guilty, because I was a bitch to Mum. I should have phoned her and apologised. She only wanted to help, and I didn't want her help, and I wanted to talk to her about you and I didn't have the nerve . . .'

Justine held her.

'Your mum will be fine. She's an amazing woman. She'll pick up the phone and talk to you when she's ready. She won't hold anything against you.'

'You don't think so?'

'Of course not. She's not that sort of person.'

'No . . .' Violet looked doubtful.

Justine was wonderful. She listened, and she didn't judge. She didn't tell Violet not to be silly, or say she was making too much of the whole thing, like a bloke would have. She cuddled her, and wiped away her tears, and made her delicious rose and cardamom tea to calm her down, then fed her the asparagus quiche that she had made. That made Violet cry again, because Justine had used one of her mum's recipes, and it tasted so good and so familiar.

Then she tucked her up in bed, in freshly laundered sheets, and stroked her brow until she slept for two whole hours in the middle of the afternoon. And when Violet woke she felt much better, much stronger, and she reached out for Justine, who hadn't left her side all the time she slept. And when they made love it was sweeter and more tender than it had ever been before.

In the middle of the night, Violet slipped out of bed and went to her piano. She wrote a song, a passionate outpouring of all the guilt and anger she felt at Raf's betrayal. It was bitter and heartfelt, very close to the bone. Violet didn't know if she could ever perform it in public. It would be like performing naked, stripping yourself bare in front of an audience. But she knew in her heart it was the best song she had ever written.

At dawn, she climbed back into bed. The birds were starting to sing. Justine stirred slightly in her sleep, turned over and instinctively slid an arm around Violet's waist, pulling her close. Violet felt safe and protected. She felt loved.

How could she reject Justine, when she made her feel like this? You didn't kick a love like that out of bed, not if you were sane.

Coco was enraged by Raf's confession, but she was determined it wasn't going to ruin her evening with Benedict. She gunned her car out of The Bower and drove at top speed to The Melksham, where she had a full body massage and an oxygen facial. She prayed she wouldn't get a chatty therapist, and she didn't. She was able to mull over the morning's events in her own mind, while undergoing the most heavenly treatments imaginable. Benedict had been right when he told her he only ever hired the best, she thought, as the girl trickled sweet-scented unguents onto her skin.

Her father's undoing had come about from the pressure of working in a tight team to a tight schedule, Coco concluded. Shooting a film was claustrophobic and incestuous. Relationships became very intense very quickly, and you had to trust people or you were sunk. She knew this from working on *Critical but Stable*. Actors had affairs the whole time. They couldn't help themselves. They were needy and narcissistic. Coco had been able to resist getting involved with any of the cast because none of them were really her type, but she could see how it might happen.

She was also pretty sure her mother would survive. Delilah was tough. She would be figuring it all out somewhere. And when she came back she would have decided what to do. She wouldn't emerge as the victim in all of this. You didn't pull off what Delilah had pulled off, against the odds, by being a victim. Coco believed implicitly in her mother's capabilities. It would take more than Pandora Hammond to knock Delilah off her perch.

So although Raf's confession had left an unpleasant taste in her mouth, Coco wasn't unduly worried. It wasn't as if he harboured any strong feelings for Pandora. She would have been more worried if it had been Genevieve he had taken up with. Genevieve Duke was definitely more of a threat, but in fact had turned out to be an incredible ally. Coco had warmed to her immensely after this morning. She seemed to have the measure of Raf, and was dealing with him firmly and sensibly. Her father would be safe in Genevieve's hands, she felt certain.

After her treatments, Coco got herself ready for the evening. It was only while she was getting dressed that she realised she felt grotty again. She decided it must be all the toxins coming out after the massage – the therapist had warned her she might feel a bit below par, and to drink lots of water to flush them away. So she ordered up a bottle of Badoit and drank it down while she did her make-up.

Then she checked herself in the mirror for the hundredth time – the skirt was sexy but not tarty, the T-shirt nicely clingy but not too revealing, her heels were high but not sluttish. She applied another layer of YSL gloss to make her lips shimmer and glisten. She wanted to look irresistible.

Benedict came to collect her at six. He led her outside, where the Bentley was waiting.

'I hope you don't mind,' said Benedict. 'I booked us somewhere out of town. It's such a beautiful evening.'

'I don't mind at all,' replied Coco, intrigued.

Benedict reached over to help her with her seatbelt, and as his hand brushed against her nipples they hardened. Their eyes met briefly, momentarily, then the driver started the engine and they both sat back.

He had found the most exquisite and tiny restaurant on the banks of the Thames.

'One of my ex-chefs,' he told her. 'It's one of my best-kept secrets. The food is sublime. Worth at least two stars, but he refuses to apply. He doesn't want the hassle. He's content to have happy customers.'

They sat out on a terrace, and were brought tiny little *amuse-gueules* to eat with their aperitifs as they watched boats chugging up and down in the evening sunshine.

Nevertheless, Coco found it hard to relax. As they moved inside to take their place at the table, she still felt under the weather. She knew perfectly well it wasn't the after effects of the massage. She knew exactly what would put her right. And she knew it was lying in her handbag. As she sipped her kir royale, she gave herself a pep talk. She had to sit it out. Eventually, the craving would leave her and she would learn to relax. For the millionth time she cursed herself for succumbing in the first place, and for letting her habit get the better of her.

She chewed the inside of her lip, as if the pain would take her mind off it.

Benedict looked at her barely touched plate, concerned.

'Are you OK? Is this not your sort of food?'

'No, no – it's lovely. And I'm sorry. I'm being very rude,' Coco told him. 'It's just . . . I'm worried about my mother.'

He frowned. 'Tell me.'

Coco hesitated for a moment, but decided she trusted him. Benedict was a man of the world. He wasn't going to betray her confidence by running to the nearest phone to alert the press.

And so she told him about Raf, and Delilah's disappearance, pouring out her heart. And he was wonderful – understanding and soothing, and even promising to see what he could do to try to find Delilah.

'I've got contacts,' he twinkled at her, and her tummy did a flip. God, he was gorgeous. So gorgeous she had almost forgotten her craving. It was him she was longing for now, not the little bag of white powder.

As the waiter took away their dessert plates, Benedict reached over and put his hand on hers. It was strong and powerful; and as he stroked the inside of her wrist with an incredible gentleness, Coco felt her insides melt, becoming as syrupy as the Sauternes they were drinking.

'I booked a room,' he told her. 'In case we didn't feel like going back.'

She looked into his eyes. They were wise, warm, sexy. The confident eyes of a man who knew damn well he wasn't going to get no for an answer.

They abandoned their table with almost indecent haste, passing the waiter who watched them go with a knowing smile.

The bedroom was minute, with a sloping wooden floor and a four-poster bed stuffed with lace-edged linen in front of a leaded bay window. But they weren't interested in their surroundings. Benedict pulled her to him and kissed her properly for the first time. Coco felt a surge go through her; a high better than any drug could give her. She unbuttoned his shirt with trembling fingers, then bent her head to kiss his chest. She could feel his heart beat beneath the warmth of his skin.

She felt his fingers on the inside of her bare thigh. She wanted to freeze this moment in time for ever.

Afterwards, he looked at her, and she thought she saw tears in his eyes.

'You don't know how long I've waited for you,' he whispered.

And as he trailed his index finger down her body, Coco knew that from now on, she was going to be able to cope. For him, she would give up breathing.

Tyger reacted to her father's bombshell by going on an insane shopping spree. Even Louis was shocked by her ability to spend. It was almost frenzied. She scarcely seemed to give any of the items she bought proper consideration. She tossed item after item at the sales assistants, asking them to ring it all up.

'Tyger.' He put a restraining hand on her arm as she picked out three more dresses. If she wore a different outfit every day for the rest of the year she wouldn't get through everything she'd bought. 'Calm down. This is comfort buying.'

'So what?' she demanded. 'I can take it all back if I don't like it.'

He knew she wouldn't. When would Tyger ever have time to pack it all back up and return it to the store? She lived on full steam ahead. She never went backwards.

'Humour me,' she begged him, and so he did.

Half reluctantly, half gratefully. All the time they were out shopping was putting off the moment of reckoning. He had made himself a promise that morning. And he was going to keep it. The longer he put it off, the worse it would be. And he had to admit that he had admired Raf for his stoicism earlier. There weren't many men who could stand in front of the three Rafferty sisters, confess their sins and walk away unscathed. He was going to take a leaf out of his father-in-law's book.

Louis reckoned Raf was a pretty good role model. He knew he had to change. The persona he had built for himself might have sold records, but it had never sat comfortably. He had been floundering in a shallow and meaningless existence for long enough, feeling the pressure to behave badly and irresponsibly.

Tyger had given his life meaning. He had something to fight for. Someone to share things with. He wanted them to have a home. Maybe even a family before long. If his record company didn't like it, then tough. Worse people than him had cleaned up their act and had continued success. Not that he was going to be as pure as the driven snow. Just knock some of his murkier excesses on the head.

But first . . .

He piled all the glossy carrier bags into the back of the taxi that was waiting. Tyger had wanted to carry on, but eventually he'd put his foot down.

'I'm knackered. And you've got enough here to open your own shop.'

As the cab made its way back to Tyger's flat, Louis felt increasingly nervous. He had to do it. If he bottled out, he would hate himself. He could feel the words stick in his throat. He had to find some way to loosen them. A drink would help. Just a shot. He didn't want to start rambling, or saying things he didn't mean.

Tyger unlocked the door. Louis followed her in, dropping all the bags in the hallway, and followed her into the living area, where she collapsed on the sofa.

He loved her flat. He loved his too, for its stark, industrial minimalism, but he loved hers for its Tyger-ness. It was a kaleidoscope of colours and textures. It was dominated by a luxurious pillar-box-red sofa in jumbo cord piled high with fur cushions, a jewel-bright chandelier dangling overhead. There was a work-station in one corner surrounded by cuttings from magazines and fabric samples. Next to it was strung a washing line where she hung interesting motifs she had found: cocktail monkeys, plastic cherries, sweets, pieces of ribbon – all things that had been incorporated into her collections at some stage. There was a cardboard cut-out of the Pink Panther in another corner. A huge range of coffee-table books – everyone from Rothko to Weber to Warhol – were spread out on a silver coffee table. There was a nineteen-fifties cocktail cabinet, a rococo sideboard, a set of Eames chairs – all eras and decades were represented and sat together. Just like Tyger, it was a crazy mishmash of influences and contradictions that somehow, inexplicably, worked.

God, he loved her.

Louis went to the cocktail cabinet and poured himself a Southern Comfort, downing it in one.

She was flopped on the sofa. She'd kicked off her shoes. Her head was resting on a zebra-skin cushion, her skirt riding up her long, bare legs. On any other occasion, he would have had his hands in her knickers before you could say knife.

Not this time, though.

He put another tiny splash of Southern Comfort in his glass and went and stood in front of her.

'Tyger,' he said bravely, 'I've got something I need to talk to you about.'

She looked up at him, frowning, unaccustomed to the serious note in his voice.

'What?' she asked.

To his horror, he could feel tears welling up. Were they a Pavlovian reaction to the memory, or in anticipation of the fallout?

'It's pretty awful, what I'm going to tell you.'

She sat up, alarmed. 'Are you ill? You haven't got cancer—'

'No, no, no – nothing like that. I need to . . . tell you something about my past.'

She laughed. 'Louis, I know all about your past. The drugs, the drink, the sex, the hotel-trashing – nothing you can say can shock me.' She grinned up at him.

He didn't smile back. 'Yes, it can.'

Twenty-Eight

When Louis was five, his father ran off and left him and his mother.

No great loss. He barely spent any time at home anyway, as he was a long-distance lorry driver. But he left them without a penny. Worse than that, he left them with debts. They watched in horror as everything was repossessed. It was only a matter of weeks before their landlord turfed them out onto the street. The council re-housed them eventually, into a grim flat in an even grimmer estate on the outskirts of Swansea. His mum never told the debt-collectors where they had gone – they had nothing else to give them even if they could be found, but the sort of collectors that were after them didn't care. They would hound you into an early grave.

The walls in the flat ran with damp and Louis – or Little Dave, as he was known then, on account of his father having been Big Dave – had a permanent runny nose and a persistent cough. In time, his mother got a job – barmaid at the ugly, flat-roofed, concrete pub on the edge of the estate, with the optimistic name of The Bird in Hand. Louis was left alone in the flat while she worked the evening shift. A neighbour was supposed to look in on him every now and again, but she was so drunk she never remembered, just took the fiver Melinda paid her for doing it regardless. Anyway, Little Dave was a good, obedient child who would never have got up to any mischief, and no one in their right mind would venture up onto the seventh floor of their block – there wouldn't be anything worth nicking, everyone knew that. Only the total dregs lived up there.

Little Dave was always ill, so he rarely went to school. He developed asthma. His eyes were huge in his pale face, and he didn't move anywhere without his inhalers. His mother sometimes held him and cried when he had a bad attack, and that was when he knew that she did love him. She rarely showed it. There wasn't time. She was working in the pub at night and in a taxi office during the day, and at last there was enough money for them to eat and to have some new clothes.

For his eighth birthday she bought him a radio/cassette player that someone had been trying to get rid of in the pub, together with a box of tapes. These kept him engrossed while he was off school. He played them over and over, a totally random selection of outdated bands – Led Zeppelin, Captain Beefheart, Pink Floyd – but they took him off into another world. He spent hours deconstructing the music, analysing the lyrics, which he often didn't understand, singing along, inventing his own counter melodies and harmonies and wishing he had a guitar.

When he was nine, he noticed a change in his mother. She was brighter, almost care-free, and she had a sparkle in her eye. She came home later and later from the pub, and a couple of times she didn't come back until the next morning, sneaking in at half past seven, thinking he wouldn't hear. She bought more new clothes, started wearing perfume, and she bought him a guitar. To assuage her guilt – he understood that, but he didn't mind. His guitar became his constant companion. His guitar would never let him down.

Eventually, his mother introduced him to the reason for her change: the guy who ran the taxi company she worked for. Little Dave mistrusted Bernie on sight. He wore low-slung jeans and cowboy boots with a big belt, his stomach hanging over the top. He had a handle-bar moustache and a lot of heavy gold jewellery. Little Dave knew that the best thing he could do in Bernie's company was to keep quiet, but he was used to doing that, so nothing much changed. Except his name. He was now called just Dave – 'Little Dave' apparently reminded Bernie that there had once been a Big Dave, and Bernie was a jealous sort. So Dave it was. He wasn't really bothered what he was called, as no one much used his name anyway. He was so rarely at school it was all his teachers could do to remember.

And then his mother told him that they were going to be moving. To Bernie's farm. Bernie was rich. He did very well out of the taxis, apparently. Dave was quietly beside himself with excitement. He had visions of a thatched house in the middle of a patchwork of green fields filled with placid cows. He would have a swing – a rope swing – and maybe a tree house. And a cat. And somewhere to ride a bike. And he could go fishing.

He should have known better than to get his hopes up. The reality couldn't have been further from what he had imagined: a stark bungalow in the middle of a concrete yard, surrounded by ramshackle buildings in various stages of disrepair. There was a field beside it – not the lush pasture he had imagined, but a dry, barren wasteland peppered with ragwort, a huge electricity pylon planted in the middle of it. He couldn't ride a bike around the yard – not that he had one. In fact, he was warned off the yard. It was dangerous, Bernie told him. There were hazardous things stored there. Dave imagined vats of noxious chemicals and stayed away. He knew whatever was in there was valuable, because people arrived day and night to deliver and take things away. But the big chain-link fence was always bolted.

The one good thing that happened was Dave's health improved, with the fresh air and the dryer environment. He was excited about going to go to a new school, too, until his mother revealed the fact that it was a Welsh-speaking school, and he had no grasp of the language.

'You'll soon pick it up,' she told him, but she didn't understand how difficult it was, to feel like an outsider, an alien. He was teased – at least, he thought he was, he didn't have a clue what any of the other pupils were saying, but from the looks on their faces he didn't think they were being particularly friendly.

He withdrew into himself even further. Books and music became his escape. There was money at last – from Bernie's taxis, and whatever was in the sheds out the back. From time to time, he heard barking.

'Guard dogs,' Bernie would say. 'Vicious. Don't go near them or they'll have your hand off, sonny.'

But as Dave grew, so did his suspicions. There was more barking from the sheds than just guard dogs. And he had seen huge bags of dog-feed in the back of Bernie's truck more than once. His mother kept the office locked and he wasn't allowed in there.

He watched and waited. Every night, Bernie and his mum got drunk in front of the telly in the lounge, or went down to the pub for Country and Western. And he knew where Bernie kept the keys: hung on a big hook in the kitchen. And so one night, while they were out, he took the keys. His heart was thumping. He felt sick with terror, both from the fear of what he was going to find and from the fear of being caught. Bernie had a sort of sixth sense and was always looking at him suspiciously. Dave reckoned he didn't trust him, but he probably didn't trust anyone.

He fumbled with the lock. It was stiff, but eventually the key turned. He pushed the gate open, slipped through and shut it behind him. He didn't want to raise Bernie's suspicions if he came back early. He crept quietly towards the big barn at the back. Again this was padlocked, so he went through all the keys until he found the one that fitted and finally opened the door.

The smell hit him full in the face. He could barely see for flies. As his eyes grew accustomed to the darkness, he could finally see what lay inside.

Cages. Dozens of cages. And inside, dogs. Bitches on their

sides, bellies swollen but the rest of their bodies emaciated. Litters of puppies scrambling over each other, desperate to suck what nourishment they could from their mothers' teats. Cracked plastic bowls of congealed drying food lay untouched, swarming with flies. Most of the cages had no water.

It was hard to tell what breed each dog was, but he managed to identify a few: a Dalmatian, recognisable by the spots but totally etiolated; red setters, judging by the colour of the coat, even though due to the condition their coats were flat and dark. And smaller toy dogs – pugs, bichon frises, schnauzers – of the type favoured by mad old ladies and Hollywood stars.

It was a puppy farm. Dozens of breeds, the bitches churning out litter after litter. Bernie's money wasn't from cabs at all. It was blood money.

Dave stepped outside the shed and vomited, his sick splattering onto the concrete. He wiped his mouth with the back of his hand and looked up. Bernie was standing there. Fear made him retch again – he'd get a hiding for this, he was certain. But Bernie just laughed.

'Well, now you know, you can help me out. I could use another pair of hands.'

And so Dave became Bernie's partner in crime. He had no choice. If he reported him, or told anyone else, or went to the police, his mum would be implicated. She knew about the puppies. It was obvious now. She did all the paperwork. She took all the phone calls. She organised the sales.

He only referred to it once.

'Why?' he asked her.

'To give you a better life,' she replied sadly, and he knew this was true. At least now he had his health; and he was warm and dry and fed and clothed. Bernie had been her way out of a miserable existence, and if she felt guilty about the puppies at least it was better than feeling guilty about her son. She did love him. Dave knew she did.

Bernie and Dave travelled the motorways, working out the

best routes on a large tattered map pinned up in the office. Sometimes they would stop in a deserted car park somewhere and hand over a clutch of puppies. Sometimes they would pull up at the back of a pet-shop, offloading their illicit cargo in the dead of night to monosyllabic men. Sometimes they flogged puppies to members of the general public through a free paper. You got the best profit this way, but the chances of being rumbled were higher. And that was where Dave came in: a good-looking young lad was far less suspicious than fat, dodgy-looking old Bernie. And if he got arrested he was under-age, and Bernie had given him a good cover story.

At least when he sold to members of the public, he knew the puppies had the chance of a better life. He could tell by the way people handled them what sort of owners they were going to be. Usually the biggest danger was that they would be spoilt. It was unlikely that they would be sent back into the sort of hell they had escaped. He prayed they were little enough to have no memory of the horrors; that they would adapt to their new surroundings and become happy and healthy.

And all the time he buried himself further and further in his music. Bernie would give him a cut – a generous cut, to give him his due – and Dave spent it on cassettes. And a new guitar, and an amp. He discovered The Smiths, David Bowie, Talking Heads, Iggy Pop, The Cure, Leonard Cohen. Springsteen, Tom Petty, Lynyrd Skynyrd. Guns 'n' Roses. He didn't home in on a particular genre – just anyone he considered a good song writer. And he began to write himself, hoping that one day, one day . . .

It was a miserable and lonely existence. He hated the guilt, the double life. He distanced himself from his school com-panions for fear of them taking too much of an interest. He lived in terror of becoming too close to someone and blurting it all out. So he became even more of an outsider, the class freak, the guy who wore black and never took off his ear-phones. It was an isolating existence, but he had become Bernie's facilitator, the one who enabled all the puppy deals, to protect his mother. It was a vicious circle, a trap, and they were all implicated. So they had to stick together.

When he turned fifteen, he began to plot his escape. He stole money at school. Even from the teachers. It was surprising how many masters left their jackets on the back of their chairs; how many mistresses forgot to supervise their handbags during class. A fiver here and a tenner there soon added up.

He never stole from his mother. And he never stole from Bernie, because he knew he would catch him, and he would do something terrible in retaliation, something that might stop him getting away.

In the meantime, he buried his head in his books and played music. Books and records provided him with an escape and took him to another place. They gave him hope. He knew from the stories and the lyrics that not everyone's life was like this. One day he would be free.

Then came the day when he couldn't take any more.

He went into the shed to do the evening feed. At least he had persuaded Bernie to keep the animals cleaner and better fed, but their conditions were far from ideal, and they were barely given any medical attention. As he looked around, he saw that one of the bitches had haemorrhaged whilst giving birth. Next to the puppies was a pile of bloody insides.

His instinct was to rush to her, pick her up, demand that Bernie take her to the vet. As soon as Bernie saw her, he scoffed.

'Put her out of her misery!'

The dog had done what she needed. Seven litters in quick succession. What was the point in wasting precious profit on trying to save her life when she could no longer make him money?

Dave knew he had no choice. There was no way he would be able to get her to the vet himself. How would he get her there? How would he pay the bill? And what about all the questions that would be asked? Could he just say he'd found her on the side of the road?

'Do it!' Bernie forced a spade into his hands. 'She's done for; better off dead. Longer you keep her alive the longer she'll suffer.'

Dave looked at the puppies, each of them barely alive, their little noses poking the air blindly for the nutrients they needed but wouldn't get.

The mother was obviously in pain. She was bleeding heavily. A vet wouldn't be able to save her. A vet would put her down. But at least she'd go with kind words, a soothing voice, a gentle stroke as the injection was administered.

Not a bloody shovel over the back of her head.

He shut his eyes, lifted the spade, prayed that he had the strength to hit her hard enough the first time, that it would be all over quickly, that she wouldn't suffer – well, not any more than she already had.

Whack.

Bernie gave a bark of triumphant glee. 'I'll make a man of you yet,' he crowed.

'Shall I bury her?'

Bernie looked at him scornfully.

'Don't waste your energy digging a hole. Sling her in the incinerator.'

The smell of burning fur stayed in his head for ever.

The next day he jumped on a train. He was driving through glorious fields full of free animals. He was on his way to a new life. With four hundred and ninety-three pounds in his ruck-sack. He wasn't afraid. Nothing could be worse than what he had escaped, just like the puppies he had released out into the world.

He didn't think about his mother and how she might feel. He shut his mind to her. She would be all right without him. She had made her choice, the day she took up with Bernie. He didn't want her to come to any harm, but he didn't love her enough to tolerate what was happening at the farm any longer, and he knew if he forced her to make a choice between him and Bernie, she would stick with Bernie. Dave was old enough now to make his own way in the world.

On the train he chose his new name. Louis, because he had been reading about Louis XIV, and he liked the idea of a Sun King – it was an image full of hope. And Dagger. Like David Bowie, who had named himself after the knife 'to cut all the lies', he chose Dagger to kill all the memories.

The train drew into Paddington. The passengers stood up and surged for the exits. The minute he stepped off the train, he would be truly free. There would be no trail.

Louis Dagger stepped onto the platform.

As he finished his story, he could barely stand to look at Tyger and see her reaction. Tears were pouring down her face. He couldn't read her expression. Horror? Disgust? Loathing? Revulsion? The realisation that this was it; it was all over between them?

It was worse than waiting for a judge to pronounce the death sentence. The pause before she finally spoke seemed like an eternity.

She was whispering something. He leaned forward to catch her words.

'You poor baby . . .'

He looked at her in surprise.

'You don't . . . hate me for it?'

'Hate you? Of course I don't. You were forced into it. You didn't have any choice. You were just a kid.'

As he realised she wasn't going to judge him, he finally broke down. All the years of shame, all the horrible memories, came flooding back; he tried to choke them back, but now he'd allowed the tears to fall, they came thick and fast. He felt Tyger's arms around him, holding him tight, and he hugged her back, unable to believe how lucky he was.

He wasn't going to lose her. Despite his heinous crimes, Tyger was still his.

'What about your mum?' she was asking. 'Do you still see her?'

He shook his head.

'I can't go back. In case I'm seen. I can't let anyone know my past.'

'She must be sad, to have lost you.'

Louis shrugged. 'When you come from nothing, like we did, you don't have a lot of choice in life. You have to make sacrifices.'

Tyger sat for a moment, chewing her thumbnail. Which meant she was thinking.

'Is the bastard still selling puppies?' she asked finally.

Louis' heart sank. This would be the sticking-point. Tyger would want him to grass Bernie up.

'I think so.' He couldn't lie to her. 'I know the paper he advertises in. I still see his number. But I can't report him, Tyger. Mum would go down with him. And none of it's down to her. She only went with him because she thought she would give me a better life. And then she got in too deep.'

'I know, I know. And I'd never ask you to dump your own mother in it. But there's another way.'

'There is?' This girl never ceased to astound him. Her understanding, her compassion. Thank God he'd had the guts to tell her at last.

She nodded, and a brightness came into her eyes.

'We go down there ourselves. And we rescue them. The whole lot.'

Twenty-Nine

Since her arrival, Delilah had barely left Gortnaflor. She curled up on the sofa in the drawing room reading Molly Keane: wonderful tales of draughty Irish houses and mad old aunts. She borrowed a too-large pair of gumboots from the porch and went walking by the lake, watching the dragonflies skitter over the surface and the large brown trout glide underneath. There was a little boat-house, much of it rotten, most of it covered in slimy green moss, and inside she found a rowing boat. She didn't have the courage to take it out – it wasn't large, but she had no idea how to manhandle it to the water's edge or how to get in or how to wield the oars.

Raf would know, she thought sadly, then told herself she wasn't going to think about him. She wasn't going to think about any of them. It was a waste of her time. She was going to think about herself, and what she wanted from the rest of her life, and how to go about getting it.

Best of all was Elizabeth's food. Wonderful and plentiful Irish food: golden poached eggs with crunchy, groaty black pudding for breakfast; sorrel soup for lunch, laced with cream, and always a plentiful supply of the cakey soda bread that Elizabeth got up at six o'clock to bake. There would be lamb or salmon or salty gammon for supper, with potatoes – she'd never tasted potatoes like it, earthy and floury with the most fulsome flavour. She could feel herself putting on the pounds, but she didn't care. It was just fabulous to have somebody else to do the cooking. Other people usually shied away from catering for her, always thinking they were going to be harshly judged. And eating out in restaurants was no better. Chefs would fall over themselves to show off and bring out their signature dishes, and then wait for a verdict. Elizabeth just seemed pleased that she enjoyed what she ate.

'My son William is coming at the weekend,' Elizabeth told her at the end of the week. 'He comes for a fortnight every summer, before the season proper starts, and helps with the jobs that need doing. He's a hotshot lawyer in Dublin.'

Delilah's heart sank. She didn't want her peace invaded. She didn't like the thought of a hotshot lawyer son around the place, asking probing questions. And possibly recognising her. With no television at Gortnaflor – only an old-fashioned wireless in the drawing room for guests – it had been no trouble keeping her identity secret so far.

'By the way, how are you doing with your history?'

'Sorry?'

'Your family tree. Are you getting on all right?'

'Um – a bit slow. I'm just enjoying the break at the moment.'

Elizabeth gazed at her and Delilah could sense her wondering just what she needed a break from.

On Friday afternoon, a gleaming silver Mercedes snaked its way up the drive and parked next to Delilah's Golf. She was in the drawing room, having devoured Molly Keane and moved onto Somerville and Ross. She watched a man in a perfectly cut navy pinstripe suit get out of the car. Late thirties, she estimated, with hair that was slightly too long for the formality of the suit he was wearing, and a tan he hadn't got in this country.

William Glass. It had to be.

She saw him register her car and take in the details – English, less than a year old, top of the range. Thank God she didn't have a personalised number plate. This was a man who didn't miss much, a man whose job it was to analyse details. She needed to tread carefully. Keep out of his way if she could. Though she didn't think there was much hope of that.

Elizabeth seemed very eager for them to meet. She watched as he pulled a nubuck travel bag out of the boot, pushed back his hair and turned to look at the house.

He stood for a moment taking it in, and Delilah tried to read his expression. Elizabeth had hinted that he was putting her under pressure to wind down the business. He thought it was too much for her. Was he assessing the house for its potential value? Probably. No doubt he was going to make it his mission this week to get her out. Move the developers in. Delilah narrowed her eyes. Why did the next generation always try to spoil things for the elderly? Why couldn't they leave them in peace?

He strode up to the front door and Delilah curled herself up into a small ball on the sofa, hoping he wouldn't look in the drawing room.

'Hello!' She heard his voice: confident, educated; British minor public school (Elizabeth had told her that) with a hint of Dublin; annoyingly attractive. 'Can I get some service from someone round here? Jesus, it's like a morgue.'

She could hear him striding around the hall.

'Mother!' he called with impatience.

Delilah knew for a fact that Elizabeth had gone into Killorglin for supplies. She had half a dozen Dutch guests arriving to stay the next morning. But if she divulged this information, she'd reveal her presence. So she kept quiet.

Mistake. He barged into the drawing room. It was his perfect right, of course, but she felt like it was her territory.

'Aha!' he exclaimed with glee. 'Another living soul. Thank God.'

And he smiled a smile that was so disarming that Delilah dropped her book, got to her feet and held out her hand.

'Your mother's gone to town. She said she'd be back in time for dinner.'

'Grand. I'm starving.' He took her hand and shook it warmly. 'William Glass. You must be the lonely lodger she's told me about.'

'Dee MacBride.'

He assessed her, just for a moment, with his lawyer's eyes. Delilah waited for a sign of recognition, but there was none.

'I'll go and get changed, then will I make you an Olympic-sized gin and tonic?'

'Sounds lovely,' murmured Delilah.

The next moment he was gone. She settled back down on the sofa and picked up her book, but she couldn't concentrate. The arrival of William Glass had totally altered the feel of the house. Her haven had been disrupted, and she felt anxious.

But a little bit of her was really looking forward to the gin and tonic he had promised.

When he reappeared he was in faded jeans and a grey sweat-shirt with the sleeves rolled up, his feet bare. He looked totally different, as if he should be leaping about on the deck of some yacht, not drafting letters in a dry solicitor's office.

'I brought my own gin. Hendrick's. With cucumber, not lemon,' he said, shovelling ice from a bucket he had found in the kitchen into two Waterford tumblers. 'So – what brings you to this neck of the woods?'

Delilah took a sip of her drink, then mumbled her badly rehearsed cover.

'I'm just taking some time out to . . . research my family. I suppose I've reached that time of life when you need to know your roots.'

He gazed at her, his eyes the same soft grey as his sweatshirt. She wondered if he was so vain as to buy it for the colour, or if it was a coincidence.

'OK,' he said, not remotely convinced. 'Moving swiftly on . . . How's my mother?'

'She's marvellous. She's looked after me wonderfully. I'm sure I've put on half a stone since I've been here.'

'Sounds par for the course.' He took a sip of his own drink, and nodded in approval. 'I don't know that she can go on much longer. She's eighty-two, you know.'

'Seventy-eight, she told me.'

'She's been lopping years off to suit herself since she turned forty.'

'She looks good for her age.'

'Yeah, but . . .' He looked around. 'This place needs someone young at the helm. I know it's got all that mad Irish country-house charm, but scratch the surface and it's all damp and cobwebs and mould.'

'I think it's perfect.'

'A surveyor would have a heart attack.'

'So?'

He looked at her evenly.

'You think I'm a rotten spoilsport, don't you? You wonder why I can't just leave her to get on? Well, I have, for the past five years. By autumn she will have run herself ragged and got her usual chest infection. I keep warning her, it will turn into pneumonia one day and that will be it, but she doesn't care. And the truth is the whole place wants gutting. It's running at the most horrific loss. She's gone through nearly all the money my father left, and I settle some of the bills without telling her. I can't do it any more. I can't leave my job and come and work for her. The maths doesn't add up. She needs my cash to keep her afloat.'

'You can't carry on doing that. It's insane business practice.'

'I know. But she's my mother. What do I say?'

He looked bleak for a moment. Delilah reached out and touched his shoulder.

'She's lucky to have you.'

At that moment they heard that crunch of tyres on the gravel and Elizabeth's battered Fiat Panda hove into view. William jumped up and rushed outside to greet her. Delilah watched as they hugged in the drive. Elizabeth's once beautiful face lit up at the sight of her son, and Delilah felt a sudden pang for her own children – the joy of seeing them after a period of absence, the relief as you pulled them to you and breathed in their familiar scent. She took another sip of her drink as William threw open the boot and took out all the shopping, not letting Elizabeth pick up a thing and shooing her into the house in front of him.

'Go into the drawing room and have a gin and tonic with our guest,' he ordered her.

Delilah got the measure of William over the next few days as he strode around the place in a ridiculous pair of khaki shorts and wellington boots. He was immensely practical, strong and seemingly tireless. He painted the guttering, laid a patio area outside the French windows, emptied two containers of fresh chippings on to the drive, planted up a load of old stone urns with bedding plants – it was like watching a speeded-up version of some garden make-over show.

One afternoon Delilah offered to help him varnish the rowing boat she had spotted in the boat house. It was total self-interest because she was hoping once it was dry he might take her out in it.

'You're a guest. You don't want to be put to work. Anyway, what about your family history?' He gazed at her, his eyes perspicacious.

'I'd rather be outside doing something while the weather's fine.' It was a glorious afternoon; she didn't want to be stuck indoors. 'Anyway, my ancestors have been dead a long time. They can wait a bit longer.'

'MacBride – that's not a Kerry name.'

'No. Well, it's my mother's side I'm researching.'

He nodded in understanding and handed her a paintbrush.

'So how long are you staying?' His voice was casual.

'I don't know.' She tried not to sound curt. 'Your mother says I can have the room as long as I want.'

She looked up as the people carrier containing the Dutch guests swooped up. They had arrived from Cork airport the previous Saturday. The three couples got out, all dressed almost identically in crisp trousers, short-sleeved shirts,

Timberlands and wire-rimmed glasses, their fair hair cropped, bags slung vertically across their bodies.

'I still can't tell which are the men and which are the women,' William complained.

'Sssh – they're no trouble. They're very sweet to your mother. Very appreciative.' Delilah tried to stifle a giggle.

William frowned. 'I thought the Dutch were supposed to be all about free love and smoking dope?'

'Well, maybe they are. Have you been into their room of an evening?'

He looked horrified at the prospect, and Delilah nearly knocked the pot of yacht varnish over, she was laughing so hard.

'I like my women to look like women, if you know what I mean.' He defended himself stoutly. And he looked at Delilah, who was wearing a very skimpy T-shirt and shorts, her hair tied on top of her head.

She blushed, and bent back over the boat, berating herself for the squiggle of pleasure his comment had brought.

It was just after six o'clock when they finally finished the boat and laid it out to dry. They wandered companionably back up to the house.

'God, I stink,' William said distastefully.

She could see the fine sheen of exertion on his chest. He had two days of stubble on his face, and his hair was tied back with a big red spotted kerchief. He wiped his brow with the back of his hand.

She could smell his sweat, his manliness.

'I hope you're going to have a bath before dinner,' she told him, and he twinkled at her.

'Run it for me, would you? I'll have some of the Radox in it.'

'Bugger off,' she laughed, but it was all she could do not to run and do his bidding.

'A man can but try,' he said with a shrug, and loped off up

the stairs. She watched him go, and felt the squiggle inside her again as she noticed just how broad his shoulders were.

The answer to an unfaithful husband was hardly to jump into bed with someone else, she told herself sternly.

The next morning, Elizabeth fell on the slippery moss of the path on the way back from the raspberry patch. When they found her, she could barely move. She kept insisting she was fine, but it was obvious she wasn't. William drove her to the hospital, stretched out on the back seat of his car because she couldn't sit properly.

He came back at three.

'She's broken her hip,' he told Delilah. 'I've had to leave her there because she's sent me packing. I've got to do dinner for the bloody Dutch. I told her we'd pay for them to go and eat at Bianconi's in town, but she practically had a fit.' He sighed. 'The one good thing is she's in great hands at the hospital. I know all the staff there. Most of them worked with my father at one time or another.'

'You know what? It's no problem. I'll do dinner.'

'You will?'

'Sure. I'm used to cooking for large numbers.'

'Really?'

She smiled to herself. He genuinely hadn't a clue. If he had any idea of the sort of things she had catered without turning a hair, he'd be amazed.

'Give me her list.' She drew it out of his hand, and began to read, turning over in her mind what she would do, and how she would do it. She opened the fridge, assessing its contents, and went to look in the cool, old-fashioned larder.

She wasn't going to go fancy. There was no point in showing off and rousing suspicion. She would stick to Elizabeth's style, which anyway was the sort of heartfelt cooking Delilah believed in.

She made a delicious cold cucumber soup, the most glorious pale green. Then salmon en croute with a tian of courgettes and tomatoes. And to finish, summer pudding, shamelessly red and served with dollops of double cream.

The Dutch were hugely appreciative, as was William of the leftovers.

'You're good,' he remarked, shamelessly shovelling in the last of the pudding. A drizzle of the red juice stayed on his lip, and she wanted to reach out and wipe it off. But she didn't.

By the end of the week, Delilah was exhausted. Elizabeth wasn't going to be allowed out of hospital for some time, and so she had wordlessly stepped in to take her place. She had done breakfast, picnic lunches, scones and cakes for tea and a three-course dinner single-handedly, as well as helping Regine with the beds and the general housework.

'I have absolutely no idea how your mother manages,' she told William, who had been carrying on with the running repairs and maintenance, only coming in for ham sandwiches and industrial quantities of tea.

'She won't be able to now,' he said grimly.

'What do they say? Be careful what you wish for?' Delilah couldn't help being arch.

He glared at her.

'What are you saying? I wished this on her? Don't be ridiculous. I don't want her to leave Gortnaflor. For God's sake, I was brought up here. I love the place. But I don't want her to run herself into the ground just to keep some sentimental dream alive. If getting rid of this place is for the best, then that's what's got to happen.'

'I'm sorry, I'm sorry.' Delilah realised she had been a bitch, and now had to mollify him. 'I'm just tired.'

William's face softened.

'I know you are. Look, I'll run into Killorglin and bring us back a take-away and a bottle of wine. How about that? No cooking for anyone tonight.'

'Until the next lot arrive.'

The Dutch had left that morning. The next lot of visitors weren't due until Tuesday. They had a bit of breathing space.

'Would you . . . stay on and keep the place running?' William was tentative.

'Sure,' said Delilah. 'I've nothing else keeping.'

'The dead relatives can wait, eh?'

She looked at him sharply and he gave her an imperceptible wink.

'Sadly I've got to go back to Dublin in a week, so I won't be much use. I've a big case coming up I can't delegate.'

Delilah felt a prick of disappointment. She had got so used to him being around the place, she couldn't imagine Gortna-flor without William's comforting male presence, shinning up a ladder or sawing up logs.

'I'll have a chicken korma. And some pilau rice. If we're still on for that take-away,' she told him by way of reply. And then wondered what the hell she'd let herself in for. Running a bed and breakfast in deepest, darkest Kerry? Life took some strange turns sometimes.

They had their Indian in the drawing room, sitting on the floor in front of the fire, sharing out the dishes. William had completely overdone the order, and even after stuffing themselves there was a mountain left over. He wouldn't let Delilah lift a finger – he cleared everything away himself and took it into the kitchen. She sat with her back against the sofa, a glass of wine in her hands, dreamily going over the time she had spent here.

Elizabeth was right. Gortnaflor was a magical place. It had allowed some sort of rapid healing process to take place in her heart. When she thought about home, it seemed a million miles away, her family people she had known in her distant past. When she thought about the reasons for leaving, it still hurt, but only like a scar that tugged every now and again when you overdid it.

There were a few things that nagged at her. The arrangements for her party, in a few weeks' time – the organisers would all be pestering Polly to death for decisions. She should really phone up and cancel everything, but she couldn't be bothered. She was tired of being responsible, tired of making the decisions, tired of having to oversee everything and make sure people did their jobs.

And the girls. Polly had been keeping her updated by email, even though Delilah still refused to respond, apart from an official notification that she had read each missive. They were all fine, carrying on with their lives. She knew Polly would let her know if anything was wrong, but she still worried about them.

And Doug. Even though strictly speaking, he was Tyger's, not hers, she missed his presence, his wide-eyed concern, the sound of his snuffling.

But none of it was enough to make her get back on the ferry.

She stretched and yawned. The tiredness she'd felt in her old life was a totally different tiredness to the one she felt now. A wonderful tiredness brought on by hard work, fresh air, good food and a little too much heavy red wine. The gentle sound of rain falling outside soothed the worries from her mind; she felt herself drifting off in the warmth of the fire.

She heard William's footsteps as he came back into the room, but try as she might she couldn't open her eyes. She heard him walk over to the window.

'Dee.' He spoke softly. 'Come here.'

She tore herself out of her stupor and struggled to her feet. He beckoned her over without taking his eyes off whatever he was looking at. She stood next to him, and he put an arm round her, drawing her close and pointing outside with the other hand.

A full moon hovered low over the lake, and an arc of light sprang from it, spanning the width of the garden and bathing it in a silver glow.

'Do you know what that is?' breathed William in wonder. 'It's a moonbow.'

'You mean like a rainbow?'

'Yes. I've heard of them, but I've never seen one before. They're supposed to be very good luck.'

'Are they . . . ?'

There was a pause, and then he slid his arms around her waist and pulled her in towards him.

'I believe so. Very good luck indeed.'

She could feel her heart triple in pace. His lips were in her hair. Not kissing, not quite. It made her shiver. She felt quite languid in his arms. Time felt as if it was going to stand still for ever. They were trapped in the radiance of the moonbow, the pair of them.

She only had to turn, and their lips would meet. He would run his fingers through her hair. She would slip her hands around his waist, feel herself against the broadness of his chest. The thought made her woozy. It was so enticing. She just wanted to—

'I'm sorry,' she whispered. 'I can't. I want to, but I can't.'

He turned her round to face him. She closed her eyes. If she looked at him, she would give in. But she knew this wasn't the answer. This way more heartbreak lay. It would throw up more problems than solutions.

'It's OK,' he answered. 'I understand.'

She didn't want him to understand. She wanted him to protest. Hell, she wanted him to force himself upon her. So she couldn't be accused of having made the decision.

The decision to commit adultery. The decision that Raf had taken so easily, again and again and again. Now she understood – how tempting it was; how easy it must be to give in. She could be in William's arms in a heartbeat, in his bed in two.

Maybe Raf wasn't a monster after all. Maybe he was simply . . . human.

William was holding her face in his hands.

'Dee . . .' he murmured. 'I can't tell you how much I want to kiss you.'

A kiss wouldn't hurt. Just a kiss. Just a dreamy, sleepy brushing of lips. Lips that tasted of wine . . .

'You've no idea who I am. What I am. Have you?' she asked him later as they stumbled up the stairs, unable to keep their hands off each other.

He stopped for a moment, feigning shock.

'You're not some sort of banshee, are you? About to bring me some portentous . . . portent?'

She couldn't help laughing.

'No . . .'

'Well, that's all right, then.' And he pulled her the rest of the way up the stairs and into the bedroom.

Thirty

You could have cut the air in the studio with a knife.

The crew stood ready for action, holding their breath. On the edges, onlookers chewed their nails – the medical adviser, the girl in charge of prosthetics, the script editor, all the people who often didn't bother turning up on set were there for today's recording. Even Lisa, the executive producer, had made it down from her office to watch.

The storylines had been building to this climax: the moment when Zak's medical condition deteriorates, and the doctors tell Emily that they must switch the machine off. The nation would be on the edge of their seats watching this tragedy in a few weeks' time. The broadcasters were hoping for record viewing figures.

So the pressure was on to get the scene just right.

Coco was pacing like a race-horse. The cameras were going to be on her all the way through the scene. There was a fine line between acting and over-acting. She had been over it with the director, and they had both decided that dignity and restraint were far more moving than hysterical weeping.

'We're ready for you, Miss Rafferty.'

She smoothed down the skirt of her nurse's uniform and took her place on the set. Neal was already on the bed, under the sheet, attached to the life support machine. As she sat on the chair next to him, he turned to look at her.

'Bye, then,' he said drily. 'It's been nice knowing you.' And he shut his eyes, ready to assume his near-death state.

According to Lisa, Neal had taken the news of his

character's demise surprisingly well. Mind you, Lisa wouldn't have stood for any whingeing. When you worked on a long-running series, you had to be grateful for whatever length of time you were employed, and you went graciously when that time was up. Lisa's philosophy was that actors had to take care of their insecurities in their own time, on their own dime. Anyone who wailed and gnashed their teeth blew any chance of a come-back, or of working on any other series Lisa was involved with.

Neal had behaved like a perfect gentleman. He hadn't bitched or blamed anyone for the fact that he was being written out.

'Hey,' he'd been heard to say, 'mine's going to be the most high-profile death on TV this year. It's great publicity.'

He had redeemed himself, with Coco and with the rest of the cast and crew. They were throwing a leaving party for him tonight, in a nightclub up the road from the studio. It was the sort of place Coco wouldn't usually be seen dead in, but she owed it to Neal to be part of his send-off. He had been if not charming, then at least polite to Coco since the tongue-biting incident, so she would go along tonight, buy him a drink, see him on his way, no hard feelings.

There was no dialogue in this final scene, as the machine was finally switched off and Zak took his dying breath. But that just made it even harder. There were no cues, just a minute and a half focused on Emily as the doctors did their thing.

In the end, they did the scene in one take. Coco didn't know how she managed to sustain the intensity of emotion, letting it build gradually until the final close-up when a single, glistening tear ran down her cheek and she brushed it away, but she knew she'd given her finest performance yet.

Yet as she walked away from the set and back to her dressing room, it wasn't pride she felt, but despair.

Her nerves had got the better of her when she arrived at the studio that morning, and she had given in. She had done so well since making the promise to herself, but the pressure had been too much. She had told herself it was the last time, that this was a one-off, a stressful situation that justified her needing a boost. And the minute she had done a line, she felt as if she could cope. Her confidence came rushing back, her fears evaporated. And it got her through.

Now, however, her mood plummeted. The applause in the studio meant nothing to her. She had let herself down. Unbeknownst to Benedict, she had let him down, too

Since she had met Benedict, she felt so much stronger. Without him, she'd have fallen apart at her mother's disappearance, would have wound herself up into a frenzy at her father's infidelity. But Benedict provided a cool, calm voice of reason. He made her feel as if everything was going to be all right and he was the first person in her life to make her feel like that.

Her own family always made her feel as if she was standing on shifting sands, that she was responsible when things went wrong. It was probably because she was the oldest of the girls. It had always been Coco reassuring Violet and Tyger. How different to have someone providing her with reassurance and support. Benedict seemed so solid; nothing could ever go wrong while he was around.

Which was why she'd decided to kick the coke. If she had any hope of a future with Benedict, common sense told her it had to go. She never wanted to be sitting in a restaurant with him again, desperate for a line, unable to think about anything else . . .

Coco looked in the mirror. How the hell had she let herself become the person that was looking back at her? Tears of self-pity welled up in her eyes, but she brushed them away. There was no point in crying.

She realised now that she wasn't going to be able to do this on her own. She was going to have to come clean to Benedict and ask for help. And if that meant losing him, she had no one but herself to blame. She began to take off her make-up. She just wanted to go home, but she had to go to Neal's party. It would be really letting the side down if she didn't. Even if she didn't owe it to him – wanker that he was – she owed it to all the others, who had been so amazing today and had given her their support, even though she didn't deserve it.

Neal's leaving party was a riot. Lisa had put a couple of hundred quid behind the bar, and there was a scrum on to see who could drink the most before it ran out. Coco tried to look as if she was enjoying herself, and desperately wished she *could*. Despite the hideously tacky surroundings, there was a real sense of team spirit and excitement that comes from being part of a success. Lisa had announced before everyone left the studio that *Critical but Stable* now had its biggest audience share since the programme started, so everyone was on a mission to celebrate. Coco mustered up her best acting talents, smiled and laughed and chattered, but inside all she could feel was a cold lump of dread at the thought of the confession she was going to have to make to Benedict. She couldn't carry on stringing him along. She respected him too much. She *loved* him too much.

By twenty past ten, she thought she could probably slip away discreetly. She'd drunk a couple of glasses of champagne – well, the revolting cava that the nightclub passed off as champagne – and danced to Sister Sledge, Chic and Earth, Wind and Fire. She managed to extricate herself from a rowing session during 'Oops Upside Your Head'. She was a sport, but she wasn't going to sit down on a sticky floor in her Roland Mouret for anyone. Everyone else was sliding into drunken riotousness and wouldn't notice if she left. She found her jacket, fumbled in her bag for her keys—

Bang! Suddenly all the lights went on, and a mass of black-clad figures swarmed into the room. With her heart in her mouth, Coco looked round for an escape, until she realised with relief that they weren't hijackers or kidnappers, but police.

Relieved, that is, until she remembered that the remains of

her stash were still sitting in her handbag. And that this was very probably the Drug Squad.

As a burly officer approached her, she saw Neal over his shoulder, a look of ill-concealed glee on his face.

It was ironic, thought Coco as she made her one phone call from the police station, that this was about the time she would have been sitting down with Benedict to make her confession. Her heart pounded as his mobile rang. He answered straight away.

'Benedict, it's Coco. Listen – I need your help . . .'

He didn't judge. He barely reacted at all. Just asked which station she was at, then promised to phone Tony and let him know what had happened.

'I'll be there as quickly as I can,' he told her.

She hung up and looked at the officer. He gave her an awkward smile, and passed a piece of paper over to her.

'I wouldn't usually ask but . . . could I have an autograph? For the missus. It would make her day.'

Coco sighed, and took the Biro he proffered. She couldn't even get arrested without some invasion of privacy. She scrawled her name, thinking that this might be the last time she was asked for her autograph. There was every chance she would be dropped from the show. She knew they had a zero tolerance policy. Having a coke-head for a star was not the sort of publicity they wanted. No matter how beautiful and talented she was. How could she have been so stupid? But that was one of the problems with cocaine. It made you think you were invincible and blinded you to the obvious.

Benedict had Coco out of the police station and all charges dropped in the blink of an eye. She wasn't sure how he did it – she didn't see any money change hands – but within fifteen minutes of his arrival she was released with just a caution.

They held hands as they came out into the street, and were immediately blinded by a barrage of flashbulbs.

'Damn them,' said Benedict, throwing his jacket chivalrously over her head and guiding her to his car.

That would have been Neal as well, thought Coco grimly as she scrambled into the back seat. Of course he'd called the papers. He would have made sure she was well and truly buried. Benedict gunned the car away from the pavement, scattering photographers in his wake.

'Welcome to my world,' said Coco wryly. He looked sideways at her with a Roger Moore eyebrow.

'It doesn't have to be this way.'

She looked down at her lap. She was ready for him to bawl her out. But he reached a hand over and patted her arm.

'I'm not going to have a go. We'll talk about it tomorrow. Right now we need to find Tony. He's waiting at The Bower. We have to do some damage limitation.'

Tony was going to be furious. He wouldn't hold back. How many times had he lectured them about drugs? About not putting themselves into compromising positions? They knew the rules. They'd been instilled in them since birth. Coco leaned her head back against the headrest and groaned.

'Tomorrow's fish and chip paper,' said Benedict. 'Just hold on to that.'

'I'm an idiot.'

'You are,' he confirmed. 'You are.'

There were a couple of photographers outside The Bower, but Coco kept her head down in the front seat and once they were through the gates, they were out of sight.

Raf's Maserati was parked next to Tony's car.

'What's Dad doing here?'

'I'm guessing Tony called him,' said Benedict.

'He's in Bath. That's two hours' drive away.'

'Not in that thing.'

Coco looked at the front door with trepidation.

'I don't want to do this.'

Benedict gave her a gentle push in the small of the back.

'It's called facing the music.'

Coco put her key in the lock. At least he hadn't called her 'young lady'.

Raf was incandescent with rage.

'Are you crazy? You've got everything in the world going for you and you throw it away on that shit.'

He was pacing up and down the kitchen, his eyes blazing with fury. Coco sat in a miserable ball on the sofa.

'You've got no right to judge me like this,' she retorted. 'No right at all.'

'I've got every right. I would have thought you'd learned by my mistakes.'

'Hold on,' Tony stepped in between them. 'Before we start blaming each other, we need to look at our options. We can stop this getting out.'

'How?' demanded Coco.

Raf and Tony looked at each other. They obviously had a plan.

'We horse-trade . . .' said Tony.

'I give them my story about Pandora,' finished Raf. 'It's worth far more than possession of half a gram of coke.'

Coco stood up. 'No way. I'm not going to betray Mum just to get myself out of trouble.'

'You're going to ruin your career.'

'That's my problem.'

'Come on,' said Raf. 'I'm happy to do it. I'm happy to face the consequences.'

Coco looked at him coldly. 'What about Mum?' she asked. 'Have you thought about her? Do you think she wants that splashed all over the papers? It would be totally humiliating. Though of course, it's not as if she's not used to it.'

Raf flinched.

Tony stepped forward.

'It's a good solution, Coco. But we need to act quickly.'

'No.' Coco stood firm. 'I don't want the world reading about bloody Pandora Hammond just to get me out of trouble.'

She turned to Benedict, who had wisely kept quiet throughout the exchange.

'Would you mind driving me home?'

'Let me take you, sweetheart.' Raf pulled out his keys. 'Or why don't you stay here. We can talk.'

'What about?'

There was an awkward pause.

'Why did you do it, Coco? I didn't think you were into coke. I thought you'd got more sense.'

'I was under pressure, Dad. It helped. You should get that – better than anyone, I'd have thought.'

'Why didn't you just . . . come and talk to me? We've always been able to talk, haven't we?'

'Well, yes . . .' She paused, then delivered the death blow. 'Except you've been too busy fucking C-list actresses just lately.'

Raf felt winded.

She turned to Benedict. 'Let's go.'

'Keep in touch, Coco,' Tony said. 'I'll do as much fire-fighting as I can but they got you bang to rights.'

'Don't worry.' She put her chin in the air. 'I know I deserve everything I get.'

Raf watched his daughter go. He'd let her down. He'd let all of them down. He threw himself onto the kitchen sofa. Tony had gone into the office to make some calls. He rubbed his face wearily.

Delilah. Where was she? He needed her so desperately it hurt. But they were no closer to tracking her down. They'd pleaded with the bank to let them have the details of where she was spending money, but they'd refused. They couldn't get onto her online bank accounts, because no one knew her passwords. They'd tried to trace her mobile, but the company said she hadn't used it since the night she had left. They even phoned the DVLA, to see if she had got any parking tickets or speeding fines, but there was nothing. They all phoned each other, every night, to see if any one of them had heard anything, but none of them ever had.

He looked at the clock. He'd make himself another coffee, swap notes with Tony, then he'd better make his way back to Bath.

Benedict drove Coco back to his house in Little Venice. They both thought it was probably best to avoid her flat, in case the paparazzi were staking her out. He ushered her inside, led her up to the master bathroom, and ran her an enormous, steaming-hot bath. While she was soaking, he made her a mug of Valrhona hot chocolate.

She sat swathed in a soft towelling robe, sipping the velvety sweetness.

Benedict looked at her.

'You were very brave,' he told her. 'And I admire you for protecting your mum like that.'

Coco rolled her eyes. 'Brave? I've been totally stupid. There's nothing to admire. I'm an idiot.'

'I have to ask,' he looked at her gravely. 'Do you think . . . you're an addict?'

She put her head to one side while she thought about it.

'I don't know. I think about it most of the time. And . . . I can't kick it. I've been kidding myself that I'm in control, but I'm not.'

A salty tear plopped into her nearly empty mug.

Benedict reached out and stroked her hand.

'I can get you help.'

Coco looked at him in surprise. 'You mean you don't want to end things?'

There was a long silence. Coco felt her eyes fill up with tears. She'd screwed up. Benedict was going to help her, but he didn't want any more to do with her—

'Definitely not,' he said finally. 'You're the best thing that's happened to me for a very long time.'

He put his arms around her and Coco buried her face in his chest.

'I wish Mum was here.'

'I know . . .'

'Everyone thinks it must be so great, being a Rafferty. But it's not. It's like a bloody computer game. Just when you think you've conquered one demon, another one pops up. Sometimes I wish I'd just been born normal.'

'Come on.' Benedict led her gently towards the spare room. It was decorated in French grey and silver, with a sleigh bed covered in sumptuous satin the colour of rain clouds. 'You need to get some sleep. We'll talk everything through in the morning.'

She felt very small in the middle of the emperor-sized bed. He piled the pillows and cushions up around her, tucked the sheets and blankets up to her chin. Her lids felt heavy. She couldn't stay awake. She closed her eyes and felt him patting her gently until she fell asleep.

Bath was coming to life in the early-morning sun as Raf came out of the front door at Collingwood. He had finally crawled into bed around dawn after flooring it back down the motorway, but he couldn't sleep. He decided he would go and check out the papers.

Joggers, dog-walkers, postmen – he passed them all on his way to the twenty-four-hour shop he knew was just three roads away. He felt envious of them all. He would have swapped places with any one of them. He, who had everything a man could possibly want. Fame, fortune, stardom, dazzling looks, three stunning and talented daughters, the woman every man in the country lusted after. A Maserati.

How wonderful, he thought, to be a postman on a bike. To wake up knowing exactly what it was you had to achieve each day, and how you were going to do it. And once you were done, once all those bills and letters and parcels were delivered, you could go home without giving any of it a second thought. Until the next morning. There was a pleasing rhythm and simplicity to it. Why couldn't God have left out the looks and the talent and the self-destruct gene when he was born, and made him a postman?

He turned the corner and saw the shop. There were bundles of newspapers still strapped up, waiting to be unpacked and put on the shelves. And there they were – the headlines. Not in *The Times* or the *Telegraph*, of course, but in the tabloids. The predictable play on words – *Coco-caine, Cocaine Coco – Top TV star in drugs bust*. Et cetera, et cetera. There were photos of Coco, looking pale but dignified, being escorted out of the station by Benedict Amador.

He didn't pick any of them up to read what was inside. He knew the editorial line. Family history of substance abuse, history repeating itself, blah blah blah. They would trot out all the old anecdotes about him. Theories about the pressures of acting. Following in her father's footsteps. The price of fame.

He should have been there for her. He should have seen the signs. He knew exactly how hard it was, to do what she was doing. He should have been checking in with her on a regular basis, making sure she was coping. He had blithely assumed, because Coco looked calm, cool and in control, that she was.

A good father should have known better. A proper father would have looked below the surface, seen the signs. Instead, he had been focusing on resurrecting his own pathetic career, preening himself, wallowing in his comeback.

Never mind, he thought bitterly. It looked as if she had found herself another father figure. No doubt Benedict would sort it all out for her. Find some therapist who would put the blame fairly and squarely on Raf.

He turned and walked away from the accusing headlines. Down to the back of the shop, where rows and rows of brightly coloured cans and bottles displayed themselves proudly, fighting amongst themselves for his attention.

He went for vodka. A cheapo brand, red and silver with mock Russian graphics. It would taste like lighter fuel, but who cared? The final effect was the same, whether it was cheap shit or Chateau d'Yquem. Raf had never drunk for the taste.

He took it up to the till.

'Are you sure you want that, mate?' the assistant asked.

He obviously recognised him. He'd clocked him and didn't want the responsibility of being the man who had pushed Raf Rafferty off the wagon.

'Are you in the business of selling alcohol, or are you just a fucking busybody?' snarled Raf, chucking a twenty-pound note on the counter.

The bloke said nothing after that, just rang up the purchase. He went to put the bottle in a bag, but Raf grabbed it off him.

'Do you want your receipt?'

He was talking to thin air. Raf was gone.

No ice. Straight from the bottle. Sitting on a park bench overlooking the city as it got ready for the day ahead.

He was a loser. He'd lost his wife. He was losing his kids. He was going to lose his career. Again. How could he ever have thought he could conquer it? Of course it was going to win, every time. You might keep it at bay for a small amount of time, but it crept back up on you, stealthy, insidious, waiting for that moment of weakness. And then it offered its slimy claw of friendship, reaching out for you, luring you back onside.

It was better than sex. Better than love. Better than the birth of your children. It was a warm golden cloak that wrapped you up and told you it was going to be all right.

Raf pulled on the bottle thirstily, gulping the raw liquid down, desperate to get in deeper, desperate to reach the state where everything was numb, where he no longer had to think or feel. He wanted to blot out Delilah's face. He could see her so clearly, the sorrow, the disappointment. Not judging him, but making him feel worse because of it. Gradually, she become blurrier and less distinct until she floated away altogether, back to wherever the fuck in the world she was . . .

And then he lay down on the bench, letting the bottle fall from his hand and onto the ground. He looked up at the sky. Looked up at the sun.

'Hello, sun,' he said, smiling his first proper smile for ten years.

It was Genevieve who found him, two hours later. Unluckily for him.

She grabbed him by the front of his shirt and pulled him unceremoniously off the bench.

'What the hell are you playing at?' she demanded.

Raf tried to get to his feet. None of his limbs would do as he told them. Confused, he tried to remember how he had got here.

'Co-co-co-co,' was all he could manage, sounded like some sort of demented pigeon. He had a dim memory of something going wrong with his daughter.

'Yes, we know. Tony's been on to me, because he couldn't get you. Jesus, Raf.' She spied the empty bottle on the ground by the bench and grabbed it. 'Did you drink all this?'

He looked at it and shrugged. It was empty, so he supposed so. She looked at him witheringly.

'When I took this job on, it was because I respected you. As an actor, and as someone who had taken control of his life. I believed in you, Raf.'

He looked at her through half-closed eyes and tried one of his disarming smiles.

'I believe in you, too, Genevieve.'

She glared at him.

'Who did you think about before you bought this?' She brandished the bottle in his face. 'Did you think about your daughter, who could probably do with some moral support right now? Did you think about your wife, who you've hurt so badly she's disappeared off the face of the earth? Did you think about Dickie, who has poured his heart and soul into this film, not to mention considerable amounts of money? Or me? Or your other girls? Or the rest of the people who are at this very moment sitting waiting for you to turn up and share your precious bloody talent with them?'

She was shouting now, earning concerned glances from passers-by, who might be right in thinking that this itself was a scene from a film. Genevieve Duke berating Raf Rafferty, waving around an empty bottle of vodka?

'Shit,' slurred Raf. 'Am I supposed to be filming?'

Genevieve sighed. There was no point in ranting. He was too drunk to take any of it in. She took his arm.

'Come on, we need to get you sobered up.'

He was swaying and stumbling against her. He could barely walk. It was going to be a long journey back to the house. She kept her head down as she walked. The last thing they wanted was for some helpful member of the public to alert the press. It was amazing how quickly they could have a photographer on the scene if they thought there was a story brewing and the Raffertys were already hot news today.

She pulled her phone out of her pocket with her spare hand and dialled.

'Dickie – it's Genevieve. I've found him. There's no way he's going to be fit for work today. He's as pissed as a bloody newt.'

She walked him back to Collingwood. It was a slow journey, because he could barely put one foot in front of the other, but they finally made it.

A pale-faced Dickie answered the door.

'I've pulled some minor scenes forward,' he told Genevieve, 'so that everyone's got something to be getting on with. I told them he'd had a dodgy curry.'

Genevieve smiled grimly.

'That old chestnut. No one will believe it.'

'As long as they don't phone the press.'

They both looked at Raf, whose knees were about to buckle. They grabbed an arm each.

'Let's get some water down him. And some painkillers. Then throw him into bed to sleep it off.'

Raf was dimly aware of the two of them tending to him. He didn't deserve it, thought Raf. He didn't deserve the support and the friendship and the care they had lavished on him. Raf Rafferty was running true to form. Trashing yet another movie.

At eight o'clock that night he emerged from his bedroom, shaky and shaken. He groped his way down to the kitchen, where he found Dickie and Genevieve sharing some pasta.

'I want to apologise,' he said to Dickie. 'I am a complete and utter cunt. It won't happen again.'

Raf would never forget the look Dickie gave him as long as he lived.

Thirty-One

Tony called all the girls over to The Bower to give them a pep talk after Coco's exposé. He gave it to them straight as they sat in a row on the stools in front of the island in the kitchen. Coco looked as if she'd just walked off a film set, Violet looked as if she had just got out of bed, and Tyger looked as if she had just fallen out of a nightclub. Which was probably the case for all three of them. Polly was sitting on the end with her laptop, taking notes. Louis, Justine and Benedict were keeping out of the way at the other end of the kitchen.

'If I've told you once I've told you a thousand times. Watch your backs. Don't trust anyone. And don't do anything that might draw attention to you.' Tony looked at the three impassive faces. 'Violet's the only one who seems to be able to keep her nose clean at the moment. But I expect it's only a matter of time.'

Violet bristled. 'That's not fair!'

On the other side of the room Justine blushed, and busied herself choosing a peach from the fruit bowl.

'Come on, girls. You know the score. And you need to be squeaky clean while Delilah's missing. We don't want any unwanted press intrusion.'

'Well, where *is* she?' demanded Violet. 'Surely we should have been able to find out by now.'

'I had another email yesterday,' Polly told them. 'It didn't say much. Only that she was fine.'

Benedict looked up from where he was fussing Doug.

'I've got people I could talk to.'

Tony frowned. 'That sounds a bit James Bond. And I can't sanction anything without speaking to Raf.'

Benedict shrugged. 'The offer's there. They know their stuff.'

'I don't think Delilah would take kindly to a crack squad shimmying down the wall of wherever she's hiding out.'

Coco sensed tension between the two men. Tony never liked people encroaching on his territory, and she could see he felt threatened by Benedict's presence. Maybe she shouldn't have brought him along, but he seemed to be the one giving her support at the moment.

'Benedict's only trying to help,' she pointed out. 'But I know what you're saying. If Mum doesn't want us to find her, I think we should respect that. I'm confident she'll surface when she's got her head together. I totally understand why she needs some space right now.' She looked at her sisters. 'Don't you?'

Violet and Tyger both shrugged.

'I miss her,' said Tyger.

'Me too.' Violet was picking at a muffin, pulling out the raspberries and leaving the sponge.

'I know it's hard for you, girls. But there's a lot at stake here. Coco, your show's a hit. Tyger, your business is booming. And Violet – I hear you've got some important industry guys coming to your show tonight.'

Violet gave the air a little punch.

'I've sent out the demo Sammy and I have been working on. We're doing my new stuff tonight.'

'Well, good luck. But remember, all of you – squeaky clean.' They all nodded dutifully.

'OK.' Tony sighed. 'Lecture over. Let's keep in touch.'

'Um – there's just a couple of other things,' said Polly, clearing her throat. 'First – do you think I should cancel Delilah's party? It doesn't look as if she's going to be back, and the invitations have all gone out. Nearly everyone has said yes . . .'

They all looked at the wall chart, where Delilah had high-lighted her birthday with stars and exclamation marks.

'No,' said Tony emphatically. 'It will just raise the alarm if we do it now. People will think it's strange. There'll be rumours. Keep it as it is, and if we need to cancel at the last minute, we can.'

'We'll lose so much money, though.' The thought of the waste distressed Polly.

'It's not a lot, in the grand scheme of things.' Tony was dismissive. 'Anything else?'

Polly swallowed.

'Um . . . yes. I'm handing in my notice.'

There was a shocked silence. Everyone stared at her.

'It's just . . . I don't think there's much room for me here any more. Now Delilah's not here. And everyone else has moved out. And there's things I want to do with my life . . .'

'Like what?' demanded Tyger.

'Like . . . I don't know.' Polly started to feel indignant. This was the first time they had paid her attention en masse for . . . years. 'But I can't just look after you lot for ever.'

'You're tired,' said Violet kindly. 'You just need a holiday. We'll book you a holiday.'

'And what about when Mum comes back?' asked Coco. 'She'll be devastated. You're her right hand.'

'We'll talk to Dad about a pay rise,' chipped in Tyger.

'You don't understand. It's not about money. Or holidays. It's about me getting a life!' cried Polly. 'Honestly, every time I book something for myself, there's a crisis and I have to cancel. And how am I supposed to arrange anything when I'm looking after Doug? Not that it's his fault.' She scooped the little dog up and hugged him. 'He's another one nobody's thought about. He's just there for your convenience.'

'Doug's my responsibility,' Tyger confessed. 'But he's not allowed in my flat. As soon as we move . . .'

She looked at Louis.

Coco stepped forward and put her arm round Polly.

343

'We hear what you're saying, Poll,' she said. 'And we'll do our best to work with you, to make things easier. But we can't do without you. You've *got* to stay.'

Polly looked round at them. It was going to break her heart. She'd worked for them for a decade. But the time had come.

'Four weeks' notice,' she said firmly. 'That's what it says in my contract. As of today.'

'Great,' said Tony. Of any of them, he understood the implications of Polly leaving. She held everything together. He'd work on her. Or get Raf to work on her.

Shit, he thought with a sigh. It was bound to happen. It always did, with these celebrity families. Sooner or later, they fell apart.

Justine was very quiet on the way back home. Violet was at the wheel, flipping through her iPod to listen again to the tracks she was showcasing that evening.

'I am so nervous,' she was saying. 'I never get nervous. But this is different. This is *my* stuff. What if they all hate it? What if they walk out?'

'They won't,' Justine reassured her. 'They won't.'

Violet looked at her.

'Is something the matter?'

Justine hesitated. She wanted to tell her that it had all become apparent to her that morning: she didn't fit into the Rafferty machine; her relationship with Violet was obviously compromising her career. But she didn't want an argument, and this was Violet's big day. She needed support, not a tiresome, whingeing, clingy girlfriend desperate for recognition.

'I'm just a bit tired . . .'

Violet seemed to accept her explanation and flipped through her iPod again to the next track.

In the dressing room before the gig later that night, Justine helped Violet get ready and tried to calm her nerves.

'You look sensational,' she told her, as she applied deep

crimson lipstick to her mouth with a brush. 'You're going to knock them dead.'

Violet pressed her lips together then tried to smile. She was trying desperately hard to show that she wished Justine wasn't there. It was nothing personal. It was just that this half-hour before the show was a time when she went into herself. She didn't want reassurance, or chitchat, or someone fussing over her. She needed space. But she didn't say anything.

Sammy arrived, looking devastating, in a black shirt with a red handkerchief in the pocket. He'd been incredible over the past few weeks, scoring her music, working out the best arrangements. He was so talented, and Violet felt guilty that it was always her name that was in lights. Not that she ever failed to acknowledge the rest of her band.

She stood up to hug him. It was funny – she didn't mind Sammy being in her space. Maybe because he understood her anxieties only too well. He was always great at the last-minute pep talk, and she found his reassurance valid because she trusted him.

'If it falls flat, we can just fall back on some of our old numbers,' she told him, with a shaky smile.

'No way is it going to fall flat.' Sammy was adamant. 'I would tell you if I thought it was shit, Violet. You know I would.'

'I know you would . . .' She grinned and gave him another hug. He was her rock, was Sammy.

Across the room, Justine watched the two of them interact. She felt like a gooseberry. Not that there was anything going on between Sammy and Violet, but she couldn't help but feel jealous that he was giving her the reassurance she needed. And she sensed that she was getting on Violet's nerves. It was probably stage-fright, she told herself. Maybe she should make herself scarce.

'I'm going to go and find myself a seat.'

The two of them looked up from their intense conversation and nodded, barely acknowledging her. She walked out of the dressing room and down the corridor, feeling tears stinging her lids, and the bile of jealousy rising in her gorge. For one moment back there, she would quite happily have stabbed Sammy.

She told herself to calm down. She was being irrational. She had to get a grip, get things into perspective.

After all, wasn't it a vicious and destructive possessiveness that had brought about her mother's demise? Justine was only too aware that this tendency was in her blood, and in her genes. She wasn't going to make the same mistake as Benedict. She walked through into the club and made her way to the table that had been reserved. None of the rest of the family was coming tonight. Violet had deliberately played it down to them, because she didn't want the Rafferty circus to worry about.

Justine sat down at the table on her own. She felt self-conscious and unsure of herself. This wasn't really her world at all. Sure, she could enjoy it as a member of the audience, but she had felt foolish in the dressing room. A spare part. She ordered a drink from a passing waiter. Maybe that would take the edge off her insecurity.

Soon, the Tinderbox was packed to the rafters. Violet had chosen it for the debut performance of her own material as the audience here were so loyal. She wanted to feel as if she was amongst friends, even though there would be some people there who would judge her harshly, because that was their job.

Violet appeared on stage, bathed in a single spotlight. She had chosen a velvet dress in scarlet, slashed to the thigh, and she looked astonishing. Like a star. Justine felt her heart burst with pride as Violet stepped up to the microphone. And her eyes filled with tears as she began to sing.

The audience gave her a standing ovation. She wasn't allowed off the stage. Four times she came back for an encore, smiling bashfully, embarrassed but obviously gratified. And when she eventually left the stage, and the lights were dimmed, Justine fought her way through the chattering crowds to get to the dressing room to congratulate her.

And there she found Violet in Sammy's arms, kissing him as if the world was going to end tomorrow. And when Violet realised she was watching, and ran after her, Justine stopped in the corridor and turned with a smile.

'It's OK,' she told her. 'It's probably the best thing that could have happened. It's my wake-up call that this was never going to be for ever . . .'

'Justine . . . honestly . . . it was just . . . I don't know. You go into this weird space when you perform together. It's not like I . . . me and Sammy aren't—'

'Hey,' said Justine. 'It's not a problem. Honestly.'

She wasn't going to break down. She wasn't going to show how she really felt. She had too much pride.

'Don't go,' pleaded Violet. 'Wait for me. I won't be long. We need to talk about this.'

Justine shook her head. 'I was thinking already . . . I'm going to go to Berlin.' She managed a smile. 'It's what I should do. For me. And you've got so much stuff going on. Then maybe, if we decide . . . one day . . .'

Violet picked up her hand and stroked it.

'I love you,' she said. 'I love you and I love having you around. But the truth is I'm not going to be much fun to be around for a while. It's not fair to expect you to support me unconditionally through all this. I'm obsessional. Selfish. A total bloody diva.'

She looked deep into her eyes.

'But I'll still be here when you get back.'

The two of them embraced, holding each other tighter than tight. Justine breathed in Violet's scent and kissed her for the last time.

'I love you,' she whispered in her ear.

Then she turned and walked away.

Violet watched her lover go, with mixed feelings: sadness,

relief, regret. Guilt – of course. Most of all, she was grateful that Justine had made the decision. Maybe it was entirely selfish, but at this stage in her life, her career was what mattered to her. She had reached a turning-point, and she didn't want her future jeopardised by a relationship she wasn't sure about. She loved Justine, of course she did, but all along she had harboured the guilty suspicion that she was just toying with her, that she wasn't giving Justine the commitment she craved. And although she would happily have gone along with things as they were, it was far better to have a clean break. That way nobody got hurt.

She turned and walked back into the dressing room. Sammy was packing away his double bass. It was hard to believe that a few minutes ago they had been kissing passionately, both high on the performance, exhilarated by what had gone between them on the stage. But that was all. There was nothing else.

'Catch you soon,' said Sammy, slinging his instrument onto his back.

'Catch you soon,' echoed Violet. And as the dressing room became empty, she suddenly felt as if all the light had drained out of her life.

On Monday morning, Justine walked into the Amador offices in Knightsbridge. Her father was behind his desk. He looked up, surprised to see her in her trademark navy blue shift dress and high heels, her hair tied back in a sleek ponytail.

'If you haven't found anyone else yet for Berlin, I'd like to go,' she announced.

He pushed back his chair and surveyed her. Should he press her for an explanation? He was fairly certain she wouldn't give him one. Instead he indicated a file on the table in front of him.

'The final contract's right here. We get the keys next Monday. You better go and get yourself packed.'

Justine smiled, and turned to walk back down the corridor to her office. She scrolled through net-a-porter and picked out some outfits she thought would be suitable for the next few months. She booked in with Alex to have her hair cut and coloured. And then she Googled Violet to read the reviews of last night's gig.

'Electrifying . . .' 'Heart-breaking and soul-baring . . .' 'A star in the making . . .'

There were tears in her eyes as she read. A mixture of pride and sorrow filled her heart. But Justine never wanted to force someone to love her. She didn't want to live like her father, consumed with jealousy. She wiped away her tears and picked up the phone to her secretary.

'Book me a ticket to Berlin for Monday. First class. One way.'

Thirty-Two

Louis had never actually learned to drive. Ever since he'd had enough money to buy a car he'd always been driven everywhere he went. So it was Tyger who had to take the wheel of the battered Jeep Cherokee he had borrowed from one of his roadies. Her pink Nissan Figaro was too noticeable to be driven on their mission through deepest, darkest Wales.

They had a plan. They were going to load up as many of the dogs and puppies as they could from Bernie's, with help from some of the guys from the rescue centre where Tyger had got Doug the Pug. She had spoken to her contact there, and made a plan to meet up under cover of darkness, once Louis had managed to get hold of the keys and was certain the coast was clear. She had made absolutely sure that the mission was confidential.

'You don't ask me any questions about where they've come from, and you don't tell the press that I'm involved,' she had instructed her contact, and they had agreed, promising her total anonymity and no reprisals.

'I give them enough publicity. And plenty of donations,' she assured Louis. 'It's not worth their while to betray me. Besides, they're good people.'

The two of them were silent on the journey down. Louis had impressed upon Tyger how dangerous this plan was. Bernie wasn't a man to be messed with. But he agreed with her they had no choice. She wouldn't countenance leaving the animals there to suffer, and reporting them to the RSPCA would inevitably involve trouble for his mother. So it was up to them to trust Tyger's contacts.

Only now they were on the road, Louis was nervous. He wasn't sure if it was the way Tyger threw the Jeep around the roads, but he felt sick.

'This isn't some Famous Five escapade,' he told her. 'It could all go badly wrong.'

'It's not going to go wrong,' she said, keeping her eyes firmly on the road. She didn't admit that she was going to have to stop again at the next motorway services and throw up. She looked at her watch. It was mid-afternoon. They were going to wait until dark before moving in on the farm. Not just so that they had cover of darkness, but because Bernie would be half-drunk by then, his reactions would be slower, he would be easier to fool.

Louis also felt sick at the thought of seeing his mother again. Had he let her down by running away like that? What was she going to say when she saw him? Would she be happy he had made contact after all those years? He couldn't deny that the outcome he was hoping for was Melinda throwing her arms around him with joy, but he was fairly sure that wasn't going to happen, so he pretended to himself that the best he could hope for was an icy amnesty.

Eventually they turned off the motorway and started driving through the countryside. It was hot inside the cab of the car. The water they'd brought with them was warm, the sand-wiches had dried and curled up long ago. Not that either of them were interested in food. Louis reached over and squeezed Tyger's arm. She gave him the briefest of smiles. Neither of them needed to say anything. They just wanted it all to be over.

At half past five they pulled over into a gateway and tried to nap. They hadn't slept well the night before, even though they'd tried to go to bed early. They needed to be alert. But it was even more impossible to sleep now, with the adrenalin coursing through them.

'Shall we stop at a pub, get something to eat?'

Louis shook his head.

'We can't risk being recognised.'

'What, in the back of beyond? Do they even have telly out here?'

Louis thumped her good-naturedly. 'You'd be surprised.'

'You're right, though. Especially after Coco last week.'

They had studiously avoided looking at each other during Tony's recent pep talk. They knew this was exactly the sort of caper he was warning against. But his salutary warning wasn't going to stop them.

Tyger put her legs up on the dashboard, one either side of the steering wheel. Her baseball cap was pulled down low over her eyes. With her skinny jeans, her biker boots and her white singlet, she looked like some crazy American rebel chick about to rob a dime-store. Louis could just imagine her pulling a Colt 45 out of the glove-box.

He shifted in his seat and looked at the clock. It would be a while before the sun even thought about going down. He fiddled with the radio.

'Turn it off,' said Tyger irritably. 'It's doing my head in.'

At last the sun began to sink in the sky, and it turned pink, then purple, then blue. Tyger started up the van again, and followed his directions. Acid burned in his stomach as they drove through the village where he'd been to school. He had nothing but unhappy memories, he realised. Not a single friend. No one had ever contacted him through his website and said, 'Hey, mate – weren't we at school together?' No one had ever taken the time to get to know him.

It doesn't matter, he told himself. You've got Tyger now, the greatest friend you'll ever have.

Then suddenly, they were there. At the bottom of the drive that led to the farm. He could see the lights on from the road.

'We've got to drive past, and go up the dirt track by the next field and round, so we come up to the back of the farm buildings. If we go up the main drive, Bernie will see the car.'

He had drawn a diagram of the layout for her, so she knew exactly how the land lay. Once they were in situ, once they had the keys and were happy that Bernie was stuck in for the night, they would phone the guys from the rescue centre, who'd be waiting in the pub car park, and give them directions.

'If anything goes wrong, if you think it's going to kick off, just get back in the car and drive. Doesn't matter if you leave the dogs behind. Your safety is the most important thing.'

Tyger nodded.

Louis suddenly panicked. What the hell was he doing, putting Tyger through this? He should have got some proper muscle in, not a couple of weedy volunteers from the dogs' home. Shit, he had enough money – he could pay people to keep quiet and do his dirty work. But he knew from experience that people always wanted more. He could trust Tyger.

And nothing was going to go wrong.

The Jeep bounced along the ill-kept track. Tyger killed the lights, just in case, and they peered through the gloom until they came up behind the compound. They parked behind a clump of trees, so the car would be obscured.

They got out. Now the sun had gone, it was chilly, and Tyger shivered in her singlet.

'OK?' asked Louis, and she nodded. Neither of them felt much like talking.

They made their way quietly towards the house, then crept round the back.

'Right – here's the downstairs toilet window. Wait here. I'll drop the keys out as soon as I can. It'll probably take a while.'

'What if you don't get them?'

'I'll get them. Then wait for me and we'll call the others when we're sure the coast is clear. Bernie's usually comatose by about ten.'

They hugged, and Louis held her as tight as he could,

pouring his courage into her. She was so fucking brave. How was he ever going to repay her?

Then he was gone. Tyger crouched down on the ground by the toilet window, wishing she had brought a sweatshirt. Wishing, in fact, that she was anywhere, anywhere, but here.

Louis pressed on the front doorbell. It didn't work. Some things didn't change. He knocked loudly on the frosted glass instead.

He waited a few moments, then saw light flood into the hall as the lounge door opened. He could hear the thunder of the telly: The Lottery – he recognised the presenter's over-excited babble, and the audience's applause. A shadowy figure approached. Louis swallowed.

The door opened.

'Bernie?' said Louis, with an awkward smile.

Bernie frowned. As well he might. Louis was eight years older than when he had left, several inches taller, considerably broader. A man, not a boy.

'Dave,' he prompted him helpfully.

'Well, shit the bed!' said Bernie, charming as ever. 'Melinda! Someone for you.'

He turned on his heel and walked back into the lounge, without asking Louis in. And a moment later his mother stood in front of him.

'Oh my God,' she whispered. 'Little Dave.'

'Hey,' he managed to croak in reply.

She looked terrible. Twenty years older than the eight since he'd last seen her. Her hair was grey, almost white. Her skin was lined, blotchy. Her eyes had sunk into her head. She was wearing too-tight leggings and a sleeveless yellow blouse, her feet stuffed into slippers.

'My baby.' She stared at him dully. Her eyes were blinking rapidly and she was swallowing repeatedly. Suddenly she put her hands up to her face and started to gasp for breath. She was having a panic attack, he realised.

'Mum – Mum, it's OK.' Instinct made him step over the threshold. Instinct made him take her in his arms. 'Mum – it's me. I thought – I'd come to say hello. See how you are. You don't have to panic. It's OK.'

'Oh my God, I've dreamed about this. I never thought it would really happen. I thought you were dead. I thought you'd probably turned into some druggy.' She took in big shuddering gasps. 'I've never forgiven myself . . .'

'Mum, it's cool. I'm OK. Very OK.' He wasn't going to tell her he was a star. Married to a celeb. She obviously had no clue, hadn't seen the photos of him and Tyger in the paper. She wouldn't have recognised him even if she had. He looked a million miles from the insignificant, mousy kid who'd left home when he was fifteen.

Bernie appeared in the door of the lounge.

'What you after? Money?' he demanded belligerently.

'Er, no,' said Louis. 'I just wanted to bury the hatchet after all this time.'

'Think you can just waltz in here like nothing's happened, do you?' Bernie was going to make this as difficult as he could. 'She's never been the same since the day you walked out, your mum. You know that?'

Louis shut his eyes for a moment. He was going to have to keep calm and focus. Not get side-tracked by all the guilt and emotion. Bernie would do his best to make it all his fault.

'Bernie, leave it.' Melinda's tone was sharp. 'I've got my boy back. Don't you drive him away again.'

'Again?' Bernie barked disdainfully. 'I gave the pair of you the shirt off my bloody back, and what thanks did I ever get?'

'Come in,' said Melinda to Louis. 'Come in and let's have a drink. Ignore him.'

Louis edged his way reluctantly into the lounge. It had been done out since he was here. A huge suite of studded burgundy leather was grouped around a massive telly. Melinda went to turn the sound down on the remote, but Bernie stopped her.

'No. I want to see if my numbers come up.'

Your number's come up all right, thought Louis, and re-minded himself what he was here for.

'Sit down.' His mum was nervous.

'Mind if I use the toilet first?'

'Course. It's still in the same place.' She laughed.

Louis went out into the hall and down the corridor. The toilet was to the right. The kitchen, where he hoped the keys were hanging, was to the left.

He could hear the sound of the lottery balls being unleashed. He reckoned he had about a minute while Bernie's attention was taken up. He walked into the kitchen, and realised with a shock that this had been done out too. Obviously the puppy farming was going well. But this also meant the keys weren't in the place he expected them to be. He looked around desperately.

A round of applause greeted the announcement of the first number.

He worked his way round the kitchen, lifting bits of paper, tea towels. Nowhere. Maybe they were in the office. Did he have time to sneak out and go further down the corridor?

More numbers. More applause. He tried to think. And then he saw them, glinting in the fruit bowl, alongside a packet of cigarettes and a lighter. He picked them up without a second thought and bolted across to the downstairs toilet, shutting the door.

He went over to the window, praying Tyger was all right. He levered it open, reached up and dropped the keys out, at the same time flushing the toilet to cover up any noise.

Then he ran the tap, washed his sweating hands, and made his way back to the lounge.

'Any luck?'

Bernie gave a humph of dissatisfaction.

'Mug's game.'

Tyger didn't know whether to be relieved or frightened when the keys finally dropped out of the window. It had seemed as if she had been waiting for ever. She picked them up and started to make her way over to the compound. She could hear the telly from inside the house. It was still on, which was good, because it would cover any noise, but they obviously weren't making much conversation.

She reached the chain-link fence and found the padlock. She felt the size of the lock with her fingers, then tried to feel for the key most likely to fit it. She tried four. No luck. Her heart started to pound. She had to find cover – this was the place where she was the most exposed.

The fifth key fitted. The lock unsnapped. She slipped through and pushed the gate closed. She ran over to the barn and repeated the procedure with the second padlock. She could hear barking inside. Sssh, she thought. Be quiet!

She slid the heavy barn door open and stepped inside, her heart heavy with dread. Only when the door was shut behind her did she turn on the torch she had brought with her. She swung the beam around.

It was worse than she could possibly have imagined – worse than anything Louis had described. Bernie had obviously increased the number of puppies he was farming, and reduced what he was spending on them. It was horrific. The beam lit up the terrified eyes of emaciated creatures crammed cheek by jowl into cages. The stench of urine and faeces was overpowering. She gagged as she opened up the first cage. The puppies yelped. She put in her hands, feeling their matted fur. Tears poured down her face.

'It's OK,' she sobbed. 'We're going to get you out.'

The pathetic beings cowered from her touch. She could see open sores on the mothers' flanks. Flies buzzed everywhere, and she batted them away.

Hurry up, Louis, she begged silently. As soon as he was here they would call the others. Then they could start the mammoth task. It was going to take hours, she estimated. She thought about carrying as many cages as she could out to the Jeep, just to get ahead, but when she tried to lift one it was impossible. She wasn't strong enough.

She placated herself by lifting a puppy out and cuddling it, stroking it reassuringly and talking in a calm, quiet voice. She couldn't even tell what breed it was, but she hugged the tiny body to her until it stopped trembling.

Louis wanted to tell his mother everything – about his life, his success, about his wonderful new wife. And about the fact that he was truly properly happy for the first time in his life. But not in front of Bernie. He didn't want to reveal any of it in front of that piece of scum. So he made up some random stuff. Said he was working in a record shop.

'Collectors' items. Rare 45s. Mostly jazz.'

'Stuff that no one wants, you mean,' scoffed Bernie. He was sitting in what was obviously his chair, his gut bigger than ever, a bottle of beer in his right hand. He hadn't offered Louis one. He'd always had the manners of a pig. 'What are you back here for, anyway?'

'I just . . . wanted to see how Mum was.'

Whatever he said, he didn't want to raise Bernie's suspicions. But Bernie had a naturally suspicious nature.

'You want money.'

Nothing wrong in letting Bernie think that. It would certainly put him off the scent for a while.

'Well . . .' said Louis slowly.

'We can give you money, love,' said Melinda, darting a sharp, nervous glance in Bernie's direction. 'Can't we?'

'Why would we want to?' Bernie lifted the bottle to his blubbery lips.

'He's my son.'

'I thought you were glad to see the back of him when he left. I thought you said he'd been a drain on you all your life.'

Melinda went pale.

Louis felt sick. Had she really said that?

'I never said that,' she told Louis.

358

Bernie gave a bark of laughter.

'Yes, you bloody did.'

'Fine,' said Louis. 'I'll go, shall I?'

Shit. This wasn't turning out how it should be. But he didn't want to stay and listen to this bile much longer.

His mother grabbed his arms.

'I've been waiting for this moment since the day you left. And I wasn't surprised you did. Good luck to you, I thought. You were braver than I was.'

'Yeah, well – you know where your bread's buttered don't you, love?' Bernie chuckled.

'I thought maybe you'd do well for yourself. Find a nice girl . . .'

He wanted to tell her. He wanted to tell her—

'He's done well for himself all right. So well he's had to come crawling back to us for cash.'

Bernie seemed to find this highly amusing. Louis wanted to smash his face in. He couldn't wait for the moment when the fat bastard found out the truth. He had to try to stay calm. His eyes flickered over to the clock on the wall. A big china clock covered in butterflies. He wanted to cry all of a sudden. His mum had always loved butterflies. He remembered that now.

'What's the matter? Scared you're going to miss your last bus home?' Bernie couldn't resist another jibe. 'How d'you get here, anyway? You parked outside?' He started to raise his fat arse out of the chair.

'Hitched,' mumbled Louis. Nearly half an hour, he'd been in here. He needed to get out and get to Tyger. But now he was here he didn't want to leave his mum. He couldn't bear the memories, or the thought that she had been left here all that time. He should never have run out on her. She had only gone with Bernie to give him a better life, and he'd sentenced her to a life of misery.

He was sweating, with the guilt and tension. He felt incredibly nauseous. The sickly scent of Bernie's cheap aftershave was turning his stomach.

'Look, Mum, I need to go. I'll come back and see you soon, I promise.'

'Give me your address. Or your number.'

She was begging him. He could see she was afraid that he would slip out of her grasp again. She didn't want to let him go.

She turned to Bernie.

'Bernie, give him some cash.'

'Bugger off.'

'Give him some bloody cash!'

Louis was quietly admiring of her bravery. He felt touched. She was standing up to Bernie on his behalf. Never mind that he had no need for it.

Bernie got up, grumbling.

'It's in the bedroom. I'll go and get it.'

When the odious presence had left the room, along with the smell, mother and son turned to look at each other. Melinda put a hand up and touched his face.

'I thought about you every hour of every day. What you were doing.'

Tears stung Louis' eyes.

'I thought about you too, Mum,' he told her. 'Has he been a bastard to you?'

She shrugged. 'Better the devil you know.'

'I've got a girl,' he said. 'A beautiful girl.'

'Course you have,' she replied proudly.

Tyger was starting to worry. The others were going to think the plan had been abandoned. Maybe they'd go home. She wondered if she should start emptying the puppies out of the cages. There were some cardboard boxes in the corner. She put the puppy she'd been holding back in the cage.

'I won't be long,' she promised.

She turned to find a man standing in the doorway. A fat bloke with a moustache and a spade in his hands.

'Who the hell are you?' he growled.

She froze, felt her legs turn to jelly. She had to run for it, but he was blocking the only way out. He stepped towards her, menacingly.

There was nothing for it but to scream.

'Louis!' she screeched at the top of her lungs. 'Louis!'

With a jolt, Louis realised that Bernie had been rather a long time, considering he'd just gone to fetch a tenner from his wallet. He'd been so engrossed with the conversation with his mother, he'd lost concentration, almost forgotten why they were here at all.

'Where's Bernie gone?'

'I dunno. He usually goes to check on the dogs about this time—'

Louis bolted out of the lounge.

'Dave?' His mother followed after him. He went into the kitchen. His heart leapt into his mouth when he saw the back door wide open.

'Shit.'

He ran as fast as he could through the darkness. He could see the gate in the fence wide open. And the barn door open too. He raced inside.

Tyger was lying on the ground. Bernie was standing over her. He looked defiantly at Louis.

'She won't have a fucking leg to stand on. She's an intruder. I had every right to hit her.'

Louis dropped to his knees beside Tyger, appalled. How could this have gone so wrong? Of course Bernie had belted her. That's the type of bloke he was.

'Tyger?' She was out cold. As pale as candlewax. And so still. Desperately he felt for a pulse.

'I might have known you'd try something like this. Fucking heroics.'

'Shut up and get an ambulance.'

'Get her inside. We'll stick some peas on her head.'

'Don't touch her. Don't move her. She needs an ambulance.'

Louis was desperately trying to stay calm, to keep a lid on his panic. He smoothed back Tyger's hair and to his horror felt sticky blood.

'What was your game anyway? A Hundred and One bloody Dalmatians?'

Bernie was sneering. Louis got his phone out. To his shock, Bernie kicked it out of his hands.

'I don't want the emergency services sniffing about. Shove her in the car and I'll drive her to A and E.'

'No way – you're not having anything to do with her.'

Louis went to grab his phone and Bernie stepped on his hand. Searing pain drove through his knuckles.

'It's OK,' came a voice from the doorway. 'I'm calling the police.'

Melinda was standing there as cool as a cucumber.

'Mum – you can't. Just get an ambulance. Hurry. If you call the police they'll arrest you as well.'

'I don't care,' she said calmly. 'I should have done it years ago. And I deserve whatever I get.'

'You call the cops and it'll be the last thing you do,' warned Bernie.

'Ambulance. And police.' Melinda spoke calmly into the phone.

'It's your name all over the paperwork,' said Bernie spitefully. 'I'm not an idiot.'

Louis looked down at Tyger. Rusty-red blood was seeping onto the concrete. He felt sheer terror, the biggest emotion he had ever felt in his life.

'I'm off,' said Bernie, and headed for the door.

'No, you're not,' said Melinda, and chucked a heavy set of car keys over to Louis. 'And you're such a fat bastard, you won't even make it to the end of the drive before they get here.'

They were astonishingly fast. Less than ten minutes, although it felt like a lifetime to Louis. His mother was amazing. She held Louis' hand while he held Tyger's, soothed him, reassured him. And when the police arrived, she was so incredibly dignified; it brought tears to his eyes.

'Don't worry about me,' she said. 'You sort your girl out.'

The ambulance-men were not impressed with what they found. Tyger wasn't responding at all. Her stats were worrying.

'We need to get her to a big hospital. We can't deal with a head injury like that here,' the paramedic told him. 'I'll get the air ambulance.'

Louis shut his eyes. How the hell could he have let this happen?

His mother stroked his arm. He threw it off.

'This is all for you,' he shouted at her. 'I've sacrificed her for you.'

Melinda blinked at him, her face crumpled and haggard.

'I didn't ask you to,' she whispered.

The air ambulance landed in the field. A young doctor quickly examined Tyger, and any hope that Louis had that the paramedic had over-reacted was soon extinguished.

'She might well have a sub-cranial bleed. We can't waste time,' the doctor told him. 'We'll take her to Bristol.'

To Louis' surprise, he was able to think clearly. Raf was in Bath. He could get to the hospital, probably before they did.

'Is there room for me? I don't drive.'

The medic nodded and Louis followed as they lifted Tyger on board. She was strapped to a stretcher, her head held in a brace.

Louis scrambled in and sat in the seat the pilot indicated was for him. As the helicopter took off, he watched down below as his mother and Bernie were escorted into a squad car. There were flashing lights everywhere. He'd phoned the guys from the rescue centre, who were also on their way, ready to whisk the inhabitants of the barn off to a safe haven. Then he looked away, the puppies forgotten, and mentally urged the helicopter on, knowing that the one thing they didn't have was time.

The helicopter chopped its way relentlessly through the night sky. The medic kept a constant watch on Tyger, checking her stats repeatedly and keeping in contact with the hospital.

'There's a trauma team ready to take her in as soon as we get there,' he told Louis. 'She'll need a scan.'

Louis nodded, mute with fear. As soon as they landed he needed to call Raf. Tell him he'd probably got his daughter killed. And all for the sake of a few bloody puppies. A few puppies who were even now being taken to the warmth and comfort of some sanctuary, while she lay there so pale and still, he couldn't imagine her ever coming back to life. He didn't let go of her hand, just in case she could feel him. Every now and again he picked it up and kissed it, as if he could somehow breathe life back into her.

The medic caught his eye. He gave him a brief sympathetic smile, then looked away.

It was all systems go as soon as they landed. Louis trailed in the wake of the trauma team, feeling completely helpless as they loaded Tyger onto a trolley, pushing her from the landing pad in through the doors of the hospital, shouting instructions at each other, comparing stats, grilling the medic who had just disembarked, grabbing the clipboard from him, talking into their radios. Louis recognised the choreography from the mayhem at a live gig. Amidst the chaos, everyone had their job, and they stuck to it. It restored his faith a little. No one seemed to be panicking. No one seemed to be giving up hope. They were all totally focused.

A pair of double door slammed shut in front of him as Tyger was taken in for assessment. He had to get in touch with Raf, let the rest of the family know. He couldn't go through this on his own.

He picked up the phone to ring, but a huge lump rose in his throat. To his horror, he was crying. A nurse came up and put a hand on his shoulder.

'Would you like me to call for you?'

He nodded, unable to speak, then sat on a chair with his head in his hands. How long? How long before he knew what was going to happen?

The Rafferty machine swung smoothly into action as soon as the news was out, almost taking Louis' breath away. Before he knew it, Raf had arrived, escorted by Dickie and Genevieve. Tony and Polly were on their way down from London, Polly on her mobile booking hotels in Bristol for them and Coco and Violet.

It was like being part of some mafia clan and he felt rather helpless. He might have married into the family, but he wasn't part of any decision-making process. It was almost as if he was superfluous. Then again, perhaps he should be grateful he was being overlooked, and not blamed.

Not yet.

Violet broke down completely when she hung up the phone after talking to Tony.

Tyger, her baby sister, was lying in hospital. Tony had sounded grim. It was serious, not an over-inflated Rafferty drama.

She'd told him she'd be fine, that she'd be able to drive, that she didn't want Benedict, who was taking Coco, to come and pick her up, because she couldn't face him, not after what had happened between her and Justine. Even though she was fairly certain he had no idea of what had gone on.

She started to look for her keys, but she couldn't find them. A random image of Tyger with her Mr Potato Head, sticking all the features on in the wrong place and laughing her head off, popped into her mind. For some reason it made her cry even harder.

Where was Mum? Where the bloody hell was their mother? Mothers were supposed to be there whatever happened. They weren't supposed to disappear off the face of the earth. They were supposed to be there for ever and ever to pick up the pieces.

Only Delilah wasn't there. And Violet didn't think she could cope with this on her own. Her little sister, so bright, so vibrant, so full of life, might die. Tony had made it clear. She was critical.

At last. She'd found the keys, under a magazine on the coffee table. But she was sobbing so hard she didn't think she'd be able to drive. Maybe she could call Tony back, get him to send a car . . .

Or maybe . . .

There was one person she knew who would get her through this. One person who would be at her side, who would understand.

She picked up the phone again, hesitated for a moment, then dialled.

Justine was laying out her packing on the bed in the spare room. She had two huge suitcases open, and was carefully going through her wardrobe, selecting which items would go best with the clothes she'd had couriered round. She didn't have time to try everything on. She didn't even bother to unwrap what she'd bought from the tissue paper. She rarely chose a mistake.

As she zipped up the lid on one of the cases, her mobile rang. Her heart jumped when she saw who it was.

She answered cautiously.

'Hello?'

'Justine?' Violet was sobbing. 'I need you. I need you to take me to Bristol. Tyger's had an accident.'

'OK, sweetheart.' Justine grabbed her bag without a second thought. 'Where are you? I'm on my way.'

'I'm at home. Oh God, Justine. What if she dies . . . ?'

'She won't die. I'll be . . . fifteen minutes, max.'

In her living room, Violet hung up the phone. She grabbed a few things and shoved them in a carrier bag. Tears were still pouring down her face. But a tiny bit of her felt reassured.

Justine was coming for her. Justine was going to be with her. What did this mean?

She ran down the stairs and out onto the pavement. She shivered in the cool of the night air, looking anxiously down the end of the street for the lights of Justine's car. And when she pulled up, and jumped out, and took Violet in her arms and told her it was going to be all right, Violet realised the truth.

She loved her.

Louis looked up as Raf walked through the double doors into the relatives' waiting room. He stood up and Raf touched him on the shoulder.

'Do we know how it's going?'

There was no reproach. This wasn't the time for recrimination.

'Not yet,' answered Louis.

The minutes seemed like hours while they waited for news. And when the neurological consultant appeared through the double doors, he headed straight for Raf. Tyger's identity was no secret. They knew exactly who they were dealing with.

'The CAT scan shows she had a sub-cranial haemorrhage resulting from her injury,' the consultant told them. 'That's basically a bleed inside the brain, which is building up pressure. We can't allow that to go on, as it may cause damage to the tissue. We need to operate to relieve that pressure, drain off the bleed.'

'You're going to operate now?'

'We can't afford to wait.'

'And what's the prognosis?'

'It's hard to say, I'm afraid. The brain is very delicate and complex. But we've got a great team here.'

As Raf and Louis took in this information, Tony and Polly arrived.

Raf turned to Tony. 'I don't care what it takes, we need to find Delilah.'

Tony nodded. 'I agree. Polly's been emailing her but we've got no idea if she will check her account, if at all. So our only option is the press.' He looked at his watch. 'If I get on the case straight away, we can get the late editions.'

Raf nodded curtly. Louis wondered if he was allowed any say at all in what happened, but decided he'd better keep quiet. He didn't care who knew what when. All he was worried about was whether Tyger would be all right. He imagined them lifting her onto the operating table – would they take off her wedding ring? What would happen to it? He allowed himself to focus on this image. It was so much easier to cope with than the thought of all that equipment, the computer screens, the trays of gleaming instruments, the tubes and bags of blood—

'Are you all right?' a nurse asked him kindly, and he squeezed his eyes shut to stop the tears from falling.

Not long after midnight, Coco and Benedict arrived, followed by Violet and Justine. They all gathered in the waiting room, silent, subdued, only speaking to ask if anyone wanted something from the drinks machine down the corridor.

It was going to be a long night.

Thirty-Three

Delilah gradually came to at the sound of the curtain rings scraping along the pole. A sliver of morning sun fell on her face. She sat up, groggy with sleep, and smiled as William put a cup of strong, dark Irish tea on the bedside table. She wondered how long he had been up. The bed next to her was cold, and he was already dressed in his jeans and one of his trademark faded sweatshirts. She stretched and yawned.

'What's the time?'

'Just gone ten.'

'What?' She threw back the bedding with alarm. 'I'd better get on with the breakfasts. Why didn't you wake me?'

'Relax! Our guests are all fed and watered and have gone off to Kinsale for the day. They're having dinner with friends on the way home. So we, young lady, are going to take the day off.'

He sat on the bed next to her.

'A day off?' she murmured.

He laughed.

'You didn't come here expecting a holiday, did you?' He put out a finger and traced the line of her collar-bone. 'Seriously, Dee – I can't tell you how grateful I am. No way could I have done it without you. The guests would have been eating cornflakes and beans on toast if it had been left to me. You're a star.'

'You know what? I've loved every minute of it. This house is . . . special.'

'I know.' His face fell. 'And I really don't want to think

about what's going to happen next. There's no way my mother is going to manage.'

They both fell silent. In the short time they'd spent together, they'd both been living in the present. They hadn't talked about the past, or the future.

William stood up.

'Let's not worry about it today. Today we're going to Dingle. It's the perfect weather to see Fungi.'

'What?'

'You don't know Fungi?'

'As in . . . mushroom?'

'Nope. As in dolphin.' He flicked back the sheets. 'So come on. Put your best dolphin-spotting outfit on. And remember you might get wet.'

Delilah scrambled out of bed, laughing. She was used to this with William – never being quite sure what was going to happen next.

'I'll go off into Killorglin and get some picnic supplies. I want you dressed and ready by the time I get back.'

Delilah gave him a mock salute.

'Yes, sir . . .'

She stood in front of the window and looked out onto the garden. It was a perfect Irish morning, the grass still wet with dew, the sun beaming down through the puffs of white cloud tinged with purple. As William drove his Mercedes out of the drive and down the pitted track, she thought how easy it had been to step into her new life. There was nothing here to remind her of her old one. They had been working round the clock to keep Gortnaflor and its guests afloat. Delilah had loved every minute of it. And William had been profoundly grateful. It was hard for him, driving back and forth to the hospital to check on his mother, trying to get on top of all the things that needed doing. Yet he still found time to show his appreciation.

And now they knew this was their last couple of days together. William was due back at the office the following week. Delilah didn't want to think about it. She turned to the wardrobe to decide what to wear. It took her two minutes to pull out a pair of jeans and a striped Breton-style jumper, topped off with an Irish tweed flat cap.

The perfect dolphin-spotting outfit indeed.

William threw bread rolls, thick hand-cut ham, salt-and-vinegar crisps and a couple of cans of cider into his shopping basket. There would be sponge cake back at Gortnaflor, and he could grab some tomatoes and cucumber from the greenhouse. He grinned to himself at the thought of the day's adventure – sure, going to see Fungi was a little touristy, but you couldn't fail to be amused by his antics, and Dingle was a charming little town. They'd stop for a pint of Guinness in one of the pubs, listen to some Irish music. Do the whole tourist thing, in fact.

He stopped by the news-stand to get a copy of the *Irish Times*, when a headline in one of the English papers caught his eye. His heart skipped a beat as he picked it up.

Search for Missing Star!

The words were emblazoned across a photograph of a laughing woman, leaning against her Lacanche cooker, wearing a sloppy cable-knit sweater that revealed her creamy bare shoulders.

Shoulders he knew only too well. The collar-bone he had run his finger along only that morning. The neck he had kissed so many times, in such a short space of time.

With mounting dread, he scanned the accompanying article with a lawyer's eye.

An appeal has gone out for the television celebrity Delilah Rafferty, who has been absent from home for several weeks, to contact her family.

'We know she was taking some time out after a difficult period – a sort of extended holiday – but we don't know exactly where she is,' said a spokesman. 'We have respected her right to privacy, but we really need her back home and would appreciate anyone who knows her whereabouts giving her this message.'

Delilah's daughter Tyger, who recently married underground rock singer Louis Dagger, is in a coma in hospital in Bristol following a head injury. Understandably her family would like Delilah by her side.

What an eejit. How could he not have recognised her? His friends always took the mickey out of William for being a bit out of touch, but he should have cottoned on. He had to admit on reflection that she had seemed a little bit familiar when he'd first come upon her in the drawing room, but people often look like other people, and celebrities didn't often tip up at Gortnaflor. He'd happily believed her story, and the name she'd given him, because she had enchanted him. She had given no hint of who she was, or what she had left behind. And he'd been happy to accept her as a blank canvas.

William realised he had to get back to her as quickly as he could. He left his basket of food, practically threw the money for the paper at the girl on the till, rushed to his car and drove back to Gortnaflor at high speed.

Delilah was clearing away the last of the breakfast things from the dining room when William walked in. She put down the butter dish and the jam pots. She could tell there was something wrong.

'What is it?'

He held the paper out to her.

'I'll take you to the airport,' he said. 'I'll get straight onto them and find out when the next flight is . . .'

Puzzled, Delilah scanned the article. As the facts gradually got through to her, so did the implications, and she choked back a sob.

'Come on,' said William. 'Get your stuff, quickly. We can be at the airport in two hours. We'll phone on the way, book a ticket. There'll be a flight to Bristol.'

'Tyger . . .' Delilah looked down at the paper, reading the terrible words again. 'I need to phone.'

William pulled out his mobile. Delilah looked at him, stricken.

'I can't remember anyone's number. I threw my iPhone into the sea.'

William didn't bat an eyelid. He dialled Directory Enquiries.

'Go and get your stuff. I'll get the number of the hospital. Go on.'

She didn't need telling twice.

William watched her as she left the room. His heart fell. The dream was over, that was for sure. It had been a great fantasy, while it had lasted, and he had known deep down that it wouldn't go on for ever. But what was life if you couldn't have dreams? And his dreams hadn't been *so* impossible: that she'd decide to take over from his mother at Gortnaflor – letting Elizabeth stay on, of course – and he would come down from Dublin at weekends, and then, eventually, when she made such a success of the place, he would give up his job and . . . Gortnaflor would rise from the ashes, become the greatest country-house hotel in Ireland . . .

For Christ's sake, William, get a grip, he told himself, and asked the operator for the number of the hospital.

Coco found it strange, how life liked to play little jokes on you sometimes.

Life imitating art. Ha ha ha. Hilarious.

It had been no time at all since she had been sitting in the very same position, in front of the very same equipment, at the hospital – only that hadn't been real. There had been an actor in the bed, the equipment hadn't really been hooked up to him, the terrible stats that had shown up on the computer had been programmed in by one of the crew. And the tear that had fallen down her face had been fake – a tear she'd managed to produce from somewhere, a tear that was down to her supposed talent.

The tear that fell now wasn't fake, nor was it single. She couldn't believe how still Tyger looked. How young. How . . .

lifeless. Her crazy, sometimes aggravating, in-your-face little sister.

Benedict had driven her down as soon as Raf had called. Polly had booked them into the Hotel du Vin in Bristol, but they hadn't checked in yet. All of them had wanted to wait to see how Tyger's operation went.

The consultant seemed satisfied. He had relieved the pressure on the brain, and was happy there didn't seem to be too much damage. Now, it was just a question of waiting to see when she would wake up. Or if . . .

Only then would they know if there had been much damage.

'I'm sorry I can't be more specific,' said the consultant. 'But it's very much a game of wait and see . . .'

Wait and see. Three of Coco's least favourite words.

She put out a finger and stroked her sister's arm.

'Hey, Tyger,' she said. Talking to the patient sometimes helped bring them round. 'It's Coco. Come on, you. We need you to wake up. There's too much going on for you to just lie there. We've got plans to make, chica. And I've got stuff I need to tell you . . .' She allowed a smile into her voice at this point. She did have stuff to tell Tyger. Big stuff. Big stuff that only sisters could share. 'There might even be a ring involved,' she told her, in a low teasing voice. If that didn't pique Tyger's curiosity and bring her round, nothing would.

But there was no response. Coco sat back with a sigh, unsure what to do next. Tyger was in the High Dependency Unit, not a private room, because she needed constant supervision. There were about eight beds, all rigged up to any number of high-tech machines, and a nurses' station in the middle. They limited the amount of visitors in at any one time, which was fair – if all the Rafferty clan were in at the same time, there wouldn't be room for anyone else.

As she sat holding her sister's hand, praying for a miracle, Benedict came in to get her.

'Come on,' he whispered. 'You need to get some sleep.

They've all promised to call if she wakes up. And your mum's on her way.'

'Mum?'

Coco stood up, and felt relief wash over her. This whole thing had been a nightmare, but it had been made even worse without Delilah holding them all together. She felt sure that Tyger was probably wondering where she was, longing for that soothing voice, that warm embrace.

She stroked her sister's hand again.

'Mum's on her way, darling,' she told her. 'Please try to wake up. It would so lovely if you woke up—'

She choked suddenly on her words. What if Tyger never woke up? It was unthinkable. But the little waxwork doll in the bed looked more like a corpse than a living being.

Benedict put an arm round her and drew her away. She immediately felt comforted by his presence; stronger. Benedict always made her feel stronger.

He'd certainly given her strength since the bust. Not that he hadn't given her hell over it – far from it. He'd been an absolute knight in shining armour on the night, but had given her short shrift the next day, when she'd slept off the trauma. And when Lisa had hauled her over the coals he'd been totally unsympathetic.

The executive producer had told her they had come that close – *that close* – to re-casting her. She had to issue all sorts of statements saying that she didn't condone the use of hard drugs – which she didn't – and sign up to weekly sessions in a treatment centre. Not a glitzy private treatment centre of the type mentioned in the glossies, but a hard-core, no-frills, take-no-prisoners place with uncomfortable chairs and ghastly coffee.

'It'll do you good,' Benedict had said briskly. 'Hopefully you'll realise that you don't need to be dependent on bloody narcotics to be a success. You'll be a success because you're *talented*, Coco. Not everyone's that lucky. Remember that.'

Benedict was definitely going to keep her real. He didn't give her any leeway whatsoever. Despite his luxurious lifestyle, there was a tough edge to him that didn't suffer fools gladly. Strangely, his tough love made Coco feel secure. And confident.

Maybe that's what her dad had needed, she thought bitterly. Someone to pull on his choke chain a bit harder, right from the start. None of them had really forgiven him yet, but the situation with Tyger had rather over-ridden his misdemeanours.

As she was about to leave, she felt sure she saw Tyger's eyes flutter.

'Nurse!' she shouted, and the nurse hurried over. 'I'm sure she was trying to open her eyes.'

The nurse busied herself taking Tyger's stats.

'We'll keep an eye on her,' she said. 'We'll let you know straight away.'

Coco looked pleadingly at Benedict. She couldn't bear to leave. What if Tyger was about to wake?

'Come on,' he said. 'It's not fair. Other people are waiting to see her.'

Reluctantly she walked away, looking over her shoulder at the small, lonely figure in the bed until the doors of the HDU finally closed behind them.

William and Delilah conducted the journey to Cork airport in a tense silence. William had spoken to Raf, and was able to tell Delilah that the operation had been a success, but they were still waiting for Tyger to come round. And he'd booked her flight. Someone would be there to meet her at Bristol airport. As he drove, at rather breakneck speed through the horribly windy Kerry roads, she sat morosely, fiddling with the zips on her handbag, chewing at her nails.

She didn't know what to focus on. She couldn't bear to think about Tyger, because she was so powerless to do anything until she got to the hospital. But the image of her little girl, unconscious, haunted her nevertheless.

Then there was the thought that she was soon going to see Raf.

She didn't know how she was going to feel when she saw him. So much had happened. She felt like a completely different person – and maybe she was. During her time at Gortnaflor, she had learned to live a more solitary existence – a life without a demanding family, without juggling a career, without having to put on a face to the outside world, or indeed, the inside world – many was the time she had to pretend she felt all right to Raf and the girls when in fact she felt under the most incredible pressure. She'd learned to work hard in a different sort of way – she looked at her hands, red raw from washing-up and preparing vegetables.

And she'd learned to enjoy simple things. She'd finally gone out in the boat, and lay back looking at the endless blue of the sky. She'd climbed one of the bruised purple mountains, clambering over the springy grass and the peaty earth, and come to another lake surrounded by forbidding granite rocks and an eerie mist – a lake that was said to have no bottom, and if you swam in it, the little people would drag you down. She had stood on the edge and shuddered, thrilled by the urge that she had to defy them, but she hadn't dared. She'd caught a fat brown trout, laughing at her ineptitude, but was delighted when it was served to her fried in butter.

All this she had done with William. And more. But all the time, there had been something missing. Someone else she wanted to share it all with. She'd tried to chase him from her mind, tell him to go away, because she wanted to share it with someone new. Someone who hadn't hurt her. But Raf wouldn't leave her mind.

And now she wanted him even more desperately. Tyger, their gorgeous, lovable, madcap daughter, their baby, was lying in hospital, in a coma. The only man she wanted by her side was Raf. The only man she'd ever wanted was Raf.

She sighed. William reached out a hand and held hers.

It wasn't a grope. It was a gesture of kindness and support.

He was a good man, an honourable man. And he'd shown her another side of herself.

But he wasn't for her.

The inevitable had happened. The paparazzi were on the case. It was a soap opera in itself, unfolding in a single location that they could home in on: a glamorous girl in a coma, her distraught rock-star husband at her side; a celebrity couple whose marriage was in peril; an actress with a recent drug problem escorted by a billionaire hotelier. They were in a frenzy of excitement, and Tony was playing hardball with them all.

The staff at the hospital were wonderful. They had tight security, but they made it even tighter, and they found a room that the Raffertys could use to be together and out of the public eye while they waited for Tyger to come round. The nurses were happy to run up and down to the canteen for sandwiches and coffee. Not that anyone could face food.

Dickie and Polly were dispatched to the airport to fetch Delilah. It was unlikely they would be recognised leaving the hospital, and so with any luck the photographers wouldn't follow them. They were going to go in Dickie's battered old Volvo.

Polly struggled to catch up with Dickie's long stride as they made their way through the hospital car park.

'This is terrible,' he said as he started up the engine. 'This is so terrible. I didn't think things could get any worse.'

'You know what?' said Polly. 'It's going to be fine.'

He looked at her sideways.

'It is?'

'It always is,' she said. 'Believe me, I've worked with them for ten years, and it's always fine. In the end.'

'How do you cope?' he asked.

She shrugged. 'By not having anything else in my life to worry about,' she replied simply.

'Well, I hope you're right,' he said, pulling onto the main road that led to the airport.

Polly's chin trembled.

'I have to believe it,' she managed. 'I couldn't bear it . . . if Tyger doesn't make it. And if Raf and Delilah don't get back together.'

To her amazement, this was true. Even though in her wildest dreams, she had fantasised about Raf spurning Delilah and telling Polly he couldn't live without her, she wasn't stupid enough to think it could possibly ever happen. It had been terrible at The Bower without the two of them. Polly had been rushed off her feet, there had been more to deal with than ever, but without Raf and Delilah around, what was the point?

She looked sideways at Dickie. With his flop of hair falling over his glasses, his earnest expression searching the roadside for signposts, he was such a dear.

'Aren't you worried about your film?' she asked.

'Desperately,' he admitted. 'There's not much we can shoot without Raf. He's in practically every scene. But I can hardly expect him to work.'

'So what will happen?'

'I don't know. There's insurance – for compassionate leave. We'd just put it on hold. But there's no saying everyone would be available to start again. We'd have to trash it.'

'That would be a shame.'

'Yeah,' he said. 'Especially as I put up half my flat to finance it.' He managed an awkward smile. 'Pretty scary.'

'You're kidding?' Polly was horrified. Dickie didn't look like the sort of person who could afford to lose that kind of money.

Dickie shrugged. 'Tyger's more important than a bloody film. I'd get some of the cash back. Probably.'

Probably not. He was running over-budget. In the hope they would make a profit. Which he had felt sure they would – the stuff they had in the can so far was fantastic. Now, however, the whole project was looking pretty shaky.

Polly didn't know what to say.

'Airport, one and a half miles,' she managed finally.

It was Violet's turn to sit with Tyger.

Justine had driven her down, but had elected not to come into the hospital. She was reticent about intruding on the family's grief. She had dropped Violet off at the hospital, and the two of them had hugged.

'We need to talk,' whispered Violet.

'It can wait,' Justine told her. 'It can all wait. Go and be with your family. I'll wait at the hotel. Call if you want me to collect you.'

Violet decided to share her dilemma with her sister. Tyger loved a bit of intrigue and a bit of scandal.

'Tyger, you've got to wake up,' she told her. 'I don't know what the hell I'm supposed to do, and you're the only person I can talk to. There's this person, you see, and it's all wonderful. Really amazing. Shag-tastic, as you would say. But it's a bit tricky. I don't know if Mum and Dad are going to approve, exactly. Not that I care if they don't. But . . . it's complicated. I was in total denial about it at first. I never thought this would happen to me, but it did. And I don't know where it's going to end up, but I can't stop it. Honestly, Tyger, the sex is to die for. I've never known anything like it. But it's not just that. It's proper L.O.V.E. love. She makes me feel like—'

Tyger's eyelids began to flutter. Violet stopped in mid-flow.

'Tyger?'

She watched in astonishment as her sister's eyes gradually opened.

'*She?*' Tyger demanded in scandalised tones. 'Did you say *she?*'

Delilah was striding down the corridor, flanked by Dickie and Polly. They'd pushed their way through the photographers outside, in through the main entrance, up in the lift. As they approached the High Dependency Unit, Raf came out of the room that had been put aside for them.

He didn't see Delilah at first. He was heading for the coffee machine. Not for coffee, but to break the monotony. He looked terrible. Unshaven. Rumpled. His eyes burned bright in his face, feverish with worry and fatigue.

He stopped in his tracks as he saw his wife. She looked different. Terribly young. Her hair was in plaits; her clothes totally out of place – jeans and a striped jumper.

She stopped when she saw him. They stood, one at each end of the corridor, staring at each other for what seemed like eternity. His heart was filled with trepidation; hers with uncertainty.

He began to walk towards her, slowly. She hung back, unsure.

And then the doors of the High Dependency Unit burst open and Violet flew out, tears streaming down her face.

'She's awake,' she sobbed. 'Tyger's awake.'

Delilah ran down the corridor. She threw open the doors, and strode into the ward, where Tyger was talking weakly to a nurse who was taking her pulse. She crossed the room in two bounds and threw her arms around her daughter.

The nurse stepped back hastily, watching the reunion.

She had to admit, she'd never have recognised Delilah Rafferty if the girl hadn't called her Mum. She looked nothing like she did on the telly. But it obviously was her, by the way she was sobbing in relief. And then the two other sisters came back in, crowding round, wanting to hug their mother and Tyger. And then Louis – the husband, who had such a filthy reputation if you believed the papers, but who had been absolutely sweet, worried sick about his wife.

She kept half an eye open for the ward sister, who would do her nut if she saw four visitors round the bed. They only ever allowed two, max. And now here was Raf. She couldn't turn him away. Everyone on the staff was half in love with him. He was so beautiful, and cut such a tragic figure. They had all fought over the chance to take him updates, ask him if he wanted coffee.

She watched with interest as he approached the bed. Delilah disentangled herself from her daughters, and looked at him. They weren't smiling. They were just looking at each other. And then Tyger caught sight of her dad, and stretched out her arms, and he went to hug her, holding her tight.

There was definitely a story here, thought the nurse, as Delilah stepped out of the way. It was almost as if she was avoiding her husband. She knew the press were all outside baying for details, but she wasn't going to give anything away to anyone. She would protect their privacy. No one deserved to go through what they had been through and have it splashed all over the papers.

She was going to have to intervene. She needed a doctor to come and check Tyger over. And the last thing the girl needed was to be tired out by her visitors.

'I'm sorry, folks. I'm going to have to ask you all to step outside. You can come back later, but I need to check Tyger over. I'm sure you understand.'

'May I stay with her?' Delilah's voice was low. 'Please. I've only just arrived.'

The nurse hesitated.

'OK. But just sit there quietly while I do her obs. The doctor will be here in a moment.'

Delilah nodded at the others to go. Raf put his arms around Violet and Coco and led them away, followed by Louis. Delilah watched them go and turned to Tyger, who was looking at her, anxious.

'Mum . . . you and Dad. It's going to be OK, right?'

Delilah put her hand over Tyger's, conscious that the nurse might be listening.

'Sweetheart, I don't know. Let's concentrate on getting you better. And I want to hear what happened. Someone said something about rescuing a load of dogs . . .'

Thirty-Four

The Temperate House at Kew Gardens had never looked so lovely.

Every branch, every leaf, every bloom was at its most succulent, bursting with life, in a tangled display of verdant ebullience. Backlit in all the colours of the rainbow, it was exotic, almost magical, the perfect backdrop for the party of the year. Down the centre of the glasshouse was the longest table imaginable, seating a hundred down each side, laid with shimmering mother-of-pearl crockery and green goblets, candelabras draped in ivy interspersed at regular intervals down its length.

The air was heavy with the mingled scents of all the guests who were assembling to take their places for dinner. A heady mix of actors, media stars, artists, fashion designers – you name it. There was no doubt that this was an A-list gathering, but there was no posturing for the cameras. These were all people who were confident and comfortable in their own skin, and with each other, and they were all here tonight to enjoy a beautiful summer's evening, a ravishing setting, wonderful food and then the chance to let their hair down.

A single photographer had been allowed in, to take official photographs, the best of which would be displayed in the magazine of Delilah's choice the following week.

He was taking photographs now, of the three Rafferty sisters, sitting in descending order of age on the Victorian spiral staircase. Coco, her arm curled round the banister, was standing, to best show off her full-length dress, silk-jersey

Halston in pillar-box red. Beside her was Violet in hot-pink ruffled Alice Temperley, her dark bob shorter and sharper than ever. And at their feet sat Tyger, her arms round her knees, surprisingly demure in lilac lace L'Wren Scott. On her lap was Tuppence, the tiny little shih-tzu puppy she had plucked out of the cage on the night of the rescue, and who now rarely left her side.

Next to them stood Louis, anxiously watching his wife. He had turned out to be a pillar of strength – the polar opposite of the dissolute waste of space his image had at first led them to expect. He had been incredibly hard on himself over the whole incident, blaming himself entirely, but everyone knew perfectly well that the caper had Tyger written all over it, and how very persuasive she could be. Besides, he had done it for the right reasons – loyalty to his mother. Although she had been arrested, he'd stood bail for her and she was now awaiting trial. He'd got her the best lawyer, and there was every chance that, although she wasn't entirely innocent, it would be Bernie who would take most of the rap.

Of course, Louis had to sell his story, and reveal the truth about his past, but by selling it to the highest bidder, and donating every penny to the rescue centre that eventually re-homed all the puppies, he redeemed himself. And the photo-shoot of him and Tyger with the rescued puppies gave the magazine that printed it their highest circulation ever. The papers loved the two of them more than ever.

Delilah looked on, dressed in a shockingly short Thomas Wylde chiffon number, her hair in a tousled mane down her back, her gorgeous legs in staggeringly high heels. Hell, this was her fiftieth birthday. If she couldn't dress like a wanton tart, then what was the point? Not that she really looked like a tart. If anyone could get away with it, Delilah could, and no one was going to judge her on her birthday. She was amongst friends, and people who loved her. After everything that had happened, she had made sure of that.

She took a sip of her cocktail. Good old Polly had gone for

the raspberry Bellinis in the end. She had staunchly carried on organising the party, never wavering in her belief that Delilah would return. Nevertheless, she had remained adamant about handing in her notice. Delilah was going to miss her, but then, so much was going to change. She'd made a lot of decisions since she'd come back from Ireland.

After dinner, Violet was getting ready to do a short set of music in the marquee before Louis and Tyger took over as DJs. She had protested volubly that she didn't want to, that it was showing off, but Delilah had begged her.

'I'd love some live music, but I don't want to pay someone else. I want you to do it, darling.'

Violet had, of course, relented in the end. Now, she was surprised to find herself nervous. She never usually got much stage-fright, but tonight was different. Tonight she was performing just for her friends and family, and it had to be perfect.

Justine held her hand as she took deep breaths. They were taking things slowly, seeing how the relationship panned out now it was official. Justine was spending the weeks in Berlin, then either flying back to London for the weekend or Violet was coming out to join her. So far, it was working like a dream. They both had space for themselves, they were both flourishing, but they cherished their time together.

As she heard Sammy tune up his double bass, she felt calm settle over her. This was her territory. This was her stage. They were her audience.

She came on to riotous applause. She knew that however badly she performed, the audience would be ecstatic. So she was going to blow them away.

She gave them everything they wanted, and more. She'd pulled together lots of stuff, some of her classics, some new things, stuff they could dance to. She did 'Mack The Knife', 'Material Girl', 'Black Velvet', *La Vie en Rose* – there was something for everyone. And then, as an encore, she steeled herself for her final offering.

'This is a song I wrote,' she told the audience. 'It's a very special song. It's about having the courage to be yourself. And about having the courage to love.'

There was a smattering of applause and some whistles.

Violet smiled, and shut her eyes, almost ready to begin.

'This is for Justine . . .'

Benedict led Coco onto the dance floor. He was, of course, the most superb dancer. They moved as one, spinning around in each other's arms, their eyes locked.

Coco still couldn't believe how lucky she had been to find this man. This man who had never judged her, who had simply supported her, and who totally understood what she needed. Her confidence was growing by the day. Offers for other parts were starting to flood in, but she had decided to extend her contract on *Critical but Stable* for another year, while she found her feet. She owed it to them for the loyalty they had shown her.

Benedict, meanwhile, was revelling in his adoration. After so many years depriving himself of a fulfilling relationship, he was drinking deep. Coco enthralled him. Everything he did now took on another dimension. He was living life to the full, instead of just living it for the sake of it. The spectre of Jeanne, the guilt, the self-blame, had faded. He would never forget her – of course he wouldn't, for he had Justine – but at last he had allowed himself to move on.

Genevieve was shocked to find her eyes welling up at Violet's performance. Honestly, she was becoming a soppy thing in her old age. Yes, she told herself, she really was. She had learned a lot on the set of *Something for the Weekend*, and the accompanying skirmishes with the Rafferty family. She had learned that there was a lot to be said for family, and companionship. And although it was too late for her to do anything about the former, she could certainly address the latter.

While she was waiting for the taxi to take her to Delilah's party, she thought long and hard. She sat in the living room of her little house in Hampstead, which she had thought so chic and bohemian, but which now seemed rather sterile and spinsterish. She thought of all the times that Jeremy had begged her to, if not marry him, then move in with him. She had kept him at arm's length, not wanting him to ruin her image, or step on her toes. But why? They got on famously, agreed over the right things and argued over the right things. Why shouldn't she bloody learn to share, after all this time?

Why, as Violet said, shouldn't she have the courage to love?

Jeremy was here, now. She was going to ask him back tonight. She never asked a man back to her house, ever. But there was a first time for everything, even at her age.

Polly was standing out on the terrace.

She wondered if she would be a party pooper if she went home. She was absolutely exhausted. It had been down to her to finalise all the arrangements for the party, what with everything else that had happened, and she was run off her feet. She was determined not to get up until at least two o'clock the next day.

Bugger. She couldn't. She had to come back up here and make sure everything was signed off in the cold light of day. She sighed, then realised that it would be the last duty she would ever perform for the Raffertys. As of next week, she was a free agent.

'That was a big sigh.'

She turned. Dickie was behind her, holding out a brandy balloon. She took it – she didn't really want it, but it was sweet of him to think of her.

'I know,' she admitted. 'I've just been thinking. As of Monday, I've got to figure out what to do with my life. They keep trying to persuade me to stay, but if I don't make a break then I'll still be working for the Raffertys when I'm ninety-three. I need to move on. But I don't know what else to do. I was thinking about teacher training college, but it's too late to apply for this year. I can apply for next, but I don't know what to do in the meantime.'

Dickie was silent for a moment.

'Well,' he said, 'I could do with someone to work for me.'

Polly eyes shone.

'Really?'

'The girl that helps me out has just left. And things are getting frantic. Early signs are that *Something for the Weekend* is going to be a real winner. I've got another couple of really hot scripts I'm lining up. And although I couldn't pay nearly as much . . .'

'Don't worry about the money,' breathed Polly. 'I've got heaps saved up. I never have time to spend it.'

'There is just one snag,' said Dickie, and her face fell. 'I'm not a great believer in mixing business with pleasure, and I'd really like to ask you out for dinner.'

The tropical heat in the glasshouse was making Delilah feel woozy. She slipped out through one of the French windows, onto the terrace and down onto the lawn. The evening air cleared her head. She reached into her evening bag.

She'd had a letter earlier in the week. A letter in a cream vellum envelope, handwritten in thick black ink, with an Irish postmark. She pulled it out again now, wanting to re-read it.

Dearest Delilah

I was delighted to read that Tyger has now been released from hospital, and is expected to make a full recovery. Please accept my warmest wishes that it will be a speedy one.

You might be glad to hear that my mother has made a full recovery as well, and is now home from hospital. However, she has decided in the light of her fall that it is in her best interests to sell Gortnaflor. I wanted to let you know before we put it on the open market, just in case you might be interested. My mother is keen for it to go to someone who would give it the love and attention it deserves, and I know you would certainly do that.

Yours ever,

William

She knew that it had been a difficult letter for him to write, and that there was as much unsaid as there was said. She had been profoundly moved by his dignity. She had telephoned him straight away.

She looked up from reading the words yet again as a figure slipped across the lawn to join her. It was a man, tall and handsome in his dinner jacket, his tie now undone. Wordlessly, he slid an arm around her, then Delilah put her hand on his chest, playing with the black enamel studs on his dress shirt. Her eyes were dancing with something approaching mischief.

'There's something I need to talk to you about.'

The man smiled down.

'Oh yes?'

'You know you didn't have time to buy me a birthday present? What with everything that's been going on. And you said, if there was something I wanted, just to let you know?'

'Yes . . . ?' The reply was cautious.

'Well . . .' Delilah held out the letter. 'It would be a long-term project. Something for me to get my teeth into. And it would be the perfect place for the girls to come and chill out. All of us, in fact. We always talked about getting a holiday home, but we never have. You will absolutely love it—'

'Delilah.' Raf reached and took the letter out of her hands. 'It's yours. Happy birthday. Now shut up.'

He bent his head and kissed her. And as they kissed, the letter fluttered to the ground.

THE END